Reginald Hill is a native of Cumbria and former resident of Yorkshire, the setting for his novels featuring Superintendent Dalziel and DCI Pascoe. Their appearances have won him numerous awards including a CWA Gold Dagger and the Diamond Dagger for Lifetime Achievement. They have also been adapted into a hugely popular BBC TV series.

MIDNIGHT FUGUE

Gina Wolfe has come to Mid-Yorkshire in search of her missing husband, believed dead. Her fiancé, Commander Mick Purdy of the Met, thinks Dalziel should take care of the job. What none of them realize is how events set in motion decades ago, will come to a violent head on this otherwise ordinary autumn day. A Welsh tabloid journalist senses the story he's been chasing for years may have finally landed in his lap. A Tory MP's assistant suspects her boss's father has an unsavoury history that could taint his prime ministerial ambitions. The ruthless entrepreneur in question sends out two henchmen to make sure the past stays in the past. And the lethal pair dispatched have awkward secrets of their own.

REGINALD HILL

♦

MIDNIGHT FUGUE

Complete and Unabridged

CHARNWOOD
Leicester

First published in Great Britain in 2009 by
HarperCollins*Publishers*
London

First Charnwood Edition
published 2010
by arrangement with
HarperCollins*Publishers*
London

The moral right of the author has been asserted

Extract of 'The Child Dying' from *Collected Poems* © The Estate of Edwin Muir and reprinted by permission of Faber and Faber Ltd.

British Library CIP Data

Hill, Reginald.
  Midnight fugue.
  1. Dalziel, Andrew (Fictitious character)- -Fiction.
  2. Pascoe, Peter (Fictitious character)- -Fiction.
  3. Police- -England- -Yorkshire- -Fiction.
  4. Detective and mystery stories.
  5. Large type books.
  I. Title
  823.9'14–dc22

  ISBN 978-1-44480-350-1

Published by
F. A. Thorpe (Publishing)
Anstey, Leicestershire

Set by Words & Graphics Ltd.
Anstey, Leicestershire
Printed and bound in Great Britain by
T. J. International Ltd., Padstow, Cornwall

This book is printed on acid-free paper

The raindrops play their midnight fugue
Against my window pane.
Could I once more fold you in my arms
You should not leave again.

Richard Morland: *Night Music*

1

accelerando

Prelude

Midnight.

Splintered woodwork, bedroom door flung open, feet pounding across the floor, duvet ripped off, grim faces looking down at him, his wife screaming as she's dragged naked from his side . . .

He sits upright and cries, 'NO!'

The duvet is in place, the room empty, the door closed. And through the thin curtains seeps the grey light of dawn.

As for Gina, she hasn't been by his side for . . . days? . . . weeks? . . . could be months.

The digital bedside clock reads 5.55. He's not surprised.

Always some form of Nelson whenever he wakes these days: 1.11 2.22 3.33 . . .

Meaning something bad.

Things go on like this, one morning soon he's going to wake and the clock will read 6.66 . . .

He is still shaking, his body soaked with sweat, his heart pounding.

He gets out of bed and goes on to the landing.

Even the sight of the front door securely in place can't slow his pulse, even the shower jets cooling and cleaning his flesh can't wash away his fear.

He tries to analyse his dream, to get it under control by working out its meaning.

He conjures up the men. Some in uniform,

3

some masked; some familiar, some strangers; some wielding police batons, some swinging hammers . . .

He gives it up, not because the meaning is too elusive but because it's too clear.

There is no one to turn to, nowhere to hide.

He looks out of the window into the quiet street, familiar from childhood, whenever that was. Now it seems strange, the houses skewed, the perspectives warped, all colour washed out, like a sepia still from some old horror movie.

He realizes he no longer knows where it leads.

Maybe that's where salvation lies.

If he doesn't know, how can they know?

All he has to do is walk away down that street. Once round the corner he'll be somewhere nobody knows about. He will be free.

Part of his mind is asking, Does this make sense? Are you thinking straight? Is this the only way?

He makes one last effort at coherent thought, trying to find an answer by looking at the past, the trail that has brought him here, but the view is blocked by a small white box. For some reason it's got a silver ribbon around it, making it look like a wedding present.

Maybe it was.

He tries to look beyond it, but it's like staring into fog rolling off the ocean at dusk. The harder you look, the darker it gets.

Time to turn his back on that box, that fog, that darkness.

Time to walk away.

08.10–08.12

'Shit,' said Andy Dalziel as the phone rang.

In twenty minutes the CID's monthly case review meeting was due to start, the first since his return. In the old days this wasn't a problem. He'd have rolled in late and watched them bolt their bacon butties and sit up straight. But if he was late now they'd probably think he'd forgotten the way to the Station. So time was short and Monday-morning traffic was always a pain. Nowt that using his siren and jumping a few red lights couldn't compensate for, but if he wasn't on his way in the next couple of minutes, he might have to run over a few pedestrians too.

He grabbed his car keys and headed for the front door.

Behind him the answer machine clicked in and a voice he didn't recognize faded behind him down the narrow hallway.

'Andy, hi. Mick Purdy, remember me? We met at Bramshill a few years back. Happy days, eh? So how're you doing, mate? Still shagging the sheep up there in the frozen north? Listen, if you could give me a bell, I'd really appreciate it. My number's . . . '

As the Fat Man slid into his car he dug into his memory bank. These days, especially with recent stuff, it sometimes seemed that the harder he looked, the darker it got. Curiously, deeper often meant clearer, and his Mick Purdy memories were pretty deep.

It wasn't a few years since he'd been on that Bramshill course; more like eight or nine. Even then, he'd been the oldest officer there by a long way, the reason being that for a decade or more he'd managed to find a way of wriggling out of attendance whenever his name came up. But finally his concentration had lapsed.

It hadn't been so bad. The official side had been slightly less tedious than anticipated, and there'd been a bunch of convivial colleagues, grateful to find someone they could rely on to get them to bed when their own legs proved less hollow than they'd imagined. DI Mick Purdy had usually been one of the last men standing, and he and Dalziel had struck up a holiday friendship based on shared professional scepticism and divided regional loyalties. They exchanged harmonious anecdotes offering particular instances of the universal truth that most of those in charge of HM Constabulary couldn't organize a fuck-up in a brothel. Then, when concord got boring, they divided geographically with Purdy claiming to believe that up in Yorkshire in times of dearth they ate their young, and Dalziel countering that down in London they'd produced a younger generation that not even a starving vulture could stomach.

They'd parted with the usual expressions of good will and hope that their paths would cross again. But they never had. And now here was Mick Purdy ringing him at home first thing on a

Monday morning, wanting to renew acquaintance.

Meaning, unless he were finally giving way to a long repressed passion, the bugger wanted a favour.

Interesting. But not so interesting it couldn't wait. Important thing this morning was to be there when his motley crew drifted into the meeting, seated in his chair of state, clearly the monarch of all he surveyed, ready to call them to account for what they'd done with their meagre talents during his absence.

He turned the key in the ignition and heard the familiar ursine growl. The old Rover had much in common with its driver, he thought complacently. Bodywork crap, interior packed with more rubbish than a builder's skip, but — courtesy of the lads in the police garage — the engine would have graced a vehicle ten times younger and five times more expensive.

He put it into gear and blasted away from the kerb.

08.12_08.20

The speed of Dalziel's departure took Gina Wolfe by surprise.

She'd been watching the house for signs of life, spotting none till suddenly the front door burst open and a rotund figure emerged. Don't be put off by his size, she'd been warned, King Henry was fat too, and like the merry monarch Andy Dalziel used his weight to roll over everybody who got in his way. But she wouldn't have expected anything so fat to move so fast.

He slid into his car like a tarantula going down a drain-hole, the old banger started first time and took off at a speed as surprising as its owner's. Not that she doubted the ability of her Nissan 350Z to match it, but on unfamiliar streets she needed to keep him in sight.

By the time she belted up, eased out of her parking spot and set off in pursuit, the Rover had reached a T-junction three hundred yards ahead and turned left.

Happily it was still visible when she too turned. A short burst of acceleration closed the distance between them and she settled down three car lengths behind. Her wanderings that morning had given her some sense of the city's geography and she knew they were heading towards its centre, probably making for the police station.

8

After seven or eight minutes, he signalled left. She followed him off the main road and found herself in a residential area, old and up-market from the look of it, with occasional glimpses of a massive church tower somewhere at its centre.

Ahead the Rover slowed almost to a stop. Its driver seemed to be talking to a woman walking along the pavement. Gina brought the Nissan to a crawl too. If he noticed, it would just look like a silly female driver terrified to overtake in this rather narrow street. A few seconds later, the Rover drew away once more. She didn't have far to follow this time. A couple of hundred yards on, he turned into a car park marked *Cathedral Use Only*.

Another surprise. Nothing she'd been told about the man had hinted devotion.

She pulled in after him, parked in the next row, and slid out of her seat. He was slower exiting his car than getting into it. She studied him across the low roof of the Nissan. He looked preoccupied, anxious even. His gaze took her in. She removed her sunglasses and gave him a tentative smile. If he'd responded, she would have started to speak, but he turned away abruptly and strode towards the cathedral.

Once again his speed caught her unawares and she lost distance as she followed him. When he stopped to speak to someone at the door, she almost caught up. Then he vanished into the building.

Inside she looked for him in the main aisle along which most of the other arrivals were moving towards the High Altar. No sign. He surely couldn't have spotted her and headed here as a diversion to shake her off? No, that didn't make sense.

Then she saw him. He'd found a seat in the north aisle where the golden October sunlight filtering through the eastern windows did not penetrate. He sat hunched forward with his head in his hands. Despite his size he looked strangely vulnerable. Something very serious must be troubling him to require prayer of this intensity.

She sat down a couple of rows behind and waited.

08.12–08.21

When Gina Wolfe's Nissan pulled out to follow Andy Dalziel's Rover, fifty yards back a blue VW Golf slipped into place behind her. There were two people in it; in the front passenger seat a man, broad-shouldered, ruddy-faced, his skull close-cropped in a gingery stubble; alongside him a woman of similar build and feature, her short fair hair packed tight into curls that could have been sculpted by Praxiteles.

His name was Vincent Delay. The driver was his sister. Her name was Fleur. On first hearing this some people were amused, but rarely for long.

She had no problem keeping the bright red sports car in sight along the relatively straight main road. Not that visual contact mattered. On her brother's knee was a laptop tuned to a GPS tracker. The bright green spot pulsating across the screen was the Nissan that she could see ahead, signalling left to follow the Rover. Fleur turned off the main road too and half a minute later braked to avoid coming up too close behind the red car. It was the Rover driver causing the hold-up. He'd slowed almost to a halt to exchange words with a female pedestrian. It didn't take long. Now he was off again.

As they passed the woman, Vincent turned his

11

head to stare at her through the open window. She noticed his interest and glared back, mouthing something inaudible.

'Up yours too, you old scarecrow,' growled the man.

'Vince, don't draw attention,' said Fleur.

'What attention? Must be a hundred. Probably deaf as a post and can't remember anything that happened more than five minutes ago.'

'Maybe,' said the woman, turning into the car park and finding a spot a few cars along from the Nissan. Here they sat and watched as the fat man made his way towards the cathedral followed closely by the blonde.

'Who the fuck is that?' said Vince. 'Can't possibly be our guy, can it?'

The woman said, 'Don't swear, Vince. You know I don't like it any time and particularly not on a Sunday.'

'Sorry,' he said sulkily. 'Just wondering who Tubby is, that's all.'

'And it's a good question,' she said in a conciliatory tone. 'But we know where he lives, so finding out won't be a problem. Now get after them.'

'Me?' said Vince doubtfully. Following was subtle stuff. Usually he didn't get to do the subtle stuff.

'Yes. You can manage that, can't you?'

'Sure.'

He got out of the car, then stooped to the window.

'What if they go inside?'

'Follow them,' she said in exasperation. 'Grab

12

a hymn book. Try to look religious. Now go!'

He set off at a rapid pace. Ahead he saw Blondie going into the cathedral.

He followed. Inside he stood still for a moment, letting his eyes adjust to the light. Blondie was easy to spot and through her he located Tubby.

When the woman sat down, he took a seat several rows behind her, picked up a hymn book, opened it at random.

His lips moved as he read the words.

> *The world is very evil,*
> *The times are waxing late,*
> *Be sober and keep vigil,*
> *The Judge is at the gate.*

Fucking judges, thought Vince.

08.12–08.25

For the first couple of miles, Andy Dalziel's reaction to the surprisingly light traffic had been relief. He should get to the meeting in plenty of time and without use of what clever clogs Pascoe called *son et lumière*.

But by the time he approached the town centre, he was beginning to find the absence of other vehicles suspicious rather than surprising. This after all was Monday morning, when traffic was usually at its worst.

Couldn't be a Bank Holiday, could it? Hardly. September had just turned into October. Last Bank Holiday, spent in a sea-side convalescent home, had been at the end of August. No more till Christmas, by which time the rest of the European Union would have had another half-dozen. Faintest sniff of no matter how obscure a saint's day, and them buggers were parading idols, wrestling bulls and throwing donkeys off the Eiffel Tower. No wonder we had to win their wars for them!

He came out of his Europhobic reverie to discover that, despite being well ahead of the clock, his automatic pilot had directed him via his usual short-cut along Holyclerk Street in defiance of the sign restricting entry 'within the bell', i.e. into the area immediately surrounding

14

the cathedral, to residents and worshippers. And now his suspicions about the lightness of traffic began to take on a more sombre hue.

There were people walking towards the cathedral with that anal-retentive demeanour the English tend to adopt when trying to look religious; not great numbers, but a lot more than he'd have expected to see at this time on a Monday morning. Mebbe during his absence there'd been a great conversion in Mid-Yorkshire. In fact, mebbe his absence had caused it!

Slowing to the pace of a little old lady clutching a large square volume bound in leather, its corners reinforced by brass triangles that gleamed like a set of knuckle-dusters, he leaned over to the passenger side and wound down the window.

'How do, luv. Off to church, are you? Lovely morning for it.'

She turned, fixed him with a rheumy eye, and said, 'My God, how desperate must you be! I'm seventy-nine. Go away, you pathetic man!'

'Nay, luv, I just want to know what day it is,' he protested.

'A drunkard as well as a lecher! Go away, I say! I can defend myself.'

She took a swing at him with her brass-bound book which, had it connected, might have broken his nose. He accelerated away, but doubt was now strong enough to make him turn into the cathedral car park a hundred yards on.

A sporty red Nissan pulled in behind him. Its driver, a blonde in her late twenties, got out the same time as he did. She was wearing wrap-around shades against the autumn sunlight. She eased them forward on her nose, their eyes met and she gave him a smile. He thought of asking her what day it was but decided against it. This one might have hysterics or spray him with mace, and in any case back along the pavement the little old lady was approaching like the US cavalry. Time to talk to someone official and male.

At the cathedral's great east door he could see a corpse-faced man in a black cassock acting as commissionaire. No backward collar, so a verger maybe. Or a cross-dressing vampire.

Dalziel moved towards him. As he entered the shadow of the great building his mind drifted back to a time when he'd been hauled along this street as God on top of a medieval pageant wagon and something like an angel had come floating down from the looming tower . . .

He pushed the disturbing memory from his mind as he reached the holy doorman.

'So what's on this morning, mate?' he asked breezily.

The man gave him a slightly puzzled look as he replied, 'Holy Communion now, matins at ten.'

Meant nothing, he reassured himself without conviction. The God-squad had services every day, even if all the congregation they could muster was a couple of geriatrics and a church mouse.

'Owt special?' he said. 'I mean, is it a special Sunday, twenty-second afore Pancake Tuesday or summat?'

He hoped to hear something like, 'Sunday? You must have had a good weekend. This is Monday!' But he no longer expected it.

'No, nothing special, sir. If you want it spelled out, it's the twentieth after Trinity in Ordinary Time. Are you coming in?'

Rather unexpectedly, Dalziel found he was.

Partly because his route back to the car would mean passing the old lady with the knuckle-duster prayer book, but mainly because his legs and his mind were sending from their opposite poles the message that he needed to sit down somewhere quiet and commune with his inner self.

He passed through the cathedral porch and had to pause to let his eyes adjust from the morning brightness outside to the rich gloom of the interior. Its vastness dwindled the waiting worshippers from a significant number to a mere handful, concentrated towards the western end. He turned off the central aisle and found himself a seat in the lee of an ancient tomb topped with what were presumably life-sized effigies of its inmates. Must have been a bit disconcerting for the family to see Mam and Dad lying there every time they came to church, thought Dalziel. Particularly if the sculptor had caught a good likeness, which a very lively looking little dog at their feet suggested he might have done.

His mind was trying to avoid the unattractive mental task that lay before him. But he hadn't got wherever he'd got by turning aside when the path turned clarty.

He closed his eyes, rested his head on his

17

hands as if in prayer, and focused on one of the great philosophical questions of the twenty-first century.

Didn't matter if it was Ordinary Time or Extraordinary Time, the question was, how the fuck had he managed to misplace a whole sodding day?

08.25–08.40

Gina Wolfe watched the bowed, still figure with envy.

He no longer looked fat; the cathedral's vastness had dwindled him to frail mortal flesh like her own.

She did not know what pain had brought him here, but she knew about pain. What she did not know was how to find comfort and help in a place like this.

She hadn't been inside a church since the funeral. That was seven years ago. And seven years before that she'd been at the same church for her wedding.

Patterns. Could they mean something? Or were they like crop circles, just some joker having a laugh?

At some point during the funeral her mind had started over-laying the two ceremonies. One of her wedding presents had been a vacuum cleaner, beautifully packaged in a gleaming white box. The small white coffin reminded her of this, and as the service progressed she found herself obsessed by the notion that they were burying her Hoover. She tried to tell Alex this, to assure him it was all right, it was just a vacuum cleaner they'd lost, but the face he turned on her did more than anything the words and the music and

19

the place could do to reassert the dreadful reality.

Neither of them had cried, she remembered that. The church had been full of weeping, but they had moved beyond tears. She had knelt when invited to kneel but no prayer had come. She had stood for the hymns but she had not sung. The words that formed in her mind weren't the words on the page before her, they were words she had seen when she was seventeen and still at school.

It had been a pre-A-level exercise. *Compare and contrast the following two poems.* One was Milton's 'On the Death of a Fair Infant', the other Edwin Muir's 'The Child Dying'.

She'd had great fun mocking the classical formality of the earlier poem.

It began with child-abuse, she wrote, with the God of Winter's chilly embrace giving the Fair Infant the cough that killed her. And it ended with an attempt at consolation so naff it was almost comic.

Think what a present thou to God hast sent.

Any mother finding comfort in this, she'd written, must have been a touch disappointed it hadn't been triplets.

Perhaps her pathetic confusion of the coffin and the wedding gift box was a late payback for this mockery.

The other poem, viewing death through a child's eyes, she'd been much more taken with. In fact the Scot, Muir, had become one of her favourite poets, though now her love for him, sparked by 'The Child Dying', seemed peculiarly ill-omened.

Back then its opening lines — *Unfriendly friendly universe, I pack your stars into my purse, And bid you, bid you so farewell* — had struck her as being at the same time touchingly child-like and cosmically resonant. But she knew now she had been delighting in the skill of the poet rather than the power of his poem.

Then she had been admiring the resonance from outside; now it was in her being.

I did not know death was so strange.

Now she knew.

And she was sure that the Fair Infant's mother, Milton's sister, must have known this too, must have felt the cold blast of that air *blown from the far side of despair.*

But did she *wisely learn to curb her sorrows wild?* Had she been able to draw warmth from her brother's poem and wrap herself in its formality? Find support in those stiff folds of words?

Had she been able to sit in a church and bury her grief in these rituals of faith?

If she had, Gina Wolfe envied her. She'd found no such comforts to turn to.

At least she hadn't fled. Unlike Alex. She had found the strength to stay, to endure, to rebuild.

But was it strength? For years her first thought on waking and her last thought before sleeping had been of lost Lucy. And then it wasn't. Did a day pass when she didn't think of her daughter?

She couldn't swear to it. That first time she'd given herself to Mick, she'd pendulum'd between joy and guilt. But later, when they holidayed together in Spain, she recalled the extremes as contentment and ecstasy with never a gap for a ghost to creep through.

Perhaps this meant that Alex had loved so much he could only survive the loss by losing himself, whereas she . . .

She pushed the thought away. She could do that.

Was that strength?

Alex couldn't. The thought pushed him away.

Was that weakness?

These were questions beyond her puzzling.

Maybe that portly figure two rows ahead, sitting as still as the statues on the tomb above him, would have the answers.

08.25–08.40

Fleur Delay watched her brother disappear into the cathedral then opened her bag and from it took a small pack of tablets. She slipped one into her mouth and washed it down with a swig of water from a bottle in the door pocket.

Letting Vince loose in a cathedral was not normally an option, but it had seemed marginally better than collapsing in the car park.

She took another tablet. After a while she began to feel a little better. All the car windows were wide open to admit the morning air. Now she closed them and took out her mobile phone. There was no one in hearing distance but minimizing risk was an instinct so deep ingrained it had ceased to be a thought process.

She speed-dialled a number. It took a long time for it to be answered.

'*Buenos días, señor,*' she said. '*Soy Señora Delay.*'

She listened to the response for a while then interrupted in English.

'Yes, I know it's Sunday and I know it's early, but I don't know where it says in our very expensive agreement that you stop working for me at weekends or before nine o clock. I'll write it in if you like, but I'll cut your fee by half, *comprende usted?*'

She listened again, cut in again.

'OK, no need to grovel. I just want a progress report. And before you start on with the crappy reasons why things move so slowly over there, you ought to know I'm looking to move in a bit earlier than planned. Four weeks, tops. That means not a day longer than four weeks, OK?'

After she'd finished her call, she opened the windows again and took another drink of water. This had not been a good idea, but turning down The Man could have been a worse one.

She leaned back in her seat and relaxed. She didn't fall asleep but drifted into a state of waking reverie that was becoming more and more common as her medication increased proportionately to her illness. The past would come and sit next to her. She could see the world as it was at present with the great cathedral towering over her, but it floated on her retina like a mirage. It was the images nudging her memory that felt like reality.

Among them she could see her father quite clearly, his eyes a shade of blue that was almost green, his lips permanently curved into the promise of a smile, his forefinger flicking his nose as he said, 'Cheerio, my darlings, keep your noses clean,' that last sunny day when he strolled out of the house and never came back.

She'd been nine, Vincent twelve.

It had taken her five long years to accept that her father was gone for good.

Their feckless mother had done her poor best, but as she slid down a spiral of substance abuse and bad partner choice, she had little time or will to give her children the attention they needed. Vince readily came to accept that it was his young sister he had to look to for the basics of hot food and clean clothing. And once he got launched on what to a neutral observer looked like a dedicated effort to become the most inefficient criminal of the age, it was Fleur, masquerading as his elder sister, who visited him inside and was waiting for him outside the many prisons he spent a large proportion of his young manhood in.

At sixteen Fleur left school. She could have stayed on. She was a bright girl with a real talent for mathematics, but she'd had enough of classrooms.

Her mother's current boyfriend, a small-time pimp, offered to find her a job. He and the girl got on quite well, so instead of telling him to take a hike, she thanked him politely and explained she would prefer to earn her money on her bum rather than on her back. He became quite indignant and assured her that he wasn't inviting her to join his team; her brain was too sharp and her body too shapeless for that. Instead he recommended her for a clerking job in the office of a local finance company.

That sounded almost as dull as school. But she knew the company he referred to and she knew it was run by The Man.

On the appointed day she went along to the company offices, located in what had once been a pet shop in a dingy street north of East India Dock Road. Determined to make a good impression she got there nice and early. The shop space still smelled of animal piss, but there was no sign of human presence. Then she thought she heard voices beyond a door at the back.

As she pushed it open, the voices died or rather disappeared beneath a loud crash and a louder scream.

She was looking into a small office occupied by three men, two black, one white. Or rather, grey.

The grey-faced man was sitting on a chair before a desk. The reason for the greyness and for the scream was that the older of the two black men, standing beside him, was holding his hand flat on the desktop, while the other black man, seated behind the desk, had just smashed the knuckle of his right forefinger with a claw hammer.

She knew who the black men were. The older one was Milton Slingsby, known as Sling, a small-time pro boxer who'd found more profitable employment for his skills as the chief lieutenant of the younger black man who was of course Goldie Gidman, The Man.

Gidman regarded her expressionlessly then made a gesture with the hammer.

Slingsby pulled the grey man upright and dragged him towards the door. As he passed Fleur, he turned his gaze upon her, his eyes wide in pleading or maybe just in pain. She realized she knew him too, at least by sight. His name was Janowski and he ran a small tailoring business just a couple of streets away. Then Slingsby thrust him through the door and heeled it shut behind them.

'Why'd you not run, girl?' asked The Man.

He was probably in his thirties but looked younger till you saw his eyes. Good looking, slim, medium build, he wore a pristine white shirt that accentuated the deep black of his skin against which glowed a heavy golden necklet, gold rings on his fingers and a gold bracelet on either wrist.

'I'm Fleur Delay,' she said. 'I've come for the interview.'

The hammer made another gesture, and she subsided on to the grey man's seat. Her eyes took in the desk's nearer edge. A series of small craters suggested that grey man was not the first to have sat here. She didn't feel safe, but she felt safer than she would have done running.

The craters vanished beneath a sheet of paper bearing a column of about twenty sums of money ranging from the teens to the thousands.

'Add it up,' said The Man. The hammer, she was glad to observe, had vanished.

She took her time. Something told her that accuracy was more important than speed.

'Nineteen thousand five hundred and sixty-two pounds fourteen pence,' she said.

'So you can add up,' said The Man, pulling the sheet out of her fingers. 'But can you shut up? The guy who was sitting there when you came in — '

'What guy?' she interrupted.

He stared at her with a blankness that could have concealed anything.

'You know who I am?' he asked after a while.

'Never seen you before in my life, Mr Gidman,' she said.

27

Slowly the blankness dissolved into a grin, then The Man laughed out loud.

'Tomorrow, eight thirty, sharp,' he said.

She stood up and as she reached the door found the courage to say, 'What about wages?'

'Let's wait and see what you're worth, why don't we?' he replied.

At the end of a week what she got wasn't much more than she could have earned stacking shelves in a supermarket, but she didn't complain.

A few days later a policeman who didn't look much older than herself came to her home. Mr Janowski was laying a charge of assault against The Man. He claimed she had been a witness to the assault. He was mistaken, she assured the cop. She knew vaguely who Mr Janowski was, wasn't sure she'd recognize him if she met him in the street, and certainly had never seen Mr Gidman assault him.

'That's OK then,' said the constable, who had a local accent and a cheeky grin.

'So I won't have to go to court?' she said.

'Shouldn't think so, darling. Though maybe Sergeant Mathias will want to talk to you himself. Just tell him what you told me, you'll be all right.'

Mathias turned up later the same day.

Unlike the constable, the sergeant had a funny accent, like somebody taking the piss out of a Pakki. 'So what you're saying is you wouldn't recognize Mr Janowski if you met him on the street, right? In that case, miss, how can you be sure you never saw Mr Gidman assault him?'

'Because,' she retorted, 'I've never seen Mr Gidman assault *anyone*, that's how.'

The sergeant looked as if he'd have liked to give her a good shaking, but she saw the young constable hide a grin behind his hand, and as he left he gave her a big wink.

She said nothing of this to Gidman but presumably someone did, for next pay-day her wage packet tripled and stayed tripled.

One night not long after, a fire broke out in Mr Janowski's workshop, quickly spreading to the flat above where the tailor lived with his wife and infant daughter. The firemen fought their way through the blaze to the smoke-filled bathroom where they found the Janowskis crouched over the bath. The mother was already dead through smoke inhalation. Janowski, who had third-degree burns, died four days later. But under a dampened blanket stretched across the bathtub, they found the child unburnt and still breathing.

At least, thought Fleur, she wouldn't have to face the pains and problems parents could inflict on their growing daughters.

Whether she would be spared the pains and problems life itself inflicted on most women was another matter.

She was feeling much better now. The past dwindled into its proper space, the cathedral descended from the sky and took its rightful place at ground level, still huge but now firmly anchored to the earth.

God's house they called it. If there were a God, then it was presumably Him who did all that inflicting, she thought. Maybe I should go inside and have a quiet word, let Him know I've decided to change his plans a bit.

But He probably got the message when He saw Vince taking a seat.

What was going on in there? she wondered.

Like so much of life, there was nothing to do but wait.

08.25–08.55

For a few seconds Andy Dalziel had felt his mind going into free fall as he contemplated his temporal aberration.

Thoughts of Alzheimer's, brain tumours, even, God help him, post-traumatic stress disorder, shrieked like bats around the tower of his understanding and the easiest solution seemed to be to jump off into the welcoming darkness.

Jesus! he told himself. It's this place putting them daft thoughts into your mind. You're a detective. Detect! Doesn't matter what you find, so long as you're strong enough not to run away from it.

First things first. This morning he'd woken up. He tried to reconstruct the waking process. It had seemed pretty normal, the mind surfacing from sleep's dark depths, thrashing around on the surface for a few moments, grabbing at flotsam and jetsam from pre-sleep memory, identifying them as belonging to such and such a day . . .

That's where it had started to go wrong.

Somehow he'd assembled these shards of memory not into the Saturday they belonged to, but into a Sunday that hadn't yet happened!

Had he simply made it up then? He tried to project himself back a day, found clear-cut

31

details hard to come by. Instead, cloudy images of sitting around, doing nothing, going nowhere floated across his mind.

That felt like Sunday all right, but a Sunday from extremely auld lang syne, the sort of Sunday he'd sometimes experienced on childhood holidays with his Scottish cousins. They'd been really happy days, most of them. His dad's family knew how to treat kids — feed them jam pieces and mutton pies till they come out of their ears, then turn them loose to roam at will, confident that they'll find their way home for the next meal. But it all stopped on Sundays. Here the will of Granny Dalziel ruled supreme. Here the bairns were expected to keep the Sabbath as she had kept it back in the mists of time. Faces scrubbed, hair slicked, bound in the strait jacket of best clothes, they were marched to the kirk in the morning and sat around with an improving book, seen and definitely not heard, for the rest of the endless day.

And that had been his Sunday . . . no, that had been his Saturday, his yesterday! Or something like it.

But why? He needed to dig deeper, go back further.

He'd returned to work a week earlier, at his own insistence and against medical and domestic advice. But he'd insisted angrily that he felt fine and was more than ready to pick up the traces where he'd dropped them over three months ago.

He hadn't been lying. Trouble was, the traces weren't there any more.

If anywhere, they were in Peter Pascoe's hands, and it had taken him a couple of days to realize the DCI's reluctance to hand them over immediately was as much protective as presumptuous.

Things had changed, both externally and internally. There might have been a sharp intake of breath across Mid-Yorkshire when he was admitted comatose to hospital, but it clearly hadn't been held for long. The old truism was true. Life went on. Criminal life certainly did, and nature abhors a vacuum.

He no longer had his finger on the pulse of things. He had a deal of catching up to do, not just in knowledge but in reputation. His famed omniscience depended on an extensive web of information and influence spun over many years, and in a couple of months this had fallen into serious disrepair. His underlings still tiptoed around him, but now their deference struck him as therapeutic rather than theocentric. He realized he was going to have to work hard to get back to where he'd been before the big bang, when he could have breezed in late to the case-review meeting, supremely confident of being able to prove yet again, as he'd once overheard Pascoe say with mingled admiration and irritation, that, like God, the Fat Man was always in the squad!

Not now. And as well as the shock of realizing how out of touch he was, he'd been dismayed to find himself completely knackered after three or four hours on the job. When Pascoe had assured him that a new roster system imposed from above required that he should have the forthcoming weekend off, he hadn't resisted. Cap Marvell, his non-live-in partner, was away that weekend, but no matter. Saturday was an easy day to fill. Long lie-in, then off down the rugger club to see some old mates. Couple of pints at lunch, watch the match in the afternoon, couple more pints after, then mebbe wander into town with a few convivial chums for a curry. Perfect.

Except the day had dawned wet and windy. Everything seemed an effort, even though everything consisted of next to nothing. Noon arrived and he was still wandering round his house, undressed and unshaven. Going out to stand in wind and rain to shout at thirty young men wrestling in mud seemed pointless. There was a match on the telly he could watch. He fell asleep shortly after kick-off and woke to find the screen full of speedway bikes. Wasn't worth getting dressed now. He summoned up the energy to put a mug of soup in the microwave and scalded his lip. Even that didn't jerk him out of his trance-like state. In fact his chosen remedy, the litre bottle of Highland Park he'd found empty on his pillow this morning, had sucked him in deeper.

And so the long hours had dragged by. Granny Dalziel would have been outraged by his dress and his demeanour, but her strict sabbatarianism could not have faulted his state of mind. *Vanity of vanities, all is vanity and vexation of spirit.*

And there was the explanation. This morning his mind, recalling the previous day as a long, vacuous, will-to-live-sapping Scots Sabbath and unwilling to thole the notion of enduring such another, had decided it had to be Monday.

Simple. Dead logical, really. Nowt to worry about there.

Except that things like that didn't happen to him. To other men maybe. There were a lot of weak, woolly, wobbly, wanked-out losers in the world, their minds in such a whirl they didn't know their arses from their elbows. But not Andy Dalziel. It had taken half a ton of Semtex to put him on his back and he'd risen up again, shaken himself down, and returned to the fray, a bit bruised and battered and mud-bespattered, but ready and able to play out the rest of the game till the ref called *no side!*

At least he hadn't made it to the Station this morning. He shuddered to think what his colleagues would have made of the mighty Dalziel turning up for Monday's meeting twenty-four hours early! They never come back, that's what popular wisdom said about champion boxers. They try, they sometimes flatter to deceive, but they never really come back. He was going to prove them wrong, wasn't he? He was going to delight his friends, scatter his enemies, and leave all the dismal doubters with enough egg on their faces to make a Spanish omelette.

He'd been vaguely aware of a continuo of faint religious murmuring beneath his thoughts, but now it stopped and was replaced by the sound of footsteps as the worshippers, unburdened of their sins, tripped lightly back down the long aisle. Service must be over already. Mebbe in this age of Fast Food and Speed Dating, the Church had brought in Quick Confession and Accelerated Absolution.

More likely, his thought processes had just slowed to a crawl.

The footsteps receded, finally there was silence, and then the organ started playing. He wasn't a great fan of organ music, something a little ponderous about it, something too diffused to cut to the emotional heart of a good tune. But here in the great cathedral, whose dim and vast prismoids of space felt as if they might have been imported from beyond the stars, it was easy to think of it as the voice of God.

He straightened up and the voice spoke.

'Mr Dalziel?'

He rolled his eyes upward. What was it going to be — the blinding light, or just a shower of dove crap?

'I'm sorry to bother you,' said the voice of God. 'I'm Gina Wolfe.'

That God should be female didn't surprise him. That she, or She, should be called Gina did.

He turned his head to the right and found himself looking at the blonde from the red Nissan. Would God drive Japanese? He didn't think so. This was flesh and blood, and very nice flesh and blood at that.

'Gina Wolfe?' she repeated with a faintly interrogative inflexion, as if anticipating the name would mean something to him.

To the best of his recollection, he'd never seen her before in his life.

On the other hand, a man whose recollection

36

could dump whole days on a whim couldn't be too dogmatic. Best to box clever till he worked out the circumstances and degree of their acquaintance.

'Nice to see you again, Gina Wolfe,' he said, thinking by the use of the whole name to cover all possible gradations of intimacy.

Her expression told him he'd failed before she said, 'Oh dear. You've no idea who I am, have you? I'm sorry. Mick Purdy said he was going to ring you . . .'

'Mick?' With relief he found a context for this name. 'Oh aye, *Mick!* He did ring, just afore I came out this morning, left a message. I were in a bit of a hurry.'

'I noticed. I really had to put my foot down to keep up with you. Look, I'm sorry to interrupt your devotions. If you like, I can wait for you outside.'

Dalziel was pleased to feel his mind clicking back into gear, not top maybe but a good third, which was enough to extrapolate two slightly disturbing pieces of information from what she'd just said.

The first was, she'd been following him.

The second, and more worrying, was she thought he'd been in a hurry to get to the cathedral to pray. Couldn't have her telling Mick Purdy that. Important operational information could vanish without trace in the mazy communications network that allegedly linked the regional police forces. But news that Andy Dalziel had got religion would be disseminated with the speed of light.

37

He said, 'Nay, I weren't devoting, luv. Just like to come here and listen to the music sometimes.'

'Oh, I see,' she said, rather doubtfully. 'It's Bach, isn't it? 'The Art of the Fugue'.'

'Spot on,' he said heartily. 'Can't get enough of them fugues, me.'

A cop could survive worse things than a taste for the baroque. There was that hard bastard down in the Midlands who collected beetles and nobody messed with him. But get a reputation for religion and you were marked down as bonkers. Even Tony Blair knew that, though in his case mebbe he really was bonkers!

'Right, luv,' he went on. 'Grab a pew, I mean a chair, not many pews left these days. Then you can tell me what it is Mick would have told me if I'd answered my phone.'

She sat by his side. Though not quite recovered to his full fighting weight, his flesh still overspread the limits of the chair and he could feel the warmth of her thigh against his. She was wearing a perfume that would probably have got her burned during the Reformation.

He raised his eyes not in supplication but simply to focus his mind away from these distractions. His gaze met that of the little marble dog who was peering over the end of the tomb as if in hope that after so many centuries of immobility at last someone was going to cry, 'Walkies!'

'OK,' said Dalziel. 'We're in the right place. Confession time!'

09.00–09.20

David Gidman the Third awoke.

It was Sunday. That was something being brought up in England did for you. Maybe it was some ancient race-memory, maybe all those church bells set up a vibration of the air even when you were well out of ear-shot; whatever it was, physical or metaphysical, it was strong enough to make itself felt no matter how many supermarkets were open, no matter how many football matches were being played.

You woke, you knew it was Sunday. And that was good.

He rolled over and came up against naked flesh.

He felt it cautiously. A woman.

That was even better.

She responded to his touch by saying sleepily, 'Hi, Dave.'

He grunted, not risking more till he was certain who it was.

Like a blind man reading Braille, his fingers traced round her nipples and spelt out her name. He gave her a gentle tweak and breathed, 'Hi, Sophie.'

She turned to him and they kissed.

This was better and better.

'So how shall we spend today?' she murmured.

The bedside phone rang before he could answer.

He rolled away and grabbed the receiver.

'Hello,' he said.

He knew who it was before he heard the voice. Like Sunday, his PA, Maggie Pinchbeck, created her own vibes.

'Just checking you're awake and functioning. I'll be round in an hour.'

'An hour?'

'To go over the timetable. Then at half ten I'll drive you to St Osith's. OK?'

'Oh shit.'

'You haven't forgotten?'

'Of course I haven't bloody well forgotten.'

He put the phone down and turned back to the woman. An hour. Long enough, but he was no longer in the mood and anyway she was regarding him with suspicion.

'What haven't you forgotten?' she demanded.

No point poncing around.

'I'm opening a community centre this lunchtime,' he said.

'You're what? I've cleared the whole day, remember? George is in Liverpool; a.m. in the cathedral, p.m. at a footie match.'

'I know. Looking to get the credit if they win, eh?'

Her husband, George Harbott MP, known familiarly as Holy George, was the Labour spokesman on religious affairs.

He saw at once his joke had fallen on stony ground.

'Sorry,' he said. 'And I'm really sorry about

40

today. Early Alzheimer's.'

He began to get out of bed.

'What's the hurry anyway?' she queried. 'Lunchtime's hours away. And you could always ring them up and cancel, tell them you've got a cold or something. Come here and I'll persuade you.'

'I don't doubt you could,' he said, standing up out of her reach. 'But no way I can cancel. This is my granpappy's memorial community centre I'm opening.'

'So? Your father's still alive, if we can believe the Tory major contributors list. Why jump a generation? Let him open it.'

'He says it's a good vote-catcher for me,' he replied. 'And it's not just lunchtime. I've got to go to church first.'

'*Church? You?* Whose idea was that?'

'Holy George's, in a way. He rattles on so much about Christian values and getting back to the good old-fashioned Sabbath that Cameron's getting edgy. What with your lot wallowing in Catholic converts and Scottish Presbyterianism, he feels he can't rely on the old religious vote any more. His last newsletter stopped just short of establishing compulsory church parades. But it was Maggie who came up with this.'

'Pinchbeck? Jesus, Dave, that woman's got you by the pecker!'

The image itself was absurd, but he couldn't deny its truth. Whatever his leader said, church was the last place he wanted to be on a Sunday. In fact when Maggie had suggested opening the new community centre on Sunday rather than

41

on Monday as proposed by the council, he'd told her she must be mad.

She'd replied, 'Monday there's showers forecast, plus most people will be at work. You'll get the council freeloaders and maybe a few bored mums with their wailing kids. Sunday's the day for good works and this is a good work you're doing. In fact, go to church first. St Osith's is perfect. Just a mile down the road, plenty of room there and I know the vicar, Stephen Prendergast. He'll be delighted to get the publicity. Service will be over by midday, so if we schedule the opening for one you should get most of the congregation along too, plus a whole gang of others with nothing better to do on a Sunday lunchtime.'

'But what about the press?'

'Leave the press to me. It will do that heathen bunch good to go to church.'

'Won't I risk alienating the ethnic vote?'

'The Muslims, you mean? No. The moderates will be delighted to see you're a man of faith. The extremists will want to blow you up whatever you do.'

She had an answer for everything, and the trouble was it usually turned out to be the right answer.

The woman was out of bed now and gathering up her clothes.

'Hey, Sofe,' he pleaded. 'Don't get mad. No need to rush off. Stay for some breakfast . . . '

'You want I should still be hanging round here like this when Pinchbeck turns up? I can feel those beady little eyes tracking over every inch of flesh, looking for bite marks. You knew about this when I rang yesterday afternoon, right? But you didn't say a thing in case I told you I didn't care to be kicked out of bed at sparrowfart like some cheap tart. Well, I bloody well don't!'

She disappeared into the bathroom. He heard the new power shower switch on. Half a minute later there was an enraged scream and Sophie appeared dripping water in the doorway.

'You some kind of masochist, or what?' she demanded. 'That shower, it's gone from red hot to icy cold of its own accord.'

He regarded her indifferently. Even a nicely put together body like hers ceased to be a turn-on when it was wet and goose-pimpled and topped by a face contorted by anger.

'Sorry about that,' he said. 'I've been having some problems. Maggie got me a couple of Poles to fix things. Looks like I'll need to have them back.'

'Maggie!' she spat. 'I might have known she'd have something to do with it!'

She vanished.

David Gidman the Third yawned then picked up a remote from the dressing table and clicked it at a mini hi-fi system on top of a chest of drawers. Terfel's sumptuous voice started singing 'Ich habe genug.'

'Now that's what I call serendipity,' he said.

He turned to a full-length mirror set in the wardrobe door and sang along for a while, studying himself in the glass.

Golden-skinned, craggily handsome, muscularly slim, reasonably well hung, and above all youthful; David Gidman the Third MP, the Tory Party's Great Off-white Hope.

He stopped singing, dropped his voice, uttered a couple of gorilla grunts, scratched his balls, leered prognathically into the mirror, and said huskily, 'The next PM but one — here's looking at you, baby!'

08.55–09.15

For what felt like a good minute the woman called Gina Wolfe said nothing, but stared down at her hands, which were nervously plucking at the hem of her short skirt. Then suddenly out came a tumble of words.

'Look,' she said, 'the thing is, I'd like to make it clear from the start, I don't want Alex dead . . . OK, I know that's the way it started out, me needing to prove he was dead, but what I mean is if I found him alive I wouldn't want him to be killed . . .'

'Just as well, missus,' interrupted Dalziel. ''Cos I need to know folk really well afore I start doing favours like that.'

That stemmed the flow. Her hands stopped their movement and she looked him straight in the face. Then she smiled weakly.

'I'm gabbling, aren't I? It's just that I didn't think I was going to have to start at the start, so to speak.'

'Because Mick Purdy would have put me in the picture, right? OK, let's see if I can get you on track with a couple of questions. First, who's Alex?'

'Of course. Sorry. Alex Wolfe. My husband.'

'And he left you?'

'Yes. Well, no, I suppose strictly speaking I left

45

him. But not really. I never *abandoned* him . . . I never thought of it as permanent . . . things had just got so bad that I needed space . . . we both did. And in a sense, he'd left me a long time before . . . '

'Whoa!' said Dalziel. 'Lots of things I need to get straight afore we get into the blame game. Where was this? When was this? What did Alex Wolfe do for a living? Why did you leave him? I think that'll do for starters.'

'It was in Ilford, we lived in Ilford. I still do. That's part of the problem . . . sorry. What did Alex do? He was like you. A policeman. Not as important. A detective inspector.'

Ilford. He'd heard of Ilford. It was in Essex. DI Mick Purdy had been with the Essex division of the Met. And Alex the walk-about husband had been a cop. Things were beginning to join up, but he was still a lot of lines short of a picture.

'And you leaving him? What was that about? A woman?'

'No! That would have been easy. Easier. It was a very bad time. For both of us. We lost . . . there was a bereavement . . . our daughter, Lucy . . . '

He could feel the effort she was making to keep herself together. Oh shit, he thought, me and my big boots. He'd have known about this presumably if he'd listened to Purdy on the phone.

On the other hand, not knowing meant he was getting everything up front, no pre-judgments.

He said, 'I'm sorry, luv. Didn't know. Must have been terrible.'

46

She said with unconvincing matter-of-factness, 'Yes. Terrible just about sums it up. Certainly not the best of times to have this other stuff at work start up. Not that it seemed to bother Alex. He just didn't seem to care. About anything. I got angry with him. I needed someone, but all he wanted was to be left alone. So I left him alone. I didn't abandon him . . . we were in it together . . . except we weren't . . . so I thought if I left him alone . . . no I didn't think that, I didn't really think anything. I just had to be with people who would listen to me talking, and going into a room where Alex was felt like going into an empty room . . . '

She was off again. Dalziel could only see one thing in this turmoil that might have anything to do with him. If it helped the woman to focus, that would be a plus too.

'This work stuff, what was that about?' he interrupted.

She stopped talking and took a deep breath. Refocusing from her bereavement to her husband's work problems seemed to bring a measure of genuine control. Her voice was stronger, less tremulous as she said, 'They called it a leak enquiry, but it was actually about corruption. Alex was second in charge of a team targeting this businessman. It was called Operation Macavity. That was a joke. From T.S. Eliot's poem. You know, *Cats*, the musical.'

Dalziel was untroubled by the presumption that the only way he was likely to have heard of Eliot was via *Cats*. There were a lot of smart people spending a lot of hard time behind bars

47

because they'd made similar presumptions.

'Yeah, loved it,' he said. 'Because he was never there, right?'

'Yes. But this time they had high hopes of getting to the man. It didn't work out. I don't know any details, but he always seemed to be several steps ahead of them. And while things were going wrong at work, at home things went into a nose dive . . . '

'Yes, yes,' said Dalziel, determined not to drift back towards the dead child. 'So the powers that be started wondering how the hell this Macavity always knew what was going on.'

'I suppose so. Why the rat pack — sorry, that's what Mick Purdy calls Internal Investigations — why they focused on Alex, I don't know. But they did.'

'Did they suspend him?' said Dalziel.

'Didn't need to. This all blew up at the same time as . . . the rest, and he was on compassionate leave, so he wasn't going into work anyway.'

'So he's at home, on compassionate leave, he's in a state, the rat pack's sniffing around, and eventually you leave him. Then . . . what? He takes off?'

'That's right.'

'And you looked for him?'

'Of course I looked for him!' she exclaimed. 'I got in touch with his friends, his relations. I talked to the neighbours. I checked out everywhere I thought he was likely to have gone, places we'd been on holiday, that sort of thing. I rang round hospitals. I did everything I could.'

'Including telling the police, I suppose?'

'Obviously,' she snapped. 'They were just about the first people I contacted. Why wouldn't I?'

'Well,' said the Fat Man, 'for a start, they're investigating him, right? It must have crossed your mind maybe they're the ones he's running from. Not sure, in your shoes, they're the first buggers I'd tell.'

She said tightly, 'I knew Alex. I believed in him. He was confused, desperate maybe. But he certainly wasn't corrupt. All I could think was he was out there somewhere, alone. So I called Mick Purdy. They were friends, so naturally I called Mick.'

He'd anticipated this was probably Purdy's connection. How had he reacted to the news? he wondered. Like a friend or like a cop?

'And what did good old Mick say?'

'He said to leave it with him, he'd make sure everything that could be done to trace Alex was done. Look, Mr Dalziel, I'm not sure how relevant all this is. We're talking seven years ago. It's here and now that I need help.'

'Aye, seven years. And there's been no sign of your husband all that time?'

'Not a whisper. Nothing from his bank account, no use of credit cards. Nothing.'

'Did he take his car?'

'No, it was still in the garage. In fact, he took nothing, so far as I could see. No spare clothes, not even his toothbrush. Nothing.'

'And the police? They turned up nothing?'

'The police, the Salvation Army, every

49

organization I could think of, none of them found any trace.'

'So, apart from being kidnapped by aliens, what did that leave you thinking happened to him?'

He watched her reaction carefully and let her see he was watching.

She met his gaze straight on and said, 'You mean it seems obvious to you he was probably dead, right?'

He shrugged but didn't speak.

She said, 'That's what Mick thought too, but I couldn't get my head round the idea. Even when I'd finally accepted he was never going to come back, I found it hard to contemplate applying for a legal presumption of death. That seemed . . . I don't know, disloyal almost, even though I really needed it.'

'Oh aye. Why was that?'

She said, 'Lots of reasons, mainly financial. The house we lived in is Alex's family house. It's in his name, so I can't sell it. There are various insurances that I can't access without proof of death. Even his police pension is being paid into a bank account in his sole name, so it piles up and I can't touch a penny of it.'

'So they're still paying his pension?'

'Why wouldn't they? Nothing was ever proved against him, no charges were brought,' she said indignantly.

Dalziel glanced at his watch. The organ was still burping out bits of tunes that chased each other round and round without ever catching up. He knew how they felt.

He said, 'I've been listening to you for a quarter of an hour, luv, and I'm no closer to understanding what any of this has got to do with me. What the hell are you doing up here in Yorkshire anyway?'

She said, 'It's simple. Next month it will be seven years since Alex vanished. My solicitor told me that after seven years we'd get a presumption of death on the nod. That made up my mind for me, so I said, let's do it. And everything was going fine, then yesterday morning I got this.'

She opened her shoulder bag and took out a C5 envelope which she passed over to Dalziel. He put his glasses on to study it. It had a Mid-York postmark and was addressed in black ink to Gina Wolfe, 28 Lombard Way, Ilford.

The envelope contained a sheet of notepaper headed *The Keldale Hotel*, attached by a paper clip to a folded page from the September edition of *MY Life*, the glossy news, views and previews monthly magazine published by the *Mid-Yorks Evening News*.

On the notepaper were typed the words *The General reviews his troops*.

A good half of the page from *MY Life* was occupied by a photograph recording the recent visit of a minor royal to the city. She was shown receiving a posy of freesias from a small girl across a crush barrier during a walkabout. A thick red circle had been drawn around the head of a man just beyond the child.

'This your husband?' guessed Dalziel.

'Yes.'

The photo was very clear. It showed a man

51

somewhere between late twenties and mid thirties, his blond hair tousled by the breeze as he observed the Royal with an expression more quizzical than enthusiastic.

'You sure?'

'It's Alex or his double,' she said.

'Right,' he said, turning his attention to the hotel notepaper.

The Keldale was the town's premier hotel, priding itself, with its spacious rooms, traditional menus and extensive gardens, on offering luxury in the old style.

'*The General reviews his troops*,' he read. 'That means summat special, does it?'

She said, 'Alex's family always liked to claim a family connection with General Wolfe . . . '

He saw her hesitating whether she needed to explain who General Wolfe was.

He said, 'The one who'd rather have written Gray's *Elegy* than whupped the Frogs, right?'

'Yes,' she said. 'Alex was rather proud of the connection and I used to make fun of him because of it, and we started playing this game . . . I was a plucky little trooper and he was General Wolfe reviewing his troops, and . . . '

She was blushing. It became her.

Dalziel handed back the magazine page and said, 'Spare me the details, luv. This something your Alex would have boasted about to his mates after a couple of pints?'

'No!' she exclaimed indignantly. 'Definitely not.'

Dalziel noted the certainty without necessarily accepting it.

'So you were convinced this was your man. What did you do?'

'I rang Mick.'

'Purdy? Oh aye. And what did he have to say?'

'Nothing. I couldn't get him. I knew he was going to be busy this weekend. He's been running some big Met op, he's a commander now. They've got to the arrest stage, so that probably meant all mobiles switched off. Anyway, I left him a message.'

Dalziel digested this. Purdy a commander. The lad had done well, but he'd had the look of a high-flier back when they'd met all those years ago. More puzzling was the woman's knowledge of him; not his promotion, that was understandable, but the details of his operational timetable.

He said, 'Sorry, luv, I'm not getting this. Seven years on you're trying to get your husband declared dead, then you get his picture through the post, and the first thing you do is ring his old boss? Why not your best friend, if it's a bit of emotional support you want? Or your solicitor, if it's professional advice. Why dig right back into the past and come up with your man's old boss?'

She said, 'Sorry, Mr Dalziel, I keep forgetting you didn't actually speak to Mick. I should have told you right away. There's another reason I need to get a presumption of death. Mick and I are going to be married.'

Vince Delay watched Tubby stand up then sit down again and start talking to Blondie.

Briefly he had a full-frontal view of the fat guy and now he dropped his eyes to compare what he'd seen with a photograph he was holding in his hymn book. It was a full-length shot of a man lounging against a tree, thirtyish, blond hair ruffled by a breeze, with the slightly mocking half-smile of a guy who knows what he wants and has no doubts about his ability to get it.

The only time Vince had seen him in the flesh, trouble had wiped that smile from his face but otherwise he'd looked the same.

Fleur had said, stick to Blondie and she'll lead us to him, and this is where she'd led.

He let his gaze drift from the photo to the bulky figure sitting close to the tart. Question was, could anything have changed this to *that* in seven years?

Didn't seem likely.

Pity, he thought. Would have been nice if things had turned out so easy. Not that it bothered him. Not his responsibility, not since Fleur took him in hand. Would have been nice for Fleur though. Or maybe not. Fleur was clever and for some reason clever people often seemed to prefer things a bit complicated. Himself, he'd

54

have been delighted if it had been Tubby. Whack! And then back down the motorway, leaving this northern dump to fall to pieces in its own time.

One thing was sure: whoever Tubby was, all that praying, he had some heavy stuff on his mind. And now it looked like Blondie was laying some more on him. This surveillance stuff was real boring.

Couldn't even light up. Not many places you could these days. No laws to stop the bastards lighting candles though. Back in the car he guessed Fleur would be on her second or third ciggie by now, probably having a coffee from the flask. Maybe a little nip in it. No, scrub that. Not Fleur. On a job you had rules and you stuck to them. You look after the rules and the rules would look after you, she was fond of saying. And if she caught you breaking the rules — *her* rules — then retribution was instant and unpleasant.

Though sending him to do the tailing was breaking the rules, wasn't it?

Maybe it meant she'd decided he wasn't just muscle, he could think for himself.

The idea was both flattering and disturbing. It suggested a change in their relationship and he didn't like change.

She'd laid down the terms pretty categorically in the prison visiting room as his last and longest stretch came within sight of the end. He'd served them years the hard way and he'd got respect, but at a price. Fleur was the only person he could share his horror with at the prospect of going back inside. In another sort of man this admission might have been linked to a resolve to go straight. Delay's resolve was different.

'I'll top myself first,' he said.

Fleur had given him the look that since she was nine had reversed the three years between them and made him feel like her kid brother.

'Don't talk stupid, Vince,' she'd said brusquely. 'Now, where are you going when you get out?'

He looked at her, puzzled, and said, 'Thought I'd come home to start with . . . '

'Home's gone, Vince. I've got my own place now. You're welcome to come and live with me, but there's rules. You do things my way, in or out of the flat. Break the rules, and you're on your own. For good. What do you say? Yes or no?'

'Well, sounds all right, sis, but a guy's got to have a bit of choice, know what I mean . . . '

'Yes or no, Vince. That's one of the rules. I ask yes or no, you answer yes or no.'

'OK, keep your hair on. I mean yes.'

'Something else. I think I can get you a job.'

'You mean, like . . . a job?' he said, horrified.

She shook her head. She knew her limitations.

'I mean like the kind of job you're good at,' she said. 'Except that what you're not good at is not getting caught. So if you come to live with me, you come to work for me too, OK? No branching out on your own. I call the shots, OK?'

'Is that a yes or no question, sis?'

'It's a yes or yes question, Vince. If you want to live with me, that is.'

'Then yes.'

It had been a good decision. There'd been a couple of rebellious moments — like he'd said, a man's got to have a bit of independence — but they'd all got sorted, and Fleur had one great argument to support that her way was the best way: for more than a dozen years now he'd stayed out of jail!

He put the photo back in his wallet and for want of anything better to do let his gaze focus on the open hymn book once more. Some of this stuff was dead easy, but a lot of it was like reading the instruction book for a computer.

A servant with this clause
Makes drudgery divine.
Who sweeps a room as for thy laws
Makes that and the action fine.

What the hell was that all about?

He sighed and shifted in the chair whose wickerwork seat felt as if it was stamping its imprint on his behind. The thought took him back to his first time inside. They'd made him strip and take a shower. One of the screws had said mockingly, 'Nice arse, Delay. You're going to enjoy yourself here.'

It had taken half a dozen of the bastards to drag him off the man and then they'd given him a good kicking. But he'd been limping round the yard a couple of days later, an object of respect, and the screw had still been in hospital.

Happy days.

But not the kind of happy days he ever wanted to enjoy again. He was going to stay out whatever it took. And if ever Fleur's way looked like failing, then he'd just have to do things his own way.

09.15–09.30

Normally Andy Dalziel was to diplomacy what Alexander the Great was to knots, but this time he hesitated the cutting edge and essayed a bit of gentle plucking.

'So you and Mick, this a long-standing engagement . . . ?'

She laughed, a pleasant sound which the old cathedral absorbed with indifference though a few human heads turned in surprise.

'What you mean is, how long have we been at it? Or even more bluntly, were we at it while Alex was still around? Very much not. Mick stayed in touch, we became good friends, we were close, I could tell he was interested romantically, so to speak, but it wasn't till the end of last year that I finally acknowledged that Alex was gone for good. Mick's told me since he was starting to think I'd never get Alex out of my system. It came as a real shock to him when I finally made the break.'

Hearing himself proposing marriage must have come as a bit of a shock to Mick, too, thought Dalziel. He recalled Purdy declaring one boozy night that the only woman worth marrying was a billionairess with huge tits, no family, and an hour to live.

Still, men often change their views on

58

marriage. He certainly had.

He went on, 'So you left Mick a message telling him to ring you. And then . . . ?'

'I called my solicitor. He wasn't all that pleased, it being Saturday. That didn't bother me. I'm paying the louse and no doubt he'll charge me double time.'

'Good lass,' said Dalziel, who loved anybody who hated lawyers. 'What did he say?'

'He said he wished I hadn't told him about the photo. Because now I had, he was bound to include knowledge of it in his plea for assumption of death.'

'Covering himself in case it later came out that Alex was alive, right?'

'Right. I asked him what I should do. He said that all I could do was make every reasonable effort to check out the possibility that my husband was alive and living in Mid-Yorkshire. He said that on receipt of my written assurance that such an effort had been made, he would go ahead with the application.'

'Lawyers,' said Dalziel, 'I've shit 'em. So what did you do then?'

'I rang the Keldale Hotel.'

'Oh aye. Why'd you do that?'

'Because I wanted somewhere to stay when I got here and it was the obvious place. Why use the hotel's notepaper unless it meant something?'

Mebbe because it meant nothing, thought Dalziel, nodding as if in agreement and saying, 'And then?'

'Then I threw some stuff in a case and drove up here,' she said.

'Don't hang around, do you?' said Dalziel admiringly.

'You might say I've been hanging around for seven years,' she said. 'But no more. I was determined to get this thing settled one way or another.'

'So you'd worked out a plan of action, had you?'

'That makes it sound a bit grand,' she said ruefully. 'At the Keldale reception, I showed them a photo of Alex, but it didn't ring any bells. The only other idea I had was to run a small ad in the local paper using the same photo of Alex and offering a reward to anyone supplying information. But it was too late when I got here, the newspaper office was closed.'

'Aye, we like to keep civilized hours up here,' said Dalziel. 'We don't let news happen at the weekend. So what did Mick Purdy have to say about all this? You must have got to speak with him if he's ringing me.'

'Yes, I did, but not till last night after I'd arrived here. When he realized where I was, he didn't sound very happy. And when I told him what I planned to do, he sort of groaned. I wasn't in the mood to be groaned at and I'm afraid I snapped at him. To tell the truth, I was really frustrated I couldn't get on with things straight away.'

'Should have thought about that afore you came rushing up here,' said Dalziel portentously. 'Could have saved yourself a couple of night's rent at the Keldale, which won't be peanuts.'

'You know, you sound just like Mick!' she said.

'It ended with me saying one thing I could do on Sunday was call in at the local cop shop and check if they were any more helpful up here than down in the Met. He asked me — asked, not told — he's a quick learner — he asked me not to do anything till he got back to me. Then he had to rush off — he was still in the middle of his op.'

'And you sat up anxiously all night waiting for your wise fiancé to call with instructions like any good girl would,' said Dalziel.

She smiled and said, 'Naturally. Actually I didn't sleep so well and I was up and out not long after seven, driving around. I know it's stupid, but I thought I might just happen to spot Alex on the street or something.'

'Aye, I've had daft buggers in the CID who thought that was how it worked,' said Dalziel. 'But not for long!'

He expected that to provoke a rueful smile. Instead she frowned and looked away.

'Come on!' he said. 'You're not saying you clocked him!'

She shook her head and said, 'No. Worse than that. I thought I did. Three times. I even followed a car for half a mile, and the driver who looked like Alex turned out to be a woman!'

'Could have had a sex change, I suppose,' said Dalziel. 'But I shouldn't let it bother you, luv. Your mind can play funny tricks when you're not quite right with yourself. Look at Blair and Bush and all them weapons of mass destruction. And I once thought I saw England win the world cup.'

That got a smile and she went on, 'Anyway,

61

chasing that woman driver convinced me I was acting stupidly. Then my mobile rang and it was Mick. When I told him what I'd been doing, I heard him start that groaning again, but he managed to choke it off. Then he told me about you.'

'Let me guess,' said Dalziel. 'He said he had this old mucker who was top-man on the Mid-Yorkshire Force and he was just the guy to make a few discreet enquiries afore you started your public manhunt, right?'

It made some kind of sense.

She said, 'More or less. That was about eight o'clock, He said it was probably better to contact you at home because this wasn't really official police business. He said he was going to ring you there to put you in the picture and would let me know as soon as he'd made contact. I told him I'd wait for his call at the hotel, but soon as he rang off I stuck the address he gave me in my sat-nav and headed round to your street. I just had to be doing something, even if I thought . . . '

She tailed off and he said, 'Even if you thought I'd probably be a waste of time. So, soon as Mick rang and said he'd talked to me, you were going to be ringing my bell!'

'That's right,' she said. 'Sorry. Anyway, it didn't work out. Suddenly you shot out, jumped in your car and drove here like you were late for a funeral.'

'How'd you know it was me?'

'Mick described you.'

'Oh aye. Young, slim and sexy, was it? Don't answer that.'

Time to review the situation. He'd been weighing up the woman as she talked. A few years older than his first assessment, well into her thirties, but she knew how to use her make-up and she kept herself in good shape. Very good shape. Bright blue eyes, teeth in good nick, hair naturally blonde and elegantly arranged by someone who probably charged a tenner a snip. Clothes to match, expensive but not designer expensive, though her shoes (he knew a lot about shoes; they were Cap's sartorial weakness and she had enough fancy footwear to kit a WAGs convention) probably cost more than he'd paid for his last suit. But then he did get very good discounts.

As for personality, she was strong. She'd come close to losing control a couple of times — and from the sound of what she'd been through, it would have been understandable if she had — but she'd managed to pull back from the brink. She was, he judged, a woman who felt that action was the better part of reaction. Heading straight up to Mid-Yorkshire in response to that weird missive, driving around the streets first thing this morning then camping outside his door, all this suggested someone who would rather do something than sit around doing nothing.

Or perhaps, rather do anything than sit around thinking about what the past had held and what the future might hold.

All in all, he liked her. Not that that signified. His life was punctuated with trouble spots that had started with women he liked.

So, decision time.

He couldn't see what this could have to do with him professionally, but it was his day off, and having someone else's confusions dumped in his lap had certainly diverted his mind from his own.

On the other hand, his knight-errant days were long past, he wasn't about to rush into anything, not even for a damsel in distress as tasty as this.

He said, 'I'll need to brood on this a bit, luv. Tell you what, why don't we meet up later? Have a bit of grub mebbe?'

Giving her the chance to say thanks but no thanks. If after meeting him she didn't care to pursue the acquaintance, it was no skin off his nose.

'OK. Where?' she said without hesitation. So he must have made an impression. Or she were really desperate!

He said, 'You're at the Keldale, right? All the best folk take Sunday lunch on the terrace there. Tell them you want a table overlooking the gardens. Any problem, tell Lionel Lee, the manager, you're meeting me.'

'Mick said you were a man of influence,' she said.

'Did he now?'

For perhaps the first time since his return, he actually felt like it.

He stood up. She remained sitting.

'You not leaving?' he said.

'I think I'll sit and listen to the music for a while,' she said.

'Oh aye?' Then recalling he was allegedly here

because he was fond of this chase-me-round-the-houses stuff, he added, 'You a fan of old Bach then?'

'Very much so. Occupational hazard. I'm a music teacher by profession.'

That surprised him. His notion of music teachers involved wire-rimmed spectacles, scrubbed cheeks, and hair in a bun. Mebbe he should get out more.

'Grand job,' he said, overcompensating for his uncharitable thoughts. 'Kids can't get too much music.'

'Indeed,' she said, smiling at him warmly. 'It's good to know we have music in common, Mr Dalziel. It wasn't something I anticipated from the way Mick spoke of you. Sorry, I don't mean to be rude . . . '

'Forget to mention I was Renaissance Man, did he?' said Dalziel. 'Mind you, all I can recall of his tastes is he fancied himself as Rod Stewart on the karaoke.'

'Still does. And he can't tell a fugue from a fandango.'

She smiled again. She really was a fine-looking woman. Mebbe his knight-errant days weren't done and dusted after all. Mebbe Sir Andy of the Drooping Lance had one last tilt in him.

He began to walk away but had only gone half a dozen steps when she called after him.

'Mr Dalziel, you didn't say what time for lunch.'

His stomach rumbled as if in response, reminding him he'd skimped on breakfast in his rush to not be late.

'Best make it twelvish,' he said. 'Folks up here stick to the old timetables, even when they're eating at the Keldale.'

And I'd not like to get there and find the roast beef had run out, he added to himself as he turned away.

He wasn't unhappy to be getting out of the cathedral. There was something weird and disturbing about all that space. But he had a curious fancy as he strode towards the door that he could hear little feet pattering behind him.

He glanced back and met the eager eyes of the marble dog peering over the edge of the tomb.

'Sorry,' he said. 'Another time, eh? I'll be back.'

And to his surprise he found he actually meant it.

Fleur Delay watched the fat guy come out of the cathedral.

No sign of Vince.

She guessed he'd be suffering an agony of indecision about whether to follow the man or stick with the woman. Vince didn't do structured thinking. Rationalizing his way to a choice was like walking across hot coals.

What he might be now if she hadn't finally decided that taking her big brother in hand was a full-time job didn't bear thinking of. Looking back, it seemed as if she'd been training for it the whole of her life, or at least since the age of nine when their father left.

To start with there'd been a lot of self-interest here. If the family fell apart, the only route for herself was into care. Someone had to hold things together, and she didn't need to be told that neither her mother nor her brother was up to the job. By the time she left school and got her job with The Man, she'd become expert at dealing with social workers who expressed doubts about the set-up. An hour in Fleur's company saw them persuaded, not without relief, that she was much better qualified than they were to save her mother from the worst consequences of her own excesses while at the same time trying with diminishing success to keep her brother out of jail and making sure he had a home to return to on release.

She'd been working for Gidman for nine years when her mother finally succumbed to a cocktail of alcohol and chemicals. Not long after the funeral, the other half of her family responsibility was put on hold by a judge deciding short sharp shocks were clearly having no effect on Vince and sending him down for a ten stretch.

His behaviour inside ensured he did the full term and, as his release date approached, Fleur found herself having to work out a strategy for the future not only for her brother but herself.

During her twenty years working for The Man her reliability and ingenuity had won golden opinions and rapid advancement. But Goldie Gidman's career horizons had widened considerably too.

Fleur's career running The Man's financial affairs had begun shortly before Margaret Thatcher began to run the country's. During the Thatcher years Goldie Gidman had come to see that this brave new world of free market enterprise offered opportunities to become stinking rich that did not involve the use of a hammer. Though the implement had changed, the principle was one he was very familiar with. Human need and greed left people vulnerable. Looking west out of the East End into the City he saw a feeding frenzy that made his own localized pickings seem very Lenten fare. And so began the moves, both geographical and commercial, that were to turn him into a financial giant.

But changes of direction can be dangerous.

It was Fleur who had pointed out to him the paradox that going completely legit left him much more exposed than staying completely bent. The movement from crookedness to cleanliness meant abandoning a lot of old associates whose faces and attitudes were at odds with the new glossy picture of himself and his activities he was preparing for the world. The trick was to make sure that, as new doors opened before him, the old doors were firmly locked and double barred behind. Fortunately he'd always tidied up as he went along and those who knew enough to do him active harm were few and far between. Now once more he scrutinized them very carefully and those he had any doubts about got visited by his long-time associate and enforcer, Milton Slingsby.

No one knew more about The Man's affairs than Fleur Delay. Her record should have made her invulnerable. But the trouble was that her professional usefulness had more or less come to an end. Her talent for manipulative accountancy had been invaluable in the days when his main financial enemies were local tax inspectors and VAT men, and she had been helpful during the early moves into legitimate areas of speculation. But as Goldie prospered, he had turned more and more to the specialized tax accountants without whom a man could sink without trace in the mazy morass of the modern markets. In their company she was like an abacus among computers, but an abacus whose database was very computer-like. While she did not believe she was in imminent danger of a visit from Sling, she knew that Goldie valued people in proportion to their usefulness, and to have dangerous knowledge but no positive function was potentially a fatal combination.

As Vince's release date approached, she saw a way to solve both her problems.

The key was Milton Slingsby.

Sling's great merit was total loyalty. Whatever Goldie told him to do, he did. But he was nearly ten years older than Goldie and his early years in the boxing ring, where he was renowned for blocking his opponents' punches with his head, were starting to take their toll. With Goldie by his side telling him what to do he could function as well as ever. But now the new respectable Goldie wanted to be as far away as possible from the kind of thing he usually told Sling to do.

So Fleur brought up the subject of her brother with The Man, not as *her* problem, but as *his* opportunity. Vince, she averred, would do the heavy work. She would do the planning, guaranteeing speed, discretion, and absolutely no lines back to The Man.

To employ someone like Vince Delay directly wasn't an option for Goldie. Such men were by their very nature likely to prove as unreliable as the unreliables they were seeing off. But the prospect of having someone as heavy as Vince under the control of someone he still trusted as implicitly as Fleur was not unattractive.

He agreed to a trial run. Three days later the designated target fell while out walking his dog and cracked his skull against a fence post with fatal results.

That had been thirteen years ago and up till now neither party had had occasion to complain about the arrangement. Rapidly the Delays' reputation for reliability and discretion drew in offers from elsewhere, some of which Fleur accepted, though as a Gidman pensioner, she had sufficient income to permit her to be choosy. But on the increasingly rare occasions The Man put work their way, she dropped everything else and came running.

It was important to please The Man, partly for pride, principally for preservation.

Her policy of keeping Vince as ignorant of the fine detail of their jobs as possible seemed to work. As a notorious ex-con, he got pulled in from time to time when the police had nothing better to do. Silence underpinned by ignorance and bolstered by the rapid arrival of a top-class brief had kept him safe. She used these occasions to point out to The Man just how ignorant Vince was. She felt pretty certain that as long as she was around and functioning efficiently, there would be no problem.

But take her out of the picture, and she knew beyond doubt that Goldie Gidman would be running his cold eyes over her brother.

She ran her own eyes over him as finally he emerged from the cathedral and headed towards the VW.

The fat guy was already getting into his ancient Rover.

Vince slid into the passenger seat beside his sister.

71

'What's happening?' she asked. 'Where's the woman?'

'Don't get your knickers in a twist,' he said. 'She's still inside. They're meeting up later for lunch at the hotel. Twelve o'clock. I heard them fixing it.'

The Rover was nosing its way out of the car park. She started the VW and followed it out into Holyclerk Street.

'We not tailing Blondie any more then?' asked Vince.

'We'll let the bug do that for us. If she stops anywhere, we can check it out. You keep an eye on the laptop. Now tell me exactly what you saw and heard in the cathedral.'

When he finished, she squeezed his arm and said, 'You done well, Vince.'

He basked in the glow of pleasure that praise from Fleur always gave him.

They had left the cathedral area behind them and were approaching the main urban highway. The Rover signalled left towards the town centre. Fleur signalled right.

'We not going to see where's he's heading?' said Vince, puzzled.

'I'm starting to have a good idea where he's heading,' said Fleur. 'What I want to see is where he's coming from.'

09.50–10.30

It was funny, thought the Fat Man. Turning up at the Station by mistake on his day off would have been disastrous, but striding in now and taking them all by surprise felt like old times.

'Morning, Wieldy,' he said breezily. 'Got a couple of little jobs for you.'

Detective Sergeant Edgar Wield had the kind of face that didn't do surprise, but there was a slight pause for adjustment before he said, 'Morning, sir. Be right with you.'

Dalziel noted the pause and thought, Gotcha! as he flung open the door of his office.

The evidence of his uncertain return to work was visible in the room's relative tidiness. Pascoe had been using it latterly and the bugger had got everything ship-shape and Bristol fashion. The Fat Man had found himself thinking it was a shame not to benefit from this orderliness and for ten days he'd been replacing files in the cabinet, closing drawers, removing clutter from his desk, and even striving to keep the decibel level of his farts under control.

That he could take care of instantly. As he sank into his chair he let rip a rattler.

'Didn't quite catch that, sir,' said Wield from the doorway.

'Would probably have broken your wrist if you

had,' said Dalziel. 'Seven years back there were a DI in the Met, Alex Wolfe, under investigation for corruption or summat; resigned, I think, then disappeared. I'd like all you can find about him. Same with Mick Purdy; DCI back then, now he's Commander. But softly softly, eh? Don't want to set any alarm bells ringing.'

'What sort of alarm is that likely to be, sir?' said Wield.

'No idea. Probably none. But you know me, discretion's my middle name.'

No it's not, it's Hamish, thought Wield. But that was a piece of knowledge he didn't care to flaunt.

'This something likely to come up at tomorrow's case review, sir?' he asked.

The Fat Man glanced at him sharply. The bugger can't have picked up on me mistaking the day, can he? No way! But that blank, unyielding face could make a nun check if her lacy knickers were showing.

'Nowt official yet. That's why I'm here on my day off,' he said. 'Pete around?'

'No, sir. His day off, too. He's going to a christening.'

'Eh? Ellie's not dropped another? I weren't out of the loop that long, surely.'

'No. They're guests. Like you, seeing as you're not official.'

'Don't get cheeky. Was a time when I'd be met with smiles and coffee.'

'Was there, sir? Can't bring it to mind. Shall I organize a coffee?'

'I'd rather have it than one of thy smiles, Wieldy. No, you get right on to Wolfe. I'll wake one of them idle buggers out there.'

He followed the sergeant to the door and looked around.

His gaze lit on DC Shirley Novello, engrossed in her computer screen.

'Ivor!' he bellowed. 'Coffee!'

The young woman looked up and replied, 'No thanks, sir. I've just had one.'

Something that on another face might have been called a grin touched Wield's lips, then he moved away swiftly.

'Now!' bellowed Dalziel. 'Why else do you think we let women into the Force?'

He went back into his office and sat at his desk. The encounter with the blonde at the cathedral had kick-started his day, but he still felt a bit out of sorts. He'd got the problem of the lost day sorted, so what was left to bug him? If he did any more internal digging, he'd be looking at his belly button from the inside, so he changed his point of view and looked around the room. After a few moments, he got it.

Problem solved, or just about to be!

Six or seven minutes later Wield dead heated with a coffee-bearing Novello at the Fat Man's door. No plastic beaker from the machine this; she'd have had to go down to the canteen to get half a pint of the Super's favourite blend in his own mug. It smelled good, but from the look on Novello's face, Wield thought it might be wise if Dalziel got her to taste it before touching it himself.

He opened the door for her and followed her into the room.

It had changed. Most of the drawers on the desk and filing cabinet were pulled out, a dented metal waste bin lay on its side against a dented wall, and in the furthermost corner as if hurled there with great force lay a file that the sergeant recognized as the one containing Pascoe's briefing notes for the case-review meeting. The window was wide open and the breeze so admitted was having a great time rustling through various loose sheets scattered across the floor.

Dalziel noted him noticing and said, 'Been doing a bit of tidying up. Ivor, you can't have much to do if you've time to fetch coffee. Run me this number will you?'

He scribbled Gina Wolfe's car number on the back of an unopened envelope that bore the Chief Constable's insignia and the words *Urgent and Confidential*.

Novello took it, turned, rolled her eyes when she had her back to the Fat Man and went out.

'Right, sunshine, what've you got?'

Wield said, 'Seven years back, DI Alex Wolfe was targeted by the Met's Internal Investigations. He was a key man in a team investigating a financier, David known as Goldie Gidman.'

'So Wolfe was a paper-chaser,' said Dalziel with the muted scorn of the front-line cop for the Fraud Squad. In the Fat Man's eyes, boardroom crime was to real crime what soft-porn movies were to child prostitution.

'Foot in both camps; he'd done his share of hard-end stuff,' said Wield. 'Commendation for bravery during the Millennium siege. Also I get

76

the impression this weren't straight Fraud Squad stuff. The officer initiating it was a deputy assistant commissioner. Owen Mathias. You know him?'

'Heard of him,' said Dalziel. 'Took early retirement and died. Dicky heart.'

'That's right. Seems to have had Gidman in his sights for a long long time, but never laid a finger on him. That's likely why he called this op Macavity. Turned out a bit too accurate. All trails banged up against a dead end, or a smart lawyer with a writ. Conclusion, Mathias's at least, someone was leaking. So he set Internal Investigations on it and they focused on Wolfe.'

'What do you mean, *Mathias's at least*?'

'Get the impression there were a lot who reckoned that Macavity were a waste of time and money. They'd not been able to touch Gidman in his early days in the East End. Now he were out of the mucky back streets and into the City, he were so squeaky clean, the Tories were accepting donations from him.'

'Proving what?' grunted Dalziel. 'So you're saying this Macavity op were a grudge thing between Mathias and Gidman?'

'I'm saying it feels like that's what a lot of people thought.'

'Did this mean Internal Investigations just went through the motions?'

'Can't say. Certainly nowt were ever proven against Wolfe. He happened to be on compassionate leave at the time, so they didn't even need to suspend him. Then he resigned. Bit later he vanished. Estranged wife reported it, they

77

looked at it, no evidence of foul play, he was a grown man, no charges had been brought so he wasn't a fugitive. I got the impression they were glad to be shot of him without the fuss of a full-blown corruption enquiry.'

'OK. What about Purdy?'

'Wolfe's DI back when he was a sergeant. Paths parted when he went up to DCI and Wolfe to DI. Wolfe more into the paperchase side of things, Purdy stayed hands on. Did well. Current job, Commander in some Major Crime Unit at the Yard.'

'Right. Operation Macavity, things improve there after Wolfe vanished?'

'Seems not. Shelved soon after. No evidence, no action.'

'And nowt since?'

'Not a word. Looks like the records have been hoovered clean. Like they'd feel embarrassed at it coming out how much time and money they'd wasted. Not surprising, considering how things have worked out for Gidman.'

'Eh? Hang about, you're not saying we're talking about yon Dave the Turd MP? No, can't be, he's still in his twenties, isn't he?'

'Goldie Gidman's his father.'

Shit, thought Dalziel. His brain really was creaking. Though in fact, he reassured himself, no reason why he should have made the leap as soon as he heard the name. In living memory he'd helped send down a Brown and a Cameron, the former for offing his boss's wife, the latter for identity theft, and in neither case had he looked at a Westminster connection.

Come to think of it, maybe he should have done.

Now he recollected a TV documentary he'd watched during his recent convalescence. It had been called *Golden Boy — The Face of the Future?*

Two years ago, David Gidman the Third had overturned a Labour majority of ten thousand in the Lea Valley West bye-election. He was a Tory golden boy in every sense. His mixed parentage had given him the kind of skin glow that footballers' wives pay match fees for. His grandfather, a Jamaican immigrant who worked on the railways, had been greatly respected as a community leader. His father was a self-made million- some said billion-aire whose predilection for investments involving gold had left him better placed than most to survive the plunging markets. Goldie Gidman was big in charity, giving generously of his wealth to educational, social and cultural projects in the East End of his upbringing. And also to the Conservative Party. No honours came his way. He did not want letters after his name, just after his son's. And if his son's nomination for Lea Valley West was his reward, then the Tories felt they'd made a good bargain, for, besides ticking all the right ethnic and cultural boxes, David Gidman was proving an attractive and energetic MP.

In right-wing journals, he was already crayoned in as a possible future leader, while in *Private Eye* his insistence on calling himself David Gidman the Third to remind everyone of his humble origins inevitably won him the witty sobriquet of Dave the Turd.

One thing was certain, thought the Fat Man. Guilty, innocent, in the modern political climate, Goldie Gidman's finances would have been gone over by the Millbank sniffer dogs before they accepted first his gift of money and then his gift of a son. With their long experience of fraud, graft, and corruption, if they ticked your approval box, you could give the finger to the police and the press. No wonder the Met felt shy about Operation Macavity.

Dalziel said, 'That it, Wieldy?'

'Yes, sir,' said Wield.

'Thanks, lad. Don't bother to close the door. This place needs an airing.'

Another man might have been offended, but Wield knew he wasn't being got at. The through-draught riffling the scattered papers was bearing away the last traces of Pascoe's ordered universe.

Alone, Dalziel sat back in his chair, clasped his hands on his lap, closed his eyes and set his mind to meditate how this changed things re Gina Wolfe, if at all.

Novello, entering a couple of minutes later, thought he looked like that huge statue of Buddha the Taliban had tried to shell to pieces, and felt some rare sympathy with the extremists.

She coughed gently.

Without opening his eyes, he said, 'You're not a bloody butler. Just tell me what you got.'

She said, 'Nissan 350Z GT, registered owner Gina Wolfe, 28 Lombard Way, Ilford, Essex. Three speeding points on her licence, no convictions.'

'Grand,' said Dalziel. 'Owt else?'

'Not on Ms Wolfe.'

'Who then?'

'While I was running this plate, I saw Sergeant Naseby. He said they'd had a call CID might be interested in. A Mrs Esmé Sheridan rang in to complain about a succession of kerb-crawlers in Holyclerk Street. She gave a description of the first one: *A gross creature with close-set eyes and a simian brow who made salacious suggestions.*'

'Sounds like a nut to me. Why'd Naseby think it was owt to interest us?'

'Mrs Sheridan took this *gross creature's* number. Couldn't be too sure of it because the number plate was as filthy as its owner — her words. The sergeant ran a check. Oddly enough, one of the possibles that came up was your number. Sir.'

'Dementia,' said Dalziel. 'Tell him to check the care homes for runaways.'

He opened his eyes and smiled as if seeing Novello for the first time.

'Ivor, you're looking well, lass. Take a seat. What time do you knock off?'

'Just got a report to finish then I'm done, sir.'

'Been on all night, eh?' he said sympathetically. 'So what are your plans?'

'Get a bit of shut-eye then meet up with some mates this evening,' she said, slightly surprised. This level of interest in her personal life was unusual in the Fat Man.

'Aye, but you'll need to eat,' he said, running his eyes over her frame as if assessing her weight. 'Growing girl needs her grub. Tell you what, how

81

do you fancy the terrace at the Keldale?'

This was a shock to Novello. Sexist the fat old sod could be if he felt like it, but one thing he'd never been was predatory. Could an unforeseen effect of his hospitalization be that he was going to turn into a dirty old man?

'Don't think I'm dressed for that, sir,' she said, glancing down at the loose olive green T-shirt and the baggy combat trousers which she habitually wore to work. On the whole her CID colleagues were fairly civilized, but there were still a few Neanderthals in the Station whose onanistic fantasies she didn't care to feed.

'Nay, tha's fine. You see some real sights around these days. Scruffy's the new smart, right?' said Dalziel. 'Any road, I don't mean right off. Thing is, I'm meeting this lass for lunch there. Twelve o'clock, high noon. What I'd like you to do is watch us.'

'Watch you?' she said. This could be worse than she'd imagined.

'Aye. Well no. What I mean is, I'd like you to keep your eyes skinned and see if there's any other sod watching us. Or watching her, more likely. Mebbe wanting to sit close enough to listen in on us. Moving when we move. Can you manage that?'

Not hitting on her then, but asking for her assistance.

Which was a considerable relief, but still odd. In matters constabulary, the old Andy didn't ask, he simply commanded.

'I suppose so,' she said hesitantly. 'Sir, is this . . . I mean, it's not a domestic, is it?'

'Like, am I having it off with a married woman and want to check if her husband's put a tail on her?' said Dalziel grinning. 'Wash your mind out, lass! Nowt like that. But it's not official, not yet. So let's keep it private. It's you doing me a favour in your lunch break. No official chitties either, so you'd best take this to cover expenses.'

He took out a roll of notes and peeled off a couple of twenties.

She looked at them in amazement — the Fat Man was not famous for his liberality — and said, 'Like I say, I normally just have a sandwich, sir.'

'On the Keldale terrace this'll just about cover that, specially if you have a glass of something nice to wash it down with,' he said.

She took the money and said, 'If I did spot someone and they moved off . . . '

'Follow 'em,' he said. 'Get a name and address; tha'll be top name on my Christmas card list. Right, twelve noon. Don't be late. Wouldn't surprise if my date gets there early; the keen ones usually do. Good-looking blonde, shoulder-length hair, thirty summat, looks younger from a distance, she'll be at a table at the edge of the terrace overlooking the gardens, so try to get sat where you can cover us and most of the other tables. Off you go now. And remember, mum's the word.'

He watched her leave. Nice bum, for all her efforts to hide it. Suddenly he realized how much better he was feeling. Mebbe it was the prospect of lunch with an attractive blonde. He wasn't yet sure what he was doing, but it definitely felt good to be doing it.

Some words popped into his mind, he couldn't remember their source, Churchill maybe, or Joe Stalin:

When the old order changeth, make sure you're the bugger who changeth it.

He got up, went out and found Wield working at his desk.

'Wieldy, I'm off,' he said. 'Man should enjoy his day of rest, eh?'

'That's right, sir. Though it's always good to see you.'

'Is it? Mebbe I really have been away too long.'

Wield watched his progress across the CID room. He looked very positive. Like some stately ship heading confidently towards the western horizon. The *Mayflower* perhaps. Or the *Titanic*.

Time would tell.

10.45–11.02

Ellie Pascoe studied the baby carefully.

It was, so far as she could see, unexception-
able. Two eyes, brown, not quite focused; a
squashed-up rather pug-like nose; a broad head
crossed by a few strands of fairish hair; rosy
cheeks and a dampish mouth from which
emerged gurgles of what was presumably
contentment; the usual number of limbs which
waved spasmodically in the air like those of a
bouleversed beetle.

Ellie had friends who, confronted by such a
phenomenon, would have dissolved into raptures
of hyperbolical praise punctuated by enough
cooing to deafen a dovecote.

It was an art she lacked. Yet, recalling how
much she had adored her own baby, and seeing
the pride and joy shining on the faces of the
infant's parents, she did her best.

'Isn't she adorable!' she cried. 'What a darling.
Goo goo goo goo goo.'

The parents, Alicia Wintershine and Ed Muir,
seemed to find her performance acceptable, but
she could feel the critical gaze of her husband
and daughter at her back and did not doubt she
was being marked out of ten for style and
content.

She got a small revenge by turning and saying,

'Rosie, isn't she lovely! So pretty. Not like you, dear. You were the weirdest-looking little thing.'

'Thanks a bunch, Mum,' said her daughter, advancing and greeting the baby like an old friend. 'Have you got her doing scales yet, Ali?'

Alicia Wintershine was Rosie Pascoe's clarinet tutor. At some point in their relationship she had moved from being Miss Wintershine, musical dominatrix, to *my friend Ali*. Ellie Pascoe took this as a mark of her daughter's progress on the instrument. Her husband, less convinced of Rosie's virtuosity, had enquired a little sourly whether dear old Ali gave a discount to her friends. But when he finally met the tutor and discovered she bore no resemblance to her lean, polished instrument but was softly rounded with big brown eyes, billows of chestnut hair, sexy lips and a laugh to match, all bundled in a package that looked ten years younger than her admitted thirty, he proved himself a reasonable man by admitting that his daughter could sometimes get as many as half a dozen consecutive notes in any given melody right, and in any case there were worse things a young girl could be putting in her mouth than a clarinet reed.

Ellie watched this softening of her husband's attitude with some amusement. He for his part was equally amused when, despite her spirited defence in public debate of the proposition that a woman needs a man like a fish needs a bicycle, she set about putting eligible young bachelors of her acquaintance in the nubile Miss Wintershine's way. Accused of attempted matchmaking, she of course denied it hotly but was caught out by her response to Peter's casual offer to trawl the corridors of Police HQ in search of possible candidates.

'A copper!' she cried indignantly. 'Do you think I could live with myself if I got another woman hitched to a copper? No, they come below estate agents and company directors, and only slightly above Tory politicians and pimps on my list.'

'So you do have a list!' said Pascoe triumphantly.

In the event, Ellie's efforts had been rendered redundant just over a year ago when Rosie came home from a lesson to say that Ali had got herself a fellow and she'd met him and he looked very nice. This news was confirmed later the same Saturday morning when Ali rang up to apologize. It turned out that Rosie's encounter with the new fellow had taken place on the landing of Miss Wintershine's house on St Margaret Street when Ed Muir, the fellow in question, had emerged from the bathroom wearing nothing but one of Ali's Funky Beethoven T-shirts.

It wouldn't happen again, Ali assured Ellie. You mean he's just passing through? enquired Ellie. Oh no, said Ali, he's here to stay, I hope. I'd love you to meet him.

And he had stayed. And Ellie had met him. And reported that he was a nice guy, quiet but bright with it, catering manager at the Arts Centre where the Mid-Yorkshire Sinfonietta, of which Ali was a leading member, gave frequent concerts.

'That was how they met,' said Ellie. 'I really like what I've seen of him.'

'Which is not as much as Rosie, I hope,' said Pascoe.

If ever Rosie glimpsed him *déshabillé* again, she kept as quiet about it as she had the first time.

Now here they were, a year later, guests at the christening. Pascoe had had to park a good quarter mile from St Margaret's and as they hurried past the Wintershine house, which was just fifty yards from the church, the door opened and the christening party emerged. Like the Magi, the Pascoe trio had turned aside for a brief moment of adoration.

This done, they went ahead and took their seats well to the rear of the fairly crowded church.

'Jesus,' said Pascoe. 'The whole of the orchestra must have been invited.'

'Not everyone will be a guest,' said Ellie. 'There'll be the usual parishioners along for the morning service.'

'Yes? That should account for six at least,' said Pascoe. 'And we're going on to the Keldale afterwards? Must be costing a fortune. You'd have thought a catering manager could have knocked up a nice little buffet in their back garden.'

'It's their first child!' said Ellie. 'You could see how excited they were. There are some things you don't even expect a copper to look for a discount on!'

'Sshh!' commanded Rosie, sitting between them. 'Can't you two behave yourselves? You're in church, remember!'

10.50–11.05

The moment the dusty, slightly battered Vauxhall Corsa pulled into the one remaining parking space in front of St Osith's, an officious policeman advanced to repel the intruder.

As he stooped to the passenger door, it opened, and the weighty reprimand about to be launched jammed in his throat.

With a commendably swift change of language, both body and actual, he said, 'Welcome, Mr Gidman,' and threw a smart salute as he pulled the door wide to let the elegant figure of David Gidman the Third step out on to the pavement.

There was a smatter of applause from the small crowd waiting by the church gate, and even a couple of wolf whistles. Gidman smiled and waved. He didn't mind the whistles. Like Byron said, When you've got it, baby, flaunt it.

'But not your wealth,' Maggie had decreed. 'You only flaunt your wealth in front of Russians and Arabs to let them know they'll have to offer you more than money to get you onside. You should never turn up at an English church in a limo unless you're getting married there.'

He'd let himself be persuaded, but he still had doubts as he walked up the path to the church door where the vicar was waiting for him.

'Stephen,' murmured Maggie in his ear as they approached.

He felt a pang of irritation. Didn't she think he was capable of remembering the guy's name? Perhaps he should address him as Stanley just to get a rise out of her.

But of course he didn't.

'Stephen, how good to see you. And what a lovely day you've arranged for us.'

'I can hardly take credit for that,' said the vicar, smiling.

They talked for a moment, long enough for Gidman to reassure the man that of course he'd have time after the service to meet a few of the more important parishioners in the vicarage garden before going on to the opening.

Now the churchwarden took him in tow and they moved out of the sunshine into the shady interior of the church.

This was the moment of truth. Two possible bad scenarios; one, there would be only a dozen or so in the congregation; two, there would be a decent crowd, but they'd all be black.

Maggie had reassured him on both counts, and it took only a second to appreciate that she'd been right again.

The church was packed. And the faces that turned to look at him as the churchwarden led him to his place in the foremost pew were as varied in colour as a box of liquorice allsorts. Maybe Maggie had called in a lot of favours, all them immigrant kids she'd helped. Maybe that pair of so called Polish craftsmen who'd fucked up his shower were here. Had to admit they were quick and they were cheap, though. And they'd certainly cooled Sophie's ardour!

The thought made him smile as he took his seat alongside the mayor and mayoress, giving them a friendly nod, before leaning forward in the attitude of prayer.

Maggie would be in the seat reserved for her directly behind him. He did not doubt that if he hesitated for a moment when the time came for him to read the lesson, he would hear her dry cough or even feel a gentle prod between the shoulder blades.

He thought nostalgically of Maggie's predecessor, Nikki. She'd been a perfect example of what he thought of as the two-metre model of PA: one metre of leg and another of bust, with shampoo-ad hair, pouting lips and a vibrator tongue. Unhappily, her tongue had been put to uses other than assisting him to the acme of pleasure. He'd been taken aback when she'd suddenly quit her job the previous year, and devastated when he started hearing rumours that she was negotiating a deal with the *Daily Messenger* for her steamy reminiscences of life under, and on top of, the Tory Golden Boy.

Dave didn't turn to his father for help immediately. A strange mixture of love and resentment kept him away. He loved and admired Goldie and had every confidence he could fix things, but at the same time he wanted to affirm his own independence.

Put another way, he was a big boy now and big boys fought their own fights.

Except, he was eventually forced to admit,

when they were up against the *Daily Messenger*, which specialized in chopping big boys down to size.

Goldie listened in silence. But he wasn't silent two days later when he summoned his son to tell him the crisis was over.

Dave the Third, the Great Off-white Hope of the Tory Party and the next prime minister but one, had to stand before his father like an errant schoolboy and listen to a long analysis of all his shortcomings without right of reply.

'Best thing for you, boy,' Goldie had concluded, 'is to get yourself a wife, someone like your mammy: loyal, home-loving, hardworking. But till you do that, if you can't keep your dick in your pants, don't stick it into anyone who doesn't have at least as much to lose as you do if word gets out. And one last thing. When you advertise for a new PA, I'll draw up the shortlist.'

That had been a year ago. The shortlist had consisted of three young men whom he'd dismissed out of hand and three singularly unattractive women, of whom Maggie Pinchbeck was undoubtedly the worst.

He recalled his first sight of her at interview, a small, mousey-haired creature who for all the clues her face, figure or even her drab trouser suit provided, could have been male or female; and undesirable in either gender. Her present job was as a senior PR officer at ChildSave, one of the big international child-protection charities. She looked the type who should be out in the desert digging latrines for fuzzy-wuzzies, he thought. This wouldn't take long.

He'd been forced to admit she interviewed well, answering every question he asked with intelligence and economy. But he still hadn't the slightest notion of employing her, a feeling reinforced when in conclusion he asked if she had any questions of her own.

'Yes,' she said. 'From time to time doubts have been expressed about the way your father acquired his fortune. In what degree do you share these doubts?'

Jesus! he thought. You take no prisoners.

He said, 'I take it you're referring to the scandal sheets in general and the *Messenger* in particular? Naturally those sad wankers would like to put a spoke in my wheel, and as I haven't offered much ammunition, they reckon that smearing my father will serve their purpose just as well. I should point out that whenever these muckrakers have dared move beyond innuendo, my pa's lawyers have made them pay heavily.'

'You haven't answered my question, Mr Gidman. Do you yourself have any doubts about the methods used by your father in establishing the basis of his fortune?'

He was tempted to tell her to sod off back to kiddy-land, then he had a better idea.

'Tell you what, why don't you ask him yourself?'

This had seemed an amusing way of getting back at Pappy. He'd brought together this gang of inadequates, let him see for himself the kind of creature his efforts had dug up. At the same time it would be a fitting punishment for this epicene dwarf's insolence. Questioning his early career always put Goldie in a bad mood. He would chew her up and spit her out!

He put the woman in his Audi A8 and watched her covertly as he drove north. To his disappointment she showed neither alarm nor surprise when he didn't head for the Gresham Street offices of Gidman Enterprises, and they had proceeded in silence till a couple of miles before Waltham Abbey he turned off on to a narrow country road. A few minutes later they pulled up before a set of imposing gates, one column of which bore the name Windrush House, while on the other a CCTV camera tilted down towards them.

Gidman waved at it, the gates swung silently open and he drove sedately up a long gravelled drive winding through an avenue of plane trees towards an imposing Victorian mansion in dull red brick that not even bright sunlight could render welcoming.

'This the family estate then?' said Maggie. 'How long has your father had it?'

'Ten years. And it's hardly an estate.'

'Whatever. Must have been quite a change relocating here from the East End.'

'It's still in Essex,' said Gidman, a touch defensively.

'Stayed true to his roots then,' she observed blandly.

At the front door a woman in a headscarf and slacks, on her knees to polish the already mirror-like brass letter box, looked up with a toothy smile and said, 'Dave, my lovely, now this is nice. We wasn't expecting you.'

Maggie assumed she was a domestic with enough service to give her familiarity rights till Gidman stooped and kissed her and said, 'Hi, Mom. This is Ms Pinchbeck, who wants to work for me.'

'Rather you than me, ducks,' said the woman. 'Nice to meet you.'

'And you, Mrs Gidman,' said Maggie.

'Call me Flo,' said the woman. 'In you go. I expect you're dying for a cup of tea.'

Maggie's pre-interview researches had told her that Flo had been a sixteen-year-old waitress in a London café when Goldie met her. By all accounts, it had been a marriage few on either side had approved and even fewer had forecast would prosper. Yet here she was, nearly half a century later, a bit plumper but with her old East End accent unrefined. 'And still doing everything around the house,' her son proclaimed proudly. 'She gets some help with the cleaning these days, but she's in total charge of the kitchen.'

The only live-in staff, Maggie later discovered, were Goldie's old assistant, Milton Slingsby, and Sling's nephew, an out-going young man called Dean who controlled the gate and other house security from a hi-tech office just off the entrance hall.

Already at this first visit Maggie was finding her expectations of baronial pretentiousness disappointed.

Goldie Gidman, in his late sixties, was as imposing a figure as his house, but a lot more welcoming. He had aged well, his lean muscular frame was supple rather than sagging, and the contrast between his vigorous white locks and almost black skin was something a lot of women might find very attractive.

To his son he said, 'Hope you haven't been spewing gravel over my lawn with that Panzer of yours.'

Maggie Pinchbeck he greeted with grave courtesy and sat there quietly observing her as Flo fussed about with teacups and home-made chocolate sponge.

Satisfied at last, Flo withdrew. She had done her job well, thought her son. If you came to see Goldie with expectations of being confronted by a jumped-up yardie, five minutes of exposure to Flo made you do a rethink.

He sat back to watch the fun.

'Dave says you got some questions to ask me, Miss Pinchbeck,' said Goldie.

She didn't hang about.

'How did you make your money, Mr Gidman? In the beginning, I mean.'

'Like most entrepreneurs, started with a little, invested wisely till I'd got a lot.'

'Were you ever a loan shark?'

'I did spend time in the personal credit business, yes.'

'You mean, you *were* a loan shark?'

'A loan shark being someone who loans out money to poor people at exorbitant interest rates and terrorizes them if they renege on repayments?'

'That sounds a reasonable definition.'

'No, I wasn't one of them. My father was what

96

is now called a community leader. Back then it just meant his reputation for good sense and honesty led other West Indian immigrants to turn to him for help and advice.'

'You saying you were a community leader too?' interrupted Maggie.

Goldie Gidman smiled.

'Not me. I was the first black yuppie, before there were white yuppies, I make no bones. But I loved my pa and when he told me members of our community found it difficult to get credit through the usual channels, I organized a neighbourhood credit club. Folk could borrow small sums on easy terms for purposes approved by the club's advisory committee. This way they kept out of the jaws of them loan sharks you talk about.'

'So where do all the rumours that you were one of the sharks come from?'

Another extremely attractive smile.

'Back then, Miss Pinchbeck, half a century ago, things were very different in Britain. Black people were expected to know their place. Physically, that place was usually a slum. Professionally it was a low-paid manual job. Sexually it was with their own kind. You saw a black man who complained about living accommodation, a black man who understood how money could be made to work, a black man who married a white girl, what you saw was an uppity nigger who needed to be put back in his place. He makes money, it must be 'cos he's a crook. He marries out of his race, that's because like all black men he has this insatiable lust to

97

bang a white woman. As for the white woman in question, everybody knows that she has to be a whore who's turned on by the thought of his eighteen-inch bone. I hope I don't shock you, Miss Pinchbeck.'

'No, Mr Gidman, you don't shock me. So all the rumours about your early career are malicious? But weren't you investigated by the police?'

'All the time! Malice don't dry up. Like floodwater, it can't find one way of getting under your defences, it looks for another. If it can't get under, it just mounts up, looking either to come in at you over the top or to break through by sheer pressure alone.'

'You sound bitter, Mr Gidman.'

'Not for myself. I've fought against it for too long. I've got its measure. In fact, I thought I'd won the battle a few years ago. But then my son comes of age and begins to make his mark in the world and suddenly the floodwaters see what looks like a breach. The rumours start again. But I'm not the target now. I'm out of reach. They tried everything they know to blacken my name, but you check the records, Miss Pinchbeck. I have no convictions for anything. Not surprising, as I never got charged with anything. My business accounts have been picked over by people more picky than hens in a coop at feeding time, and none of them ever found a single decimal point out of place.'

'So why are the rumours so persistent?'

'Like I say, because of David here. Me they can't touch because they need proof to touch me. But they don't need no proof to harm David. Let the rumours grow strong enough and they will do the trick. Look at him, people will say, throwing his money around to buy advantages for himself. And we all know where that dirty money came from. You hear what I'm saying, Miss Pinchbeck?'

'Yes, I do, Mr Gidman. But I'm wondering why you're bothering to say it to me.'

Now at last she'd asked a question Dave the Third was interested in. He couldn't believe that Pappy was letting this chit of a girl get away with her impudence. His father's answer was even harder to believe.

'I'll tell you why. Because my boy needs taking care of. He don't like me saying that, but he can pull faces all he wants, it's the truth. I've been out there in that world and I know what it's like. He'll find out eventually, but I'd like him to find out without too much pain. I haven't worked hard all these years and put up with all the crap I've put up with to sit back and see my son suffer the same. He needs someone like you, Miss Pinchbeck. That's why I'm talking to you.'

'I think you are mistaking me for someone else; I'm not a bodyguard!'

'Bodyguards I can buy ten a penny. You're the kind of guard he needs the kind of places he goes, the kind of people he meets. I know, I've had you checked out. No need to look offended. I bet you've spent a bit of time checking me out too — am I right?'

'I did do a bit of checking, yes.'

'And you found nothing bad, else you

99

wouldn't be here. And I found plenty that was good, else you wouldn't be here either!'

He glanced down at a sheet of paper on the arm of his chair.

Maggie said, 'That my life story you've got there, Mr Gidman?'

'Not all of it,' he answered, unperturbed. 'Just from the age of eighteen. You were doing one of them gap years, working with VSO in Africa, when you got news that your mammy and daddy had been killed in a car accident, right?'

She went very still.

He leaned forward and looked into her eyes.

'You miss them, don't you?'

'Yes, Mr Gidman,' she said quietly. 'I miss my parents very much.'

'I can see that, and I'm truly sorry for your loss. Theirs too, not getting the chance to see what a great job they'd done bringing you up. But what I want to ask is, why, after you done your college course, did you go for an office job at ChildSave rather than heading back out to Africa or somewhere to work on the ground?'

Good question, thought Dave, recalling his own uncharitable thoughts about her suitability for a career of digging latrines for fuzzy-wuzzies.

'I don't see that it's relevant, Mr Gidman,' she replied, 'but I looked at my abilities, such as they were, and decided I could do more good by looking after ChildSave's profile at home than being a general dogsbody in a Third World village.'

'Good answer, Miss Pinchbeck,' said Gidman. 'And by all accounts, you done so well at

ChildSave, I bet that soon as they got a notion you were getting restless, they started throwing money at you to try and keep you. Which brings me to my next question. You such a bright girl, knowing your own abilities like you do, why would you want to leave ChildSave and work for my boy? Whatever else he is, he ain't no charity!'

The pair of them, the dignified old man and the slight, unprepossessing young woman, exchanged a smile.

'No, he's not,' said Maggie. 'But from what I read, your son could end up having more power to do good than all the UK charities put together, if he's steered right. And I'd like to be around to help with the steering. So, pure self-interest, Mr Gidman.'

'Hey, you two, I am still here,' protested Dave the Third, feeling excluded.

'We know that, boy,' said his father. 'And if you've been paying attention, you'll be about to offer this young lady the job. If she doesn't like the salary, up it and I'll pay the difference, OK?'

'I'm not worried about the money, Mr Gidman,' said Maggie.

'Maybe you're not, but how you value yourself is one thing, how other folk value you is something else. If I thought you could be bought, I wouldn't waste a penny on you. So why don't you go and have a think while I talk to my boy? You got some deciding to do. Either you believe all them rumours, in which case I'm sorry. Or you think they're crap and you'd like the job. It's been a real pleasure talking to you. You'll find Flo in the kitchen. With luck she'll be

101

doing apple turnovers. Try one. You won't have tasted better. So remember this before you decide. Work for my son, and you'll never be further than a phone call from them turnovers!'

Maggie left the room, looking slightly shell-shocked.

Dave, always keen to learn, said, 'Why'd you tell her to see Mom before we left?'

''Cos after ten minutes talking to your mother, sometimes I find myself believing I can't be all that bad! You hire her, boy. She's what you need. Bright as a button and she'll work for you 'cos she believes in you.'

And so it had proved. And now she was indispensable.

But like the song says, sometimes the honesty's too much. Having someone to keep you straight's fine. But straight can get boring; occasionally a man needs to stray.

Once, early on in her employment, he'd asked her to factor a diversion into a Continental trip so that he could contrive an assignation with the wife of a British Embassy official. She had simply refused, leaving it up to him to react as he would.

If she'd preached about the dangers of such activities, he'd have carried on regardless. But she said nothing. After that he didn't try to involve her in his private life.

He'd come to see what his father had spotted at once. Maggie Pinchbeck had all the qualifications. Super efficient, very bright, a smoother of paths, a sniffer of perils, an organizer sans pareil, she knew all the tricks common to PR and politics — the spinning, the wheeling and dealing, the compromising, the short-cutting. But she was only willing to play those ambiguous games if and when she believed the end was just. That was the quality that Goldie had spotted. You couldn't buy that.

But sometimes he still found himself fantasizing about those two-metre models . . .

As now, when that dry cough, which others probably never noticed but which rang out to him like the Lutine Bell, warned him he'd spent long enough in prayer. Any longer and people would be wondering what he had to pray about.

He straightened up. As if this were a signal, the organ boomed, and the congregation rose as the vicar and the choir made their way up the aisle singing the processional hymn, 'Now thank we all our God, with heart and hands and voices'.

David Gidman the Third joined in lustily, aware that he had much to be thankful for. Already blessed through birth with countless gifts of love, wealth and opportunity, he could not doubt that it was his destiny to enjoy many more wondrous things.

Truly his future shone so bright it took the eye of an eagle to look into it.

Bring it on!

10.55–11.20

As soon as Andy Dalziel entered his living room, he knew something was wrong.

He stood in the doorway and tried to isolate it. But his mind, though building up to its old speeds, was not quite there yet. He moved from intuition to examination. By the time he'd checked everything off and found nothing missing, nothing moved, nothing open that had been shut, or shut that had been open, no muddy footprints on the carpet, no greasy fingerprints on the door handle, he had to admit that everything was exactly as he'd left it, which meant that his sense of something not right was a load of bollocks, just another example of the continuing fragility of his mental processes.

'Oh well, Rome weren't rebuilt in a fortnight,' he reassured himself, and sat down next to the answer machine with the intention of listening to Mick Purdy's message.

But as his finger hovered over the *playback* button, it came to him.

Yes, everything was exactly as he'd left it, but it shouldn't have been!

He'd heard the start of Purdy's message as he made for the front door. When Purdy rang off, the presence of a new message on the machine should have been registered by a red light

104

around the *play* button.

There was no light, meaning someone had played the message.

Or maybe the red bulb had simply failed.

He pressed the button and found himself listening not to Purdy but to a message Cap had left six days ago, reminding him to eat a casserole she'd put in his fridge.

This confirmed it.

When the red light showed, what you got was new messages.

Otherwise when you pressed *play*, you got all the messages unerased from your tape, the oldest first.

He left the tape playing, armed himself with a heavy brass candlestick, and went through every room in the house.

Two conclusions: one, the place was absolutely empty; two, it was becoming a bit of a tip. His regular cleaner had defaulted during his long lay-off. Cap Marvell had seen that the place was spick and span for his return, but if you leave a horse to muck out its own stable, you'll soon be knee-deep in manure. Time to get organized afore Cap organized something for him. He liked to pick his own staff, in and out of work.

The machine was playing Purdy's message when he returned to the living room. Now he was listening to it rather than leaving it behind him, it struck him that there was a note of strain here with the attempt at banter sounding false and forced.

He sat down, and dialled the return number.

It answered on the second ring, a terse, 'Yeah?'

'That you, Mick? Andy Dalziel here.'

'Andy! Hang on.'

There was a pause, then Purdy spoke again.

'Sorry about that. At the fag-end of an op. Been on the go since sparrowfart yesterday, so forgive me if I yawn from time to time.'

'Get a result?'

'Way to go, but it's looking promising. How about you? Happy with your enquiries so far?'

'Sorry. Not sure what enquiries that 'ud be,' said Dalziel.

'Come on, Andy, soon as you'd talked to Gina you'd be straight off down the nick to trawl through the records.'

'You've spoken to Gina then?'

'Briefly. Couldn't talk long though. I gather she gave you the basic facts?'

'Aye, she gave me summat, and you're right, I've dug up a bit more. But what I haven't found yet, Mick, is any hint of what the fuck it might have to do with me.'

'Yeah, I'm sorry. Thought I'd be able to have a chat with you before you saw Gina, but she's not one for letting the grass grow under her feet, know what I mean? OK, let me give you the facts, though I've strong suspicion you won't need them. Alex Wolfe was a good mate and a good cop. But like you know, even good cops can come under suspicion. Nothing was ever proven, there was no smoking gun, just enough smoke to make it necessary to take a closer look.'

'Resigning and doing a runner smells very smoky to me.'

'He was under a lot of pressure. Not just the

investigation. I reckon that was just the straw that broke him. Look, what exactly did Gina tell you?'

'Something about a family bereavement. A kid. No details.'

'No, she wouldn't want to get into that. All those years and it's still painful, so we can only guess what it must have felt like back then. It was their daughter, Lucy. She'd been diagnosed with a rare form of acute leukaemia. They tried everything, travelled everywhere; it was a real switchback for a couple of years. And just when they thought that maybe this time they had it licked, bang, she was gone. She was six, by the way.'

'Jesus. What a fucking world.'

'Yeah. A thing like that takes people different ways. Some couples turn to each other. Some turn on each other. I think Gina wanted all the support she could get, but Alex went right back in on himself. He just wasn't there for her, and didn't want anyone to be there for him. He got compassionate leave. Then this investigation thing came up.'

'Nice timing,' said Dalziel.

'Oh yes. I'm sure those Internal Investigation rats thought so. They had to box clever. Pressurizing a bereaved cop at his most vulnerable doesn't play well. Unless they got cast-iron proof of corruption out of it, they'd end up with a lot of egg on their faces.'

'And they didn't? Get proof, I mean.'

'I never saw the paperwork, but obviously not. When Alex took off, there was a debate about classifying him as a fugitive, but his boss put his foot down. That was Owen Mathias. Did you know him?'

'Heard of him. Died, didn't he, soon after he retired?'

'Yeah. Always a bad move that, retiring. On the job you don't have enough time to die. I think Owen felt a bit guilty about Alex. Operation Macavity was Mathias's baby. He was obsessed with Goldie Gidman. Thought the guy was laughing at us. So when Macavity started getting nowhere, Owen called foul and asked Internal to check it out, and they looked for an easy target and turned up Alex.'

'So Mathias didn't point the finger himself?'

'I don't think so. And after Alex vanished, he told the rat pack that, seeing as they'd found nothing to charge him with while he was in their sights, they weren't going to blacken his name when he wasn't around to defend himself. So, no warrant.'

'What about media coverage? Them sharks can smell blood at a Scotch mile.'

'A bit of local interest, but we had it covered. Alex had written a letter of resignation when they put him on compassionate. Mathias had stuck it in his desk drawer till he saw how things panned out. When the time came, he dug it up and slipped it into the files. So when the press started asking questions, all they found was an ex-cop who'd resigned because of personal problems, then walked away. Worth a para or two on a bad day.'

'And you personally, Mick? What did you

think had happened?'

'Breakdown, maybe. Losing a kid's devastating for anyone, and Alex was the sensitive sort — university entrant, bit of a bleeding heart, you probably know the type.'

'Yeah, I've got one of them, but mine's come along nicely. Like they say, you can do a lot with a graduate if you catch the bugger young.'

'True, and I had high hopes of Alex, but it wasn't to be. So, as I say, some kind of breakdown seemed favourite, but as time went by and there wasn't the slightest trace, no movement on his bank account, nothing on credit cards, no contact with Gina . . . '

'You knew that for certain?'

'I believed her then and, since we got close, I've been absolutely sure. Anyway, as time went by I stopped thinking breakdown. Something doesn't move for that long, it's got to be dead.'

'Right,' said Dalziel. 'Educated guess at how he might have died?'

'Could have cracked under the strain and topped himself,' said Purdy. 'Could have been an accident. Guy in his state of mind is quite capable of walking under a bus.'

'Except bodies under buses get noticed, and even suicides usually draw attention to themselves. All Wolfe's details would be on record, so even if they found him bollock naked, it wouldn't be long before the magic box popped him up, would it?'

'Still on the ball, eh?' said Purdy admiringly. 'Gina said you struck her as being very sharp. Made an impression there, Andy.'

'Save the bullshit for your roses,' said Dalziel. 'If he is dead and hasn't been found, then it's likely 'cos someone didn't want him found. Any suggestions, Mick?'

'You're thinking Gidman, right?'

'It's a motive.'

'Only if Gidman is a wrong 'un, and Alex was bent. I don't think so.'

'Either or both?'

There was a silence, then Purdy said, 'You and me have been around a long time, Andy, and we've seen a lot of good coppers caught with their hands in the till. Circumstances change people. You got a dying kid on your hands, there's not much you won't do to try and buy a cure.'

'So a maybe there. And Gidman, what's your take on him?'

'Pure as the driven snow, on paper at least. Lots of stories about his younger days, several accusations, but nothing ever proved. And since he got into the big money game, what with doling out cash on a regular basis to good causes, and sitting on financial advisory boards, he's fast approaching sainthood.'

'Not surprising if you can afford the best PR firms,' said Dalziel cynically.

'He can certainly do that,' said Purdy. 'My reading is, if they really want to get rid of MRSA, they should give Goldie Gidman the NHS cleaning franchise.'

'So you do think he's got things to hide?'

'We've all got things to hide, Andy. All I know is the Met gave it their best shot. And long after everyone else had given up on the job, old Owen Mathias kept on niggling away. But try as hard as he could, in the end he didn't even lay a parking ticket on him.'

'Why was Mathias so obsessed then?'

'Well, he was always a man of principle, Owen. Signed up with South Wales but got himself transferred to the Met in the late seventies. Operation Countryman time, remember? Robert Mark cleaning out the stables. Owen reckoned Mark was the new Messiah. Wanted to be around to do his bit. Cynics said that he was a wily Welshman who worked out that all the corruption sackings meant lots of opportunity for quick promotion.'

'And what did you say?' asked Dalziel.

'I saw him close up. Believe me, he was the real thing, a full-blown zealot! He started in the East End, he was mid-twenties then, just made sergeant, and one of his first jobs was dealing with an allegation of assault against Goldie Gidman. I was not long in the job myself and I worked under him for a bit. Came to nothing, of course. The guy who'd made the accusation died in a fire that gutted his flat. Accident, they reckoned; the electrics were shot, but Owen was convinced Goldie was behind it. Couldn't prove anything, but never stopped going after Goldie till the end of his career. Got to be a bit of a laugh in the end.'

'So you think he just got it completely wrong?'

'It happens. I heard of this guy up north was convinced that the England selectors had been bribed to keep Yorkshire lads out of the team

111

— come think of it, that was you, wasn't it? Me, like everyone else down here, I just came to the conclusion that if all them smart lawyers at the CPS and at Tory Party Central Office couldn't find anything niffy in Goldie's linen basket, then it wasn't worth looking.'

'You take notice of lawyers down at the Yard these days? Jesus!'

'I take notice of Gidman's lawyers, that's for sure. I tell you, Andy, if this call's bugged, then I'm in deep shit! Even the papers have had their fingers burned too often to risk more than the obliquest of innuendoes. In fact, they wouldn't even bother with that if it wasn't for his beloved son.'

'Oh aye. Dave the Turd MP, the soft crinkly buttock of Conservatism.'

'That's the one. Andy, why am I telling you all this when obviously you've dug it up already? Don't you have anything better to do on a Sunday?'

'Aye, I'm going out to an intimate lunch with this smart tart. Your fiancée, I believe. That were a surprise.'

'To me too, if I'm honest. But a great one. You won't want the soppy details, not unless you became a Mills and Boon fan same time as you started digging swinging old Bach. Couldn't believe it when Gina told me. What were you really doing in that cathedral, Andy?'

I'm not the only one who's stayed sharp, thought Dalziel.

'Mebbe I were praying for guidance,' he said.

'Girl guidance, perhaps,' said Purdy, laughing.

112

'And you're too old to get one of them. Well, a man's entitled to his operational secrets.'

'Not you, not if you want my help,' said Dalziel. 'Listen, you don't sound like you've changed your mind about Wolfe being dead. So what about this photo? Gina says it's definitely him.'

'That don't stop it being a fake. You checked it out yet?'

'No,' admitted Dalziel. 'It looks fine to me.'

'Andy, they could give you tits like Jordan and they'd look so real, you'd be shopping for a cantilevered bra. No, I'll bet you'll find it's a fake.'

'OK. And if I do, what then?'

'Listen, I think this is more about me than Gina. My money's on the whole thing being set up by someone down here who doesn't like me and has heard about me and Gina getting it together, so he decided to stir things up and jerk us about a bit.'

'Hard to believe with someone as lovable as you, Mick.'

'Ha ha. You know we have to deal with some pretty sick fucks, Andy. In fact, one or two of the bastards we even have to work with! My first guv'nor warned me, keep your eyes wide open, especially in the office. Working in the Met's like having your drink spiked with roofies. Doze off and you can be pretty sure someone's fucking you.'

'So why'd you not just tell Gina this when she rang?'

'If she'd been able to get hold of me when she

got the photo, I probably would have done. But I was on this op, mobiles off, security silence, all that crap.'

'Sod's law, eh?' said Dalziel.

'Maybe not,' said Purdy. 'Maybe it was part of the plan. Anyway, when I got back to her and found she was already up there, I could tell she was in a hell of a state.'

'Seemed pretty calm to me,' said Dalziel, unwilling for reasons he didn't altogether recognize to share his own diagnosis of Gina's mental state.

'That's her way. Believe me, Andy, underneath the surface, she's really seething. No wonder, with all that background stuff I've given you. I could tell if I'd suggested this was about someone getting at me, she'd probably have erupted and ended up on local telly flashing Alex's picture and asking anyone who recognized him to get in touch.'

'Aye, they'd have lapped that up down at MYTV,' admitted Dalziel.

'Exactly. And I'm sure you've got plenty of loonies up there who'd be ringing in to say they've seen him, he's living next door, he drinks down their pub, he looks just like their local vicar. Our sick joker would be rubbing his hands to see this all get into the public domain. And once he's got the taste of blood, who knows what he might try next?'

Dalziel digested this, then said, 'So what exactly do you want from me, Mick?'

'I need someone to keep the cap on things. I'd been reading about you recently when you had

114

your little blow-up. You back to full fighting fitness now, I hope?'

'Nice of you to ask. Yes, I'm getting back into the swing.'

'Great. Andy, if I'd been able to get away, I'd have been up there myself by now. But I'm stuck here on this job and I'll be tied up a good few hours yet. I don't want this to be official because that would just complicate things. But if you could check that photo out, that would be great. Learning it was fake is something she'd probably take better from you.'

'And if it's not a fake?'

'Then I'd be even more grateful to have someone up there I can trust to keep an eye on her. Look, Andy, put simply, I'm just asking a favour from an old friend. OK, I know that's maybe putting it a bit thick, seeing as we only ever met over a few days and that was a long time ago. But that's how I've always thought of you.'

'Glad we don't have video,' said Dalziel. 'Can't bear to see a grown man crying.'

'Listen, got to go. They all think this must be some important operational message I'm dealing with and even so, they're looking impatient. So you'll do what you can?'

'I'll see how it all looks after we've had lunch.'

'Thanks, Andy. Only wish I could be there to pick up the tab.'

'Not to worry, lad. This being unofficial, I'll send you an expense claim. Cheers!'

Dalziel put the phone down. There was stuff going off here he didn't yet understand. Be nice to have some input from Mr Clever Clogs and Mr Ugly, but not till he was sure if it amounted to owt or nowt. As things stood, he could ill afford to let himself be seen flapping around on a wild-goose chase.

At least he now had something to get his teeth into over lunch aside from the Keldale's famous Aberdeen Angus beef.

He rose and went upstairs to his bedroom. Here he regarded himself in the long wardrobe mirror. He'd told Novello scruffy was the new smart, but that didn't apply to overweight fellows in advanced middle age. There, scruffy was just the old scruffy.

As he stepped into his shower he felt an urge to break into song.

Bit of Bach might have been appropriate. From what he knew about the old Kraut, he'd had about fifty kids, so likely he'd written a tune or two to celebrate the prospect of having lunch with a well-stacked blonde *Mädchen*. Gina Wolfe would probably know.

In the meantime, it was the thought that counted.

He opened his mouth and in a bass-baritone more leathery than velvety but nonetheless melismatic he boomed out the opening lines of 'Happy Days Are Here Again'.

2

con forza

Prelude

Happy days are not even a memory for him. He does not have memories.

Merlin-like, he lives backwards.

He clings to the present, would make it infinite if he could, but inexorably he advances to the past.

Once he woke to flee from dreams. Now he sleeps to hide from visions.

If he pauses to study how he feels, the best answer is he feels safe.

He does not ask safe from what? for knowing what you are safe from means you no longer are.

Forgetfulness is his friend.

For a man in fugue is like a beast of the plains that takes refuge in a dense wood.

He can move but not freely. Trunks impede, roots trip, briar hooks, mire sucks.

He can see but not clearly. The canopy of foliage filters the light and each gust of wind fragments and scatters it.

Forgetfulness is his friend and fear is his companion.

Fear tells him when to move, when to keep still. Fear shows him how to blend with the forest.

He survives by limitation and simple repetition. He makes the unfamiliar familiar by staying in one area. He makes his own existence familiar by following patterns as strict as a square dance.

119

From time to time a brighter light through the crowding trees tells him he is looking towards the boundary beyond which stretch the sunlit pastures where he once roamed free.

But he looks and turns away, for though he has forgotten who they are, fear tells him there are hunters out there, and he lies very still for fear tells him also that once his presence among the trees is suspected, they will send in their dogs to flush him out.

Yes, forgetfulness is his friend, fear is his protector.

Anything that challenges fear and forgetfulness is dangerous. So the first faint scent of the possibility of happiness sets off alarms like the first faint scent of a distant forest fire. He is not sure what it is, but instinct warns him that it means change and change means movement and movement brings the past closer and the past is pain.

How he knows this he does not know, but he knows it.

But happiness is insidious, it does not make a frontal assault, it creeps up gradually. And because it is gradual, he feels he can control it, just a little step at a time, just the tiniest relaxation with each step, advancing like a wild beast towards the proffered hand, ever suspicious and ready to flee at the breaking of a twig.

And suddenly, without realizing it, he is there, close up, in contact, the hand caressing his head, the fingers combing his hair.

The past is closer now, but no longer does it feel like a pain that must be relived. It begins to

120

feel like a tale that can be re-told.

Then in the space of a few words, happiness explodes into joy.

Joy clears memory but clouds judgment, joy lets him see the sunlit fields but dazzles his eyes so that they miss the hidden hunters.

Joy makes him feel whole again, brings him love again.

But love is his betrayer.

12.00–12.15

Shirley Novello had not been convinced by her boss's assurance that scruffy was the new smart.

Refreshed by an hour's sleep followed by an alternating scalding freezing shower that left her skin glowing like a sun-ripened apricot, she had dressed with care. She didn't overdo it. When you were on a surveillance job it was daft to draw attention to yourself by wearing your shortest skirt and tightest top. But she certainly looked good enough to make the young man checking lunchers on to the Keldale terrace return her smile with more than professional enthusiasm.

'Hi,' she said. 'Table for two, please.'

One meant you were either a hooker or just sad.

'Have to be on the upper terrace,' he said in a rather sexy Italian accent. 'Garden terrace she is all booked up. Sorry.'

The terrace was on two levels, the upper one protected from the weather by an awning, the lower open to the skies. Today, with little breeze and lots of warm autumn sunshine, it was the al fresco area that was most popular. Already, just after twelve, most of the tables here were occupied. At one of them, in the right-hand corner overlooking the gardens, sat a striking blonde wearing a frock that looked like it would have cost Novello a month's pay and sunglasses that would have eaten up another week's. Fat Andy knew how to pick them!

'That's fine,' said Novello, checking the empty tables on the upper terrace. 'Could I have that one there?'

'Sure,' he said, smiling. She smiled back, full beam. His name tag read Pietro, and he was fairly dishy in a Med kind of way. Bit too slender for her taste, but no harm in being friendly.

He led her to her chosen table, which was right at the edge of the upper terrace. From here she had a good view of both levels.

He said, 'I'll keep an eye open for your friend, Miss . . . ?'

'Smith,' she said. 'Yes, she shouldn't be long.'

She opted for *she* because when no one else appeared she didn't want him thinking she'd been stood up. A girl has her pride, even a WDC on an op!

A glance at the menu told her Dalziel was right about the prices. She felt quite hungry, but it was probably best to go through the motions of waiting for her imaginary friend and when a waitress approached a moment later, all she ordered was a Bacardi Breezer.

On the lower terrace, the blonde was still by herself. There was a water jug on the table from which she topped up her glass from time to time. Maybe she wanted to keep her head clear for the encounter to come. The only table close enough to permit meaningful eavesdropping was occupied by two couples engaged in a conversation so animated it verged on the raucous. Novello let her gaze slide over the other tables. Apart from the blonde there were no solitaries on the lower terrace and only one besides herself on the upper, a brawny gingery man, yawning his way through one of the Sunday Supplements. As she watched he was joined by a woman who, tight blonde curls apart, looked like the other half of a matched set.

Of course no reason why watchers shouldn't come in pairs. In fact, Sunday lunchtime, it was solitaries like herself that were going to stick out.

It was nearly ten past twelve when Andy Dalziel swept past her table without the slightest flicker in her direction.

There was something different about him. Like herself, he had smartened up. This morning he had been decently dressed but with little care for colour coordination or the location of creases, and though his face had been in recent contact with a razor, the effect had been that of a badly mown lawn. Now his drumlin chins were smooth as a bowling green and he wore a dazzling white shirt tucked into pale green slacks whose crease fell like a plumb-line on to matching deck shoes.

Novello made a bet with herself that everything below the waist at least had been bought by the Fat Man's partner, Cap Marvell. She wasn't quite so confident that Cap would know, or approve, the occasion of what looked like their first airing.

She watched carefully to see how Dalziel greeted the blonde. Disappointingly (not that she bore Cap Marvell any malice, but what a

124

story it could have made!) there was no embrace, not even the airiest of air kisses. So his decision to smarten himself up didn't seem to be sexually based. In any case, he'd hardly have invited a subordinate to witness the encounter. Unless of course he didn't trust himself and she was really there as a kind of chaperone . . .

She grounded these flights of fancy and once again checked out possible watchers over her Breezer.

Dalziel had attracted a few glances as he made his way across the terrace, but that was only to be expected. He had never been one of Mid-Yorkshire's blushing violets and his close brush with death in the Mill Street terrorist explosion had got most of the local media trailing their prepared obituaries. But none of the lunchers showed any sign of continued interest.

Pietro passed by, ushering a middle-aged couple to a nearby table. The man, hook-nosed and balding, protested that he'd asked for a table overlooking the gardens. Pietro apologized profusely saying there must have been a mix-up but now, alas, all the al fresco tables were booked. Hook-nose, who gave the impression of a man used to getting his way, looked ready to make an issue out of it, but his companion, slightly younger though that might have been down to her make-up, uttered soothing noises and gave him a consoling stroke of the crotch area which, in view of their advanced years, Novello assumed was the result of age-related myopia rather than erotic targeting. But when she observed that under the table the man was responding in kind, Novello closed her eyes in horror. They had to be over fifty, for God's sake!

'No sign of your friend then?'

She opened her eyes. Pietro, having disposed of the lusty geriatrics, had paused alongside her.

'No. Typical. Maybe I'll start without her. What're the open prawns like?'

'Opened fresh every day! I'll order one for you, shall I? Such a shame a good-looking girl should have to eat alone though.'

'You trying to wangle an invite to join me?' she said, smiling.

'Love to, but I'd get fired,' he said. 'Don't work all the time though . . . sorry, got to go.'

He headed back to his station where some new arrivals were waiting impatiently.

Doesn't work all the time, she thought. Unlike me and all the rest of us sailing on the Good Ship Dalziel.

Mind you, she could do with a lot of work like this. The sun was shining, she had the Fat Bastard's money in her purse, there was even some music drifting up from the garden; not the kind of music she'd have dreamt of listening to normally, but here in this place it fell very pleasantly on the ear.

She found herself wondering what time Pietro got off, then pulled herself together.

He wasn't her type, and she had a job to do.

Once more she started checking off the other lunchers, one by one.

Result as before. No one suspicious.

Now she let her gaze return to Dalziel and the

126

blonde, and then beyond them to the source of the garden music.

There seemed to be some kind of buffet party going on, with tables set up on a square of lawn at the centre of which stood a gazebo that held the musicians. Occasionally a cork popped; everyone seemed to be having a good time. She felt quite envious. Being a cop could be a lonely business.

Then she saw someone who wasn't entering into the swing of things. A guy standing on the edge of the lawn. Maybe he just didn't like that kind of music either. Or that kind of drink. He had 'phones on his ears, a bottle of lager in his hand, and he was nodding his head so that his black Zapata moustache and his matching shag of hair bounced up and down as though in time to a beat from his MP3.

Hard to tell precisely what he was looking at as he was wearing big reflective sunglasses, but he was facing the hotel and there was an uninterrupted line of sight between him and Dalziel's table on the lower terrace, a distance of twenty or thirty yards.

Maybe she was being over-cautious, but those 'phones were a bit too big for the general air of *cool* the guy seemed to be trying to project. And the Zapata moustache was a bit *démodé* too.

She took out her mobile, brought up her phone book and selected Dalziel.

127

12.10–12.20

Dalziel was not a religious man but he felt grateful to *something* that a day that had started so badly had taken a distinct turn for the better.

Certainly, sitting in the sun with a good-looking young woman opposite you and the prospect of a tasty meal ahead of you was not the worst way to spend a Sunday lunchtime, not unless you were his old Scots granny, of course. She wouldn't even have given him brownie points for his visit to the cathedral. A kirk should be small and homely. Those overblown buildings said more about man's vanity than God's greatness.

Well, it were twenty years since she'd gone to her long home, so now she'd know for sure if she'd been right. Which she probably had been, according to the eschatological model Dalziel sometimes liked to propound at the end of a long night in the Black Bull. In the Gospel according to St Andy, after death, *everybody* discovers they've been right. In other words, we all get the afterlife we believe in, whether it's eternal harping or eternal oblivion. Even suicide bombers, except that in their case when they find themselves exploded into the midst of their seventy-two doe-eyed virgins, they find the one bit missing after the reassembly process is their dicks.

But for all his mockery of formal religion, today it somehow felt as if his brief unplanned visit to the cathedral had won him the reward of this lunchtime.

It was tempting just to relax and enjoy it, but how much he could relax rather depended on whether he was working or not. If, as he suspected, someone had been in his house, and if that intrusion had anything to do with this woman, then certainly he was working. But if the phone thing had just been a technical glitch . . .

Gina said, 'So did I check out?'

'Eh?'

'Come on. Since we talked, you'll have checked me out to make sure I haven't been sent by Professor Moriarty to bewitch you into a compromising situation. If you haven't, then I can't see you being much good to me.'

Clearly she was completely back in control.

'Fair enough. Aye, you checked out, more's the pity.'

'Why do you say that?'

He gave her his best leer and said, 'It's a long while since I've been bewitched into a compromising situation. Bothered and bewildered, yes, all the time. Like now. But bewitched doesn't come round as often as it once did.'

'I know the feeling. But I know you've spoken to Mick. He rang me afterwards. I'm sure he filled out the picture. So why should you feel bewildered and bothered?'

'I'm a cop, Mrs Wolfe,' said Dalziel heavily. 'I catch criminals. Nowt criminal going off here, according to you and Mick. Unless you know something I don't.'

'Such as?'

'Such as Alex, your dear departed husband, was definitely on Goldie Gidman's payroll and getting reunited with him might also reunite you with some large sums of dirty money only he knows the location of.'

He'd seen the vulnerable emotional side of her, now let's take a look at how she stood up to a bit of rough and tumble.

She regarded him steadily for a moment then said, 'And if that was my motive, why on earth would I be sitting here talking to the local king of the cops?'

'Wasn't your idea to contact me, luv. It was Mick Purdy's.'

'So I'm keeping stuff from Mick too?'

Dalziel shrugged and said, 'All women keep stuff from their men. And vice versa. As you found out. Usually doesn't matter. No, the big test will come if you find Alex and get faced with the choice: do I take off with the bad cop who's got the big bucks, or do I stay true to the good cop who's just got his pension to look forward to.'

'Is that what you really think might happen, Mr Dalziel?' she said.

'How should I know? This show's been running for seven years and I've just strayed in from the wings.'

A waitress who had been hovering said, 'Are you ready to order yet, or would you like a little more time?'

Gina said, 'I'm fine. I'll just have the beef carpaccio with a green salad.'

'I'll have beef as well, luv,' said Dalziel. 'But I'll have mine roast with Yorkshire pud and lots of spuds. And we'll have a bottle of Barolo to wash that down.'

'Actually I'd prefer a white, a Montana sauvignon blanc, perhaps,' said Gina.

'Fair enough. We'll have one of them too,' said Dalziel.

They sat in silence for a while after the waitress had gone. There was a buffet party going on in the gardens. The chatter reached them, not loud enough to be distracting, more like a treeful of birds or the babbling of a brook. And there was music, too; classical but tuneful with it and live not canned — this was, after all, the Keldale. He traced its source to a small group playing in the pagoda.

'That Bach?' he said.

'Mozart,' she said. 'Mr Dalziel, let's talk straight. One way and another I know cops. I reckon a good police technique here would be to start with a bit of provocation to see if it would shake anything out of me. Then lull me with a bit of idle chitchat about music, say. Then try to catch me with some more provocation. Eventually, over coffee, we might get down to some constructive talk. Good technique, perhaps, but it won't make for a very enjoyable lunch.'

Dalziel's mobile rang. He took it out of his pocket, glanced at the display then put it to his ear and said, 'Yeah?'

He listened for a moment then said, 'Thanks

for that. Just keep a close eye on him OK? A very close eye.'

He replaced the phone and smiled at the blonde.

'You don't look the shakeable type to me,' he said. 'So let's drink to constructive talk.'

He picked up the heavy crystal water jug and topped her glass up, then did the same with his own. There was still some water left in the vessel, but he raised it above his head and waggled it at a waitress who was serving a nearby table and called, 'Refill here, luv, when you're ready.'

Gina Wolfe watched him, puzzled. He didn't look like a man who made toasts in water. A change in the buffet music from lively Mozart to dreamy Strauss drew her attention to the party in the garden. They seemed to be enjoying themselves. There was a colourful semi-formalism about the way they were dressed. Not a wedding party; no buttonholes, no one in morning suits. Then she saw a woman holding a baby. The child was wrapped in a long white robe that floated in the gentle breeze.

A christening. Her heart made a little movement in her breast and she felt tears forcing their way upwards into her eyes.

Then her breathing stopped and she blinked furiously to try to remove the watery veil through which she was peering.

And at that moment the jug slipped from Dalziel's fingers and crashed on to the table.

12.15–12.25

The claims to quality made by the Keldale were more than justified by the noise produced by the shattering jug.

No unbreakable plastic this, nor cheap glass which dissolves into powder, but genuine high-tensile crystal that exploded in a scintillation of diamantine fragments, turning heads not only on the terrace but in the garden too.

Peter Pascoe was already on his third glass of champagne and his sixth lobster ball.

'Enjoying yourself,' said Ellie, coming up alongside him.

'You know, I do believe I am,' he said. 'These fish fingers are really rather nice. As for the bubbly . . . you did say you were driving us home, right?'

'Yes. My turn. I'm measuring the units carefully, which, considering the quality of this stuff, is a real sacrifice. I may expect to be rewarded for my relative temperance when we get home, so don't go over the top, so to speak.'

'You interest me strangely,' said Pascoe. 'Talking of temperance, I hope Rosie's sticking to the juice. We don't want her doing her Gigi act.'

'No problem. Nothing alcoholic or even bubbly with her performance coming up.'

'Performance?' said Pascoe, alarmed. 'You

didn't say anything about a performance.'

'Didn't I?' said Ellie innocently. 'It's just a little clarinet duet Ali put together for Rosie and another star pupil. It'll give the Sinfonietta quartet the chance to get some refreshment.'

'Oh God. I need another drink.'

As if in response, Ed Muir approached with a champagne bottle at the ready.

'Top up, Peter?' he asked.

'You bet.'

He watched approvingly as the man took his glass. He'd only met Muir a couple of times previously, hadn't felt able to relate very closely to him, perhaps because of the gap between his appearance and his manner. With his shaven head and five-o'clock shadow he looked like someone you'd step aside for if you met him on a lonely street. But his quiet speech and self-effacing manner faded him into the background when you met him in a group. Today, however, at his daughter's christening, he was so full of joy and pride that he generated more warmth than the pleasant autumn sun.

And if any doubt about his clubbability remained, the way he tipped a champagne bottle tipped the balance.

Ali Wintershine had picked well!

'Great party, Ed,' said Pascoe effusively. 'The perfect way to launch little . . . '

For a moment the baby's name escaped him. Then he saw Ellie mouthing something at him.

' . . . Lolita,' he concluded triumphantly.

Ellie rolled her eyes upwards in exasperation while Muir looked slightly puzzled as it came to

Pascoe that the child's name was Lucinda.

To correct or not correct? But before he could reach a decision God intervened in the form of an explosion somewhere behind him.

Sensitized by the anti-terrorist briefings which were now a staple of police life, Pascoe span round.

Whatever had happened had happened at a table right on the edge of the terrace. Attention centred on a large fat man and a willowy blonde, both on their feet, she looking a touch damp down the front of her dress, he mouthing what were presumably apologies as he tried to wipe her dry with his napkin.

'Oh my God,' said Ellie. '*Et in Arcadia ego!*'

'What the hell's he doing at the Keldale?' said Pascoe, assuming the high tone of the habitué. 'And who's that with him?'

'I don't know, but if he doesn't stop trying to massage her tits, I think he might get his face punched,' said Ellie hopefully.

This entertaining possibility was unhappily brought to nothing by the rapid arrival of a darkly handsome young man who, assisted by a couple of waitresses, smoothly restored calm and order to the table. Pascoe worked out that something fragile and heavy, a bottle perhaps or a jug, must have been dropped and shattered. Andy getting clumsy in old age? That from a man who for his size had always been incredibly nimble and dextrous was yet another cause for concern about the extent of his recovery.

And Dalziel chatting up a young blonde while his long-time partner was away for a few days . . .

135

Didn't the trick cyclists say that a sharp reminder of mortality often sent a man in desperate search for earnests of potency?

No problems himself in that field, he thought smugly. Though with the afternoon stretching ahead of him and the sun warm on his back and Ellie getting that languorous look, he should perhaps take her advice and slow down a little on the bubbly.

But not yet!

He turned to retrieve his glass from Ed only to discover that that particular temptation had been removed. His host had disappeared and with him Pascoe's refill. Perhaps, he thought charitably, after the explosion, he'd felt constrained to rush and reassure his young wife that all was well.

Ellie, disappointed in her hope of seeing the Fat Man assaulted, was now concentrating her attention on her husband.

'What?' said Pascoe.

'*Lolita!*' said Ellie, shaking her head. 'What are you like?'

'Your fault,' he said. 'The longer I look at you, the younger you get.'

He waggled his eyebrows at her and tried for a salacious leer.

She couldn't help smiling. But Pascoe's instincts had been right. The warmth of the sun and the single glass of bubbly she'd allowed herself were combining very nicely to make a bit of salacity seem not such a bad idea.

'Keep working on it, Mr Humbert,' she said huskily. 'Who knows? You may get lucky.'

12.20–12.30

Not all heads had turned at the sound of the exploding jug.

Shirley Novello's gaze had remained fixed on the black moustached man at the edge of the lawn.

As the jug shattered, she saw his head jerk back and his hand go up to the headphones.

'Gotcha,' she said.

Now she turned her attention to the Fat Man's table and watched the pantomime of Dalziel apologizing to everyone in hearing distance and making ineffectual attempts to dry his lunch date down. In no time at all, Pietro was on the scene, directing operations. Novello wondered idly if he were as efficient in everything as he clearly was in his job. He had the glass cleared, the table re-laid, and Dalziel and the blonde re-seated in just a couple of minutes.

Down on the lawn, the listener seemed to have got over his shock. He was back in his former mode, standing looking vacant, his head nodding as if he were mesmerized by some disco beat. But he had a mobile phone in his hand and, as she watched, he slipped the headphones off one ear and started speaking into the mobile.

She let a couple of minutes pass till the corner

table was no longer a focus of interest, then took up her phone once more and thumbed in the Fat Man's number.

'Hello?'

'I was right,' she said. 'You're bugged.'

'Grand. I'll sort it.'

'What do you want me to do now?'

He thought a moment then said, 'Stick to the bugger. But don't get close.'

'I'm on him.'

The bugger had his headphones back on. Then something happened; nothing as violent as the shattering of the jug, but enough to make him remove the 'phones and give them a shake. Service interrupted, guessed Novello. When the Fat Man said he'd sort something, it usually got sorted.

The bugger gave up on the 'phones but now he had his mobile to his ear again, receiving this time, not calling. So he wasn't a loner, he must have back up. Would he continue as an observer now he could no longer listen in?

Her view was blocked by Pietro, who set an open prawn sandwich and a glass of white wine before her. This guy really was efficient.

'You serve table as well as clean up?' she said, smiling up at him.

'Depends on the table,' he said.

'I didn't order any wine.'

'On the house. To make up for the disturbance.'

'So everyone will be getting a glass?'

'Only the sensitive ones. Any news of your friend?'

138

'Definitely not coming,' she said indicating her mobile. 'That woman, at the table where the jug got broken, has she been on telly or something? I'm sure I've seen her.'

'Mrs Wolfe? Don't know. She's certainly got the looks, but I don't watch too much telly. I prefer real life.'

'Me too,' she said. 'She's a hotel guest, is she?'

'That's right. And the guy with her's some sort of cop. Mr Lee, the manager, was around when she asked if she could book a table overlooking the garden, and I told her, Sorry, those tables are all taken. And she said, My guest, Superintendent Dalziel, will be disappointed. And suddenly Mr Lee got in on the act and told me he was sure there must be a table available. So I looked again, and there was.'

'Theirs, was it?' said Novello, glancing at Hook-nose and his partner. At least the exploding water jug seemed to have distracted them from their heavy petting. Maybe it had reminded them of their stolen table. Whatever, they were now deep in conversation.

'Shush! Don't want to start him on at me again,' said Pietro.

His wish wasn't granted. The couple rose and headed for the hotel entrance. As they passed Pietro, Hook-nose said, 'After cocking up our table, the least I expected was efficient service. We'll find somewhere decent to eat.'

They moved on. Pietro made a face at Novello and said, 'Better cancel their order. Enjoy your prawns.'

'Oh, I will,' said Novello.

But even as she spoke she realized she wouldn't.

For as Pietro moved away opening up her sightline to the lawn again, she realized to her horror that the man with the 'phones had vanished.

12.20–12.35

Gwyn Jones sank back on the sofa and felt the voluptuously soft leather upholstery embrace his naked flesh.

Life was good. Back home in the sleepy Mid-Wales township of Llufwwadog they would probably still be in the chapel now, perched on pews as narrow and hard as a cliff ledge, listening to an interminable sermon that started at *hwyl* and built up to hysteria, and made the hell it threatened seem like a welcome deliverance.

Outside it would be raining. He knew the Met Office had declared that there was an anticyclone stationary over the British Isles, guaranteeing the continuation of the Indian summer right into the middle of October, but as all natives of Llufwwadog knew, such fair-weather forecasts did not apply to them. When the wind was in the east it pushed the rain clouds over the Black Mountains before they burst, and when it was in the west, it punctured them as they reached the foothills. He supposed there must have been days when the Welsh sky was as perfectly blue as the one he could see now backing the topless towers of Canary Wharf, but his memory seemed to have scrubbed them all.

What it hadn't scrubbed was his waking resolution from an early age — birth, it seemed

141

like now, but that was probably pushing it — to get out of Llufwwadog as quickly as he could. The conventional exit routes for a growing *hogyn* of sport, art and education were closed to him. He was hopeless at rugby, couldn't sing or act, and had very little academic ability. So it was either the army or journalism. He had gone for the latter on the grounds that you didn't have to get up so early in the morning and there was less chance of being shot at.

It had been a happy choice. The disadvantages of a dreadful prose style and an excitable stutter were negated by a huge natural curiosity, a complete insensitivity to rebuff, and an acuity of eye, ear, and nose that took him places others did not care to tread.

After an apprenticeship on his local rag, he had moved to Cardiff, where he rapidly made a name for himself by pulling the lid off a little pot-pourri of financial and sexual improprieties in the Welsh Assembly. This it was that got him his move to London, where six years later he was established as one of the *Daily Messenger*'s famous team of investigative journalists, his particular remit remaining the political scene.

He was well paid but not well enough to be able to even dream about a pad in Marina Tower, one of the most exclusive developments on Canary Wharf. To do that you needed an editor's screw, or, failing that, you needed to screw an editor. If she had a bit left over from an extremely profitable divorce, that didn't do any harm either. This combination of qualities came together in the person of Beanie Sample, the driving spirit behind *Bitch!*, the glossy mag which for eighteen months now (a long time in magazine life) had contrived to win the hearts, titillate the senses, and open the wallets of readers of both sexes and all ages from eighteen to thirty-eight.

Beanie, known both eponymously and epithetically as *the Bitch*, had a reputation for devouring young journalists, then dumping them when she'd had enough. Gwyn Jones had no problem with this. As he told his friends, why would a virile youngster want a long-term relationship with a woman twenty years his senior? Nonetheless, since moving into her Docklands apartment, he'd come to the conclusion that maybe long term wasn't so bad. A man could put up with a lot of this luxury. Also it was within a fit man's strolling distance of Canary Tower, which housed the *Messenger* offices. Compared to this, his own flat above a dry-cleaners in Bromley seemed like a particularly remote and ascetic monk's cell.

Somewhere his phone was ringing. He recognized the ring tone, the opening bars of 'Cwm Rhondda', chosen to remind him he need never listen to a male voice choir again.

The ringing stopped and Beanie came out of the bedroom. She had slipped a robe on. That was the difference between twenty-six and forty-seven, he told himself complacently. She was holding his phone.

'Someone called Gareth,' she said. 'Says he's your brother.'

'Yeah. Then probably he is.'

He held out his hand for the phone.

'You never said you had a brother,' she said as if it were a major infidelity.

'You never asked.'

She tossed the phone into his lap with some violence.

'Ouch,' he said.

That seemed to mollify her a little.

'I'm going to run through the shower. Some coffee would be nice when I'm done.'

At least the command still came over lightly disguised as a request.

'Gar, boy,' he said. 'Shouldn't you be praising the Lord?'

Unlike himself, Gareth had been a lovely treble who'd broken into a fair tenor.

'No, today I'm pursuing the ungodly and watching them in their ungodliness.'

'What? You're actually doing it? Great. Rung up for some advice, is that it?'

'No, I'm managing very well, thank you, bro. But something's come up I thought might interest you.'

'OK, boyo, but make it quick. Me and Beanie are on our way to Tris's party . . . yeah, Tris Shandy, eat your heart out. So shoot.'

Jones listened for a couple of minutes, hardly interrupting at all. Then he heard the shower stop.

He said, 'OK, Gar. Thanks. No, I don't know if it means anything . . . yeah, sure I'm grateful . . . How grateful? That depends . . .'

He listened again and said, 'Jesus, Gar, if you're going to be Sam Spade you need decent wheels! OK, I'll sub you, but you hang on to the

144

bill. Of course I think you're trustworthy — about as much as I was your age!'

He saw Beanie come into the room, towelling down and concluded hastily, 'Got to go, Gar. Any developments, keep me posted. Take care now.'

'So where's that coffee?' said the Bitch.

'Sorry,' he said. 'Got to talking. Family stuff. Kid brothers can be a real drag, eh?'

'Much younger than you, is he?'

'Nearly eight years. He was an afterthought.'

'And he does what?'

'Wants to be a journalist. In fact, he's in much the same job I started in.'

'With his eyes on London eventually, no doubt. Maybe I can help him when he gets here.'

Help yourself to him, you mean, thought Jones. Publicly, his attitude to his brother was one of weary exasperation, but beneath it he was, and always had been, fiercely protective. No way he was going to let the Bitch get her claws into young Gareth till the boy had been properly schooled!

'Doubt he'll ever make it,' he said dismissively. 'One genius a family, that's the ration.'

'Oh, he'll make it. I know you thrusting Welshmen.'

'We like a good thrust, that's true,' he said, looking at his watch.

'Man should have what he likes, darling,' she said, misinterpreting. 'And it will be another hour before Tristram's party really warms up . . .'

She let the towel slide to the floor and slipped on to the sofa beside him. To her surprise he stood up.

145

'Beanie,' he said. 'I'm sorry, but I've just remembered. Somewhere I've got to be, so I'll have to give Tris a miss. Say I'm sorry, OK?'

She had learnt long ago never to let a man think he had the power to irritate her.

'Don't suppose anyone will notice, darling,' she said indifferently.

She watched him leave the room. Nice tight bum, lots of other useful accessories. Made you wonder what the nineteen-year-old model might be like.

But while the sensual part of her being was toying with that interesting speculation, the journalistic part was wondering what was important enough to make Jones stand her up. He'd left the phone on the arm of the sofa. She picked it up, brought up the last call number and rang back.

'Gar,' she murmured in her most seductive voice. 'Hi. This is Beanie. Beanie Sample. We spoke briefly earlier.'

She listened, grimaced, but didn't allow any of the grimace to get into her voice as she said, 'Yeah, that's right, Gar. Gwyn's girlfriend. And he's told me all about you too. I'm really looking forward to meeting you when you get up to town. Listen, Gwyn was going to ring you back but he has to smarten himself up for this party we're going to . . . yeah, Tris Shandy's do, that's right, Gwyn told you, did he? Anyway, we were talking about your call and there were a couple of things he wanted to check with you, make sure he got them right. So as we're a bit pushed for time, he asked me to ring you back, OK?'

12.20–12.35

Apart from a little dampness and a few shards of crystal down the front of her dress, Gina Wolfe had taken no harm from the accident.

'The sun will soon dry me off,' she said in face of the Fat Man's repeated offers to rub her dry.

The mess was quickly cleared up, the broken glass removed, and the table dried off. Almost immediately, a waiter appeared with their wine, opened the white, and asked Dalziel if he'd like to try it.

'No,' said the Fat Man. 'That's for the lady.'

She watched the waiter pour a taster, downed it all, nodded and drank half the refill.

'You look like you needed that,' said Dalziel, taking the red from the waiter's hand and pouring his own.

'It was a shock,' she said.

'Yeah. Sorry. Didn't have you down as the nervous type, but.'

His phone rang again. He listened, said, 'Grand. I'll sort it.' Listened again. And said, 'Stick to the bugger. But don't get close.'

When he put the phone back in his pocket, his hand did not reappear and she realized he was leaning forward with his arm reaching under the table. She pressed her knees tightly together in

147

instinctive defence against a potential grope, but felt nothing. And now he was straightening up, glancing at something between his finger and thumb, before dropping it to the floor and grinding it beneath his heel.

He said, 'Bit of glass got stuck underneath. Didn't want you scratching your knee.'

'What? Oh yes. Thanks.'

She wasn't really paying attention. She seemed much more interested in the garden.

He said, 'You sure you're all right, luv? You look a bit pale to me.'

Now she met his gaze and with a visible effort at composure said, 'Yes, really, I'm fine.'

He regarded her doubtfully but once again she was looking down into the garden. He followed her gaze but saw nothing to explain her interest. Then he thought he glimpsed a familiar figure. And the surprise of recognition sparked a suspicion of what might be troubling Gina.

'It's not just me dropping the jug,' he said. 'You thought you saw him again, didn't you?'

She didn't deny it, just nodded.

'Like you thought you saw him when you were driving around first thing. And there'll have been other times?'

She didn't deny it. In fact she seemed glad to talk about it.

'At first it was every day,' she said. 'Then less and less frequently — till today, that is. Before that the last time it happened was nearly a year ago, the start of November . . . '

Now she paused, and he said, 'Tell us about it, luv. No need to be embarrassed. Think of me as

148

a priest. Or a doctor. That way I get to take your pulse.'

That should have been worth a smile, but she clearly wasn't in the mood for smiling. Hesitantly, not looking at him, she went on with her story.

It had been a winter night. Mick Purdy had taken her out for a meal at their favourite *trattoria*. They had fallen into a regular pattern somewhere between friendship and dating. She'd no idea where it might lead, but she knew she enjoyed his company.

That night perhaps they'd drunk a little more wine than usual. On her doorstep, she'd asked if he'd like to come in for coffee. He said lightly, 'Better not. I'm up at the crack tomorrow.' But she'd sensed the real reason behind his refusal was he didn't trust himself not to try and move their relationship along faster than he thought she wanted. Tonight, though, he'd got it wrong, and when he leaned forward to give her his usual formal goodnight kiss, she'd responded with a far from formal pressure. A few moments later she'd found her hands were inside his clothes and his inside hers, and she'd felt him hardening against her, felt herself softening against him, felt ready to give herself to him, here, now, in the doorway, standing up, like a pair of teenagers with nowhere better to go.

Then over his shoulder in the vaporous wintry glow cast by a streetlight she'd glimpsed a figure, muffled, indistinct, not much more than an outline, but she had known it was Alex.

She'd closed her eyes as Mick's lips found hers

again. When he broke the contact she'd gasped, 'Let's go inside before you have to arrest us.'

And as they'd practically fallen across her threshold, she'd glanced along the quiet street once more and of course the phantom figure had vanished. And when she woke in the morning with Mick's arms around her, she'd felt the past and all its sorrow had vanished too.

But of course it hadn't. How could she have fooled herself? It had been lurking, in the mist, behind the lamplight, ready to step forward once more when summoned by something as simple as a magazine photo through the post.

She told Dalziel this, or a version of it, bowdlerized, but she guessed he got the picture.

'And now I've started seeing him again,' she concluded. 'Crazy, eh?'

Her attempt at being casually dismissive was unconvincing.

'Can you still see him?'

She looked into the garden and shook her head.

'Not to worry, luv,' Dalziel reassured her. 'Happens to us all. Look at any crowd of strangers, you're sure to see some guy who looks like some guy you know. I mean, when I looked just now, I saw someone who's a dead ringer for my DCI.'

The difference being, of course, that Dalziel was absolutely sure it was Pascoe he'd seen, and could still see.

Things had become very interesting, he thought. Had it been the 'bugger' Gina had clocked? He could have asked, but at this stage he wanted to keep ahead of the game, particularly now he was certain there was a game, and a complex one at that. And telling her about the bugger would have meant telling her about Novello, and she was a card he definitely wanted to keep up his sleeve.

That the woman might be watched didn't surprise him. Someone had brought her here, so presumably they'd want to keep an eye on her. But from keeping an eye on someone to bugging them was a large step, suggesting a worrying level of fore-planning.

'So where do we go from here?' he asked.

He had detected how troubled she was and from his own reading of the woman and from what Purdy had said about her, she needed an action plan, or at least the prospect of activity, to keep her demons under control.

She said, 'I've thought about what you said this morning. I don't want to turn my search into a circus that could frighten Alex off. But I've got to let him know I'm here so that, if he wants to see me, he can make up his own mind.'

For the moment he let pass her implied assumption that her husband was still alive, and close.

'Mebbe you don't need to let him know you're here,' said Dalziel casually.

She said, 'You mean, it might be Alex himself who sent me the picture? But if he wants to contact me, why doesn't he just pick up a phone?'

'Mebbe he wants you up here to take a closer look without you seeing him,' said Dalziel.

'Check out if you're likely to be tying a yellow ribbon round the old oak tree.'

At last she smiled and said, 'Bach, *Pal Joey*, and now Tony Orlando. You've very catholic musical tastes, Mr Dalziel.'

'You should hear my Al Jolson imitation,' said Dalziel. 'So?'

'So, if that were the case, what form do you think the yellow ribbon or its absence might take?' she asked.

'Wedding ring, for a start. Which you're not wearing. On the other hand, you're not wearing an engagement ring either.'

'To see that would mean getting pretty close,' she said, glancing round uneasily.

'Nay, good pair of field glasses would do the trick,' said the Fat Man.

The plaintive wail of some reed instrument came drifting up from the garden.

'Listen,' she said. 'Clarinet. I love the sound it makes.'

'Aye,' he said. 'Like the bagpipes: fine at a distance out of doors if someone else is paying for it. What's your weapon?'

'Piano, mainly. But I play the violin too, and I can tootle a flute if I'm pushed.'

'A real one-woman band,' he said. 'Alex musical too?'

'Not so you'd notice. I mean, he doesn't play anything. But he likes to listen.'

'Good husband material then,' said Dalziel. 'So how'd you meet?'

'At college. I was secretary of a music group. I wanted to book a room in the Union for a concert, Alex was on the Union committee, he was in charge of bookings, he had that kind of head, he was a very good organizer.'

Good enough to organize his own disappearance? wondered Dalziel.

'So how'd you feel when he let on he wanted to be a copper?' he asked.

'No problem,' she said, surprised. 'Should there have been?'

He shook his head, smiling. He'd been drawing parallels with Peter and Ellie Pascoe. They too had met at university, but from what he'd gathered, the news that Pascoe was joining the Force had been greeted with rather less enthusiasm than if he'd announced he planned to make a living flogging his ring round Piccadilly Circus.

'This job of yours,' he said. 'In a school, is it?'

'No. I'm what you call peripatetic; that means I'm employed by Education Authorities to go round several schools. I give private piano tutorials too. What about you? Do you play anything?'

He grinned at her and said, 'Only games that two can play. Thank God, here's our grub. I'm fair clemmed.'

The waitress had appeared with their order. He checked the level of the Barolo. All this talking must have given him a thirst; it was well down. He was still working his way back to full capacity since his recent little set-back, and if he'd been officially on duty, he might have exercised restraint. But what the hell, this was his day off!

He picked up the wine bottle and flourished it in the air, causing the waitress and Gina a moment of serious alarm.

'Another one of the same, luv, when you've a moment' he said.

12.20–12.40

When Dalziel dropped the water jug, Vince Delay turned his head to look and said, 'Clumsy bastard. Probably got the DTs. Only time them cunts hold their hands steady is when they're getting a backhander.'

His sister said, 'Don't swear, Vince. And if all cops were as thick as you think, you wouldn't need me to keep you out of jail.'

She was facing the garden terrace and had observed the Fat Man's brief conversation on his mobile immediately before the accident. When, shortly after the table had been reset and the debris removed, she saw him take out his phone again, she leaned back in her chair and took a long pull on her glass of mineral water, letting her gaze drift round the other diners. She spotted three using mobiles, but two of them continued talking after the Fat Man had switched off.

The third was a young woman sitting alone on a table quite close to the Delays at the edge of the upper terrace. As Fleur watched, the Iti waiter who fancied himself approached with a tray bearing an open prawn sandwich and a glass of white wine. He engaged the young woman in conversation, gently flirtatious from his body language, and she smiled back as she replied, but

155

she seemed to be asking questions, one of which made the young man glance across the garden terrace to the couple on the corner table.

Finally he made as if to move away, but the woman, instead of settling down to her lunch, started up from her chair, an expression of dismay on her face. She was looking across the lower terrace towards the gardens where a buffet party was taking place. Then she said something to the waiter and dashed past him into the hotel.

Fleur said, 'Vince, sit tight. Make sure your phone's switched on. OK?'

She stood up, nice and easy with no sign of undue haste, but she still moved fast enough for the young woman to be in sight as she went through the door into the hotel.

She followed her out into the car park, digging the VW keys out of her shoulder bag in anticipation of another pursuit. But the young woman ignored the ranks of parked cars and made straight for the exit on to the road. Here she paused and took a mobile out of her pocket and started talking into it. But she hadn't touched the number pad. She was faking it, Fleur guessed, giving herself an excuse to be standing in the car park.

Fleur worked out the reason simultaneously with having her conclusion confirmed. A man approached the exit on a small motor bike. Most of his features were hidden by his helmet and goggles, but she could see he had a moustache. As he passed the young woman, her gaze followed him. The bike turned left, passing the entrance gap close to where Fleur was standing.

She took out a ballpoint and scribbled its number down on the palm of her hand.

Could it be as easy as this? she wondered. She needed to move quick. If, as she assumed, the young woman was working for Tubby, then it would only take a single phone call for her to get all known details of the motor cyclist.

Two could play at that game if you had the right contacts, and one thing Fleur Delay had was the right contacts. The young woman didn't seem in any hurry to get on the phone. In fact she was standing in the same place, giving every impression of uncertainty over her next move. So there could still be time here to get ahead of the game.

She put a number into her mobile as she walked towards the VW.

'I need a vehicle check,' she said. 'Quick as you can.'

She rang off then speed-dialled her brother.

'Vince,' she said, 'come to the car.'

'They're still at the table,' he protested. 'And my pudding's just arriving.'

'The car, Vince. Now!'

She opened the door of the VW and slid into the driver's seat.

The young woman was on the phone now but she looked as if she were having a conversation rather than simply making a request.

Vince came out of the hotel, looking sulky.

Fleur's phone rang.

'Alun Watkins, Flat 39, Loudwater Villas,' she repeated.

By the time Vince got into the car, she'd

entered the address into her sat-nav.

'What's happening, Sis?' asked Vince.

Fleur started the engine and smiled at him.

'We may be going home sooner than you think.'

12.35–13.15

The Fat Man rarely needed an excuse to be hungry, but this morning he'd been in such a rush that he'd scrimped on breakfast. Now he tucked into his roast beef with relish. And with horseradish too.

Gina on the other hand merely poked her fork at the wafer-thin slices on her plate, but nothing got near her mouth except her wine glass.

Finally she said, 'If Alex is behind this, then I don't need to worry about getting his picture in the paper or on the box, do I?'

He said, 'I'd say not.'

She went on, as if thinking aloud, 'But I can't make that assumption, can I? If the photo didn't come from him, then I've got to do everything I can to find him.'

'Why?' said Dalziel.

For a second she looked at him as if he'd asked a stupid question. But the look faded as she started to answer and discovered her reasons were not so clear cut as she'd imagined.

'Because . . . because I need . . . because of what we felt for each other . . . what we went through together . . . Because I need to know!'

She stared at him defiantly, as if challenging him to ask, *know what?*

Instead he said, 'What about him? Mebbe he

doesn't want to be found.'

'We don't know that. He may still be in a state of fugue.'

'Like old Bach, you mean? Thought you said he weren't all that musical.'

'I think you know very well what I mean,' she said dismissively.

Reckons she's got my number now, he thought complacently. That was OK. He liked dealing with folk who believed they knew how his mind worked.

He said, 'So if he's in trouble, all mixed up, don't know who he is or what's gone off or owt, you'd like to help him, right?'

'Of course I would.'

'And if you find he's alive, but not in trouble, what then?'

She took another drink of wine then said, 'I may just kill the bastard!'

She spoke with deadly emphasis. Dalziel pursed his lips as if pondering the idea before nodding in approval. Now her features relaxed into a smile and finally she laughed out loud.

'Sorry! What am I like? Mixed feelings is putting it lightly, Andy. Can I call you Andy?'

'Why?' said Dalziel.

'Because Mick says it's your name. Also because anyone overhearing me call you Mr Dalziel will imagine you're either my boss or my sugar daddy.'

'And calling me Andy 'ull make them think I'm your toy boy, is that it?'

She laughed again. A couple of glasses of wine had really loosened her up. What might a third do? It occurred to him that if Pascoe was keeping an eye on him, he might be getting the wrong idea about this lunch date. Serve the bugger right!

Gina said, 'The thing is, Andy, you're Mick's idea, not mine. When he suggested contacting you, I thought that probably it would be a complete waste of time.'

'And you don't now? Why's that?'

'You're not the only one who's done some checking up,' she said provocatively.

'You've been checking on me, you mean? How'd you manage that?'

'For a start, I spoke to Mick. I asked him to tell me all about you.'

'Can't have been that much to tell, we only ever met the once.'

'Your reputation seems to have spread pretty widely in police circles, Andy. Do you like cowboy movies?'

'Sometimes.'

'Mick's a great fan. John Wayne, Clint Eastwood. We often spend a night watching old DVDs. When it's my turn, it's *The Red Shoes* or *Tales of Hoffman*. With Mick it's *Unforgiven* or *True Grit*. That's his favourite.'

'Aye, I've seen it. Good movie.'

'You remember the bit where the girl is looking for a marshal to pursue the man who killed her father? Depends what she's looking for, she's told. But if it's true grit she wants. Rooster Cogburn's her man. That's what Mick said about you.'

Dalziel massaged his chins reflectively.

'I told you already, I don't kill people, not unless I really don't like them,' he said.

'Same as Rooster, then,' she said. 'Anyway, I put together what Mick said with what I'd picked up from you in our short meeting. And I decided I'd be mad not to accept any help you can give me, if you're up for it, that is.'

Dalziel looked at her over his wine glass. Were Mick Purdy and this woman jerking him around? But he had to admit the *True Grit* bullshit gave him a warm glow.

'So what might you want me to do?' he asked.

She became very businesslike as she said, 'Well, here's how I see things. There are only two possibilities that concern me. One, Alex is alive and will want to make contact with me if he knows I'm here. Two, Alex is alive and either won't want to make contact or isn't in a fit mental state to recognize me.'

Three, Alex is alive and doing the horizontal tango with some bit of dusky chuff in Buenos Aires, thought Dalziel. Or four, he's a seven-year-old corpse.

He said, 'Sounds reasonable. So?'

'If it's the first, I can take care of that myself. But if it's the second, I'm going to have a hell of a job tracking him down on my own. Whereas someone with your experience and resources . . . '

'You reckon? Any tips where I might start?'

She produced the envelope containing the page from *MY Life*.

'You could start here. There are other people standing around him. I'm sure you've got the

162

resources to blow their faces up then set about tracking some of them down. They might remember him, even know him.'

'Mebbe,' he said, taking the envelope. 'Worth a try.'

Though he'd been planning to get the photograph from her so that he could test Purdy's theory that it was a fake, getting it this way made him feel slightly uncomfortable. But it wasn't his job to suggest to her that this might all be a put-up job with Mick as the main target. Was it?

He was saved from further debate by his mobile ringing once more.

'He's left,' said Novello.

'You mean you've lost him?'

'He's on a motorbike. I've got the number. Shall I run it?'

Dalziel took the point without need of elaboration. All requests to run vehicle numbers were logged and an off-duty DC would be expected to explain herself.

He could of course by a mere word turn this from unofficial to official. Even if Purdy's notion that it was nothing more than a sick joke were right, the fact that their table had been bugged upped the ante considerably. But it could still be either owt or nowt. A couple of months back he could have shrugged off *nowt* with an even-Homer-nods indifference, but now he felt himself being weighed in the balance of his colleagues' judgment.

Sod it. He was king of the castle, wasn't he? And being king meant not having to explain yourself.

He said, 'Give it to me.'

He scribbled it on his hand.

'I'll get back to you,' he said.

He disconnected, thumbed Wield's speed-dial number.

'Wieldy, check this for me. And get back to me soonest, OK?'

He put the phone on the table and smiled apologetically at Gina Wolfe.

She said, 'This is like being with Mick on his so-called day off. You never know when his phone's going to ring.'

'You must have got used to it during your marriage,' he said.

'To some extent. But after Alex moved up to DI, he was much more concerned with paper chases than blues-and-twos hot pursuit. It was good for a while. No more long white nights wondering what he was up to. Then we had other reasons for long white nights. And days.'

He said, 'That must have been a terrible time. Hard to imagine worse.'

'Mick told you the details about Lucy, did he?'

Her recent brightness had faded. He found he wanted to bring it back, and he had to remind himself that he wasn't on a date.

He said, 'Aye. So no need to talk about it if you don't want to.'

'No, that's OK. Talking about it's better than keeping it all inside, eating you up. That's what it did to Alex. It ate him up. Which in a way was good for me. Keeping an eye out for Alex gave me a function.'

'But you left him all the same.'

'Because he'd gone beyond my help. There was an edge he was close to falling over. I knew if I stayed I'd probably go after him. I left to find strength to come back and save him. At least, that's what I tell myself. But by the time I came back, he'd gone. Literally. I still wonder . . . '

'Nay, lass, don't. You don't measure how you feel pain by how you bear it. Surviving don't mean you're less sensitive, just that you're stronger.'

Jesus, Dalziel! he admonished himself. Might not be a date, but there's no need to sound off like a big-tent preacher!

She said, 'Maybe. Maybe his weakness has given him the chance to start over from scratch while all my so-called strength does is leave me bearing it forever. Just because I've reshaped my life doesn't mean I've escaped from the past, Andy. Not a day passes but I think about little Lucy. But I still find it hard even to refer to what happened directly. I hear myself skirting around. Like in the cathedral.'

'You're not skirting now.'

'No. I suppose in the cathedral I was talking to a stranger.'

'And now?'

She smiled even though there were tears in her eyes.

'Now I'm talking to Rooster Cogburn.'

'You'll not get me on a horse,' he said, seeking an escape route from this intensity.

She was glad to take it.

'Don't need a horse to be a perfect gentle knight,' she said, only half mocking.

'I've been called a lot of things, but not that. Here, where's my grub gone?'

The Fat Man had no problem eating and talking at the same time, but the problem with this simultaneity was that often the food went down without him really noticing it.

She said, 'You can try mine, if you like. I'm not really hungry.'

He looked suspiciously at her plate.

'Beef, is it? How's it cooked?'

'It's not.'

'Bloody hell! My dad used to warn me, never get mixed up with a lass who eats raw meat!'

'Perhaps you should have listened to him,' she said. 'But it tastes fine. Really.'

'Well, I'll try owt, except for incest and the Lib Dems.'

He cut off a sliver, chewed it, said, 'Not bad,' and pulled her plate towards him.

His second bottle of Barolo was almost gone.

She on the other hand was showing no inclination to push beyond her second glass. Pity, perhaps. But waste not, want not.

He said, 'The rest of yon white stuff, you're not leaving that too, are you?'

Smiling she pushed the bottle towards him.

He had made good inroads into the raw beef when his phone rang again. He looked at the display and said, ''Scuse me, luv. Private,' stood up and descended the steps towards the garden before answering.

'Wieldy,' he said.

'That number, I've got a name and address,' said the sergeant.

166

Dalziel scribbled it down into his notebook. 'Thanks, Wieldy.'

'No problem. Owt I should know about, sir? Or Pete, mebbe?'

'Talk about it tomorrow,' prevaricated Dalziel. 'And if I need to talk to Pete, as it happens I'm looking at the bugger right this minute. Thanks, Wieldy. Cheers.'

It was true, more or less. He could distantly see Pascoe's head among a group of people at the buffet party.

He thumbed in Novello's number.

'Ivor, here's the name and address. Alun Watkins, 39 Loudwater Villas. Listen, see what you can find out, but softly softly, OK? Good girl. No, no need to get back to me. Unless something really important comes up, it'll keep till the morning. Enjoy thasel!'

He suddenly felt very relaxed. Maybe it was the fact that he'd sunk two bottles of lovely Italian plonk, but relaxing here in the sun looking out over a garden where the glories of summer were enhanced rather than threatened by the first touch of autumn, with that pleasantly mazy music drifting up from the gazebo while behind him, impatient (he hoped) for his return, sat a golden-haired damsel begging him to ease her distress, he found he'd shed all the doubts and concerns that had beset him since his return to work.

And there was still pudding to come!

Once more master of his soul and captain of his fate, he could do anything he wanted.

Except maybe drive home.

But sufficient be the evil . . .

He turned round and realized Gina Wolfe had risen too and was standing close behind him. Close enough to have overheard? Mebbe. But it didn't matter. He'd said nowt that suggested the calls had anything to do with her.

She said, 'This is a lovely spot, isn't it? It seems somehow, I don't know, *ungrateful* to be unhappy in such a place on such a day.'

'Then let's try not to be unhappy,' he said, leading her back to the table and pouring an inch of golden wine into her glass and filling his own to the brim. 'Let's have a toast. To a bright future, eh?'

'No,' she said seriously. 'Don't tempt fate by bringing in the future.'

'You're right,' he said. 'Wise man sticks to here and now. So, let's see. Here's to Iti wine, English weather, and a little chance music out of doors. Cheers!'

'I'll drink to that,' she said, smiling.

13.00–13.40

David Gidman the Third stepped up to the microphone and acknowledged the applause.

Pinchbeck had been right. Again. The crowd at the opening was at least fifty per cent larger than the church congregation. The bloody woman had probably also been right to run interference when that dishy deaconess had tried to top up his glass on the vicarage lawn. The notion of pleasuring a woman in canonicals was strangely appealing.

He shook the thought from his mind and concentrated on carrying his audience back to 1948 and the arrival in England of the *Empire Windrush*, bringing with it David Gidman the First and his young son, not yet known as Goldie.

Maggie listened critically as he outlined his grandfather's early days in the East End, his emergence as a community leader, his rise from railway cleaner to guard on the *Flying Scotsman*. She had to acknowledge he was good. More convincing than Cameron, beefier than Brown, less lachrymose than Blair, he had it all. In the right hands he could really go far.

He made the transition from his grandfather to his father with consummate ease, projecting Goldie as a hard-working, selfmade entrepreneur who'd used the opportunities offered by a benevolent state to get an education and make a fortune.

'There was one other thing my dad shared with his dad as well as a capacity for hard work,' he declared. 'Neither of them ever forgot where they came from. They always gave something back and the more they earned the more they gave.'

'Now here am I, the third generation of the UK Gidmans. By their standards, I've had it easy. Not for me the long journey across a wide ocean to a new land, a new life. Not for me the long journey from the back streets of the East End to the boardrooms of the City. No, I stand before you, benefiting from the advantages of going to a first-rate school and a first-rate university.'

'Yet I do not feel any need to apologize for these advantages. They've been paid for, and paid for with interest, by the love and the devotion and the damned hard work of my father and his father.'

'But I'm always aware that, if I'm to show myself worthy of their efforts, their love, their sacrifice, then I too have payments to make.'

'I'm proud of my pappy and of my granpappy, and I want to make them proud of me. It's people like you standing here before me today who will tell me by your comments and your votes if I succeed.'

'But I won't be doing my political career much good if I keep you any longer from the refreshments waiting inside! So without further ado, I would like to declare the David Gidman the First Memorial Community Centre well and truly open.'

He took the scissors that Maggie handed him and flourished them for the cameras, making sure his head was inclined slightly to the right. Both profiles were good, but the left was slightly better. Silently he counted up to three, then he snipped the white silk ribbon stretched across the open double door of the ultra-modern reflective glass and white concrete building squatting like a crash-landed space cruiser within world record javelin-throwing distance of the no man's land that was allegedly going to blossom into the London Olympic village.

He acknowledged the applause, then stood aside and waved the public in towards the promised refreshments.

First to the barricades, last to the refreshments, that's the way to win hearts and minds, Maggie said. He looked for her now, and saw her making sure that the Centre manager had taken control of the official civic party so that she could give her full attention to the much more important posse of journalists.

She'd vetoed Dave's suggestion of a formal press conference.

'That would make it look like it's all about you,' she said.

'But it is,' he objected. 'That's why Pappy said he'd stay away.'

'Yes, but we don't want it to look like that. It's OK, you'll get the coverage.'

To this end, she stage managed a series of

171

semi-private conversations as they trailed in the wake of the civic party. All PAs like to claim they can deal with the press. Maggie was one of the few who actually could. So unobtrusive you never knew she was there till you stepped out of line, she was gaining a reputation for never failing to deliver on a promise, or a threat.

First up was the *Independent*. Not their top political man; you needed something a bit meatier than an upwardly mobile young politician opening a community centre to get him off his wife's Norfolk estate on a Sunday. No, this was a pleasant enough young fellow called . . . he needed Maggie's whisper this time.

'Hello, Piers. Good to see you.'

'Thank you, Mr Gidman. Your father must be disappointed he couldn't be here today. How's he keeping?'

'He's fine. Just a touch of cold. Thanks for asking.'

'Hope he shakes it off soon. But we don't seem to have seen a lot of him recently anyway. Not leaving the field clear so you can shine, is he?'

'No one shines brighter than Goldie Gidman, isn't that what they say? No, he just likes the quiet life nowadays.'

'Quiet? I understand he's in and out of Millbank all the time, helping the shadow chancellor get his sums right in the current crisis.'

'He's always available when his country needs him, but today he really is treating himself to a day of rest.'

'Unlike you, eh? Busy busy, in and out of the House. Where do you get the energy? Your friends must be worried you're taking too much on.'

'You know what they say — if you want something done, ask a busy man.'

'I'm sure the PM agrees with you. There's a rumour going around that there may be something for you in the next reshuffle. Any comment?'

'I am at my Party's and my country's disposal.'

'And the rumour . . . ?'

'Almost impossible to stop a rumour, Piers, so do keep spreading it.'

Now Maggie Pinchbeck materialized between them and with a sweet smile indicated that the reporter's time was up. Obediently he moved aside.

Next up was the *Guardian*. Again second string, though his well-worn bomber jacket and balding suede shoes looked as if they'd been handed down by his superior.

He too wanted to focus on Goldie Gidman's contributions to the Tory coffers. When he started getting aggressive, suggesting that if Goldie wasn't looking for some payback to himself, maybe he regarded it as an investment in his son's career, Maggie stepped in again, turning as she did so to signal the next journalist on her list to move forward. It should have been Gem Huntley, a rather pushy young woman from the *Daily Messenger*. Instead it was Gwyn Jones, who was to political scandal what a blow-fly is to dead meat, and he'd been trying to settle on the Gidmans ever since Dave the Third burst on the scene.

'Gwyn,' she said, 'good to see you! What happened? Shandy not sending double invites then?'

It never did any harm to let these journalists know that they weren't the only ones who kept their eyes and ears open. She knew about the Shandy party because Gidman had been sent an invitation which she'd made sure never reached him. While fairly confident she could have persuaded him that cancelling the Centre opening to attend what the tabloids were calling the mega-binge of the month would have been a PR disaster, it had seemed simpler and safer merely to remove the temptation.

Jones smiled in sardonic acknowledgement of the suggestion that he would only have been invited on Beanie's ticket and said, 'Man cannot live on caviar alone. Give me a good honest sandwich any time. Anyway, young Gem wasn't feeling too well this morning so they asked me if I could step in.'

He made as little effort to sound convincing as Maggie did to sound sincere as she replied, 'I'm sorry to hear that, hope she's OK. David, we're honoured today. The *Messenger's* sent their top man to talk to you.'

She had to give it to Dave. Not by a flicker did he show anything but pleasure as he smiled and said, 'Gwyn, great to see you. Must have missed you at St Osith's.'

'Didn't make the service, Dave, sorry. Good to

see you're taking your leader's strictures to heart. What was it he said? *Religion should have no politics. We will all stand naked before God. When doubtless we will find if size really does matter.*'

Gidman's heart lurched. Could the bastard be on to Sophie?

But his smile remained warm and his voice was light and even as he replied, 'You're talking about majorities, of course. So what do you think of the Centre?'

'Looks great. No expense spared, eh? Folk round here must be very grateful.'

'Gratitude isn't the issue. We just want to put something back into the area.'

'Yeah, I can see why you'd feel like that. Though it does raise the question, would it ever really be possible for your family to fully put back in everything you've taken out? You'd have to build something like Buck House, wouldn't you?'

Maggie was taken aback. The *Messenger* was never going to be Gidman's friend, and Jones hated his guts, but even so his approach here was unusually frontal.

Her employer's initial reaction was relief. Sexual innuendo would have bothered him. Anti-Goldie slurs were old hat and easily dealt with.

'Do what you can then do a little more, isn't that what they say?' he declared.

'Is it? Who was that? Alex Ferguson?'

'Someone even older, I think. Confucius, perhaps.'

'That's really old. But we should always pay attention to the past, right, Dave? You never know when something's going to come up behind you and bite your bum. Man with a bitten bum finds out who his real friends are. Of course, it depends what's doing the biting. A flea would just be irritating, but something a bit bigger, like a *wolf*, say, that could be serious. You wouldn't have a *wolf* trying to take a bite somewhere behind you, Dave?'

Why the hell was he stressing *wolf*?

'Not even a flea to the best of my knowledge, Gwyn.'

'Lucky you. Talking of the past, I heard a rumour your dad was thinking of writing his autobiography.'

'Another rumour! Definitely nothing in that one, Gwyn. I once suggested it to him and he said, who'd want to read about a dull old devil like me?'

'Oh, I think there's quite a lot of people who'd like to hear the whole moving story, Dave, *wolves* and all. If he ever does go down that road, I'd be more than happy to help him out with the research. It's never easy digging up the past. People move on, disappear. That's where a journalist could come in really useful. We've got the skills. Finding disappeared people's a bit of a specialty of mine.'

'That's a kind offer. I'll be sure to mention it to him, Gwyn.'

His gaze flickered to Maggie, who took the hint and brought the interview to a close by advancing the friendly face of the *Daily*

Telegraph. For which relief much thanks, thought Gidman. The *Telegraph* loved him. But as he answered the bromidic questions, the voice he was hearing in his mind was still Gwyn Jones's.

13.00–13.50

Goldie Gidman watched his guest's reaction to the food that Flo had set before him with an amusement he took care to hide.

The man had been an hour late for his eleven o'clock appointment at Windrush House. As his purpose was basically to beg for money, it might have been expected that he would be punctual. On the other hand, as a peer of the realm condescending to visit the tasteless mansion of a self-made black man, he perhaps did not feel that the courtesy of kings need apply. Certainly his explanation for his lateness with its casual reference to the number of roadworks between Sandringham and Waltham Abbey had more of condescension than apology in it.

Goldie Gidman was not offended. When asked as he frequently was by journalists why a man with his background should be such a staunch supporter of the Conservative Party, he had a stock reply that included references to traditional values, British justice, fair play, equal opportunity, enlightened individualism, and cricket.

Privately, and not for publication, he had been known to say that he'd looked closely at British politics and seen that the Tories were his kind of people. Folk he could deal with, motives he understood.

Internally, in that core of being where all men hide their truths and which will only be laid completely open at the great Last Judgment, if such an event ever takes place, Gidman believed that all politicians were little better than reservoir dogs, so you might as well run with the pack that fed off your kind of meat.

The peer was what is known as a fund raiser. His purpose in visiting Goldie was to discover why in recent months his hitherto generous donations to the Party had diminished from a glistening flood to a muddy trickle. It should not be thought that the Party's ringmaster was so naïve as to think that Gidman was likely to be impressed by an ancient title. Rather his thinking was that, by hesitating his payments, Gidman was taking up a bargaining position. In consequence of recent scandals, such negotiations tended to be delicate and oblique, with the attendant danger of misunderstanding. When a man who thinks he has bought a villa in Antibes finds himself fobbed off with a time-share in Torremolinos, dissatisfaction at best, and at worst defection, will follow. So this particular peer had been chosen because he gave out such an impression of intellectual vacuity that Goldie might feel constrained to explain in words of at most two syllables what precisely it was he wanted in return for his largesse.

But an hour had passed and the peer was no further forward.

So when Goldie looked at his watch and said, 'Any second now my wife's going to call me in to lunch. Thinks if I don't eat regular I'm going to

179

get an ulcer. You're very welcome to take pot luck with us if'n you ain't got somewhere better to be.'

'How kind,' said the peer. 'I should be delighted.'

He meant it. Though this was his first visit to Windrush House he had heard that his host kept a fine cellar and that his wife, who apparently had a professional connection with the catering trade, could dish up some of the tastiest traditional fare a true blue Englishman could desire. This he imagined would be an old-fashioned Sunday lunch to remember.

He was right in one respect.

The pot from which he had agreed to take his luck held nothing more than a thin beef consommé. This was backed up by some hunks of wheaten bread and a wedge of hard cheese, all to be washed down by a small bottle of stout — a special treat, Goldie assured him, as on normal days Flo permitted him nothing but still water.

After a cup of lukewarm decaffeinated coffee, the peer was eager to be on his way even though, with regard to his mission, he felt he now knew less than he thought he did when he arrived.

As he rose to take his leave, Gidman said, 'Almost forgot. Must be getting old.' And he produced a long white envelope.

It was unsealed and, after an enquiring glance from the peer had been met by an encouraging nod, he opened it and examined the contents.

'Good lord,' he said. 'My dear fellow, this is extraordinarily generous.'

'I like to help,' said Gidman.

'And you do, you do. Don't think we're not appreciative.'

Here he paused, expecting to receive at the very least a strong hint as to how this appreciation might best be shown.

But as he was later to explain to the ringmaster, 'He just smiled and said goodbye, didn't hint at a gong, never even mentioned young Dave the Turd. I mean, can it really be he's not looking for anything in return?'

And the ringmaster said with that insight which had put him at the centre of the circus, 'Don't be silly. Of course he wants something, and I don't doubt we'll find out what it is sooner or later.'

He was right, but not wholly so.

Back at Windrush House, Flo Gidman, who was more susceptible to the glamour of a title than her husband, rattled on about what a nice man the peer had been, and how you could see the family connections in his nose and ears, and finally asked, 'Did your talk with him go well, dear?'

'I think so,' said Goldie. 'He got what he came for.'

'The donation, you mean. I hope they show their appreciation.'

Though she would never press her husband on the matter, the prospect of being Lady Gidman was not altogether disagreeable to Flo.

'Maybe they will,' said Gidman, smiling fondly at her. 'Me, I hope they won't have to.'

His wife smiled back, not really understanding what he meant.

She was not alone in this, for even the subtle mind of the ringmaster only partially grasped what had gone on.

The reason for the recent scaling down of the

Gidman contributions had been that Goldie didn't care to be taken for granted, except in matters of retribution. When it came to largesse, it was his judgment that regularity and reliability bred first disregard, then disrespect.

It was always his intention when the right moment came to remind the Millbank mandarins what an important contributor he was. Today he felt the moment had come.

A couple of hundred miles to the north, two of his employees were dealing with a potential problem. If, as he thought most likely, they dealt with it satisfactorily, then that was an end to the matter.

But if, as was always possible, things went belly-up, and if, as was most unlikely but still just about possible, all his other safeguards proved to be flawed, then a wise man would be found to have grappled his influential friends to him with bands of gold.

That was why he'd been able to remain underwhelmed by his visitor. He might have a title and a name that ran so far back into antiquity its spelling had changed at least three times, but in the Gidman scheme of things, he was nothing more than the Man from the Pru.

He had been selling insurance.

And having made such a large down payment on his policy, Goldie Gidman felt able to head up to his private sitting room for a cigar and an afternoon with Jimi Hendrix, confident that nothing happening up in darkest Yorkshire could disturb the pleasant tranquillity of his day.

13.00–13.30

Loudwater Villas was an Edwardian terrace converted to flats in the loadsamoney eighties. It derived its name from its proximity to a weir on the Trench, one of the two rivers that wound through the city. Had it overlooked the other, the placid and picturesque Till, the outlook might have added value to the property. But when the industrial revolution began to darken the skies of Mid-Yorkshire, geography and geology had dictated that the deeper, narrower, speedier Trench should be its power source. All you saw across the river from the upper windows of Loudwater Villas was a wasteland of derelict mills that successive Bunteresque city councils promised to transform into a twenty-first-century wonderland of flats and shops and sporting arenas as soon as this postal order they were expecting daily turned up.

Fleur Delay knew none of this, but her eye for detail told her this wasn't the kind of apartment block that had high security.

No main entrance security cameras; no concierge cum security man behind a bank of screens checking out visitors; no bar to unobtrusive entry but the locked front door.

She knew it was locked because she'd just seen a man walk up to it, insert a key and enter.

Simplest was to wait for someone else to approach, then follow them in. But she was keenly aware of the woman cop standing in the Keldale car park. She'd been talking on the phone. Presumably she'd rung in for instructions.

And if eventually the instruction was to head for Loudwater Villas, then she could be close behind.

Fleur made up her mind. This was after all just an initial check-up, so while a low profile was still preferable, invisibility wasn't of the essence. The subject identified, then the serious business would begin. It had already occurred to her that the accident rate for young men on motorbikes was pretty high. Not that an old Yamaha 250 was exactly a high-performance machine, but you can break your neck hitting tarmac at forty miles an hour almost as easily as you can at eighty.

But that was getting ahead of herself. Now she needed to get in there quick, even if it meant ringing someone's bell.

She said, 'Vince, sit tight. I'll go and take a look.'

'Sure you don't want me along, sis?'

'Not yet. Have your mobile handy, keep your eyes skinned, and if that woman from the car park shows, give me a ring, OK?'

'Sure.'

She got out of the car. As she straightened up she swayed slightly. Then she was OK. Vince hadn't noticed. Sometimes Vince's ability not to notice things was irritating, but this time she was grateful.

184

She set off for the entrance. Her luck, always good on a job, held. A car drew up behind her. She glanced round to see its driver, a young Asian man, get out. He was in a hurry, passing her without a glance, inserting a key in the lock and pushing the door fully open as he entered so that she was able to reach it before it swung shut.

She was in a small hallway with a staircase rising from it. No sign of a lift. This had been a conversion with no economy spared. A notice headed LISTON DEVELOPMENTS with a logo resembling the Sidney Opera House confirmed what she'd guessed: the flats in the thirties were on the second floor.

She headed quickly up the stairs. The faster she moved the less chance there was of meeting somebody. Ahead she could hear the young Asian's footsteps. He was making for the second floor too. She stepped out into the corridor just in time to see him entering a flat, calling, 'Devi, what are you doing? Ma's expecting us at one,' to which a woman's voice replied, 'In a minute, in a minute, your ma's not going anywhere, worse luck!'

The door closed as Fleur approached. Number 38.

She passed on to number 39, which was the last along the corridor. So, neighbours on one side only and they sounded as if they were on their way out.

Beyond the door she could hear the sound of a television copshow or movie, the kind that involved screaming women and screeching cars. There was a bell push. She leaned into it, then stood back. No security cameras, but the doors did have peepholes. She composed her face to smiling housewife mode. It didn't come easy and wouldn't stand close examination, but it should do for a one-eyed squinter.

The peephole darkened. After a moment it lightened again. Thirty seconds passed. Adjusting his dress, or didn't like the look of her? She was starting to fear the second when the door opened.

She made a rapid assessment of the man who stood there.

He had an unruly mop of hair whose blackness was of an intensity you rarely met outside of a priest's socks. But his eyebrows she noticed were light brown. And surely he'd had a moustache when she glimpsed him leaving the car park?

His build was right, just under six foot tall, quite muscular, no evidence of any middle-age spread around the belt of his jeans. Age hard to say, though his skin tone looked like that of a young man. Too young? Maybe he used male moisturizer.

He said, 'Yes?'

She said, 'Mr Watkins?'

He said, 'Who's asking?'

She said, 'I'm glad to find someone at home. I was beginning to think the whole block was empty. I'm Jenny Smith, Mr Watkins. From Liston Developments. It's about the proposed improvements. We will have to ask you to vacate your apartment for a couple of days, I'm afraid. I'm here to discuss timings and alternative accommodation with you. Do you have a few moments?'

As she spoke she moved forward with an assurance it would have taken a tank trap to deny. The man retreated before her. Her gaze took in the tiny room. She got no impression of permanency. Furnishing was minimal: television set with a lousy picture and distorted sound, one balding armchair next to a rickety coffee table on which stood a telephone, no pictures on the wall, no curtains on the window.

After seven weeks this would have looked good. After seven years it was puzzling.

He said, 'Look, I'm a bit busy, couldn't you do this some other time . . . ?'

He had a bit of an accent. She wasn't too good at accents. Bit up and down, like that nosey cop who used to get up Goldie's nose. But accents were easy to put on if you had the gift for it. Vince did a great Arnie Schwarzenegger.

'Sorry,' she said. 'Health and Safety — they need everything yesterday. God, they're the bane of my life these days. How long have you been here, by the way?'

'Why? Isn't that on your records?'

'Of course it is.'

He was sounding edgy. The furnishings apart, it was looking good. But between looking good and absolute certainty there was a gap a rash jump to conclusions could easily tumble you in.

He said, 'Look, just for the record, could I see some identification?'

Real edgy!

'Of course,' she said. 'No problem. You're

187

quite right to ask. In fact, you asking reminds me I should have asked too. So I'll show you mine if you show me yours, all right?'

A bit of jocular innuendo was always distracting, especially when accompanied by a menacing leer. She rarely had difficulty facing down guys who liked to talk big.

He said, 'No, I'm sure you're who you say you are. But listen, I've really got things to do . . .'

Her phone rang.

'Mind if I answer this?' she said, opening her shoulder bag.

She took the phone out. As she pressed the *receive* button the room swayed and this time didn't level off immediately.

'Oh God,' she said.

The phone fell to the floor and she followed it down, cracking her forehead against the TV set which, as if in sympathy, let out a blood-curdling shriek. The warm trickle oozing over her left eye suggested it hadn't curdled hers.

'Oh fuck!' he said, kneeling beside her. 'You OK?'

'Yeah, sure, that's why I'm lying here bleeding,' she grated.

'You look bad. Shall I call an ambulance?'

Her wig had come askew. No wonder he was worried about the way she looked!

'No, I'm fine,' she insisted. 'A glass of water maybe.'

He rose and went out of the room.

She needed to be out of here too. She scrabbled for the phone to confirm what she suspected, but there was no one at the other end. Which meant . . .

She didn't like to think what it might mean.

She really needed to be out of here. Strength was returning to her legs, but not enough yet.

The man came back with a cupful of water.

She took it from him, squeezed a tablet from the bubble pack and washed it down.

She saw him looking at her and she said, 'Aspirin.'

There was a tap at the door.

'Don't answer . . . ' she started to say, but he wasn't taking any notice of her. Why should he?

She got on all fours to try and push herself upright as he opened the door.

Then for about two and a half seconds, everything happened in single-frame audio-visual flashes.

The young female cop in the doorway wearing the kind of phoney smile Fleur had tried for earlier.

Vince behind her swinging a short metal cylinder against the side of her head.

The girl falling into the room.

The man taking two steps back and standing on Fleur's hand.

Fleur hearing herself scream.

Vince raising the cylinder that was the sawn-off barrel of a shotgun.

The flash.

The bang.

The man falling backwards.

'For God's sake, shut that door!' grated Fleur.

One thing she'd trained Vince up for was instant obedience. He kicked the door shut. Still on her knees, she swung round to the TV set and turned the volume up.

Then she sat and waited, counting up to twenty.

Nothing happened.

The TV set was showing a night scene. She studied herself in the darkened glass. The streak of blood down her face was dramatic but its source was a lesion the size of a peanut.

She adjusted her wig, turned the TV sound up higher, and got to her feet. Vince opened his mouth and she quietened him with a look.

She went to the door and listened.

She heard a door opening, a male voice saying, 'Don't be silly, it's the television. Come on, we're half an hour late already. Ma will be furious.' To which the shrill female replied, 'So what? Can't we be an hour late, or better still two hours? In my condition, how can I hurry?'

The voices faded away down the corridor.

Now Fleur turned and took in the room.

The man who might be Wolfe was gone beyond recall. The shotgun blast had all but removed his face. There was no way they were going to identify him by comparing him to a photo.

The female cop had fallen on her left side. Blood oozed from a long contusion on the right temple where Vince had struck her. A shallow bubble of saliva formed at her lips, sank, then formed again very slowly, so for the time being at least she was still alive.

Vince stood there, weapon in hand, regarding her with an expression she was all too familiar with, the look of a small boy who suspects he has done wrong but isn't yet sure if his actions merit mild reproof, stern reproach, or severe punishment. She had to bite back the angry invective forming in her throat.

Then he said, 'I thought he was hurting you, sis,' and her anger dissolved.

He is what he is, she thought, and for better or worse she loved him. In fact he was the only person on the face of the earth that she had any positive feeling for, and his need to be protected was matched by her need to protect him. These two, the dead man and the probably dying woman, were so much collateral damage, the high but necessary price that had to be paid for the love between her and her brother. Everything came second to that. Love was a harder taskmaster than even The Man, promising small reward at the end of the day. But you knew when you entered his service that you signed all your rights away.

She said wearily, 'We'll talk about it later, Vince. For now, let's get things sorted in here then be on our way.'

3

misterioso

Prelude

She says I'm pregnant.

The words bring such an explosion of joy that it shatters the barriers his mind had built against pain.

She sees only the pain and turns away.

But he turns with her, and now she sees the joy, and it's so great that in a moment she thinks she must have imagined the pain.

He knows once more who he is . . . no, not is . . . he knows who he was, for now the nowhere existence in which he had felt himself shadowy, insubstantial, has sent out roots and will grow like the seed in her belly, while that other existence in that other world of pain proves to be the world of shades, inhabited by ghosts, himself nothing more than ghost when he visits it.

He knows he has to visit it, for that ghost of himself needs to be laid. So he descends into the shadowland to seek his old love, and when he sees her there, safe and secure in another shade's arms, he turns away and climbs back to the light, not fearing to look over his shoulder because he knows she will not be following.

His new love waits for him, radiant to see him return, not questioning where he has been for no doubt lies between them, and he tells her no lies for how can a man lie about a world that no longer exists?

195

He feels the new world of her ripening belly under his hands.

Lucinda, *he says.*

What did you say?

Lucinda. That's her name.

But we don't even know that we'll have a girl!

Yes we do, *he says with the smiling certainty of one who knows that that other existence had been but a dress rehearsal whose disasters were a necessary prelude to a triumphant and lengthy run.* And her name will be Lucinda. And from the moment she is born, she shall have nothing but the best.

So easily in joy and love a man plots his own betrayal.

13.45–14.50

Gwyn Jones left the community centre without troubling the buffet. When he had the scent of a story in his nose, he lost all other appetite. Also his unexpected presence had aroused unwelcome curiosity from some other journalists. Bumping Gem Huntley off the assignment hadn't been a problem. Not long up from the provinces, she was still eager to please. Very eager. He'd taken advantage of her eagerness in the traditional style only last week when Beanie was out of town for a couple of nights. She wasn't bad looking, in a peasant kind of way; carrying a bit too much flesh perhaps, but it was young flesh, and while a man might grow tired of such a plain diet every night, she was touchingly eager to learn. It had made a pleasant change from the Bitch's *cordon bleu* menu. So a squeeze of her buttock and a promise that he would meet up with her later to explain everything had been enough to get her out of the way.

The others were more of a problem, the trouble being that his antipathy for Gidman was so well known that his presence at such a bland public relations affair was bound to spark interest.

The groundwork for his dislike had been laid on his first arrival in London six years before.

His mother, the one person from whom he'd hidden his delight at leaving Llufwwadog, had been worried that her eldest son might not survive the inevitable pangs of homesickness he must feel alone in a great foreign city. So before parting she extracted a solemn oath from him that, as soon as he settled in, he would make contact with her cousin (twice removed) Owen Mathias. Owen, she averred, being a recently retired policeman, would be able to provide good sound advice as well as a reminder of his beloved home country.

When, after much maternal cajoling, Jones finally travelled out to Ealing to pay his respects, he saw at a glance why the man had taken early retirement. Mathias, in his mid-fifties, could easily have been taken for eighty. The upside was that he showed no sign of wanting to wallow in Celtic nostalgia and proved an entertaining and generous host, so Jones was happy to accept his invitation to come back soon, much to the delight of his mother.

His reward for this filial piety was that on subsequent visits he was introduced to many of Owen's former colleagues, young and old. True, several of them shrank away as if from a wandering leper when they heard he was a journalist, but a few showed signs of sociability which he hoped to cultivate into a mutually beneficent relationship. One thing they all did was wince and look for excuses to leave whenever the subject of Goldie Gidman came up. This man, of whom Jones had never heard, was evidently Owen's King Charles's head.

'I could never lay hands on him,' the 'old' man complained after they'd got to know each other better. 'But you're an investigative journalist, you can sort him out, boyo. You can make those blind bastards at the CPS see what's plain to all honest men. He's a bad job, a crook through and through.'

Scenting a possible early scoop, Jones had listened closely to the ex-policeman and mentioned Gidman in the office. There he had been warned in no uncertain terms that Gidman was off limits unless you had an absolutely water-tight story to tell.

Then within a year of their first meeting. Owen Mathias died. On learning that he had been mentioned in the will, Jones for a while had pleasant hopes of a modest legacy. What he got in the event was a box of CD-roms on to which had been downloaded so far as he could see everything in the Met's records about Goldie Gidman and his associates.

Recognizing that possession of these probably constituted an offence under several Acts, he stashed them away behind his wardrobe. And there they remained till the famous bye-election that signalled the eruption of David Gidman the Third on the political scene.

Warned of a possible upset, Jones in company of many other journalists had been on the spot. It wasn't till well into the victory celebration that he'd managed to get close enough to the Golden Boy to ask his questions. When he introduced himself, Gidman, not yet a finished product of the Millbank School of Charm and flushed with success and champagne, cried, '*Jones*? Why is everybody in Wales called *Jones*? Only way they can sort the buggers out is by calling them Dai Grocer and Nye the Nutter and so on. From the *Messenger*, you say? I shall think of you as Jones the Mess!'

A feeble joke in doubtful taste, but certainly more of a birdbolt than a cannon bullet. He had smiled with the rest and carried on with his questioning. And afterwards, it had seemed to him that he was doing no more than his job when he joined the journalistic pack in digging around to see what murky secrets might lie in the new boy's past.

When their combined efforts failed to turn up any drug convictions, dodgy dealings with right-wing extremists, or documented instances of sexual deviancy, most of his fellows gave up the chase.

But Jones found he couldn't let it alone. Eventually he tried a bit of self-analysis. It had to be more than the initial slur. He wasn't a professional Welshman, for God's sake, no supersensitive Celt eager to take umbrage at the merest sniff of an Anglo-Saxon attitude. No, there had to be something more, something chemical as much as political. Perhaps it was in the blood, perhaps he had inherited it from the same source as cousin Owen.

Whatever the cause, he came to recognize that the young MP was his Dr Fell, his heart's abhorrence. And so began his anti-Gidman campaign.

Unable to find a weakness in the MP's

defences, he turned his attention to Goldie Gidman, and now Owen Mathias's downloads became useful. He managed to get in a few sneers about the dubious nature of Goldie's early financial dealings, but it was soon made very clear to him by the *Messenger's* lawyers that there was a line he wasn't going to be allowed to cross. His only success had been an article suggesting that the late David Gidman the First would have been outraged to know that his son was making substantial contributions to the Conservative Party and devastated to learn that his grandson was a Tory MP. Goldie's briefs had huffed and puffed, but there was nothing they could do. You can't libel the dead.

But it was the living he wanted to get in his sights.

And then the rumour reached him that Gidman MP was banging his PA. She, it was reported, had dreams of what would have been a very lucrative marriage, but when Dave the Turd got wind of this, he made it brutally clear it wasn't going to happen. So perhaps she might be in the market for an alternative offer . . .

Jones had masterminded her subornation. Not that what she had to tell was necessarily a career breaker. Since Clinton, the fact that a politician had a big dong and liked to exercise it in unusual venues was at most a peccadillo, might in some instances even be a vote-catcher. But the *Messenger's* spinners and weavers had been hopeful that with a little embroidery they might be able to hint at S&M tendencies, Nazi sympathies, and even the possibility of security risks.

Then, on the day the deal was due to be signed, the woman's agent announced she'd changed her mind and had no story to tell. No prizes for guessing why. The woman had got the message that, whatever the paper could offer, Goldie would top it. When Jones argued for getting into an auction, his editor ordered him to back off, adding cynically, 'One thing we can't offer the tart is guaranteed health insurance. Goldie can. But I never said that.'

Jones, who hadn't been able to resist boasting among his colleagues that Dave the Turd was in for a nasty surprise, lost a lot of face. Perhaps it was this feeling of irritation that caused him to be less than diplomatic shortly afterwards when he found himself on a *Question Time* panel with Dave Gidman. He did not doubt that the juxtapositioning was deliberately provocative, but both he and Gidman were so determinedly polite to each other that the normally urbane chairman who'd been promised blood began to let his frustration show.

When Gidman with charming modesty refused to take seriously a suggestion by one of the other guests that he was *if not yet the Tories' heir apparent, at least their heir presumptive*, the chairman reminded Jones that he'd once described the MP as *a modern Icarus, soaring high on wings created by his father.*

'Did you mean to imply,' went on the chairman with his charming smile, 'that, like Icarus, the higher he flies, the more he will be in danger of crashing to earth?'

Jones had replied urbanely, 'Some people

202

might say that, but I couldn't possibly comment.'

And then, almost as if in a dream, he'd heard himself adding, 'Of course, as a classical scholar, you will doubtless recall that Icarus' father, Daedalus, was mixed up in some very dodgy activities, and indeed as a young man he had been banished from Athens for murdering one of his apprentices.'

While this fell short of being actionable, it made a nice headline in many of the papers, but from his own editor it had won only a stern reproof.

'Don't even dream of writing anything like that in my paper, not even if it's in fucking Welsh!'

So he'd gone quiet. But he continued to add to the police files he'd inherited from Owen anything else that came up about either of the Gidmans. Secretly he still felt that it was his mission in life to do radical chiropody on their feet of clay, but now the only person he trusted enough to share this feeling with was his young brother. The eight years between them meant there was little or no sibling rivalry, just a strong current of affection, protective from the elder and hero-worshipping from the younger. Gareth sometimes asked for advice and usually took it, occasionally asked for a loan and always took it, and if ever the chance arose to impart something that might impress his brother, he always took that too. Hearing the name Wolfe mentioned in connection with that of Goldie Gidman had sent him rushing to his phone.

Jones tried to get in touch with Gareth as he

drove back to Marina Tower, but there was no response. As he'd expected, the flat was empty. Might have been nice to find that Beanie didn't feel the Shandy party was worth going to without his company, but he'd known better than to count on it. To tell the truth, he was quite glad to have the place to himself. Beanie would have required explanations, and even in their closest moments he never forgot that she too was a journalist. You might share your body and the deep secrets of your heart with a fellow hack, but you stopped short of sharing a story.

He switched on his laptop and accessed his Gidman file. He'd already done a quick check after Gareth's call to confirm that Wolfe was there.

Now he ran through the relevant section again. Operation Macavity. Possible leak. DI Wolfe under investigation. Nothing proved. Wolfe's domestic troubles. Breakdown, Retirement. Disappearance. State of fugue posited by medical experts. Goldie's involvement posited privately by Owen Mathias, but no supporting evidence whatsoever. No trace of Wolfe ever found. (Owen's personal note read: *Murdered?*)

Then there was the wife. Gina Wolfe. She was looked at very carefully after her husband went walkabout, both by the police and even more so by the papers, who'd given her such a hard time, she complained to the Press Complaints Authority.

Nothing from either source. No unexplained increase in bank balances. No sudden trips to faraway places. No untraceable phone calls.

Nothing suspicious. She was either totally innocent or a consummate actress.

His mobile rang. He picked it up, expecting it would be Gareth. But the caller screen read *Paul*, which was just as good.

Paul was one of the sympathetic Met officers he'd encountered at Owen's sickbed. An investigative journalist is only as good as his contacts and he'd worked particularly hard on this relationship over the past few years. Paul was a chief inspector, not all that high on the police totem pole, but he worked in the communications centre and what he didn't overhear, he could usually find out. Jones had rung him on his way to ambush Gidman and asked him to check the current status of Gina Wolfe to see if there was any continuing interest in her.

Paul had laughed when he understood the link to the Gidmans. It amused him considerably to think that Jones had inherited the Mathias obsession. But it didn't prevent him from doing a good job, though unfortunately it was pretty negative.

'Had to go way back to find any mention at all,' he said.

He then proceeded to give Jones the stuff he already had, though, of course, the journalist made sure that neither Paul nor any other policeman was aware of this breach of security.

So if there was nothing since, this presumably meant she was rated lily-white.

'One thing, though,' Paul continued. 'The name rang a bell, I'd heard it recently, so I asked around. Probably nothing, but it seems one of our commanders, Mick Purdy, has got something going with this Gina Wolfe. I checked and it's definitely the same one. Maybe she just likes cops.'

'Maybe. Thanks, Paul.'

He fed the new name into his laptop, told it to search the Gidman file.

It came up twice. Thirty years ago, Owen Mathias, newly promoted to sergeant and not long arrived in the Met, had investigated an allegation of assault against Goldie. A DC Purdy had interviewed one of Gidman's employees who'd been cited as a witness. Result, negative, and despite Mathias's conviction that the man was guilty, no case was brought.

The second time was more interesting. Purdy, now a DCI, had been interviewed in the course of the internal investigation into Alex Wolfe. It seemed to have been merely a background interview. Purdy had been Wolfe's boss during his early years with the Met and the investigators were checking to see if there'd been any previous doubts as to his reliability. Purdy had given him a glowing testimonial.

Now, seven years later, Purdy and Gina Wolfe were an item.

Significant? Probably not, but he added a note to the file. *By indirections find directions out.* A favourite quote of an old English teacher who fancied himself as a Richard Burton *manqué*.

What to do now? He tried Gareth's number again. Still nothing. Probably needed a top-up. How many times had he told the stupid sod that his mobile was a tool of the trade?

So all he had was what his brother had told him. Not a lot, and when he'd tried to bluff it into something bigger, Dave the Turd had been puzzled rather than alarmed. He certainly hadn't reacted like a guilty thing surprised. It was Goldie he should have gone for. No doubt young David would be hurrying to complain to Daddy that a big boy had hit him then run away. Perhaps it had been a mistake to gate-crash the Centre opening.

But it was done now. And the question remained — what next?

He couldn't let it go. He liked the smell of this, and he'd learned to trust his nose. But he doubted if he would find anyone else at the *Messenger* who shared that trust, not when the name Gidman was mentioned.

So keep it to yourself till you've got something concrete. The advice he'd pumped at Gareth — *Don't tell a soul your story till you're sure you've got a story to tell* — still held good.

But it was pointless hanging around here. If there were to be any action, it was going to be up in Mid-Yorkshire.

He started tossing a few essentials into a small grip. As he did so he debated how to deal with Beanie. The key to her luxurious apartment nestling in his pocket wasn't something to give up easily and, despite her efforts to appear indifferent, he'd seen she was seriously irritated by his defection from Shandy's party. Returning home to find he'd taken off into the wild blue yonder could seriously piss her off. He'd need to think of a really good story; family emergency, maybe. She knew that Gareth had rung, so that could provide a firm basis. It was always best to have enough truth in your lies to hold them together. Old gran dying would probably sound too corny not to be true!

But not a note. A phone call. A besotted admirer had once told him he had the kind of vibrator voice that could sell bacon futures to an ayatollah. His old English teacher wasn't the only Burton *manqué*.

As if issuing a challenge, 'Cwm Rhondda' played. He checked the name: Gem Huntley. He'd promised to meet up with her later. No time for that now. He couldn't be bothered to talk to the girl, but he'd better not leave her totally disconnected. For one thing, she'd be expecting some feedback from the opening to put into her piece. Not that she'd be getting more than a couple of paras.

The phone stopped ringing. He thought for a moment then tapped out a message on his laptop.

Hotlips, hi! Opening went fine. Gidman made moving speech about his family's origins, said his father felt affection and loyalty towards the community as did he etc etc. Universal applause. Centre a joy to behold. Sorry, something's come up, family emergency, gran about to snuff it but won't go without seeing me first, so need to head west. Look forward to catching up with you soon as I get back. Anticipate I'll be emotionally vulnerable and in

need of a lot of TLC!
Love G x

There, that should keep her on hold. One excuse fits all. The economy of genius!

He sent the message, closed the laptop, began to put it into its case, then changed his mind.

Nowadays there were computers wherever you went. Lugging a pricey bit of kit like this around was a liability. Up there in the frozen north they lifted everything that wasn't nailed down. He had no fears about leaving it here. Marina Tower had better security than Westminster Palace and another thing he certainly hadn't shared with Beanie was his access code.

He stuck the laptop at the back of the top shelf of the wardrobe and headed down to his car.

As he drove away he felt that surge of excitement that always accompanied the start of a trail. This was what made him the success he was. Brought up in a strict nonconformist socialist tradition, it was easy, and useful, to claim a moral imperative for what he did. Sometimes he almost believed it himself. But this time he revelled in acknowledging to himself at least that it was completely personal.

Getting some dirt on Goldie Gidman and making sure it spread out wide enough to hit his son would be a real pleasure.

He selected one of the discs in his CD player, found the track he wanted, pressed the *play* button.

The tremendous opening bars of 'The Ride of the Valkyries' thrilled out.

The image it brought to his mind had nothing to do with buxom divas and grand opera, which he disliked almost as much as male voice choirs. It was the helicopter squadron in *Apocalypse Now* signalling its devastating approach to the Vietnamese villagers.

Whatever was going on up there in the frozen north, the bastards were in for a real shock when they realized who it was that had them in his sights.

He turned the music up full blast.

'Here I come, ready or not!' he cried.

12.25–15.00

Ellie Pascoe wasn't happy with the way her Sunday had gone and she blamed Dalziel.

The explosion of glass that proclaimed his imminence to the pastoral idyll of baby Lucinda's christening party should have warned her. This was a promise of disruption as clear as thunder on an east wind. But bathed in the golden glow of the autumn sun, not to mention the golden glow of the Keldale's champagne, she had refused to let it dissipate her feelings of mellow fruitfulness. Peter had never looked more attractive and the afternoon stretched out before them like a fair field over which they would wander to that most private corner of their garden where a suburban Adam and Eve could imparadise themselves in one another's arms with no witness other than the lusty sun.

But things started to go downhill thereafter, slowly at first, then with gathering momentum.

The baby grew fractious, a condition that spread rapidly to his parents with an interesting role reversal in that it was the anxious dad urging that the best place for little Lucinda was home and the laid-back mum retorting that this was nonsense, babies were like viola players, they cried to get attention, but if you left them alone, they usually fell asleep.

Whoever said that music has charms to soothe a savage breast clearly hadn't heard the clarinet duet now played by Rosie Pascoe and a stout young woman called Cilla who had been less abstemious than her partner. All went well till Cilla was assailed by a *sforzando* set of hiccoughs which might in less musically sensitive company have passed for an amusing experiment in syncopation. Baby Lucinda, who had shown signs of nodding off, came back to screaming life and a vengeful violist observed loudly that if these were Ali's *primas*, he would not care to hear her *secondas*. The duet limped to its end with Rosie winning by several bars. Cilla left the pagoda in tears, Rosie in a rage.

When her parents caught up with her, she refused to be consoled, declaring her conviction that this must inevitably signal the end not only of Ali's friendship but of her tuition, in acknowledgement of which she threatened to break her clarinet across her knee, prompting Pascoe, who'd found the duet quite hilarious, to say brightly, 'Not all bad then,' which did nothing to improve the moment. Nor did it help that the Sinfonietta quartet who were back in the pagoda now broke into a schmalzy rendering of 'The Last Rose of Summer.'

It had taken the direct intervention of Ali Wintershine to lift the girl from the depths of despair, for which Ellie was grateful. But her gratitude grew somewhat dusty when Rosie, now revelling in her role as justified sinner, demanded yet one more reassurance that she was truly forgiven and Ali said, 'A few of my very dearest friends are coming to the house for a cup of tea after we finish here. Why don't you join us, Rosie? And your mum and dad, too, of course.'

Refusal would clearly have tipped the girl back into the depths, so Ellie had put mellow fruitfulness on hold, gritted her teeth, and said brightly, 'That would be nice.'

Pascoe had taken the diversion fairly philosophically. Though looking forward with much enthusiasm to the promised bliss awaiting him at home, the afternoon was young, not yet half past two, and he didn't mind a brief interval of tea and cake to neutralize the side-effects of too much champagne.

It was quickly apparent to Ellie that the alleged tea-party was little more than a ruse to complete Rosie's restoration. There were only two *very dearest friends* there: a timpanist with a roving eye and a habit of testing all surfaces he encountered for resonance, including, whenever he got the chance, those of the other musical friend, a bassoonist too intoxicated to know her Arne from her Elgar. Ed Muir, perhaps thinking of the large cost of what hadn't turned out to be a totally successful celebration, appeared somewhat distracted, provoking a *sotto voce* reproof from his partner, who clearly felt he wasn't pulling his weight as co-host. Only Rosie looked unequivocally delighted. Getting her out of there, Ellie realized, was not going to be easy.

At this stage, though already feeling Dalziel's unexpected appearance as augurous, she was still far from ascribing to him full responsibility for the day's divagations.

Then Pascoe's mobile rang.

Ellie sometimes claimed there was a ring tone undetectable by ordinary people. Only a policeman's wife could catch it, and she heard it now.

He looked at the display, mouthed 'Wieldy' at her apologetically, and left the room at the same time as Ed Muir who'd vanished a little earlier re-entered to tell Ali there was a small catering crisis at the Arts Centre that required his presence. Ali started demanding details and there was no saying where this debate may have led if Pascoe hadn't appeared in the doorway looking distracted and said, 'Ellie, sorry, I've got to go. Can you get a taxi?'

'Yes, sure,' she replied instantly. She knew it had to be serious stuff to bring the afternoon to such a sudden conclusion.

Ali, sensing this too, backed off her confrontation with her partner, who said, 'I can drop Ellie and Rosie off.'

'But it's out of your way,' said Ellie. 'We live north. You'll be driving into the town centre.'

This seemed to nonplus him for a moment, then he said, 'No problem,' reinforcing his assurance with a rare smile.

'Then thank you very much, Ed,' Ellie replied, returning his smile. Generally she found him reserved to the point of diffidence, but as she got to know him better, she was beginning to see what Ali saw in him. And his tranquillity provided the perfect foil for Ali's usual ebullience.

Ellie followed Pascoe out into the hall.

'What's happened?' she murmured.

'There's been a shooting. Someone dead. Shirley Novello hurt.'

'Oh shit. Not again.'

A few years earlier she'd actually been present when Novello was shot.

'How bad?' she asked.

'Don't have too many details, but it doesn't sound good.'

Ellie felt all the residual warmth of the day fade from her body. She and Novello weren't best buddies, but for a policeman's wife, hearing of a serious injury to any officer is like a rehearsal of that moment when the bad news will be yours alone.

'Was it an op?' she asked.

He hesitated then said, 'Nothing I knew about. Wieldy thinks Andy might have been using her for something.'

This was untypically vague.

'Why don't you ask him?'

'We will, when we can raise him,' he said neutrally. 'Wieldy's tried. He's not answering his mobile.'

Many questions were buzzing through her head. Already these uncertain references to Dalziel were shifting his role from ominous apparition to guilty first mover.

'You mean the fat bastard's up to his old tricks?' she said. 'Need-to-know rules, except he's usually the only one who needs to know?'

'Could be,' he said. 'Look, I've got to go.'

'I know. Come here!'

She put her arms around him and drew him

215

close, crushing him against her body. This had nothing to do with mellow fruitfulness. This came out of the dreadful awareness that only when she had him in her grasp like this could she be sure of him. Out of her sight he was at the mercy of whatever malignant Fate cared to hurl. She would never forget, could never forget, the moment they had come to tell her that he'd been caught in the same explosion that comatized Andy Dalziel.

'Careful,' he said. 'Or I may have to do you for perverting the course of justice.'

'Do me any which perverted way you like, so long as you come back safe,' she said.

He broke away and went out of the front door. Without his supporting strength she felt faint and dizzy.

How much easier life would be without love, she thought. The Holy Joes are forever preaching that it's love that makes the world go round. It isn't. It's love that stops the world in its tracks. Be faithful in love, they tell us, and all will be well. Travel with love in your heart, and you'll never walk alone.

They're right. You'll have a shadowy companion, invisible only at the moments of greatest ecstasy, but otherwise constantly present. His names are fear and loss and pain.

One way or another, love always betrays.

13.35–15.25

By the time Fleur Delay got back to the hotel, she was close to collapse.

The adrenalin rush of having to deal with the aftermath of Vince's violence had kept her going till they reached the car. Then she'd said, 'You drive,' and sank into the passenger seat.

Vince said anxiously, 'You OK, sis?'

'Yes, sure, I just banged my head.'

She put her hand to her brow and looked in the rear-view mirror. There was a small cut there with a trickle of blood which she wiped away with a tissue.

Vince, reassured, drove carefully away from Loudwater Villas. He was normally a flashy driver, but he knew that his sister would get seriously pissed if he did anything that drew attention.

Sometimes Fleur felt it as a blessing that he was so easy to fool. Sometimes it filled her with fury and resentment. Anyone else living as close to her as he did would have been aware for a couple of months at least that there was something seriously wrong. There had been times after the fatal diagnosis when she had come close to telling him that she hadn't been away from home for a minor woman's operation, that the drugs he sometimes saw her taking

217

couldn't be bought over the counter at the local chemist's, that the wigs she'd started wearing weren't a belated fashion statement in reaction against the onset of middle age. If she could have hoped for loving support and comfort, she might have given way to the temptation. But she knew that when the time came to say, 'Vince, I've got news for you. I have an inoperable brain tumour and I'm going to die,' the support and comfort would be all one way.

She wanted to have him safe and secure when she told him, she wanted him to be a long way away from London, and most of all she wanted him to be a long way away from Goldie Gidman. Spain wasn't all that far, but it was as far as she could hope to remove Vince, and even then she had found it hard to get him to share her enthusiasm for the idea of buying a villa on the Costa del Sol and settling down there. For a holiday it suited him very well with its sunny beaches, cheap booze, and unending supply of succulent bimbos who'd left their inhibitions behind at Luton Airport. But as for living there . . .

She'd countered with economic arguments. This was the perfect opportunity for them to invest some of their hard-earned savings in a bit of truly palatial real estate. The Spanish property boom had gone into a nose-dive as the credit squeeze left lots of ex-pats unable to keep up payments. Making a sale even at a substantial loss was better than repossession and for someone with Fleur's long experience of the economics of distress it had been easy to snap up a real bargain: four bedrooms, sea views, private garden, swimming pool, games room, all mod cons, at just over half the price the owners had paid three years ago.

The deal was close to completion, but the way she'd felt over the past few days, the sooner it was done the better.

'We're here, sis,' said Vince.

She opened her eyes. They were in the Keldale car park.

In the next row she spotted the red Nissan, so that was all right.

She said to Vince, 'Take the laptop up to your room. You can keep a check on her in case she goes out again.'

'Me?' said Vince dubiously. Like following Blondie and Tubby into the cathedral, this wasn't the kind of task he was usually given. 'What are you going to do?'

'I'm going to get cleaned up, then I'll take a close look at the stuff I took off that guy you shot, and then I'll report in to The Man. That OK with you, Vince?'

She spoke sharply. She'd always felt the need to be firm with Vince, but lately firmness had drifted into irritability.

'No need to get in a strop,' he said. 'All I meant was, how long will you be? If the guy I offed is our man, we'll be heading for home, right?'

He sounded hopeful.

She said, 'Maybe.'

She checked herself in the mirror. She looked a bit pale, but the cut on her forehead had stopped bleeding. Taking a deep breath, she got out of the car and willed herself to walk steadily towards the hotel.

It seemed to take an age, but finally she was in her room with the *Do not disturb* sign on her door. She kicked her shoes off, went into the bathroom and bathed her face in cold water. Then she took a couple of tablets. How many had she taken today? She couldn't remember.

Back in the bedroom she looked longingly at the bed. It invited her to lie on it. Instead she spread across the duvet the trophies she'd brought with her from Loudwater Villas. A hip wallet, a mini recorder, and a phone.

First she examined the contents of the wallet.

A few pounds. A pack of condoms. Cards in the name of Gareth Jones.

Jones. Not Watkins. Was that good or bad?

Then she listened to the conversation on the recorder.

Nothing she heard there surprised her.

Finally she checked the incoming and outgoing numbers on his phone, wrote them down, accessed his messages, checked out his phone book and made notes.

She tried to make sense of what she'd found, or rather make of it the kind of sense she wanted to make. It was no use. No way she was going to sell this to The Man as job done. Best she could look for was damage limitation.

She took out her phone and rang Goldie Gidman.

When he answered she gave no name but started straight in with her report, editing out all references to timings and her collapse, and editing in a version of events that made Vince's reaction absolutely essential. She was as selective as she dared to be with the details of the contents of the wallet and the info she'd gleaned from the phone, but she needn't have bothered. He'd always had the knack of smashing through no matter how thick a coating of verbiage to the essential truth of thing. At least he wasn't close enough to reinforce the process with a hammer.

'It's not the guy,' he said.

'Probably not,' she agreed wearily. 'So what shall I do now?'

There was a long pause. In her mind's eye she could see him sitting there, the phone in his hand, staring into space. His mind would be checking over the known facts, formulating the possible outcomes. Eventually he would reach a decision about the best course of action. She'd known the process to take several minutes. She'd learned early not to interrupt with speech or movement, not even if your bladder was bursting or the ciggie in your fingers had burnt down to the skin.

He said, 'Where's the woman?'

'In her room. Vince is keeping an eye on her.'

'Let's hope he doesn't decide to shoot her.'

A joke, or serious? Without a video phone, she couldn't tell. The plus was, he couldn't see her sitting here, bald as a snooker ball.

If he was waiting for a laugh, he was disappointed.

He said, 'Question is, if it wasn't Wolfe, why the fuck was he bugging Gina?'

'Don't know, Goldie.'

'Makes no odds, I still need Wolfe. And fast. Don't let the wife out of your sight.'

The phone went dead.

She looked in the dressing-table mirror and saw that the dome of her head was beaded with sweat.

'You look like you just landed from Mars,' she told herself. 'Pity you don't have a return ticket.'

She had a sense of things falling apart, but when you felt like that the only thing to do was stick with the plan. Not that there was much of a plan. Follow the woman. If Vince saw the tracker moving on the laptop screen he'd bang on the door. Fleur hoped to hell the blonde cow stayed put for another hour at least. She needed the rest.

She swept the Jones/Watkins trophies to the floor, fell across the bed, rolled over to wrap the duvet round her, and closed her eyes.

In the room next door Vince had obediently set up the laptop. He realized he didn't have its mains lead. That would be in Fleur's room, but he didn't want to risk worsening her mood by disturbing her. It wasn't that he was scared of his sister, but no denying she could be scary! There was plenty of juice in the batteries anyway, so it didn't matter.

The pulsating green dot that showed the Nissan's position remained steady in the car park. He turned his TV set on, keeping the sound low. There was nothing on the sports channels that he wanted to watch, so he checked out the hotel's entertainment channel and accessed an adult movie. Its title promised a lot more than it gave.

A few nice boobs, no pubes, and the kind of simulated passion that wouldn't have fooled a myopic nun; all it did was put him in the mood for something that was really for grown-ups! After ten minutes of grunt and groan, he switched the set off and turned his attention to the laptop. The green dot was still in the car park.

Most likely the blonde tart was in her room, sitting on Tubby's face, he told himself. The thought did more for him than the movie had, and he ran his fingers over the keyboard and a few moments later he was into one of his favourite sites. He rose, went to the interconnecting door between his room and Fleur's and made sure it was bolted. Then he stripped his clothes off and lay on the bed with the laptop to enjoy the fun.

Over the next ninety minutes, he fetched himself off three times. The first had been an almost spontaneous reaction to the images on the screen, the second came after a long languorous build-up as he navigated his way through progressively more extreme sites, and the third time had been pretty mechanical to confirm that his recovery speed was as good as ever. Shooting that guy in the face had really turned him on; stuff like that usually did. Some hotels he knew, he could have come back and whistled up a woman, but the Keldale didn't feel like it offered that kind of service, particularly on a Sunday afternoon. Anyway, with Fleur next door and likely to come calling, it was out of the question, so it had to be DIY time.

He glanced at his watch. Coming up to half

three. Rest a bit then go for number four? No, this movie stuff was all right and often provided some instructive tutorials, but it didn't come close to a real woman. Blondie now, he wouldn't mind an hour of grunt and groan and maybe a bit of slap and scream with her.

The thought reminded him he was supposed to be watching the tracker screen.

He exited his porn site and there it was, the green spot pulsating merrily in the car park. Probably still trying to coax Tubby into his first orgasm, he thought complacently. Might appreciate a real man.

But no point thinking about that with Fleur calling the shots. Bit of a prude, old Fleur. He assumed she must have had it, because on the streets he grew up in, he'd never met any tart over fourteen who hadn't. But where or who with he had no idea. Maybe The man had given her one. He certainly wasn't going to ask.

He rolled off the bed and went into the bathroom. Nice refreshing shower, then downstairs for a cup of tea and a club sandwich. He sang 'Maybe It's Because I'm a Londoner' as he soaped himself. He felt surprisingly happy. And why shouldn't he be?

Soon, with a bit of luck, they'd be out of this godawful town heading back to the civilized south where people knew who he was and showed him respect and didn't speak like a bunch of fucking sheep with hiccoughs.

And one thing was certain.

Like with prison, once he was out of fucking Yorkshire, no way he was ever going back in!

14.45–15.45

Every time David Gidman the Third tried to prise himself away from the new community centre, someone got in his way. Several times he'd thrown Maggie Pinchbeck a desperate glance, appealing for rescue. All he got in return was an encouraging nod of the head.

But at last he made it to the car. The charming smile with which he said farewell to his civic escort did not flicker till Maggie had driven beyond the range of prying eyes, then it broadened into a huge yawn.

'God, that was mega boring,' he said.

'I noticed. Let's hope no one else did.'

Exaggerating his sulkiness because he feared he couldn't altogether hide it, he said, 'OK, sharp-eyes, on a scale of ten, how did I do?'

'Six out of ten, six point five, maybe,' she said promptly.

He chewed on this for a while, then said, 'Why do you imagine that relentless honesty makes your job more secure than fulsome flattery?'

'I don't. But if it doesn't, I don't want to work for you anyway.'

He gave her a smile which if it had been any tighter might have cracked his teeth.

OK, she was never going to give him the kind of comforts the two-metre model could provide, but at least she might do the occasional bit of ego-stroking.

He said accusingly, 'You didn't warn me Jones was going to be there.'

'That's because I didn't know. He wasn't in church. In fact, I'm sure I saw Gem Huntley there, but she vanished afterwards. Not feeling well, he said.'

'Yeah. You believe him?'

'No.'

She waited to see if he'd follow it up, but he didn't.

She drove in silence for a while then said casually, 'That stuff Jones was spouting about wolves from the past biting you, what do you think that was all about?'

He wasn't surprised she'd latched on to it. She had a very sensitive radar.

He said, 'How the hell should I know? Probably came along for the free sandwiches. Why does the bastard hate me so much? I never did anything to harm him.'

Maggie let this pass. After a moment she said, 'Still, it's strange. And he did give the impression he thought he was on to something.'

'Part of his trade,' he said dismissively. 'The others call him Nine Ten. Knows more about tomorrow than he does about today. And he's probably rattled his brain to jelly shagging Beanie the Bitch.'

He closed his eyes and pretended to doze for the rest of the journey to his Holborn flat. *You should live in the constituency*, Maggie had advised. *Not fucking likely*, he'd replied.

226

Holborn was a concession.

As he got out, Maggie said, 'Shall I come in? There's stuff we need to go through for tomorrow.'

'Later,' he said. 'I'm knackered. Think I'll get my head down.'

Not on Sophie Harbott you won't, thought Maggie, who'd arrived early enough that morning to see the woman departing in what looked like high dudgeon. It was a liaison Maggie disapproved of more than most of her boss's adventures. If the tabloids got a sniff he was shagging the wife of the Labour spokesman on religious affairs, they would fall over themselves to top each other's headline: WHO'S CONVERTING WHO? . . . CROSS-BENCHING MODERN STYLE . . . COALITION COITION . . . the possibilities were endless.

But that was, literally, Gidman's affair. She'd made it clear that, so far as his love-life was concerned, she wasn't getting involved in either arrangements or clean-up.

'OK,' she said. 'Six thirty? Seven?'

'Whatever. By the way, did you get hold of the Chuckle Brothers?'

This was the term he used for Kuba and Drugi, the two young Poles who'd done the work on his shower that had completed the cooling of Sophie's ardour. They had been recommended by Maggie, who said she'd met them when working for ChildSave on immigrant families. Gidman had not been altogether displeased to have been able to complain about an arrangement made by his usually tediously efficient PA.

'They'll be there tomorrow,' she promised.

'Meanwhile I'll just have to take a cold shower, I suppose,' he grumbled.

'Might do you good,' she said. 'See you later.'

David the Third watched her drive away, then went up to his flat. For once he had time on his hands. He could do a bit of work on a speech he was making next week. Or read a book, watch a bit of telly, or even ring Sophie, see if she'd be interested in taking up where they'd left off. Probably not. Anyway, he didn't feel much interested himself, in that or any of the other options. Jones the Mess had really got to him, he realized. What he needed were answers, and there was only one place to get them.

Ten minutes later he was in his Audi A8 heading north. There are no good times for moving through London outside the small hours, but Sunday afternoon comes close and it wasn't yet half three when he came to a halt before the high gates of Windrush House.

The camera on the gate column viewed him for a moment then the metal gates swung silently open and he sent the car moving slowly forward up the long drive, careful as always not to provoke his father's wrath by spraying gravel over the manicured lawns.

As Gidman went up the steps to the front door, it was opened by a young black man dressed in immaculately creased burgundy slacks, a beautifully cut suede jacket and a white shirt so bright it made you blink.

He said, 'Hello, Mr Gidman, sir. You're looking well.'

'Hello, Dean. And you look like you've got something really special lined up.'

Dean grinned. He and Dave the Third had identified a common interest in the pursuit of love. He said, 'Yes, sir. Another hour and I'm off duty, then I'm driving out to Romford to pick up this new gal I met last week, real looker, training to be a hairdresser. We're heading up West, got a table booked for a nice meal, do a club, then it's all in the lap of the gods.'

'The only thing in the lap of the gods is a divine dong,' said Gidman, smiling. 'Sounds like yours is ready for action.'

'Hello there, young Davey!'

He looked round to see another much older black man who suddenly flung a left hook at him which he only just managed to fend off with his right forearm.

'Nearly got you! You come down the gym after you done your homework, we'll soon sharpen you up.'

'I'll look forward to that, Sling,' said Gidman.

Milton Slingsby had been part of his life since childhood. As well as the boxing, Sling had always been on hand to play cricket and football with, to drive him to school, to pick him up when he'd been out with his friends in the evening. The precise role he played in Goldie's affairs had never been quite clear to Dave. He'd heard him described at various times as driver, handyman, even personal trainer. Nowadays he was never far away from Goldie who, if asked, would probably say, 'He's my old friend.' If pressed to explain exactly what he did, Dave had

229

heard his father reply, 'Any damn thing I ask him to,' with a laugh to signal a joke, though Dave wasn't certain he was joking.

Just how much Sling's treatment of Dave as a schoolboy was a joke and how much down to his mild dementia, Gidman hadn't worked out. Certainly his mental condition would have been a lot worse if it hadn't been for Goldie. 'Your pappy bought my contract,' Sling often told Dave. 'And he say to me, 'From now on in, no more boxing rings. From now on you fight only for me.''

By one of the little jokes that time likes to play on its subjects, as Sling's brain paid the penalty for those early rattlings, his body aged in quite a different way. No flat-nosed, cauliflower-eared, punch-drunk pugilist this; long and lean, with silver-grey hair and an academic stoop, he could have been a retired professor whose occasional abstractions were the mark of a mind voyaging through strange seas of thought alone.

'Where's Pappy, Sling?' asked Dave as he moved into the house.

'Upstairs with Jimi. You home for the holidays now, young Dave?'

'That's right, Sling. Home for the holidays. I wish,' said Gidman. 'Dean, have a great night!'

The young man gave him a thumbs-up and went back into the security control room. It sometimes bothered Dave that Sling and Dean were all the household staff there were, but his mother was adamant she didn't want help cluttering up the place. Goldie acknowledged his wife's domestic authority with a meekness that would have amazed those who knew him only through business. *Couldn't hire a better cook,* he'd say. *Which makes it all the worse she got me on a lunchtime diet!*

As for security, Dave Gidman knew the alarm system was state of the art.

He ran up the stairs to a darkened first-floor room set up as a home cinema. Here he found his father watching a video of Jimi Hendrix at Woodstock. It was a taste they didn't share. Another was the pungent Havana cigars which Flo had decreed could only be smoked in this one room.

Goldie didn't take his eyes off the screen where the great rocker was deep into 'Message to Love', but raised his right hand in the imperious gesture which those around him had learned meant *stand still, don't speak, I'll get round to you when I'm ready.*

A wave of resentment surged up in his son. One thing to be seen as a school kid by Sling's defocused gaze, quite another to be fossilized in that role by his father.

Out in the world he was the golden boy, expecting and receiving deference, even from those who disliked him. Why make an enemy of a man who was the hottest long-term bet for Downing Street in the last fifty years?

It was only those most intimately linked to his political career who refused to defer. Like Cameron and his attendant clones. And Maggie bloody Pinchbeck, who tried to control him like a performing dog. At least he could sack her. Maybe.

But his father was the worst offender. Sometimes the appellation David Gidman the Third sounded more pecking order than genealogy. OK, he couldn't sack Goldie, but maybe it was time he understood that the wide and glittering world of political power into which he'd launched his son didn't end at his mansion gates.

He picked up the remote and stopped Hendrix in mid-syllable.

'OK, Pappy,' he said, already appalled at his own boldness. 'I need to know what the fuck's going on.'

Goldie Gidman turned his head and regarded his son blankly. Inside he wasn't displeased at this show of spirit. Life had given him only two things he wouldn't ruthlessly discard in the interests of his own comfort and security. One was Flo, his wife, and the other was his son. He'd kept them at a very long arm's length from the world he'd grown up in, a world where you learned to survive by being harder than those trying to survive around you. With Flo, it had been easy, despite the fact that she was by his side almost from the beginning. Her love was unconditional, she saw nothing he did not invite her to see, asked no questions, passed no comments.

Dave the Third was harder. Brought up to a life of privilege, it was simple to put a firewall between him and his father's colourful past. But protection was no protection if it weakened what you were trying to protect. In the career he was launched on, he would need the same skills as

232

his father — a nose for danger, an eye for the main chance, and a ruthless instinct for survival at no matter what cost to others.

By this small act of defiance he was showing himself flesh of Goldie's flesh, blood of his blood, and that was good.

On the other hand, he needed to be reminded from time to time that, whatever power he now wielded and would in the future wield in the great world out there, in his father's world he was and must remain a cipher.

He said, 'What you talking about, son?'

'I'm talking about Gwyn Jones ambushing me at the opening.'

'Jones?' He could see he'd caught his father's attention. 'That Jones the Mess?'

'The same. The last guy a politician wants to see at his door if he's got anything he needs to keep hidden. Have I got anything I need to keep hidden, Pappy?'

'Just tell me what this Jones fellow said. I mean, the words he used.'

Dave Gidman had a power of recall that came in very useful in the House and he was able to repeat the journalist's words almost verbatim.

When he finished, Goldie said, 'What did Maggie say about this?'

Dave felt hugely irritated. The degree of respect, indeed of affection, both his parents showed to Pinchbeck really pissed him off.

He said, 'Nothing. Why the fuck should she say anything?'

'It got you worried, son. Anything you see, Maggie would see two minutes earlier, that's for

233

sure. Now go and see your mammy. Tell her you'll be staying for supper.'

'Is that it?' demanded Dave, incensed by the implication that his PA was brighter than he was.

'Yeah, that's it. Nothing for you to worry your head about. You just concentrate on kicking them government bastards while they're down.'

Dave the Third took a step closer to his father and glared down at him. Goldie stared back up at him with a lack of expression that those who had received the hammer treatment in his youth might have recognized. It felt like a defining moment.

Which in a way it was.

It was the younger man who broke off eye contact first and stalked out of the room.

Goldie felt almost disappointed but not quite. Now wasn't a good time for young Dave to be rocking the boat. Way things were going, it would take a steady hand on the wheel and a clear eye at the helm.

Maybe, he thought, I should have left this alone.

But all his life he'd dealt with stuff as it came along. Tidy up behind you and you didn't leave a trail.

Except sometimes, if things didn't fall right, the trail could be the tidying-up.

Long way from that here, and anyway, he thought confidently, he'd got friends in high places who'd make sure the trail got brushed out long before it reached him.

Politics was a lot like fucking. Same rule about relationships applied here that he'd tried to drum into young Dave after the business with his tell-tale PA. Always make sure the woman you're boning has got more to lose than you have if you get found out.

It had taken a conversation with Fleur Delay to show that would-be blabbermouth, Nikki the Knockers, just how much she had to lose. In the world of politics and finance, you got heavy in a different way, but it came to the same thing in the end. Over the past few years he'd made sure that Westminster and the City were full of folk who would shit bricks if they thought that Goldie Gidman was running into trouble. Couple at the Yard too. And his lunch today with that poncy peer had reinforced his protection. So he was fire-proof.

Not young Dave, though. A political career was like a delicate flower. Leave the wrong door open and a cold draught could kill it off overnight.

He'd sent Fleur Delay up to the frozen north to close a door. No one he trusted more than Fleur. So there'd been a glitch. Despite her efforts to cover for him in her phone call, it was clear that the glitch had been down to that dickhead brother of hers. But you could rely on Fleur. She always came through in a crisis. And if she didn't, well, all relationships that aren't blood relationships come to an end.

How did Jones the Mess play here?

No way to know yet.

Jones. The name might mean something, might not. Like young Dave had said, every second fucker in Wales is called Jones.

235

Time would tell.

He picked up the remote and pressed the start button. On the screen Hendrix sprang once more to noisy life.

As always when he watched this video, his mind drifted back to the sixties. He'd started them as a skinny teenager, subject to all the conflicting impulses of the time and of the times. Change had been in the air, particularly for the young. He'd wanted to be part of it, but wanted even more to be able to afford all the new goodies on offer. He'd known one or two kids who'd actually made it to the States, been at Woodstock. By '69 he could have afforded to fly over there first class. But of course he hadn't. Too much business to look after, too much wheeling and dealing to be done, too many people to keep in line. What the hell, those kids probably ended up in dead-end jobs, were sitting even now in some shitty little house, seeing their grandchildren yawn as they started to reminisce about Woodstock.

But watching the video, listening to Jimi, it always felt like an opportunity missed.

One thing was certain, his boy was never going to look back on missed opportunities. The world was his inheritance and his father was going to make sure he got it.

And if that long-gone loser, Wolfe, really had come crawling out of the past to threaten young Dave's future, he'd quickly find that Goldie Gidman could still wield a mean hammer!

He pushed these thoughts from his mind and settled back to enjoy the music.

15.20–15.30

Andy Dalziel opened his eyes.

His old sleeping patterns had taken some time to re-establish themselves after his long sojourn in the strange never-never-land of coma, of which he had no memories but which occasionally sent him brief visionary flashes.

He wondered if he was having one now, but it seemed more than a flash. Perhaps he had suffered a complete relapse?

He was lying beneath a silky smooth feather-light duvet with his head buried deep in a mountain of soft pillows. The air was sweetly perfumed, there was music sounding in his ears and through the dim religious light surrounding him moved a lovely blonde angel in a diaphanously revealing negligee.

He applied his mind to a cool consideration of the possibilities.

Did he wake or sleep?

Was he dreaming or dead?

The angel dropped something on to his face.

It bounced off his nose. He said, 'Ouch.'

'At last,' she said. 'This thing's been ringing ever since I got back. I'd have chucked a bucket of water over you if it hadn't been my bed.'

Her bed. Slowly it came back to him. By the end of the meal he'd felt definitely languorous.

237

Coffee had had no restorative effect. Mebbe the fact that it was accompanied by a large malt hadn't helped. As they left the terrace, he checked his watch. Their early start meant it was only just after half past one.

'You got any plans for this afternoon?' he'd asked.

'Plans?' she said, as if not recognizing the word. 'Why?'

'Just that I could do with getting me head down for half an hour afore I set off driving. Snoring in the lounge might be a bother. Some people are funny. So I wondered, any chance of crashing out on your bed?'

'As long as I'm not in it,' she said. 'And as long as you're out of it in half an hour.'

'Cub's honour,' he said gravely.

Only he'd never been a cub.

But he really had thought that his internal clock would wake him after thirty minutes. It always had in the past. Instead, he realized as he stared blearily at his watch, he'd been sleeping for nigh on two hours.

'I'm now going to have a shower,' said Gina. 'When I come out, I definitely don't expect to find you still here.'

She drifted out of his line of vision.

He sat up and threw back the duvet, realizing as he did so that, apart from his shoes and his jacket, he was fully clothed. His phone had stopped ringing so he didn't need to bother about that.

He swung his legs off the bed and stood up.

The movement made him aware of two things.

He had a bit of a headache and he needed a pee.

The headache was nothing that a breath of fresh air and a cup of strong tea wouldn't take care of. The pee was rather more urgent.

It occurred to him that Gina Wolfe was unlikely to feel the enjoyment of her shower in any way enhanced by the arrival of a fat policemen in her bathroom, no matter how urgent his need.

He slipped his feet into his shoes and put on his jacket. There was a notepad by the room telephone. He scribbled a couple of lines on it and tucked it between the pillows on the double bed, then headed for the door.

By a great effort of will he made it to the ground-floor toilet without incident, then he headed out on to the terrace.

As he sat down, a young man he recognized as Pietro, the highly efficient restorer of order after his demolition of the water jug, appeared at his side.

'*Buon giorno, Signore* Dalziel. Can I get you something?'

Remembered names too. That was good.

'Pot of strong Yorkshire tea, thanks. And mebbe a parkin.'

'*Subito, signore.*'

'By the by, did I settle up for the lunch?'

'No problem, sir. *Signora* Wolfe said to charge it to her room.'

Shit. Would a knight errant let a distressed damsel foot the bill?

Probably not. But it wouldn't bother Rooster Cogburn.

'Grand,' he said. 'Quick as you can with the tea.'

He remembered about his phone and took it and checked for messages.

There were several, the first couple from Wield asking him to ring back urgently.

Then the message repeated in Pascoe's voice.

And finally, 'Andy, where the hell are you? I've got search parties out. We've an emergency here. Get in touch the second you get this, understand? This is important. Don't muck me about!'

This was not the language of a deferential 2 i.c. to his superior. This was angry and imperious.

He brought up Pascoe's number.

'OK, lad,' he said. 'What's all the panic? Forgot where I keep the key to the stationery cupboard? It had better be good — this is my day off, remember?'

If he'd hoped by his bluster to fend off bad news, he was disappointed.

Pascoe said, 'Andy, thank God. Listen, it's Novello. Someone's bashed her over the head and she's in Intensive Care. It gets worse. She was found lying next to a man's body. He's had his face shot off!'

'Oh Christ. Found where?'

He knew the answer before he heard it.

'Loudwater Villas. Number 39. Wieldy says he ran a number plate for you this lunchtime and that was the address. Andy, what the hell's going on?'

'You there now?' said Dalziel, ignoring the

question because he couldn't answer it.

'Of course I bloody well am!'

'I'm on my way.'

He set off, passing en route without a glance Pietro bearing a silver tray on which rested a pot of tea and a freshly baked parkin.

It had been a crazy day, thought the young waiter. This was the third time someone had ordered then rushed off without touching a thing!

But at least the good-looking young woman who'd abandoned her prawn sandwich had said she'd be back. Pietro prided himself on recognizing genuine interest when he saw it.

Oh yes, he told himself complacently.

That one would definitely be back.

14.45–15.35

As Maggie Pinchbeck drove away after dropping Gidman, she hadn't been happy.

Normally she might have been as dismissive of Gwyn Jones's unexpected appearance as her employer had appeared to be. Journalists spent much of their time chasing will-ó-the-wisps. The only sin was to miss a story, and if that meant spending tedious hours exploring dead-ends, that was the price they had to pay.

In newspaper circles it was generally agreed that Goldie Gidman was fireproof. Some cynics averred this meant he had to be dirty because nobody could be so clean, but majority opinion held that if there really had been any dirt to be found, the combined excavatory skills of the police and the press would surely have dug it up years ago. Of course it was potentially such a great story, conjuring up the prospect of bringing the Tory's new Icarus crashing to earth, that it would never entirely die. Great truths may burn eternally, but great lies too retain a heat in their embers that stubbornly refuses to be quenched.

So Jones had probably caught a fragment of a whisper, half overheard and wholly misinterpreted. Being a dedicated Gidman-baiter, he'd tossed it into the water and stood back to see if anything surfaced.

Disregardable then, thought Maggie. If it hadn't been for Tris Shandy's party.

Tristram Shandy (real name Ernie Moonie) was a former Irish boy-band singer who had survived changing fashion, waning hair and waxing waist with a flexibility worthy of the Vicar of Bray. In turns record producer, *Celebrity-Up-the-Creek* winner, comic novelist, Live Aid activist, panel game player, soap star and confessional autobiographer, he was now, rising fifty, revelling in his latest metamorphosis as chairman of *Truce!* this season's mega-successful TV show. Its ostensible aim was to bring together warring parties ranging from quarrelling neighbours, divorcing couples, kids at odds with parents, and families divided by wills, to individuals in dispute with corporate bodies such as supermarkets, estate agents, manufacturers, hospitals, lawyers, politicians.

The resulting melange of glutinous sentimentality when disputants were reconciled, and blood on the carpet when they weren't, was so much to the depraved taste of twenty-first-century Britain that Shandy had now joined the crowded ranks of those minutely talented, monstrously ego'd 'media personalities' whose contracts were worth millions.

Maggie knew that today he was spending some of his loose change on a luncheon party on the *Shah-Boat*, the former Shah of Persia's luxury yacht, found rusting in a remote backwater of the Black Sea by a Russian oil millionaire, restored to its previous opulence, and towed to its present location on Victoria

243

Embankment where it had rapidly become the location of choice for those who liked to combine the maximum of privacy for their parties with the maximum of publicity for their personal wealth.

Anybody with pretensions to being somebody would have been invited. Beanie the Bitch certainly fell into that category, and presumably, as her current server, Gwyn Jones too.

So whatever it was that had brought the journalist to the Centre opening had been worth missing the party of the week for, as well as presumably pissing off the Bitch.

If something was brewing that might affect her employer, Maggie Pinchbeck wanted to know. The potentially most fruitful line of enquiry had to be via Beanie Sample. Of course she might know nothing, but if she did, there were two reasons why she might be persuaded to share it.

The first was that Jones's defection had probably left her feeling seriously irritated, and the Bitch was famous for not getting mad but getting even.

The second was that she owed Maggie Pinchbeck.

At an early age Maggie had looked at herself, accepted that she was insignificant and turned insignificance into an art form. Raising funds for ChildSave had been her training ground. 'She's like a bloody pickpocket,' one Captain of Industry had said wonderingly. 'You hardly notice she's around, then a bit later on, you realize your wallet's disappeared!' Working for Dave in that twilight zone where politics meets

244

the media, she'd soon discovered that shadowiness got you places that brashness couldn't reach. Thus it was that Maggie, seated unnoticed in the corner of a Fleet Street pub much favoured by the press before the great migration south, found herself listening to an alcoholic conversation between three old journalists haunting the place where whatever honour they'd ever possessed had probably died.

Their subject was the Bitch, who had clearly trodden on each of them at some point with more than usual violence. Their theme was revenge. Their proposed method was to put in her way a young man possessing all those attributes guaranteed to set her juices flowing. He, armed with the very latest surveillance gear, would make a detailed audio-visual record of their encounters. No journal with any sense would touch this stuff, but the Internet has neither fears nor loyalties, and the knowledge that everyone she knew was revelling in these images must, the trio felt, pierce even the Bitch's famous defences.

Stage One, Maggie gathered, had been successful. The bait was on display. The Bitch was showing interest. But she was a wily old tigress who knew better than to pounce on any tethered goat. She would do a lot of checking first and the merry threesome were congratulating themselves on the thoroughness of their preparation, which they were sure would soothe even the most suppurating doubts.

Maggie debated what to do, but not for long. She knew Beanie Sample only by reputation and didn't much like what she'd heard. But she'd been fostered in infancy, and though treated by her foster parents with much kindness, her two foster sisters had never let her forget her status. The result had been a sensitivity to injustice on a par with Jane Eyre's.

She rang the Bitch at home. Getting through to her at work, though not impossible, would have taken a lot of time and effort. It was easier to extract her unlisted number from a common acquaintance who also owed Maggie a big favour.

To start with, Beanie's sole concern was to discover how Maggie had come by her home number, which she dispensed like an oenophile sharing a 2001 Yquem. Ignoring this, Maggie stated the facts baldly as she had overheard them and rang off.

She then dropped the matter from her consciousness until it resurfaced a week later when the Bitch appeared at her flat with a huge bouquet of roses and a magnum of Mumm. They talked, but not for long. Both were too realistic not to face the fact that they didn't warm to each other. But as the Bitch left, she'd said, 'Remember, I owe you.'

'You've paid me,' said Maggie.

But that wasn't really true. Being pollen allergic, she'd passed the bouquet on to the ancient lady who lived next door. As for champagne, the bubbles gave her hiccoughs and the magnum was still in her fridge.

Now as she drove back to her modest flat in Southwark, Maggie contemplated her next move.

She could ring Beanie at her apartment again, but when she would return from the party was anybody's guess. Also she'd probably changed her number. Anyway, getting was different from giving information. For getting you wanted face-to-face.

She parked the car and climbed the stairs to her flat.

In the corner of her living room was a filing cabinet in which she kept anything she didn't want her employer to have access to. From this she took an envelope, and out of the envelope she took an invitation to Tris Shandy's party.

David Gidman the Third was definitely a somebody. Also, he'd appeared on *Truce!* to be confronted by a couple of angry constituents whom he had placated with considerable aplomb. The whole event had of course been carefully stage-managed, otherwise Maggie wouldn't have let him anywhere near Shandy.

But the *Shah-Boat* party was something different. No way was Maggie going to risk seeing Dave head off from the Centre opening to such a potentially scandalous event, so she'd simply hidden the invitation.

Now it could come in useful.

She thought of changing her clothes, decided nothing in her wardrobe was going to make her look more like one of the Shandy crowd, and contented herself with adding an *a* to *David* on the invitation.

The security guards by the gangplank had clearly been chosen for their muscle rather than their political awareness. They checked her

247

invitation against the guest list, showed no surprise that *Davida* should have been misprinted there as *David*, and even less that a female Member of Parliament should be plain and drably dressed.

On the boat the party was in such full swing that probably no one would have noticed if Captain Jack Sparrow himself had come mincing up the gangplank at the head of his band of cutthroats, but this did not stop her from taking precautions as she went in search of Beanie Sample. Moving unnoticed among crowds of people whose sole desire was to be noticed might seem an easy option, but there were dangers. She was long practised in the art of scia-mimicry, but the sight of Gidman's shadow moving independently of Gidman might provoke someone to draw attention to her presence in order to draw attention to himself.

At one point in the main saloon she passed close to Tris Shandy and felt those shrewd Irish eyes register her. Happily before he could rummage through the bran tub of his memory for her identity, one of the three bimbos competing for his attention upped the ante by letting her left boob loose from the confines of its halter with all the subtlety of a cannon ball bursting out of a paper bag.

As Shandy, with the scholarly wit for which he was justly famous, called, 'Fetch a warm spoon someone — better make that a shovel!' Maggie slipped out of the saloon and found herself on a narrow walkway on the seaward side of the boat. Her luck was in, for there was

248

the Bitch in all her flesh-flaunting finery, talking to a pretty black man Maggie recognized as a premiere league star. Coming between the goddess and her prey was not a good idea, and Maggie was preparing herself for a long wait when from the other direction arrived a young woman who clearly had no such inhibitions. Bearing all the episematic markings of the WAG, she shouldered Beanie aside with the gentle courtesy of Wayne Rooney on a bad day and bore her man along the walkway, filling his ear with the sedimentary vowels of estuary-speak from which Maggie, who could interpret whispers at fifty paces in a gale, excavated the phrases *old enough to be your gran* and *fuck knows where she's been.*

The Bitch was ready, Maggie decided. Getting no joy from the substitutes bench, she would be in no mood to feel protective about her absent Welsh striker.

Plus she owes me!

But for all that, as Beanie Sample came along the walkway towards her, Maggie felt about as confident as Androcles in the Coliseum. Just because you'd once helped a lion didn't always mean it would be grateful next time you met.

The editor's mood as evidenced by her greeting didn't hold out much promise.

'So Dave the Turd came after all, did he?' said Beanie. 'Rattle the swill pail, even the fattest pig comes running.'

One of the few things Maggie found to admire about the Bitch was that she'd stated publicly she'd rather bed a porcupine than a politician.

She said, 'In fact I'm here by myself. I wanted to talk to you.'

'Yeah? You want a job on *Bitch!*, hon, you'll need to smarten yourself up.'

'Thanks, but I've got a job. That's why I'm here. I want to know what Gwyn Jones is up to.'

Beanie's face went blank.

'What makes you think he's up to anything?' she asked.

'Because he came to the opening of the Gidman Memorial Community Centre instead of strutting his stuff here as your Stud of the Month.'

There was no point, Maggie had decided, in beating about this bush. Directness would get her what she wanted, or get her thrown overboard.

For a moment she thought the odds were on the latter.

Then a phone rang.

Beanie dived into her Vuitton bag and plucked out a mobile whose diamond-studded case matched her earrings and choker.

She checked the display then turned away from Maggie and walked out of earshot, or so she thought. But the acoustic of the walkway, plus her priceless acuity of hearing, allowed Maggie to catch Beanie's half of the conversation.

'*Hi, honey. Where are you?*'

'*Jesus! So what's going on?*'

'*Hell, that's truly terrible. How long will it take?*'

'*No, I understand. Families are important. Of*'

course you've got to put them first.'

'Yeah, it's OK here. No fun without you, though. I probably won't stay long.'

'I love you too. Hope everything goes OK. You take care now. Bye.'

Her tone as she spoke was affectionate and concerned, but her expression as she made her way back to Maggie was gorgonian.

'Bad news?' said Maggie.

The Bitch glowered at her for a moment, then her features relaxed into a smile that would have made Jones nostalgic for Llufwwadog.

'Not for me,' she said. 'You got a car? Don't know about you, but I'm ready to abandon this rust bucket before I get sea-sick. You can drive me home and on the way we'll have a nice little chat about Jones the Mess.'

15.50–16.15

Dalziel looked out of the window of 39 Loudwater Villas.

The view of industrial dereliction across the Trench wasn't pretty, but it was preferable to the view inside. Even his normally cast-iron stomach had experienced a spasm as he looked down at the body. It wasn't just the ruined head that made him queasy, it was the idea that he'd been responsible for putting Novello close to this carnage.

'Shotgun — sawn-off, from the spread,' said Pascoe. 'Death instantaneous.'

'Often is when you lose most of your head,' said Dalziel.

It was a feeble attempt to assert control.

On arrival he'd found the street in front of the Villas had been cordoned off. This was easy to do as it was a dead-end for vehicle traffic, narrowing down within fifty yards to a rutted track following the course of the river. An incident room caravan had already arrived, reminding the Fat Man how far behind the game he was. Pascoe emerged from it as he approached. Before he could speak, Dalziel had barked, 'What's the news on Ivor?'

'Still unconscious, but active signs are good. They'll let us know soon as there's any change. Sir . . . '

'Save it, lad. Need to take a look for myself first.'

The DCI hadn't demurred, merely produced a couple of white sterile cover-alls from the caravan and said, 'We'll need these. SOCO's up there already.'

So, agreement, obedience, just what a senior officer arriving at the scene expected. But as they made their way up to the second floor, Dalziel had a sense of being escorted rather than being in charge.

The feeling had persisted in the flat. Pascoe, usually the sensitive plant when it came to gore, had taken him through the details of the fatal injury without a tremor, his gaze fixed on the Fat Man as if determined to register every reaction.

What's he want? A confession? Dalziel asked himself. But he knew that if the circumstances were reversed he'd be doing exactly the same.

He said, 'Who found him?'

'Two uniforms. A neighbour called in to say she was worried, the TV set was on playing very loud but when she knocked at the door to ask Mr Watkins . . . '

'Watkins?' interrupted Dalziel. 'That the dead man?'

'Alun Watkins is the name of the man renting the flat,' said Pascoe carefully. 'As I was saying, when she couldn't get a reply, she decided to ring the emergency services. Couple of uniforms turned up. They couldn't get an answer either. Then one of them thought he smelled gas, which was odd as there isn't any gas connected here . . . '

'Probably the drainage,' said Dalziel. A sensitive nose came in handy when you needed to get into premises without a warrant.

'Whatever, it was as well they did. First thing they saw was Novello lying on the floor, bleeding from the head. They reacted by the book, one of them did what he could for her while the other called up an ambulance, told them exactly what the situation was so they came prepared. Their quick actions probably saved her life.'

'Thank Christ we've got a few buggers we can trust,' said Dalziel fervently.

'Yes, that is a comfort, isn't it?' said Pascoe, looking at him pointedly.

Fuck, thought Dalziel. He's not going to make this easy.

He made himself concentrate on the body.

He said, 'Any identification?'

'Nothing found. He had no ID on him.'

'Nothing at all? No wallet. Meaning mebbe it were stolen?'

'Possibly. So, probably Watkins, but we'll need to wait for positive identification.'

'You'll not be asking his mum,' said Dalziel, forcing himself to look unblinkingly at the ruined face.

'Dental records should do the trick if there's enough of his teeth,' said Pascoe. 'Or fingerprints maybe.'

Dalziel stooped lower.

'Hey, look at this,' he said. 'I think the bugger's wearing a rug.'

'So it would seem,' said Pascoe neutrally.

The Fat Man delicately tweaked the black wig

to reveal the true close-cropped blond hair beneath. Then he straightened up with a sigh.

'Pete,' he said, 'are you going to tell me everything you know, or are you going to play clever buggers to see if I let slip summat I couldn't know without knowing a lot more than I'm letting on to you?'

'Don't think I need to play clever buggers to reach that conclusion, sir,' said Pascoe.

'Because of the address, you mean?'

'That will do for starters. Why don't we step outside and let these good people get on with their work?'

Dalziel took a last look round the room. There were signs of a search, drawers open, papers scattered, a rack of CDs emptied on to the floor. Just inside the door a body-shaped outline had been marked on the carpet. He stepped carefully over it and went out. Behind him the CSIs who had been waiting patiently recommenced their painstaking examinations.

Outside as they took off their cover-alls, they saw Ed Wield come out of the caravan. Pascoe made a beckoning sign, then opened the door of his car. Dalziel got the message. There'd be other officers in the caravan and the DCI wasn't sure he'd want them to hear everything his boss was going to say.

He sat in the back seat with Pascoe next to him. Wield got into the front passenger seat and twisted round. At least, thought Dalziel, they haven't locked the doors.

'So fill me in,' said the DCI.

Wonder what he'd do if I said, *No, you go*

first? thought Dalziel. Arrest me? Wouldn't put it past the bugger!

He said, 'That woman you saw me with at the Keldale, her name's Gina Wolfe . . . '

He told the story fairly straight, though he did omit his confusion about the day, and glossed over the fact that he and the woman had met in the cathedral.

His involvement of Novello in the business, his subsequent phone contact with her, the whole sequence of events at the Keldale he described in exact detail. With the lass in hospital, glossing over things wasn't an option here, not even if they made him look foolish or irresponsible. But he found himself over-stressing that when he passed on Watkins's address to Novello, he'd told her to find out anything she could about the man but to avoid any direct contact.

When he finished, Pascoe said peremptorily, 'This photograph you mentioned, you'd better let me have it.'

Have it, not *see* it.

He took the envelope out of his inner pocket. Pascoe put his gloves back on before taking it.

'Blond hair,' said Pascoe. 'But not wearing a wig. Though, if what you say about Gina Wolfe thinking she saw him watching her at the Keldale is correct, it wasn't much of a disguise anyway. Of course we're only guessing that Watkins is Wolfe.'

'Same initials,' said Dalziel.

'Andy, Wieldy's got the same initials as Esther Williams but that doesn't mean you want to see him in a figure-hugging swimsuit.'

That was better. First name, a joke, altogether more relaxed. Or mebbe it was just part of the clever bugger's technique.

He said, 'Any road, Mick Purdy thinks this is likely a fake.'

'But you haven't checked yet?' said Pascoe.

'Not had time,' said Dalziel defensively.

'No, you have been rather busy. Eating and sleeping,' murmured Pascoe.

Before the Fat Man could decide how to respond to this piece of insolence, Pascoe handed the magazine page to the sergeant and said, 'See if you can check this out, Wieldy. Who've we got at HQ?'

'Seymour's there.'

'Just the man. Tell him to get himself a WPC then head off to the Keldale to bring Mrs Wolfe in. And we'll need a team to look at her stuff. Car, clothes, the lot. What was she wearing when you last saw her, Andy?'

'A sort of negligee,' said Dalziel. 'I explained . . . '

'I don't mean that,' said Pascoe. 'Though her having a shower might be significant. So what was she wearing last time you saw her fully dressed?'

Dalziel bit back an angry response. In Pascoe's shoes, he'd be asking the same.

He described Gina's dress as best he could.

'Right. Particular attention to that, Wieldy.'

'Right,' said the sergeant. 'By the way, what are we going to do with the Duttas?'

'They still here? I thought he was taking her back to his mother's till SOCO got finished going over the corridor.'

'She's not keen to go. Don't think she cares for her ma-in-law and she's loving being at the centre of things here. I got her out of the caravan after taking their statement, but they're still sitting round the back.'

'I'll have a word.'

The sergeant got out of the car and headed for the caravan.

Dalziel said, 'Pete, I think you're barking up the wrong tree about Gina Wolfe . . . '

'It still needs barking up,' said Pascoe. 'Woman's in the middle of getting her runaway husband declared officially dead so she can inherit his estate and remarry. She thinks she sees him in or around the same place as Shirley Novello spots a man who's bugging your table. This man is later found murdered. He is wearing a wig, presumably to disguise his appearance. The woman had possibly overheard you passing on this man's address to Novello. What would you do, Andy?'

'I'd want to ask her what she'd been doing all afternoon,' admitted Dalziel.

'Of course you would. Right, let's go and talk to the Duttas.'

Inclusive, but not subordinate. Go with the flow, Andy, till you see where the flow is going, he told himself as he eased his bulk out of the car.

Behind the caravan they found an Asian man standing alongside a woman seated on a fold-up canvas chair. The man, dressed in a Technicolor beach shirt and off-white Nadal-style shorts, looked rather anxious, but the woman, bright-eyed and beautiful in a shot-silk kaftan under

258

which she was heavily pregnant, could have been relaxing in a holiday caravan park.

'Mr and Mrs Dutta, this is my colleague Detective Superintendent Dalziel,' said Pascoe. 'Perhaps you could tell him what you told me earlier. Excuse me, Andy, I'll be back in a minute.'

The cunning bastard's leaving me stuck with this lot while he gets on with God knows what! thought the Fat Man. But he wanted to hear it anyway.

Mr Dutta began to speak rapidly.

'Yes, on Sundays we go to have lunch with my mother. She lives in Bagley Street near the post office, and usually we would stay there all afternoon, sometimes into the evening, but Devi was not feeling so good when we arrived, so we hardly had any lunch at all and came home early only for all this to happen and I am very worried about Devi who should not be put under any strain because of her condition as you can see.'

Devi, from Dalziel's observation, did not look to be suffering from anything other than a keen desire to find out what was going on and a certain amount of excitement at being at the centre of it. His guess was she was milking her condition for all it was worth to minimize contact with her mother-in-law.

He said, 'Right, we'll keep it short then. Tell me about Mr Watkins. Did you know him well?'

'Not very well,' began Ravi Dutta.

'Not very well?' his wife cut in. 'I think I've seen him once! Number 39 was empty when we moved in six months ago; we looked at it because

259

the rent was much cheaper than our flat, but that was because it is so small, and we needed the extra room with baby on the way, and Ravi has a good job so we can afford it even though his mammy did not want us to leave — we used to live with her, you see, and that was bad enough when there were just the two of us but soon as I knew I was carrying, I said to Ravi, this will not do at all . . . '

Dalziel said, 'So how long has number 39 been occupied?'

'I am not precisely sure . . . ' began Ravi.

'Four months ago I started hearing noises, television and radio, the walls are very thin, but not so loud I needed to complain,' said Devi. 'In any case, it was not every day; a lot of the time there did not seem to be anyone there, then I would hear the TV again, then another few days or a week and nothing. I thought he must travel a lot . . . '

'So tell me what happened today.'

Now Mr Dutta got a short innings. To save his wife the walk, he had gone to get the car, which he kept in a lock-up a minute's walk away. He'd expected to find her waiting outside the Villas. When she wasn't there, he had gone back inside to fetch her.

'See anyone hanging around outside?' asked Dalziel.

'No, I do not think so. Though I think someone came into the building behind me.'

Now Devi took over again.

'There was noise from the TV next door, it was a movie, it sounded an exciting movie, lots of shouting and shooting and loud music, and I was thinking how nice it would be to sit and watch a movie this afternoon instead of making a visit, and then there was a noise like someone falling and a big bang and voices and suddenly the music and everything got much louder, and I said to Ravi, What is that? And he said, It is the television, come on we are late, and I said, It sounded different from the movie, but he was so anxious not to be late at his mammy's that I did not have time to knock on the door and ask if everything was all right.'

Lucky you, thought Dalziel.

'But when we came back early because I was not feeling well, while Ravi was parking the car, I went up to the flat and the TV next door was still playing as loud as ever, so I knocked at the door but no one came, and when Ravi came up he knocked too, but still no one come, so I said, Now we must tell someone. Ravi did not want to cause a row but I said, No, this we cannot put up with, in any case maybe Mr Watkins is ill, so I went into our flat and rang 999. Soon your men came, they made us stay in our flat then they brought us out here. What is happening, Superintendent? Is Mr Watkins dead? Did he attack the lady they carried out? When shall we . . . '

'Hold on, luv,' said Dalziel. 'What you're saying is very important, I think mebbe we need to get you down to our headquarters so you can make a proper recorded statement. Excuse me.'

He walked away and climbed into the caravan.

Pascoe and Wield were standing together looking at a creased and soiled copy of MY

Times open at the page containing the picture of the loyal citizens cheering the royal visitor.

'By God, Wieldy that were quick,' said Dalziel admiringly.

'There's some recycle dumpsters round the side of the building,' said the sergeant. 'I set a couple of lads to go through the paper skip. Take a look, sir.'

He held it up alongside the page that Gina Wolfe had received through the post to show that, in the genuine copy, the face in the space occupied by Alex Wolfe was that of a balding middle-aged man.

'Mick were right then,' said Dalziel.

'Why would someone go to all the trouble of faking this?' wondered Pascoe.

'Not much trouble,' said Wield dismissively. 'Kid could do it with a decent scanner and printer.'

'Purdy reckons someone might be wanting to have a pop at him,' said Dalziel.

'Blowing a man's face off and putting a cop in hospital's a bit more than a pop,' said Pascoe. 'I think it's time to have a long chat with Mrs Wolfe.'

A phone rang. The constable who answered it called, 'Sarge — Seymour for you.'

'So what do you make of the Duttas, Andy?' asked Pascoe.

'You got a problem. Keep them here and they'll drive you mad and she'll be into everything. Turn 'em loose and she'll be on every channel, spilling everything she's seen and heard. I'd get her taken down to HQ and let her talk

262

her head off to some poor sod. Paddy Ireland's a good listener. With a bit of luck, eventually she'll go into labour, then we'll be shut of her for a while.'

'Andy, you're all heart. But it's not a bad idea. I'll get Wieldy to sort it.'

But the sergeant had other things on his mind as he rejoined them.

'That were Seymour from the Keldale,' he said. 'Seems Mrs Wolfe checked out half an hour back.'

Pascoe turned on Dalziel.

'Well, Andy,' he said. 'How's your instinct feeling now?'

'Bearing up,' said the Fat Man. 'Likely it means nowt. Decided she wanted to get out of reach of everyone to consider her options.'

It sounded so feeble he almost smiled apologetically as he said it.

Pascoe said, 'Wieldy, put out a call. You should be able to get the details of her car from the hotel . . .'

'No need,' said Wield. 'Call's out. I knew the details already. Super asked me to check them this morning.'

'So he did. Lucky to have him around, aren't we?' said Pascoe savagely.

But this chunk of heavy irony fell short of its mark.

Dalziel had moved away and was talking urgently into his mobile.

'Mick,' he said. 'When you get this, don't care if you're saving the fucking universe from aliens, ring me!'

13.35–17.30

Finding Dalziel still in her room when she returned had been a serious disappointment to Gina Wolfe.

She hadn't expected a senior police officer to drop everything and devote himself totally to her concerns, but the degree of interest shown by the Fat Man over lunch had given her hope that he'd do everything in his power to help. Lying in her bed, sleeping off an excess of booze, did not strike her as a very promising start.

Her mood had not been improved by her afternoon. She'd gone out into the Keldale garden and rung Mick Purdy to give him a progress report. His phone was switched off so she left him a message. She sat for a couple of minutes longer, trying to work out if she was any further forward. Then her phone rang. It was Mick.

He said, 'Sorry. Still at my desk, tying up loose ends.'

He sounded very tired, not surprising as she guessed he hadn't had much sleep for the best part of two days. But he listened very carefully to her account of what had happened, constantly interrupting with questions, till in the end she got a strong impression that he had a better understanding of what was going on than she

264

did. Maybe he was able to put himself in Dalziel's place and create a whole picture out of disconnected fragments.

In the end she got rather annoyed with his insistent questioning and said, 'Look, Mick, I'm not in one of your interview rooms, OK? I've told you what happened and the net result, so far as I can see, is that I've got another boozed-up cop snoring in my bed!'

'You've never complained before,' he said.

'That's not funny.'

'No. Sorry. Listen, I'll talk to Andy when he wakes up . . .'

'To get a truly professional picture, you mean? The things I've missed, or maybe the things he's not telling me?'

'Hey, don't be so sensitive. We're cops, we speak the same language, that's all. Listen, what are you doing now?'

'I'm sitting in the hotel garden talking to you on my phone.'

'That's fine. Good idea to stay there, don't go wandering off. Look, I need to finish stuff here, then I'll get back to you . . .'

'No need. I'm perfectly capable of managing myself. And you sound like you could do with getting your head down for a couple of hours at least.'

'Couple of days would be better. Listen, keep in touch. And remember what I say. Until we're sure what's going off here, be careful. Don't go wandering off by yourself.'

Maybe she should have been touched by his concern, but all it did was irritate her.

What right did he have to start dishing out instructions? So he was worried on her behalf. How much more worried would he have been if she'd told him about her several *sightings* of Alex, both the obviously fallacious ones this morning, and especially the much more powerful image she'd glimpsed just before Dalziel dropped the water jug.

This was one of the reasons she'd come into the garden, to stare at the space the image had briefly occupied in hope of recreating it.

It didn't work. She looked at her watch. Two o'clock. The christening party looked as if it was breaking up. Dalziel would soon have had his half-hour, but she suspected he might need a little more. Dissatisfied with herself and also with the tone of her conversation with Mick she rose from the bench she was sitting on and headed for the car park. Aimlessly driving around wasn't going to advance matters but at least it was doing something in a world where men expected her to do nothing without their imprimatur.

It was of course totally non-productive. This time she didn't even imagine she'd spotted Alex. So finally at half past three she'd returned to her room, not in the mood to make any allowances whatsoever if she found the fat slob still in her bed, which of course he was.

The shower soothed her bodily and mentally. As she was towelling herself down she heard the phone ringing in the bedroom. Checking first that the Fat Man had definitely gone, she picked up the receiver and said, 'Hello?'

There was no reply, just a faint sound of breathing.

She said, 'Room 25, who is this, please?'

Distantly a voice said, 'Gina?'

She froze.

After a while the voice said, 'Gina, you there?'

She managed to relax her throat muscles sufficiently to say, 'Alex, is that you?'

Now it was the caller's turn to pause. When he finally spoke, he said, 'Yes, it's me,' but hesitantly, like a witness whose certainties begin to crumble in the witness box.

Gina heard the doubt and forced herself to restrain the torrent of questions welling up in her head.

She said, 'Alex, it's so good to hear your voice. Where are you? Can we meet?'

Another long silence made her wonder if even that had been a question too far, then the voice said, 'Why are you here?'

She said, 'Someone sent me the photo of you in *MY Life* magazine.'

'Photo? Which photo?' He sounded puzzled, with a faint note of alarm.

She said reassuringly, 'The photo of you in the crowd during the royal visit last week. I thought it might be you who'd sent it. You were right at the front, I knew at once it was you. Like I did when I saw you today, in the garden at the Keldale.'

Silence. Am I losing him? she wondered. Again.

Then he spoke and for the first time the voice was that of the man she'd married: alert, positive, forceful.

'Gina, what are you driving?'

'A Nissan 350Z. Red.'

'Give me your mobile number.'

She obeyed.

'Now get out of there. Check out and leave. Drive north. Leave your phone switched on. I'll be in touch. Gina, don't hang about!'

The phone went dead.

She sat on the bed because her legs had lost all strength. Despite everything she'd done since getting the photo, everything she'd said to Mick and to Dalziel, in her heart she'd refused to believe that Alex could really be alive. Even all those 'sightings' of him had been good. The ones she knew for certain were false reinforced the chances that the ones that were doubtful were false too.

And now she'd heard his voice. Could that be a delusion too? She wanted it to be. Over the past seven years she'd built up a barrier against all the pain of that time of loss, she'd buried it as deep, so she thought, as the small white coffin. But now she knew — had known as soon as she saw the photo — that the barrier she'd built wasn't the sturdy bulwark clad in tempered steel of adamantean proof she'd imagined, but a rice-paper wall a dead child could poke a finger through.

She felt herself on the edge of the state of shock, but she must not succumb, not while there was still doubt. There were questions to ask. Questions were good. They forced the mind to work at seeking answers.

First, was it really Alex?

Every instinct told her it was. The voice was his.

He had offered no proof of identity, but even that was a kind of proof.

Yet he didn't seem to know anything about the photo.

So that was a maybe.

Second, why had he told her to check out?

She recalled Dalziel's suggestion that maybe someone else had a reason for getting her up here. She hadn't taken it all that seriously, but now . . .

That might explain Alex's alarm, his desire to get her out of there.

Or could it be that someone else was keen to get her out in the open?

She thought of ringing Mick, but what good would that do? She could formulate his response without bothering with the conversation. *Don't do anything, stay put, contact Andy Dalziel, he'll know what to do.*

Perhaps he would. But she didn't need external input into her decision. Which in fact wasn't a decision.

She didn't have a choice.

She had never been a subservient wife. She'd once told Alex, if he wanted instant obedience, he should have become a dog handler. But now she saw no way forward but to assume it was his voice she'd heard and to obey his instructions. The only way to settle all doubts was to see him face to face. To do anything that might drive him back into his hidey-hole, whether it were mental or physical, was not an option. She'd lived

269

through uncertainty into certainty once. It had been a slow painful journey and it wasn't one that she wanted to have to start making again.

She rang Reception, told them she was checking out and asked them to charge everything to the credit card they'd swiped on her arrival. Then she got dressed, bundled the rest of her stuff into her case and headed out, descending by the service lift that deposited her next to a door opening on to the car park.

She slotted her mobile into the Bluetooth connection and drove away from the hotel. He'd said drive north so she turned right to keep the sun on her left. At last her Brownie days were coming in useful!

After a few minutes the phone rang.

'Where are you?' he said.

It was Alex. She was sure of it. Wasn't she?

She said, 'I'm on the outskirts of town. There's a roundabout ahead. Left is Leeds and Harrogate, right Scarborough, straight on Middlesbrough.'

'Carry straight on. Don't disconnect.'

Other instructions followed at regular intervals. Soon she was off the main highway into a maze of narrow country roads passing through hamlets whose names meant nothing to her. She would have been completely lost had not her Brownie fix on the sun told her she was now to the east of her starting point and heading south. Finally after three quarters of an hour she was told to turn west on to a road which ran arrow-straight between low hedges of burnished hawthorn. By her rough geographical calculations, if she carried on in this direction for four or five miles, she would intersect with the main north — south motorway she'd started out on. She'd worked out that the purpose of all this meandering was to shake off any possible pursuit. Well, she hadn't seen another car either in front or behind for miles, so perhaps now he was simply directing her back to town.

A mile or so ahead the narrow road breasted a steep hill on whose summit silhouetted against the declining sun she could see a building. As she got nearer she could see an inn sign swaying in a gentle breeze.

At the foot of the hill he told her to stop and wait.

She obeyed.

Time passed. Five minutes. Ten. Half an hour. Nothing happened. No traffic overtook her, none came towards her. With each passing minute her certainty that it was Alex's voice faded. She wound down the window. There was no sound except for the call of a single bird, far away, repeating the same phrase over and over again. She tried to analyse it musically but it defied annotation. It had no connection with humanity. It belonged in a world where all the humans were dead. She felt totally alone. Abandoned.

It hadn't been Alex. It was nobody. And nobody was going to call.

She would sit here till it got dark, and then she would . . .

She didn't know what she would do.

16.35–16.41

Once more Andy Dalziel drove into the car park of the Keldale Hotel but this time his mood was very different. Last time he'd been anticipating a leisurely al fresco lunch with a good-looking woman who'd presented him with an intriguing little mystery, just the right size to take his mind off his own troubles.

He'd felt completely justified in keeping the whole daft business to himself. Involving an off-duty Novello had seemed harmless enough. Of all his DCs, she was the one whose discretion he most trusted. She was very ambitious and therefore unlikely to risk his wrath by shooting her mouth off. The same could be said of the lads, when sober, but after a few jars down the Black Bull he wouldn't trust any of them to keep their mouths shut about their boss's dalliance with a beddable blonde!

Before the bomb, it wouldn't have bothered him. A man with a hide like a rhinoceros doesn't fear pinpricks of laughter. A rhino might look a bit comic wandering around among all them elegant antelopes, but let him turn his sagacious eye in your direction, and you soon stop smiling.

On his return to work, however, he found that Mid-Yorkshire, which had once stretched around him like the wild savannah, had contracted to an enclosure at the zoo. People were now looking at the beast with curiosity, or, worse, with pity.

So they had to be re-educated.

Back to basics first; keep them guessing what you're up to, make them jump a bit, remind them you're answerable to nobody but yourself. Respect! Wasn't that the cant word these days? Get some respect!

After this morning's visit to the Station, he felt he'd taken a good stride in the right direction. He'd come to the Keldale at midday feeling more like his old self than he had for a long time.

And now as he drove into the car park, he felt like a petty recidivist crook returning to the scene of his pathetic crime.

Pascoe was certainly treating it as a crime scene. He'd upgraded the search of Gina Wolfe's room to full SOCO examination.

'You sort that, Wieldy,' he'd commanded as if his commanding officer were not present. 'But first off, get on to Seymour and tell him to make sure Mrs Wolfe's room is left untouched. Don't want a chambermaid getting in there and stripping the bed, do we?'

Stripping the bed? Was that a crack? wondered Dalziel.

'You're still giving the room the once-over, are you, Pete?' he said. 'Mebbe I should take a look first afore SOCO gets to work.'

'Why's that, Andy?'

'Because I've been there, remember? Could be I'd spot summat.'

It had sounded weak and Pascoe hadn't bothered to try and smooth over the fact.

273

'Oh, I see. Maybe you'd notice a subtle change out of the corner of your eye, some slight discrepancy that would eventually turn out to be the clue that cracks the case, like in one of Agatha's novels? No, I think on the whole it might be best for all our sakes if you weren't around when the CSIs start poking about.'

Best for all our sakes? That was definitely a crack!

'Why? What do you think they're going to find? Semen stains on the sheets?'

Pascoe shrugged and said, 'I just need to be sure there's nothing to find, OK?'

'Listen,' said Dalziel, 'I told you, I were knackered. Not fit to drive. I dossed down by myself. For Christ's sake, if Gina had been there, whatever else I gave her, I'd have given her an alibi, wouldn't I? And you'd not be wasting time with this daft notion that she might have blown Watkins's face off and put Novello in hospital.'

Pascoe had looked at him with half a smile and said, 'No need to get your knickers in a twist. All right, if you're so desperate to go back, let's go. Wieldy, you keep an eye on things here, OK? Anything comes up, ring me.'

'As opposed to keeping it all to myself, you mean?' said the sergeant ironically.

'Why not? Seems to be in fashion nowadays,' said Pascoe.

They weren't going to leave it alone, thought Dalziel. And he couldn't complain, he had it coming.

Pascoe, who'd parked alongside him, was out

274

of his car already and opening his boss's door for him.

'Come on, Andy,' he said impatiently. 'Work to do.'

This was too much. Pascoe had followed him to the hotel. Followed, not led the way, thought Dalziel. Like he was scared I was going to do a runner. Time he had a little reminder of the divine order of things.

God seemed to agree. Even as the Fat Man looked for a way to slow things to his own pace, the good Lord sent him one.

'Here,' he said, looking across the car park to where a man was putting a suitcase into a BMW X5, 'I know yon face.'

He set off with Pascoe in close attendance. As they approached, the man straightened up and looked round. He was an imposing figure, broad-shouldered, grey-haired, with a Roman emperor's head and a nose to match.

'How do, Hooky!' boomed Dalziel. 'Long time no see!'

Pascoe was a good reader of reaction and it struck him that this Roman emperor was reacting to Dalziel's approach as if he'd just noticed Alaric the Visigoth trotting up the Appian Way.

Conclusion: he was a crook whose acquaintance with the Fat Man was purely professional. Question: what kind of crook was he, and could his presence here have anything to do with Gina Wolfe?

But even as the question formed in his mind he was revising his conclusion as Dalziel took the man by the hand and shook it vigorously.

'So what are you doing here, Hooky? Bit off your patch. Can't be official, else we'd have baked a cake or summat.'

The man managed a wan smile and said, 'No, just a visit. Old chum's daughter got married.'

'Oh aye? Job, is he?'

'No, no. Some of us do have friends outside the Force,' said the man, his eyes straying to Pascoe, who coughed in the Fat Man's ear.

'Oh aye, I'm forgetting me manners. Hooky, this is Peter Pascoe, my DCI. Pete, drop a curtsey, this is Nye Glendower, king of the Cambrian cops!'

'Good to meet you, sir,' said Pascoe. 'I've heard of you, of course.'

Aneurin Glendower, Chief Constable of the Cambrian Force. Not a household name outside of Wales, but one well known in police circles as a man of strong views who might rise even higher if he could find a PM on the same wavelength.

They shook hands and Glendower said, 'You boys got something going on here? I noticed a bit of activity in the hotel.'

Seymour and a WPC. They couldn't have caused much of a stir, but you didn't get to be CC without having well-tuned sensors, thought Dalziel. He opened his mouth to reply, but Pascoe cut in.

'Just a little local difficulty,' he said breezily. 'But we'd better get it sorted. Good to meet you, sir. Andy, when you're ready . . . '

The bugger's worried in case I shoot my

mouth off! thought the Fat Man indignantly.

He said, 'With you in a minute, lad. Us old buggers need the young 'uns to keep us on our toes, eh, Hooky? Sorry I didn't know you were here. We could have cracked a bottle and had a chat about the good old days when we mattered.'

'Yes. Would have been nice, Andy — not that I had much spare time. Got to shoot off now and burn a bit of midnight oil when I get home so that I'm up to speed when I hit the desk in the morning. Good to see you. Nice to meet you, too, Pascoe.'

He slammed his boot, got into the X5 and accelerated out of the car park.

'He's in a hurry to get home,' said Pascoe.

'Well, it's Wales,' said Dalziel. 'Probably shuts at half past seven. Here, watch out!'

He pulled Pascoe out of the way of a white Mondeo backing out of its parking spot at speed. The middle-aged woman driver scowled at them, then sped off towards the exit.

'Bloody women drivers,' said the Fat Man, shaking his fist after it. 'Most on 'em couldn't push a pram straight.'

Racist and sexist in the same ten seconds, thought Pascoe. Nothing new there then, except it came across rather mechanically, as if the old sod were becoming a parody of himself. And all that stuff about the good old days when he mattered! He really should have taken a few more weeks convalescent leave. Or maybe months.

Or am I just behaving like Henry the Fifth looking for arguments to invade France?

But Glendower's reaction had certainly contained something of the embarrassment of the successful man on meeting the one-time equal he'd left behind. In the past their leader's national reputation had always been a source of pride to his colleagues in Mid-Yorkshire CID. Could the truth really be that he was regarded as a bit of a joke by the upwardly mobile, a cop who'd found his relatively low level, a grampus puffing his way around a small provincial pond?

Pascoe shook away the disloyal thoughts.

'Let's find Seymour,' he said.

16.35–17.05

It had been a funny kind of day, thought Edgar
Wield.

The unexpected appearance of Dalziel early
that morning should have rung a warning bell.
Looking back now, it seemed that there had been
something a touch manic about the fat sod's
speech and demeanour, and there was that
business about the old lady, Mrs Esmé Sheridan,
ringing in with a complaint about a kerb-crawler,
and giving a car number and description that
pointed the finger at the Fat Man. But on the
whole Wield had been happy to accept his arrival
as evidence that normal service was about to be
resumed.

That the superintendent had come back too
early from convalescent leave the sergeant did
not doubt. But when others, including Pascoe,
had expressed concern as to whether the great
man could ever truly get back to where he had
been before, Wield had kept his counsel. In his
eyes it was just a matter of time. The others saw
it in terms of a champion boxer trying to make a
come-back. He saw it in terms of Odysseus come
to reclaim his kingdom.

He had sufficient self-awareness to acknowledge he might be emotionally biased.

Pascoe was very close to the Fat Man.

Romantics — there are a few of those even in the modern police force — analysed this as a vicarious father/son relationship. Dalziel had no children, or at least none he acknowledged, and years ago Pascoe's father had confirmed the distance between himself and his son by opting to emigrate to Australia with his eldest daughter and her family.

The Romantic analysis of the D and P relationship went something like this: as initial distrust and dislike had moderated, via reluctant acknowledgement of detective skill and technique, to mutual respect and even affection, the residual ability to get up one another's noses had been rendered innocuous by subsumption into a quasi-familial mode. You may at times loathe your parents or kids, but that doesn't get in the way of loving them.

Wield felt it was maybe a bit more complicated than that. What he was certain of was that he owed his own progress, perhaps even survival, to the Fat Man. He had congratulated himself for many years on the skill with which he'd concealed his gayness from his institutionally homophobic employers. It was only late on, around the time he decided — without marking the occasion with a ticker-tape parade — to come out, that he realized he'd never fooled Andy Dalziel. Looking back, he began to understand how much he'd benefited from the Fat Man's protection. Nothing obvious involving civil rights and liberal declarations and such. Just an invisible circle drawn round him which said, He's in here with me, touch him at your peril.

He'd never said thank you because he knew if he had, all he'd have got back was, *For what?* And indeed, for what? The right to function like any other copper? Surely he had that anyway. So, no thank yous. But what he did give the Fat Man was unconditional trust that, whatever he was, so would he always be.

Trust was one thing, reality another. There was no getting away from it, the way things had turned out today meant there was a big dark cloud hanging over Dalziel, and Wield doubted it was about to burst in blessings on his head. Nowt he could do but get on with his job.

He had disposed of the Duttas as the superintendent had suggested and now he was sitting collating statements from the other Loudwater Villas tenants.

The sound of a rackety engine caught his ears and he looked out of the caravan window to see a dusty white Bedford van pull up in front of the building.

A young man got out, early twenties, dressed in baggy jeans and a red T-shirt. He stretched his arms and yawned, then pulled a grip off the passenger seat and headed into the Villas.

Wield frowned. He'd set up a checkpoint on the approach road. They couldn't keep people out who had a genuine reason for going in, such as, they lived here. But where there was doubt, the officer on duty would ring in to check; and where there was no cause for doubt, he would make a note and ring in with the details to indicate there was somebody new to interview.

None of the caravan phones had sounded in

the last five minutes.

The sergeant said, 'Smiler, who's on the checkpoint?'

The constable so addressed, glanced at a list and said, 'It's Hector, Sarge. Everyone got called in for this one.'

The last sentence was significant.

In a case of murder accompanied by a serious assault on an officer, everyone was expected to turn out and help. Indeed, everyone wanted to turn out and help. But if Wield had been consulted, he'd have advised that the best way Police Constable Hector could help was to continue to devote himself to whatever unimaginable activity occupied his mind on his day off.

The sergeant rose and opened the caravan door. From this elevated position he could see down to the checkpoint quite clearly.

There was no one there.

The air was very still and a distant splash drew his attention down to the river bank. There he was, that unmistakable figure, lanky and skinny, with a head set slightly beneath the level of the shoulders, as though like a terrapin's it could fully retract in time of trouble.

He was throwing stones into the water. No, on closer observation of the throwing style, it seemed likely he was trying to make stones skip across the surface of the water, only they never rose out of the initial splash.

This time I'll kill him, thought Wield. But that pleasure would have to wait.

He jumped down from the caravan and headed into the building.

As he ran up the stairs he could hear raised voices drifting down from above.

He found their source on the second floor outside number 39.

The young man from the white van was having a row with PC Jennison, who was on guard outside the fatal flat. The SOCO team had finished and now its sole occupant was the faceless corpse waiting to be bagged and transported to the morgue. Joker Jennison had risked a peep and wished he hadn't. Now the door was firmly closed and he was concentrating on his appointed task of keeping unauthorized personnel out.

At sixteen and a half stone, he formed a pretty effective barrier, but while he was winning the battle he was clearly being worn down by the argument and he spotted Wield's arrival with relief.

'Sarge,' he called. 'This gent says he wants to go inside and he won't take no for an answer.'

'No, I bloody well won't!' exclaimed the man, turning. 'You in charge here? Then tell your pet ape to let me in.'

He had a lilting Welsh accent and a fiery Welsh tone.

'I'll do what I can, sir, but first why don't we calm things down a touch, and take a close look at this thing together?' said Wield.

His words were softly spoken and would have won plaudits in a bedside manner contest. But he knew it wasn't his soft answers that turned away wrath but the agate-hard face they came out of.

'Yes, all right, it'll be good to talk to somebody who's got two penn'orth of sense for a change,' said the man, shooting a twelve-bore glance at Jennison.

He allowed himself to be led away to the far end of the corridor.

'Now, sir, I'm Detective Sergeant Wield of Mid-Yorkshire CID,' said Wield, producing his ID.

He let the man study it for a moment, then put it away and took out his notebook and pen, by these small rituals providing a space for the more volatile vapours of anger to dissipate.

'OK, sir,' he said, pen poised. 'Could you start by giving me your full name and address, and then explain why you want to get into number 39?'

The man let out a long sigh, but his voice was relatively calm as he answered.

'My name is Alun Gruffud Watkins,' he said. 'My address is Flat 39, Loudwater Villas. And I want to get inside because that's where I bloody well live!'

16.00–16.30

Maybe I ought to play the lottery today, thought Maggie Pinchbeck. Clearly I'm on a roll.

Her first stroke of good fortune had been the timely phone call from Gwyn Jones.

The reasons for the Bitch's anger had been made clear on the journey from the *Shah-Boat* to Marina Towers.

'Family fucking emergency! His old gran seriously ill. Got to go back to fucking Wales to help sort things out. God, you could almost hear the tears in his voice! And all the time he's heading up to Yorkshire chasing a story! Bastard! There's got to be trust, hon. Once a man starts treating you like an idiot, that's finito.'

Maggie noted that it wasn't the lie that bothered her, it was the assumption she wasn't smart enough to spot it.

It had been an easy job for Beanie to get Gareth Jones to repeat a full account of what he'd overheard when bugging the terrace table, almost as easy as it was for Maggie to get the Bitch to repeat the story.

'Like any kid, he really wants to impress big brother,' said Beanie, 'and knowing that Gwyn's got this thing about Dave the Turd, soon as he heard the name Gidman, he couldn't wait to pass the info on to Gwyn.'

285

In fact there wasn't all that much to pass on, and from what Beanie relayed to her, Maggie wasn't any clearer why the possible resurfacing of an amnesiac cop should have got Gwyn Jones salivating. From Dave the Third's reaction, she was pretty convinced the name Wolfe didn't mean a lot to him either. She didn't anticipate getting much more from Beanie Sample, but she was presently her only link to what was going on in Yorkshire. So when they got to Marina Tower, and the Bitch got out of the car still talking, Maggie followed her up to her apartment.

Inside, Beanie poured herself a large vodka and invited Maggie to help herself. She matched the size of Beanie's drink but hers was mostly soda.

The Bitch went wandering off. Maggie followed her into a palatial bedroom.

She was noticing a change in the tone of Beanie's complaint. The initial fury had died away and though the descriptive language used about Jones was just as colourful, the target area of complaint seemed to be shifting from his demeaning attempt at deception to the fact that he hadn't shared a possible scoop with her.

'Shit, I was breaking front-page stories before his balls had dropped,' she declared. 'I could have run things down here for him while he was pissing about up in Yorkshire. Cover your back, hon, that's rule number one. No fucker's a fucking island.'

She'd pressed a button that set the doors of a wall-length closet sliding silently open.

'Look at that,' she said, indicating the few

hangers from which men's garments hung. 'Some women cut up their guy's clothes when he pisses them off. This fucker, I'd be doing him a favour. Only decent things he's got are a jacket and shirt I bought him, and the cunt's wearing those.'

She reached up and took a gleaming silver laptop off a shelf.

'Let's see if he's got anything in here to show what he thinks he's up to,' she said.

'That's Gwyn's laptop?' asked Maggie as the woman opened it and turned it on.

'Right,' said Beanie as the screen lit up and invited her to enter a password.

Without hesitation she hit the keyboard.

'He gave you his password?' said Maggie incredulously.

'Not so's he noticed,' said Beanie, smiling. 'But when I invite a man into my house, I expect him to give me *everything*. Now let's see. No, not you, hon. He may be a creep, but he's my creep and even a creep's got right to some privacy.'

She turned the computer so Maggie couldn't see the screen. This wasn't a good sign, possibly signalling a further softening of her attitude to her lover that could make her regret sharing her initial anger with an interested stranger.

Well, unless she tries to silence me by chucking me out of the window, it's too late to do anything about it now! thought Maggie as she admired the view. To see the sky out of her own bedroom window, you had to open it and lean out backwards. She didn't envy Beanie much, but this she certainly envied.

Behind her she heard a hiss of rage.

She turned to see that the relatively mellow mood into which the woman had been drifting had vanished like March sunshine.

'Oh, the lousy bastard. It's not his fucking clothes I'll take the scissors to. The bastard!'

Maggie moved forward quickly and looked at the screen.

It contained an email. And this, she instantly realized, might be her second stroke of fortune.

Hi lover, sorry to hear about gran. Yes I'll be ready with the TLC when you get back tho not sure what it means. Try Licking my Cunny maybe?!!! C u soon Gem xxxxx

She picked up the laptop and moved out of Beanie's reach. The Bitch looked ready to hurl it through the window if she got her hands on it.

'Can you believe it? I give him a key to my apartment and he's doing this to me! Who the fuck is this Gem, you got any idea?'

She glared at Maggie so accusingly that she found herself answering, 'There's a junior on the *Messenger* staff called Gemma Huntley . . . '

'A junior? You mean he's humping some kid then coming here to stick his cock into me? Jesus, I need another drink!'

She stormed out of the bedroom. Maggie didn't waste time. While she doubted there'd be an early restoration of sympathy for Gwyn Jones, it seemed wise not to take the risk. Within a matter of seconds she'd located a folder marked

Gidman, typed in her email address, attached the folder, and sent it.

It was still being downloaded when Beanie returned.

'What you doing there, hon?' she asked.

'There was some stuff here about the Gidmans that I'm sending to my computer. That OK with you?' said Maggie, thinking that if she kept the woman talking just a few minutes longer it wouldn't matter if it were all right with her or not.

She needn't have worried.

'You get all you want. Anything you can do to stiff Jones is all right by me. And when you're done, I'm going to send little Miss Gem a reply that will put her off playing with the big girls forever!'

16.30–18.05

Fleur Delay woke out of a dream in which she saw a man get shot in the face by her brother.

But when she stooped to look at the body, the ruined features belonged to Vince.

And when she turned to look at the gunman, it was her own pale face she saw.

She rolled off the bed and staggered into the bathroom to pee. Then she removed her clothes and got into the shower, letting it run cold then hot then cold again. Dried off, she got dressed in fresh clothes, disguised her pallor as best she could with make-up, adjusted her wig carefully, then tried the door that communicated with her brother's room. When she realized it was locked, she tapped on it gently, then hard.

There was no reply.

She took out her mobile and thumbed in Vince's number.

'Hi, sis,' he said.

'Where are you?'

'Downstairs having a sandwich.'

She didn't reply, but switched off and hurried down the stairs.

Vince saw her before she spotted him. He was in the spacious lobby, settled deep in the kind of armchair whose soft leather upholstery embraced you like a good woman. Seeing the look on his

290

sister's face confirmed his feeling that he'd rather be rolling around on a thin mattress with a bad woman as long as the action was taking place two hundred miles south of here.

'Hi,' he said. 'Like a club sandwich? They know their meat here, got to give them that.'

'How long have you been down here?'

'Half an hour, maybe,' he said vaguely.

'Where's the woman?'

'Her car's still in the car park,' he assured her. 'No way she can come down the stairs or out of the lift without I see her. I reckon she's got Tubby in her room, trying to give him a heart attack.'

She sat down next to him. He was right, he did have a good line of vision on the staircase and lift.

'So what's The Man say?' he asked.

'He's thinking about it,' she prevaricated.

Vince frowned.

'What's to think?'

'He needs to be certain it was Wolfe.'

Vince said, 'Makes no difference. You always say, you down a guy, you should put space between you and the body soon as you can. So why're we hanging around?'

'Because I say so,' she snapped. 'I've told you before, Vince. Just do as you're told and we'll be all right. And no one told you to off that guy.'

'I only shot him 'cos he was hurting you,' he protested.

'Yeah? Don't think I'm not grateful, 'cos I'm not,' she retorted.

291

They sat in separate silences for a while, hers irritated, his hurt.

Fleur thought, Box clever, girl. This is getting us nowhere. If I want him to be able to look after himself, I've got to stop putting him down.

She forced a smile and said, 'Fancy a ciggie?'

'What about the woman?' he said, still sulky.

'We'll just be outside.'

They went out of the French window on to the terrace, then down the steps into the garden. There were several other addicts there already, their progress along the gravelled walks marked by clouds of tobacco smoke. They lit up and joined the parade. After a while they sat down on an elegant rustic bench and talked as they smoked. As usual, Fleur chose the topic, and as usual it was their Spanish villa.

For once Vince seemed genuinely enthused. Normally he started yawning whenever Spain was mentioned. OK, it was great for holidays, but he couldn't understand his sister's desire to move out there permanently.

What he did understand, however, was that when he and she disagreed, almost inevitably events proved her right. Not that he went in for statistical analysis. He just knew that submitting wholly to her judgment had kept him out of jail for well over a decade, which compared very favourably with the year and a half that was his previous longest non-custodial period since leaving school.

Sitting here, listening to her rattling on about her plans for their life together, gave him a sense of continuity, of family, that his early upbringing had lacked. And being marooned in this grotty northern town made the prospect of retirement to Spain with its bars and beaches and clubs and dark-eyed senoritas seem very attractive.

So he responded with more interest than he'd ever shown before. For Fleur, it was one of the pleasantest times she'd ever spent with her brother. So enthusiastic did he sound about the villa that all her doubts vanished and her plans for their future, or more precisely, Vince's future, seemed perfectly feasible.

Time flew by and it wasn't till she glanced at her watch that she realized nearly an hour had passed.

'Better get back in,' she said.

'Yeah, I'm feeling pretty hungry,' said Vince. 'That sandwich was OK, but I need a real meal or I may faint.'

'Always thinking of your belly,' she said, regarding him fondly. 'I want to pick up my jacket from the car.'

They walked round the side of the hotel to the car park.

As she opened the car door and reached inside for her jacket, she glanced at the next row to check on the red Nissan.

It wasn't there.

Panic starting in her stomach, she ran her eyes over the other cars in case she'd misremembered its location.

Finally there was no doubt. It had definitely gone.

Vince was untroubled.

'So she's gone for a drive again,' he said.

'How come you didn't notice her?'

'She probably went out while we were in the garden,' he said. 'So she can't be far. We'll pick her up on the laptop. Come on, sis. Don't always be looking for trouble!'

He led the way up to his room. Fleur followed, thinking, Sometimes he gets it right. It might do me good to listen to him for a change. Maybe then I can stop lying awake wondering what's going to become of him.

The laptop was on the bedside table where he'd left it, but the screen was blank, not even a screensaver.

He tapped a key. Nothing happened.

'What's up?' demanded Fleur.

'Nothing. Must have gone into hibernation,' said Vince.

'Let me see.'

She touched a couple of keys, frowned, picked up the laptop and shook it in his face.

'You're on battery and you've run the batteries flat. Why didn't you plug it in, for God's sake?'

'The mains lead's in your room and I didn't want to disturb you,' he explained. 'I was just being thoughtful.'

'No you weren't. Thoughtful means being full of thought. How come the batteries have run flat anyway? Should have lasted another hour at least, just checking the tracker. What the hell have you been doing, Vince? Have you been downloading your mucky videos again?'

'No,' he denied unconvincingly. 'Maybe I did do a bit of surfing for a couple of minutes; it gets boring just looking at that green blob all the time, especially when it isn't moving . . . '

'It'll be moving now!' she screamed at him. 'Only we can't see it.'

'Hey, I'm sorry . . . '

She wasn't listening. She unlocked the communicating door, went through into her own room and returned with the mains lead. Stooping, she dragged the bedside lamp out of its socket and inserted the plug. Then she connected the other end to the computer.

It glowed back into life. She went online, entered the tracker code.

The sat-map came up. The green dot was stationary.

'There,' said Vince triumphantly. 'No problem. She's stopped.'

'And that's not a problem?' said Fleur, studying the screen closely. 'Why do you think she's stopped, Vince?'

'Run out of petrol? Needs a slash?'

'How about she's stopped because she's met up with her longlost husband and they're sitting in her car, having a nice heart-to-heart?'

She went into her room again, this time returning with an OS map.

'Now let's see exactly where they are. Got you! Come on, it's going to take us about twenty minutes, half an hour, depending on traffic. Let's hope she doesn't move off before we get there!'

'No problem,' said Vince. 'We can track her through the laptop.'

'And how are we going to manage that, Vince? You ran the battery flat, remember? It won't work in the car.'

'It's working here,' objected Vince.

'Great. So all we've got to do is find a way of moving the hotel! Come on!'

'So I shan't bring the laptop then?'

She felt an urge to scream at him, but what was the point?

'Shove it under the bed out of the way. Leave it switched on. At least it'll be charging up the battery while we're out. Though let's hope we get there quick enough not to need it again.'

She led the way out of the door. Vince followed. They didn't wait for the lift but hurried down the stairs, not the main stairway but a service stair that would bring them out at the rear of the hotel, near the car-park entrance.

Of course, thought Fleur, if Gina Wolfe had come down this way, she wouldn't have passed across Vince's line of vision. Why hadn't she thought of that earlier? Why had she sat in the garden, smoking and babbling on about Spain, instead of heading straight out into the car park to confirm the Nissan was still there?

Because you're sick, she answered herself. Because you're losing the capacity to think straight. Or to walk straight, for that matter, she thought, staggering a little as she hurried towards the VW.

Behind her, Vince noticed the stagger. It wasn't the first time he'd seen it. Not so nimble on her pegs as she used to be, he thought. With anyone else he'd have suspected too much booze, but not Fleur. Probably her age; she was in her forties now. Probably a woman's thing, that stuff that happened when they stopped having their periods.

It would pass, he told himself confidently. One thing you could be sure of with Fleur, she wouldn't go funny with it like some women did. No, not good old Fleur. She'd deal with it, take it in her stride. He hadn't learned much in his life, but one thing he had learned.

No matter what shit came at him, he could always rely on Fleur.

16.41–17.15

When Dalziel and Pascoe entered the Keldale, they found Seymour waiting for them.

Clearly not certain who he should be reporting to, he diplomatically aimed at a spot midway between their heads and said, 'It's Room 25, sir. I've got it sealed off like you said till the SOCO team gets here. Talking of which, the manager would like a word. Think he's a bit worried about SOCO worrying the guests.'

'You'd best see to that, Pete,' said Dalziel. This was ambiguous, both deferring and commanding. It was also suspicious as Lionel Lee, the manager, was, like most men in charge of premises licensed to sell intoxicating liquor, a close acquaintance of the Fat Man's. But the suspicion didn't really surface till Pascoe emerged from Lee's office to find Seymour alone.

'Where is he?' he demanded.

'The Super took the key and said he'd go on up,' explained the DC nervously. The Dalziel/ Pascoe relationship was a much-favoured subject for analysis among the intellectuals of the locker room, but the favoured conclusion was they didn't know what the fuck was going on.

Pascoe bit back an irritated response. How could he expect a lowly DC to exert control where chief constables had failed? A moment

298

later he was glad of his restraint when Seymour said, 'By the way, sir, when I did a quick check round the room, I came across this tucked behind the pillows.'

He took a small evidence bag out of his pocket and handed it over, his face a mask of studied neutrality.

Pascoe examined it for a moment then said, 'Thanks, Dennis. You wait in the car park for SOCO. Take them up in the service lift; let's keep the management happy, eh? I may want to buy you a drink here some day.'

Which, interpreted, meant, You've done well, but this is between us, OK?

He found Dalziel standing in Gina Wolfe's room looking pensively at the bed.

Pascoe said, 'No, she didn't find it, Andy. Seymour did.'

He held up the plastic bag.

It contained a note scrawled in a hand as familiar to members of Mid-Yorkshire CID as their own.

It read *Sorry to pass out on you, put it down to old age. Next time I'll try to stay awake! I'll be in touch. A.*

'I did wonder,' said Dalziel, apparently unfazed. 'Was a time when Dennis would have handed it over to me.'

'*Tempora mutantur*,' said Pascoe, who often armoured himself with pedantry in anticipation of a verbal skirmish with the Fat Man. 'So you thought you'd get up here first just in case it was still lying around. And your exquisite reason, knight?'

'Nowt that you'd call exquisite, but reason enough,' said Dalziel. 'It's nothing to do with the case, but it could be misinterpreted.'

The two men stood and looked at each other. Dalziel was not used to feeling vulnerable but he felt vulnerable now. That his unofficial activities might have put a junior officer at risk was bad enough. The fact that he admitted to sleeping off an excessively vinous lunch in a suspect's hotel room made matters worse. But the inference drawable from the note that he had passed out as he attempted to have sex with Gina, still giving her the time to head out to Loudwater Villas and confront her errant husband, added an element of black farce that he might find hard to survive both personally and professionally.

To a ruthless rival to his throne, this was a perfect opportunity to achieve his goal with the gentlest of pushes. Even someone as upright and decent as Peter Pascoe had to do nothing but play things by the book to make his boss's position very difficult.

Pascoe put the bag back in his pocket and said wearily, 'From now on, just talk to me, Andy, OK? One more time I'm left not knowing what's going on will be one time too many. Now bugger off out of here. I'll see you downstairs.'

Dalziel left. He felt good, not because of what he'd done — nothing to feel good about there — but because of his part in making Pascoe what he'd become. It was going to be hard, but it was time to let go. Not step aside, that would be too easy. And in any case, he was far from ready to step aside. This too would pass and the *tempora* would bloody well *mutantur* back again! But his first task once he was safely back on the throne must be to make sure his loyal lieutenant got lift-off.

Meanwhile he was a cop and he was still on the case.

He went downstairs to reception and asked the woman on duty to get hold of the car-park security video for that afternoon. While she was sorting that, he checked the record of incoming phone calls and made a couple of notes. The receptionist then took him into her inner office where she'd linked the car-park video to her computer. It was a good system. When they'd had their bit of bother a year back, he'd read the riot act to Lionel Lee. 'You'd not give your guests nylon sheets and scratchy bog-paper, would you? So why sell 'em short with cheap security?' It was a message Lee had taken to heart. There'd been an attempt to break into the hotel office only last weekend, but it had been thwarted by the new levels of security installed since Dalziel's lecture.

First he checked the period immediately after Gina had thrown him out of her bedroom. It didn't take long to spot her departure less than thirty minutes after he'd left. Then he went right back to lunchtime and studied what he found there with great interest.

'Anything else I can help you with, just ask, won't you?' murmured the receptionist in his ear. She was keen to know what was going on.

'Can I print some stills from this video?' he asked.

301

'Of course. Like me to do it for you?'

She leaned over him, her soft bosom resting on his broad shoulder.

'There,' she said huskily. 'Anything else you want?'

She were either very nosy or she liked the cut of his rig. Odds on the former, but he didn't have time to find out.

'Aye,' said Dalziel. 'That lad, Pietro, who were in charge of the terrace this lunchtime, he still around?'

While the woman was checking that, he helped himself to the guest registration book. One thing he found there made him laugh out loud, causing the receptionist to glance at him curiously. Get a grip! he admonished himself. This is serious business.

Pietro arrived and Dalziel sat down with him in the reception lounge. As he sank into the chair, his elephantine buttocks obliterated the imprint left by Vince Delay a little time before.

'Right,' said the Fat Man. 'I've got a lot of questions and not much time, so let's not bugger about. Answer me straight and you and me will stay friends, and I'm a good friend to a likely lad. But fuck me around and tha'll be on an early boat back home to sunny Italy, OK?'

'Bus, sir.'

'Eh?'

'It' ud be a bus back home to 'uddersfield.'

His accent had changed from Mediterranean mandolin to Yorkshire tuba.

Dalziel laughed out loud.

'I think thee and me are going to get along

famously,' he said. 'First, who does the table selection on the terrace at lunchtime?'

'That would be me, sir. Guests state their preference and I try to oblige them.'

'So how come I got the best table overlooking the garden even though it weren't booked till this morning?'

'That were Mr Lee, the manager. He told me to change it.'

'That must have meant you bumping some poor sod.'

'Yes, sir. A Mr and Mrs Williams. They're staying at the hotel.'

Dalziel nodded, unsurprised, and said, 'Take a look at these pictures. Recognize any of 'em?'

He showed him the photos he'd printed from the security video.

Pietro picked out three faces he recognized as belonging to hotel guests.

'Any of them on the terrace at lunchtime?'

'The only one I can be sure of is Mr Delay,' said Pietro. 'Him and his sister.'

'Have they been staying here long?'

'A week, I think.'

'Oh aye?' said the Fat Man, rather disappointed. 'But they were definitely around at lunchtime?'

'Yes, sir. On the upper terrace. They left without having their puddings.'

'More fools them, Notice a young lass by herself? Brown hair, nice knockers.'

Pietro grinned.

'Yes, I did. She were another one who shot off before her order came.'

They spoke a little longer, after which Dalziel took out his mobile and began making calls.

When Pascoe joined him a few minutes later, Dalziel said, 'Gina Wolfe had a call fifteen minutes after I left. I've checked the number. Unregistered pay-as-you-go. A few minutes later she rang down to say she were leaving. She used their express check-out which meant she didn't have to come down to the desk. Security video shows her in the car park at twenty past four. She seems to be checking around like she's worried someone might be watching her. Then she drives away.'

'But where to? No word that she's been spotted yet?'

'If she stays on the main roads, we'll soon have her,' said Dalziel confidently.

'Fine. Anything else?'

'Mebbe.'

Pascoe gave him his more-in-sorrow-than-in-anger look and the Fat Man said, 'Nay, lad, I'm not holding out on you. Just I don't want to waste time chatting about stuff that may be owt or nowt till I'm sure of it.'

Pascoe was saved from having to decide whether to make a stand or not by his phone ringing.

He looked at the display and saw it was Wield.

'Pete,' said the sergeant, 'we've got a problem.'

Pascoe listened for a while, then said, 'He's talking, you say?'

'Real gabby. It's shutting him up that's going to be hard.'

'Let him talk all he wants. I'll be back soon as I can.'

He switched off and said, 'We're needed back at Loudwater. It looks like our corpse is neither Watkins, the flat tenant, who has appeared on the scene, nor indeed a Wolfe in borrowed hair. Andy, have you been practising not looking surprised?'

'No. Just comes natural, specially when I'm not.'

'Is that so? I thought we'd entered on a new era of transparency.'

'Nay, lad,' protested the Fat Man, 'I'm not holding owt back. I can't help it if occasionally I make a lucky guess.'

'And in this case, what might your guess be?'

'About the dead 'un? I'd say, Welsh and a journalist. Nay, don't lose your rag, Pete. You know me, always a lucky guesser.'

'I'll tell you one thing, Andy, much more of this and your luck is really going to run out,' said Pascoe in a low, hard voice.

'Pete, trust me. I'll never keep owt from you that I think you need to know, OK? Now you'll be wanting to get back there quick to talk to this Watkins. I'll join you soon as I can. Couple of things I need to check first. OK?'

'OK,' said Pascoe reluctantly. 'But don't make me come looking for you, Andy.'

The two men stood staring at each other for a long moment.

It was Dalziel who turned away.

16.42–18.05

Nye Glendower drove westward along the roads of Mid-Yorkshire at a moderate speed in keeping with his standing as a respected Chief Constable and pillar of a community that expected its pillars to be strong and upright and based on good Welsh granite. After a few minutes his mirror showed him a white Mondeo coming up fast behind him.

He gave a wave and for an hour they drove in close convoy. Finally, with the Yorkshire border behind him and the declining sun beginning to be a trouble to his eyes, he signalled left to pull into a lay-by separated from the main road by a line of scrubby trees.

The Mondeo drew in behind him. Its driver got out. Glendower followed suit and stood by the X5 as she came towards him.

Myfanwy Baugh, Chief Executive of the Cambrian NHS Trust, a solidly built woman in her early fifties with a natural authority and unbending will that made many a man who'd tasted the sadness of her might say grudgingly, 'That Myfanwy, she's got balls.'

But Nye Glendower knew she hadn't.

She opened her mouth to speak. He took her in his arms and stopped her tongue with his.

After a long moment she pushed him away

and said, 'Somebody might see us.'

'All racing home,' he said, indicating the traffic flashing past beyond the trees. 'Anyway, who's to know who we are round here?'

'That fat slob you were talking to, for one. It was that cop who ruined our lunch, wasn't it?'

'The same. Bad luck he should have been in the car park just then. Could have been worse, though. He could have seen the two of us together. You did well to hang back, Myfi.'

'Is that meant to flatter me? Nye, the point of going to that dump was that nobody knew either of us there and we'd be able to relax for a change. Instead of which we end up doing a runner like a couple of petty crooks!'

'Hey, we didn't do a runner, I paid the bill, girl!' he laughed. 'Listen, there's nothing to worry about. Just a precaution once I got a sniff there was some sort of op going on round the hotel. Anyway, the fat bastard's just filling in time till he gets his pension, so forget him. Point is, we've still got a night in hand. I was thinking maybe head down into the Peak District? Should get in somewhere nice, Sunday evening, lot of weekenders will have checked out. And it's on our way home, more or less.'

She was shaking her head emphatically.

'I think we should head home now, Nye. We've got away with one close encounter. Let's not push our luck.'

He didn't argue. Myfanwy Baugh hadn't got where she was without being able to signal when she'd made up her mind and wasn't to be budged.

But he too had had to fight his way up the rocky promotion mountain, and he hadn't got to the top without learning that the way to deal with immoveable obstacles was to push them in a new direction.

He opened the rear door of the X5.

'OK,' he said. 'But get in. Let's at least say goodbye properly.'

She said, '*Here?* You must be mad!'

But she wasn't resisting as he put his arms round her thighs, lifted her up and laid her across the back seat, in the process forcing her short skirt up around her buttocks.

He said, 'See you're wearing my favourites, girl. You know what the red silk does to me. What were you thinking when you put them on, eh?'

'For God's sake get in and close the door,' she said hoarsely. 'And we'll have to make it quick.'

He smiled as he pulled the door to behind him. He knew his Myfi. Once they got started, goodbye caution. She'd want it to last as long as he could make it last.

For a brief moment his mind went back to his meeting with Andy Dalziel. They were of an age and there had been a time when Dalziel was regarded as the sharpest knife in the box, the man with the starry future. But you never knew what time was going to do to a man. It had been a shock to see what he'd become — a grampus puffing around in a very small pond, a ready-to-be superannuated superintendent who let himself be bossed around by his pushy young DCI. What a contrast with his own continuing rise to the stellar heights! What pain it must have caused Dalziel to come across his contemporary in the car park of a posh hotel, stacking designer luggage into an expensive car, and looking at least a decade younger than the poor fat sod!

And if he could see me now, he thought triumphantly, still getting it on in the back seat with a sexually rampant woman, he'd probably have a heart attack!

Then the red silk panties slid down to Myfi's ankles and Aneurin Glendower erased all thought of Andy Dalziel from his mind forever.

Or at least for a minute and a half.

For it can't have been much longer than that before the rear door was pulled open and a polite but forceful cough halted him in mid-stroke with Myfanwy's legs round his neck, one of her feet waving the red panties like a May Day banner.

He turned his head, not without difficulty — she was a strong woman — and managed to bring one angry eye to bear on the intruder.

He saw a uniformed constable standing to attention, his gaze firmly fixed somewhere above the car roof. Behind him alongside a police Range Rover stood another constable, his face bearing the emotionless unfocused look that can only be put there by a waxwork sculptor, or by the awareness that, if you let it relax for a millisec, you will collapse to the ground and roll around in fits of ungovernable laughter.

'Chief Constable Glendower, sir?' said the first constable in a broad Lancashire accent. 'Sorry to bother you, sir, but there's an urgent message from Detective Superintendent Dalziel of Mid-Yorkshire CID. He'd like for you to ring him. As soon as it's at all convenient. I've got his number here. If you've got a pen handy. Sir.'

Behind him the other constable gave up, did a smart right turn and marched away, stuffing his fist into his mouth. Out of the gathering dusk came a noise like the hoarse barking of a hyena.

At last Glendower found his voice.

'Shut . . . the . . . fucking . . . door!' he said.

17.35–17.55

When Mrs Esmé Sheridan opened her door, the sight that met her eyes made her recoil in shock. But indignation triumphed over fear and, pausing only to select a walking stick from the elephant-foot umbrella stand in her hallway, she began to advance, crying, 'You vile creature. Not content with making our pavements unsafe to walk along, you now dare to defile our very doorsteps! Go away or I shall summon the constabulary.'

'Madam, I am the constabulary,' boomed Andy Dalziel, holding his warrant card before him like a talisman. 'I've been sent by the Chief Constable to thank you personally and explain to you exactly what's going on.'

It took several more minutes to convince her that this wasn't simply a cunning masquerade to gain admittance to her house and have his wicked way with her, and even when she finally allowed him in, she insisted on leaving the front door wide open.

'Now the thing is this, Esmé . . . can I call you Esmé?'

'No, you may not,' she said emphatically. 'I deplore this instant familiarity which is not the least of the evils America has infected us with.'

'Sorry, luv . . . I mean, Mrs Sheridan. Like I

were saying, this morning when you saw me I were on an op — that's an operation . . . '

'Yes, yes, I know what an op is. Just because I deplore many modern trends does not mean I am out of touch. I feel it is my duty to keep up with what transpires in the world about me, even if it means watching plays and films of dubious artistic merit and ambiguous moral import.'

Dalziel had noted the 42-inch HD plasma screen that struck a rather jarring note in the stolidly Victorian décor of the room. God knows what she'd been watching the previous night to stimulate her lively imagination into identifying him as a kerbcrawler at half past eight this morning!

'Nay, that's my point,' said Dalziel. 'Bright as a button, that's how they described you after you called in at the nick . . . that's the . . . well, tha'll likely know what it is. And that's why I'm here. This morning, like I say, I were undercover following a suspect and somehow or other they got behind me . . . '

'As in *Bullitt*,' she said. 'Though, now I come to think of it, in that case it was the policeman being followed who managed to get behind the criminals.'

She looked at him dubiously as if her earlier fears were reasserting themselves, and he said quickly, 'Aye, likely he were a lot sharper than me.'

Now she nodded as if this were a persuasive argument and said, 'So because of your incompetence, the op went pear-shaped. You see I'm completely *au fait* with the *argot*, Superintendent. And now you are here to ask for my assistance, am I right?'

'Aye, spot on. They were right. Bright as a button. Down the nick, as well as giving them a fair description of me and my car, you mentioned that I weren't the only one to cause you concern in Holyclerk Street this morning, and I wondered if mebbe you could be as precise about some of the others.'

She said, 'Well, you of course were the only one who actually accosted me . . . why did you accost me, by the way?'

'Playing for time,' replied Dalziel, 'while I collected me thoughts. Sorry if I alarmed you. I were in disguise, of course, because of being under cover.'

She let out a little incredulous snort, then went on, 'But there were two other cars behind you. The first was bright red, low slung, of oriental manufacture, I would say. The driver was a woman. Blonde but not tarty. Behind her was a dark blue Volkswagen Golf — my nephew Justin drives a similar vehicle. Also driven by a woman, though it may have been a man in drab . . . '

'I think you mean drag,' corrected Dalziel daringly.

'Drag? Are you sure? Why should it be drag? Drab in its sense of slattern or whore has some kind of logical link. I think you may be misinformed there, Superintendent. Which would hardly surprise me. Where was I? Yes, the driver had a square, distinctly masculine cast of feature, but it was the passenger who caught my attention. He peered out at me through the open window and if ever I read the mind's construction in a face, there was evil intent in those grotesque features.'

'You'd know him again then?'

'Oh yes. Just as I was instantly able to recognize you, Superintendent.'

Deciding it was neither timely nor useful to protest this comparison, Dalziel reached into his inner pocket and drew out the envelope into which he'd put the stills from the Keldale carpark video.

Mrs Sheridan glanced at the pictures and pointed straight away at one of them.

'Yes, that's him,' she said. 'No doubt about it.'

'That's grand, Mrs Sheridan,' he said. 'You've been a great help.'

With any other little old lady he might have expressed his delight by giving her a hug and a smacking kiss on the forehead, but in this case his courage failed him and he contented himself with an effusion of thanks and flattery as he headed for the door.

'Pulled your irons out of the fire, have I?' she said, not without complacency when he was safely over the threshold. 'Good. Now I suggest you go home and remove the rest of your disguise before you spread any more despondency and alarm in the neighbourhood, Superintendent.'

The door closed firmly in his face.

They don't make 'em like that any more, thought Dalziel as he returned to his car. More's the pity!

He slid on to the driver's seat. He was getting somewhere at last. He had a face and he had a

314

name. He didn't yet have any direct connection between their owner and his lass, Ivor, lying in hospital with her head cracked open, but if there were a connection he reckoned he knew half a dozen not very subtle ways of finding it.

He realized he was gripping the steering wheel so tightly his knuckles were white. Deep breath, Andy, he admonished himself. This could still be owt or nowt. Deep breath, then drive back sedately to the Keldale.

But first he'd better bring Pascoe up to speed as promised, else the lad might go into one of his strops.

He took out his phone, but before he could thumb in the number, it rang again.

For a moment he was tempted to hurl it out of the window.

The bloody things had their uses, but sometimes they got on his wick end!

He bellowed, 'What?' into it, listened, then said, 'Mick, where the hell have you been? We got problems.'

Mick Purdy awoke with a start. The room was almost totally dark, but that meant nothing. In a job that turned night into day, the wise detective quickly learned to buy curtains that turned day into night.

He turned his head so he could see the digital read-out on his bedside alarm.

He'd been asleep for nearly two hours.

The deputy assistant commissioner who was his immediate boss had come into his office and found him slumped at his desk, his eyes open but clearly not focused on the file that lay open before him.

'Mick, what the fuck are you trying to do? It's been a very successful weekend and I don't want it ruined by having my main man drop dead of exhaustion. You've done all that was asked of you, now it's up to those plonkers at the CPS. You're out of here, and that's an order.'

It was nice to feel appreciated even if he'd hardly turned a page of the file since Gina had rung him.

His mind had chased round and round her account of her lunch with Dalziel. What was the fat bastard up to? All that stuff about dropping a water jug and getting lots of phone calls, what was that all about? Purdy knew what he'd have

316

done in Dalziel's shoes. Was he still the sharp knife he'd been when they met nine years ago or had time and his recent explosive experience blunted his edge? Drinking so much that he had to lie down suggested the latter. Back on the Bramshill course, he'd amazed everybody by the amount he could put away without the least visible reaction. Or maybe this present debility had been a ruse to get access to Gina's room. Maybe as soon as she left him there alone, he'd been rifling through her stuff.

His attempts at analysis, as non-productive as the efforts of a hamster on a wheel, only added to his sense of exhaustion, and he was almost comatose when the AC had intervened.

He'd come home and fallen on to his bed. His two hours' sleep felt like two minutes and he woke to find his mind still trapped on the hamster wheel.

He switched on a bedside lamp and checked his mobile, hoping to find Gina might have rung again.

There was a message, but not from her.

Andy Dalziel.

He listened.

'Don't care if you're saving the fucking universe from aliens, ring me!'

Not a friendly chat then, not a simple progress report. One thing he was certain of was that the Fat Man didn't do pointless hysteria. Something had happened. He tried Gina's number without any expectation of a reply. When he got the answer service, he said, 'Ring me. Please. Soon as you can.'

317

Then he accessed Dalziel's message again, but he didn't press the hash key to return the call. Between sensing and knowing disaster there's a space where a man can linger, can even imagine he might be able to take a backward step and press the *delete* button.

He wished his head were clearer. He went to the bathroom and threw handfuls of cold water over his face. God, how great it must be to have a job that didn't leave you constantly fatigued. It wasn't just the bastards you were working against but the bastards you were working with that demanded your total concentration. Sleep and someone would fuck you! Practise and a steady supply of Provigil had minimized his rest needs and helped his nimble progress up the main-mast of promotion. With luck — and luck was what it came down to when you got within striking distance of the top — one day soon he might be able to haul himself into the secure crow's nest of deputy assistant commissioner level.

But sometimes when the seas got rough and your fingers got cold, the deck below became a small round mouth seductively inviting you to fall.

Jesus! Where did that come from? he asked himself. It's all them books Gina has cluttering up the place. You'll be writing poetry next!

He'd managed to push Gina to the back of that space for a nanosecond, but here she was again. There was nowhere to escape to. He needed to know what was going on, and there was only one way to find out.

He went back into his messages, listened to Dalziel again, then pressed hash.

After a moment a familiar voice boomed, 'What?'

'Andy, it's Mick.'

'Mick, where the hell have you been? We've got problems.'

'Problems? Has something happened to Gina?' His voice on a rising scale.

'Don't get your knickers in a twist, lad,' said Dalziel. 'She's checked out of her hotel, that's all. When did you last talk to her, Mick?'

'This afternoon. She said you'd crashed out on her bed. Jesus, Andy, I thought you were having lunch with her to get on the case, not to get pissed!'

'I wasn't pissed,' retorted Dalziel defensively. 'And I was on the case — and a funny fucking case it's turning out to be. Let me tell you about it. I'd set one of my WDCs to watch us, and what she spotted was some sod bugging us.'

'Bugging? You sure?'

'Of course I'm bloody sure. You think I'm playing games? Just listen to what happened next and then tell me I'm playing games! When the bugger left, my girl went after him. An hour or so later, the pair of them were found in his flat, her with her head cracked open, him with half of his face blown off. In the meantime, Gina checked out of the hotel and took off.'

'Oh Christ,' said Purdy. Suddenly that space between guessing and knowing seemed very attractive. This was worse than his worst imaginings.

319

'Mick, you still there?'

'Yes,' he said, trying to keep his voice controlled and professional. 'Listen, have you put a call out on Gina?'

'Now why should we do that, Mick? Presumably she's on her way home.'

Purdy tried to sound casual, wasn't sure if he succeeded.

'I just thought you'd want to talk to her, in connection with this case of yours.'

'The murder? You mean in case the dead man turns out to be Alex Wolfe? You want us to put out a call on her as a suspect?'

Is he taking the piss? thought Purdy.

'Don't be stupid. Of course it's not Alex. I mean, why should it be?'

'No reason. Oh, by the way, Mick. Does the name Delay mean owt to you? Brother and sister, Fleur and Vincent?'

There was a long pause necessary for him to make sure the panic he felt surging up his gut didn't leak out through his larynx. Then he said, in a tone so controlled it was probably a bigger giveaway than panic, 'Why do you ask? Are they up there?'

'Aye, Been staying at the Keldale for a week now. So you do know them then?'

'Know of them. There's a Fleur Delay used to work for Goldie Gidman. Looked after his finances for years, both the stuff he let the taxman see and the stuff he didn't. As he got bigger and went legit, Fleur dropped out of the picture. Spending more time with her family, to coin a phrase.'

'Her family being this Vince?'

'That's right. Got a lot of form, but nothing recently to my knowledge. Listen, Andy, if they're around, could just be coincidence, but I'd give them a pull. Keep them close. But you've probably got that organized anyway, haven't you?'

He found he couldn't — in fact no longer wanted to — keep the deep concern out of his voice.

'Don't worry, lad,' said Dalziel. 'We've got 'em in our sights.'

'Good. And listen, Andy, do me a favour. Put out that call on Gina anyway. Please.'

'OK, no need to get on your knees. I'll make sure my lads are out there looking for her. If you make contact first, be sure to let me know, all right?'

'Straight away. And you'll get in touch with me, right?'

'Of course I will. First on my list. OK, Mick, got to go now. Unless there's anything else you want to tell me . . . ?'

'I don't think so. Andy, thanks for putting me in the picture. I'll not forget it.'

'I'll not let you. And I'll try to keep you posted. But, Mick, remember this is official now, so at some point we may need to talk to you officially. You hear what I'm saying? Get your act together. Cheers.'

The line went dead.

Purdy switched off, hurled the phone on to his bed, and let out a sobbing, snarling cry that contained all the doubt, anger and fear that had been repressed during the conversation. It made him feel better, but not much.

He retrieved the phone and tried Gina's number again. Still nothing. He brought up another name and looked at it for a while before cancelling.

Some things needed to be done face to face.

He went back into the bathroom, turned the shower on cold and stripped off. From the wall cabinet he took a small plastic bottle, shook a couple of Provigils into his hand, tossed them into his mouth then stepped under the jets, his head thrown back to let the icy water drive the tablets down his throat.

Until this lot got sorted, until he knew where Gina was and that she was safe, sleep wasn't an option.

Edgar Wield was not a man who boasted about his skills, but he took a quiet pride in his ability to get the best out of a witness. Dalziel's analysis of his success was typically direct.

'The bugger's got a head start, hasn't he? Seeing yon face t'other side of the table is like being shown the torture kit in the Tower of London. It doesn't half loosen the tongue!'

After viewing the documentation produced by the new arrival to prove that he was in fact Alun Gruffud Watkins of 39 Loudwater Villas, Wield had rung Pascoe then settled down to extract a detailed statement. The trouble was that, after learning what had happened in his apartment, Watkins's tongue was not so much loosened as liberated. It was hard to get him to stop talking, which might not have been so bad if he hadn't moved rapidly from offering answers to requiring them. His favourite, most frequently iterated question was, 'Why will you not let me see the body?' and he grew progressively more irritated each time Wield steered him away from the topic.

He was seated in the caravan, Wield facing him, his back to the window, which any fan of crime fiction knows is the approved interrogation set-up with the interrogator's face in shadow and the light streaming into the interrogatee's eyes.

It has the disadvantage that the latter can see out of the window while the former can't. So it was that over the sergeant's shoulder, Watkins saw an ambulance arrive and two paramedics enter the building, bearing a stretcher.

He stood up, saying, 'I need a breath of air,' went to the door, jumped down from the caravan, and then he was off and running towards the Villas.

Wield was fit and had the high muscular tone of a sprinter, but even moving at full speed he didn't get the man in his sights till he burst through on to the second floor and saw him vanishing into his apartment behind the stretcher bearers.

Jennison was inside, holding the door open, so he couldn't be blamed for not bringing Watkins to a halt. But once in the room, no human agency was needed.

The sight of the near faceless body lying on the floor stopped him in his tracks.

'Oh Christ,' he said. 'Oh Christ.'

His legs were buckling and Wield and Jennison had to practically carry him back down the stairs and out into the open air, which he drew into his lungs in great rasping gulps.

A constable came hurrying from the caravan.

'Sarge,' he said, 'there's a TV crew turned up at the barrier.'

It was bound to happen sooner or later, thought Wield. Sooner, if Mrs Dutta had anything to do with it. Thank God he'd ordered the tape to be replaced by a metal barrier and removed Hector from duty. He'd have probably waved the TV van through!

But even from a distance their cameras would be nosing up close.

He said, 'Let's get you back into the caravan, sir. What you need is a cup of hot sweet tea. Give him a hand, lad.'

By the time Pascoe arrived a few minutes later, the Welshman was looking a lot better, but he hadn't spoken another word. Wield had seen this kind of reaction before — imminence to tragedy triggering logorrhoea, sight of a bloody corpse producing lingual paralysis. But Wield's skill at plucking relevant facts from a flood of verbiage meant he already had plenty of information to offer the DCI.

The two policemen stood outside the caravan. It had a door at the back as well as at the side, so they were able to descend unseen by the inquisitive media cameras. Sunset was over an hour away, but the day was clearly in decline. A light mist rising from the river turned the derelict mills on the far side into romantic ruins. The air still retained something of its earlier warmth but there was in it a hint of a chilly night to come.

Pascoe said, 'Right, Wieldy, so now it looks like we've got ourselves a dead journalist. Let's have the grisly detail.'

Wield said, 'Like I told you, the guy in the caravan is this Alun Gruffud Watkins the Duttas told us about. Age twenty-three, he works as a rep for Infield-Centurion, the agricultural supplies company. The dead man, subject to

325

forensic confirmation, seems likely to be Gareth Jones, nineteen, a reporter with the *Mid-Wales Examiner*. He has been staying with Mr Watkins since Friday last.'

He paused, seeing that Pascoe had a question. He knew what the question was going to be, but he also knew that, whether dealing with superiors or suspects, it generally paid to give the impression of genuine dialogue.

Pascoe said, 'This Watkins, how's he look?'

Not an enquiry after the man's health but his status. Witness or suspect.

Wield said, 'Mr Watkins has been working this weekend. He left on Friday lunchtime and has not been back since. I have the address of the farm he claims to have been visiting this afternoon. It's just south of Darlington. I've got the locals taking a statement, but a telephone call has confirmed Mr Watkins' story that he was there from two until four thirty, which takes him out of the frame.

'He was here when Jones arrived on Friday morning. The young man's old banger just made it and Watkins got a local garage to send someone round to check it. They took one look and said they would need to take it in, start work on it straight away and hopefully finish on Monday morning. Mr Watkins didn't want to leave his friend without transport so he offered him the use of the Yamaha which he normally takes with him in the back of his van on his trips.'

'So we've got Watkins out of the frame,' said Pascoe. 'And we know how Jones came to be riding his bike. But why, if his friend was coming for the weekend, did Watkins take off and leave him?'

'Because Jones invited himself,' said the sergeant. 'He rang up mid-week to say he had to be in Mid-Yorkshire at the weekend and asked if he could doss down on Watkins's floor. Watkins said he could do better than that, Jones was welcome to his bed as he was going to be away. I asked him if he knew why his friend was coming here. He said Jones indicated he was working on a story. No details and he didn't press.'

Pascoe said sceptically, 'Didn't press? And him an old mate?'

Wield said, 'Seems that Jones's older brother, Gwyn, is an investigative reporter . . . '

He paused to see if this rang a bell.

Pascoe said, 'Gwyn Jones, you mean, on the *Daily Messenger*?'

'That's the one,' said Wield. 'Mr Watkins knows the Jones family well, he's from the same village, three years younger than Gwyn and the same older than Gareth. When Gwyn started in journalism, he was always quoting some famous reporter who said, Never tell your story till it's ready to be told. That became Gareth's motto too when he started following in big brother's footsteps. So Watkins reckoned asking questions was pointless. Also, he was in a hurry.'

'Does he work a lot at weekends then?' asked Pascoe.

'Business and pleasure, I gathered. Farming's a seven-day job, so the farmers don't mind. And I'd guess he's got at least a couple of girlfriends scattered around the county that he likes to keep happy. He's a bit of a chancer, I'd say. That so-called apartment's pretty basic, and he's got a camp bed in the back of his van. But when I was checking his laptop, I found he'd got templates for the letterheads and account invoices of good class hotels all over the North, plus several local garages. Looking at the expense claims he makes to Infield-Centurion could be instructive.'

'Perhaps, but not to us. Not unless we need something to put a bit of pressure on the guy,' said Pascoe. 'Let's concentrate on making sense of what we've got, which appears to be a young journalist come all the way from Wales to snoop around this woman, Gina Wolfe. Does that make sense to you?'

'Mebbe. Snooping around's what journalists do, isn't it?' said Wield.

'I can't see how there's anything here to interest the readers of the *Mid-Wales Examiner*,' retorted Pascoe.

'What if he weren't working for his local rag? What if he were doing a bit of moonlighting on brother Gwyn's behalf?' said Wield. 'Something to do with the Gidmans, for instance? That would really get the *Messenger*'s sensors twitching.'

'Maybe,' said Pascoe thoughtfully. 'I've got a feeling we need to tread carefully here, Wieldy.'

'Not worried about treading on someone's toes, are you?' said the sergeant, regarding him doubtfully.

'No, but I'm worried about being warned off anyone's toes before I've had the chance to give them a good treading,' grinned Pascoe. 'Didn't you say that when you started digging for info about Macavity, you felt things had been very carefully tidied up? From what I've read about him, this Goldie Gidman wields a lot of influence now. Any whiff of a scandal touching him, them buggers in London will be covering themselves like tarts in a raided brothel!'

Wield hid a smile. There were times when Pete sounded so like the Fat Man it was hard to tell the difference.

'What?' demanded Pascoe, eyeing him sharply.

This was another area where they'd grown together, thought the sergeant. Was a time when only Dalziel came close to being able to read his face, but now the DCI was starting to get the knack.

As he opened his mouth to prevaricate, the caravan door burst open and DC Bowler jumped down the steps, his face split by a huge smile.

'Just had a bulletin from the hospital, sir. Seems Shirley's woken up and they say she knows who she is and where she is and everything. Probably too woozy to answer questions before tomorrow, but she's definitely off the critical list. She's going to be all right, sir!'

It was good to see his pleasure. Bowler and Novello were fierce rivals in their work, each determined to be the leader in the race for advancement. But when it came to mutual support and comfort in times of trouble, neither had ever been found wanting.

'Great news, Hat,' said Pascoe. 'Spread it around, will you.'

'The Super will be mighty relieved to hear that,' said Wield after the DC had gone back into the caravan.

'Yes. I must remember to tell him,' said Pascoe, but not in a tone which suggested putting the Fat Man out of his misery was a high priority.

Oh dear, thought the sergeant. He's really got it in for Andy at the moment. OK, so the fat sod has it coming to him, but the sooner these two get themselves sorted, the better it will be for all of us.

As he mused on how he might contribute to establishing peace in our time, Pascoe's phone rang.

'Talk of the devil,' he said, glancing at it. 'Hi, Andy. How's it going?'

Friendly informal, or familiar impertinent? wondered Wield.

Then he saw Pascoe's expression change as he listened, and he knew it didn't matter which.

'No, Andy, for God's sake, wait for me to . . . Andy? Andy!'

He took the phone from his ear and said, 'The bastard's rung off.'

'What did he say?' demanded Wield.

'He said he thinks he knows who killed Jones and attacked Novello, and the guy's staying at the Keldale, and he's on his way there now. He rang off before I could tell him to stay put till I whistled up an Armed Response Unit. You know what that means, Wieldy!'

'He's being John Wayne again,' said the sergeant. 'I'll organize the ARU and look after things here. You'll want to get back to the Keldale quick as you can, Pete.'

Sometimes you didn't have the time to wait and let them speak for themselves.

'Right, Wieldy. Thanks. I'll keep you posted.'

He headed off towards his car, trying not to look in too much of a hurry in case that aroused the watching journalists' interest.

'Hey, Pete, don't forget to tell him Novello's on the mend,' Wield called after him.

Over his shoulder Pascoe rasped, 'I'll do better than that, Wieldy. I'll maybe put him in the next bed so he can find out for himself.'

17.00–18.00

Maggie Pinchbeck sat in her flat, which in total occupied about the same space as Beanie Sample's bedroom, and downloaded Gwyn Jones's folder on Goldie Gidman. The greater part of it consisted of confidential police intelligence reports. It occurred to her that you'd probably get a longer sentence for having this stuff on your computer than you would for downloading child pornography.

She had her own file on Gidman, compiled when putting in her application for the post of Dave's PA. She had confronted the man himself and been impressed by the way he answered her questions. Subsequently she had found much to admire in him and she'd become really fond of his wife, Flo. Personal feelings apart, she knew that, when he became a donor, the Millbank mandarins would have sent in their most experienced investigators to run their beady eyes over him. They would probably have seen everything in Gwyn Jones's Gidman file and found nothing that came close to usable evidence of wrong-doing.

Nor did Maggie.

Yet underpinning everything in the folder was the unswerving certainty on the part of at least one policeman, Owen Mathias, that Goldie

Gidman was a villain. Operation Macavity had been Mathias's last throw of the dice before Gidman moved lock stock and barrel away from his shadowy beginnings into the sunlit uplands of the commercial Establishment.

And Macavity failed. Either because there was nothing to find, or because someone had been keeping Goldie two steps ahead of the investigation.

Mathias, naturally, had gone for the latter option. Internal Investigations had looked for the man most likely and picked on DI Alex Wolfe, although there did not seem to have been a scrap of real evidence against the man. Even his disappearance was less suggestive than it might have been when you considered the tragic circumstances of his family life.

She Googled Mathias. He had retired from the Met a year after the failure of Macavity. Perhaps that had contributed to his going. Or it might have been ill health as he died just a year later.

She guessed that he had been the source of all these confidential files in Jones's folder. And from him also she presumed Jones had inherited his strong antipathy towards the Gidmans, *père et fils*.

Not that it mattered why Jones was so obsessed. What mattered was where his investigation was going to lead.

She started reading again, this time selectively, making notes.

What she ended up with was just one name to put alongside that of Alex Wolfe.

Mick Purdy.

Purdy's name occurred only three times.

Thirty-odd years ago DC Purdy, no initial, had taken a witness statement — or rather an *alleged* witness statement, as the alleged witness denied having seen anything.

Forward a couple of decades and it's DCI Purdy now answering the questions from Internal Investigations and giving DI Alex Wolfe a glowing testimonial.

Jump to the present and Commander Mick Purdy is in a close relationship with Gina Wolfe, wife or, as she probably imagined until recently, widow of Alex Wolfe, tragic father and/or bent copper, who vanished without trace seven years back.

Did it mean anything? She knew from study and observation that many of the great political scandals arose because someone got spooked into believing that something meant something it didn't. And by the time the error was realized, it was too late, the hounds were loose, and they were not going to let themselves be whipped back into their kennel before they'd torn something to pieces.

Another chance to quiz Goldie might be helpful, but she could hardly ring him up and demand an interview.

She sipped on a can of orange juice and nibbled at a wedge of cheddar. It seemed a long time since she'd had a real meal. Coffee and a stale muffin for breakfast had been supplemented by a snatched half-sandwich at the Centre opening. She thought of ordering in a pizza. Then her phone rang.

It was Dave Gidman.

'Maggie, that stuff you said we should do tonight. Is it urgent?'

'Pretty urgent. Why?'

'Thing is, I'm not at home. I'm at Windrush House. Thought I'd probably spend the night here, make an early start in the morning. That way I can really explore Pappy's disgustingly expensive cellar. And I don't have to worry that my shower is suddenly going to freeze my bollocks off. You're sure the Chuckle Brothers are coming to fix it in the morning?'

'Yes, they'll be there, don't worry,' said Maggie. 'I can come up to Windrush now, if you like. Best we get things done before you start popping corks.'

'If you're sure it won't keep,' said Dave, without a great deal of enthusiasm.

'Unlike Goldie's wine, it certainly won't improve with keeping,' said Maggie. 'I'll be there about half six.'

She sat still for a moment after the call. Her earlier feeling that she was on some kind of lucky roll had evaporated. Or rather it had changed into a sense of being pushed towards some place she might not want to be. First the lying call from Jones just before she spoke to Beanie on the *Shah-Boat*. Then the email from Gem Huntley stoking up the Bitch's resentment again and giving her access to the Goldie folder.

And now, just when she'd been thinking another chat with Goldie Gidman would be useful to clear things up, Dave had given her the chance to revisit Windrush House.

Perhaps the wise move would be to delete the computer folder, ring Dave and say the morning would do after all, and settle down to a night with the telly.

Except she had a job to do, and she'd decided a long time ago that doing your chosen job was the only thing that made sense out of life.

Correction.

The only thing that might for some portion of three score years and ten delude you into thinking life made any sense at all.

4

furioso

Prelude

It is like waking.

Waking is odd. Sometimes sudden, like bursting through the surface of a pool after long minutes swimming under water. Light, air, sound, all in a terrifying triumphal confusion.

Sometimes so slow and gradual that there are stages when you still do not know if you wake or sleep.

He has been waking gradually.

That moment when he thought love and joy had brought him fully back to the waking world he now realizes was only a partial waking, the border country where dreams and reality meet and are still confused.

Such certainty of happiness, such a sense of renewal, of leaving the old far behind and striding forward joyously towards the new, had made him feel invulnerable, had led him to take the risk, which of course he did not see as a risk.

He sees it now.

As clearly as he sees the long straight road tapering downhill before him, empty except for the bright red car.

There is nothing in sight behind it. He has summoned it here to make sure it is alone. That piece of planning, of forethought, belongs to that old world he now knows he has to wake into. He hasn't left it behind him. He'd been fooling himself to think there was any way he could ever do that.

The final act of waking will take place when he speaks into his phone.

He waits. And he waits. Then he waits some more.

He tells himself this long wait is necessary. He has to be absolutely sure nothing has followed the red car. But he knows in truth it has nothing to do with being secure, at least not in that sense. He needs to be confident that the barriers he has built to protect his new world are strong enough to resist all onslaughts from the old.

So still he waits.

Then finally, knowing if he does not speak now, he may never speak, he raises the phone to his lips and says, 'Leave the car. Walk up the hill to the pub. Go to the car park.'

The late afternoon has an autumn chill at its edges. The car park has only a handful of cars in it, mostly parked near the entrance to the pub. His is parked in the corner furthest away. He is the only person out here.

He watches the blonde woman get out of the red car and start walking up the hill.

He puts his phone in his pocket and gets himself ready for the final waking.

'Hello, Gina.'

'Hello, Alex.'

This was the real, the final waking. Here they were, face to face, standing awkwardly, like a pair of youngsters uncertain where their first date is going to take them.

He made no attempt to touch her. A handshake would have been absurd, a kiss obscene. What would he say? What would for him be the most important thing to say?

He said, 'Let's sit in my car.'

She followed him to an old pale grey Astra in need of a good scrubbing. She remembered that when she used to complain about the condition of his vehicle, he'd grin and say, 'Man in my line of work wants a car nobody takes notice of.' She remembered . . .

She dug her nails into the palms of her hands. Once let memories take control and all the pain she had fought her way through seven years ago would come rushing in again, and she did not know if she had the strength to fight it a second time.

She got into the passenger seat, he got behind the wheel.

He looked straight ahead and said, 'I came to see you . . . to see how things were.'

She turned her head to look at him. It was definitely him, but different. Concentrate on the differences, they would help anchor her in the here and now. Head shaven, nothing remaining of those light fair locks so easily ruffled by even the gentlest breeze. Face slightly fatter. Strange. She would have looked for it to be thinner. She knew hers was.

She said, 'Last year.'

'Yes.'

'You were in the street . . . late one night . . .'

'Very late. I'd arrived earlier in the evening. No one was in. I waited. I needed to see . . . how things were . . .'

'And you saw me and Mick. You saw us embracing. You saw me take him into the house.'

'Yes.'

'How did that make you feel?'

He didn't answer and she said impatiently, 'It must have made you feel something.'

Interrogation. Take control, set the agenda. Mick had said that. Or was it Alex? Did it matter? Somehow it felt that it did.

He said, 'It made me feel relieved. It confirmed who I was, where I was.'

He turned his head now and looked straight at her.

'I'm sorry. I don't want to hurt you.'

'Not hurt me?' she cried incredulously. 'You disappeared. All those years without a sound. And suddenly you feel you don't want to hurt me!'

He shook his head and said, 'Back then, to start with I knew nothing, I was nothing. I didn't

342

think about hurting you because I didn't know anything about you. Or about anything. Even when things started coming back, they had nothing to do with feelings. For a long time I was just a sackful of fragments trying to learn how best to reassemble itself.'

Take control, set the agenda. Well, that didn't last long, she mocked herself.

'Fragments?' she echoed.

'I was in pieces. I didn't just run away and hide from you, Gina. I hid from myself. You have to believe that.'

'Of course I believed that,' she said. 'I couldn't let myself think you'd simply abandoned me without a word. I told myself it had to be something in your mind, or . . . '

'Or?'

'Or you were dead. I didn't think that at first. It took me a long time to come round to that. But after so many years of nothing, that became the easiest thing to believe.'

'So Mick was . . . '

'A long time after I gave up on you. Not until I was sure you were never coming back. You know what made me sure? It was seeing you that night in the street. For a moment you were so real I knew you had to be an illusion. Does that make sense?'

'Yes,' he said. 'Yes, because seeing you, and Mick, made me realize that to me, the new me, you were an illusion too.'

She wanted to scream, But I was there! I hadn't run away! You could have stepped out of the shadows and spoken to me, how the hell dare

343

you say that I was an illusion too?

Instead she said, 'And that's why you were relieved. Because you decided I was . . . what? Unreal? Unimportant? *What?*'

'You were with Mick. You'd moved on. You weren't letting the past rule your life. We had nothing to give each other except pain. Better for both of us that we ceased to exist to each other.'

They sat in silence for a moment, their eyes averted, then she burst out, 'So why are you here now, Alex? What's going on? You say you decided we had nothing to give each other but pain. So why the hell are we sitting here now?'

He turned his head to meet her gaze once more.

'Not to hurt you, believe me,' he said. 'I'm truly sorry . . . '

'Forget it,' she interrupted him. 'Just tell me what happened, what's happening, tell it straight. We'll save the apologies and recriminations for later.'

He looked relieved and settled back in his seat.

'OK,' he said. 'Except telling it straight isn't easy because of the gaps. All I can do is say what I know, or think I know. I was at home. Then I wasn't at home, I didn't know where home was, I didn't know who I was, or rather I suppose I knew I didn't want to know. Does that make sense? What I mean is, I knew I was lost, but I never felt an urge to go and ask anyone for help in finding me.'

'That sounds more like hiding than lost,' she said.

'Maybe. I had a lot to hide from.'

'Meaning?'

'Meaning Lucy's death.'

Someone had to say it. She was glad it was him. She'd always thought of herself as the stronger one, but seven years on it was Alex who had the strength to say it. She'd have thought this mention of her daughter's name would be the trigger to open the floodgates, but instead it seemed to give her the strength to maintain her control.

'And not just that, though that was at the centre of everything,' he went on. 'Once I knew she was ill, everything shifted, perspectives changed, I changed, you changed too I daresay, though I was too absorbed in my own pain to really see that. I thought that you were strong, that you had the strength to be resigned, but I see now that all that was just a different way of dealing with the pain.'

'Yes,' she said. 'Alex, this corruption thing, were you guilty?'

He looked at her impatiently, as if this were a diversion from the important stuff.

'Of course I was. You must have known that.'

She shook her head. Somehow this felt like the biggest shock of all, not because it was more important than anything else but because, amidst all the debris of their shattered lives, she'd always clung to the certainty of his innocence.

She said, 'I thought . . . I thought . . . '

'Come on!' he said. 'We needed the money. From the start we knew the good old NHS was only with us so far along the way. If we wanted the newest and the best treatment, we went looking for it, remember? Here, there, everywhere, chasing a hope. Hope doesn't come cheap. Where did you think the money was coming from?'

'You got a bank loan, you were applying for a mortgage on the house . . . '

'The loan went nowhere, mean bastards. And they were making me jump through all kinds of bureaucratic hoops to get a mortgage, then Gidman made his offer. There it was: instant money, no strings attached. I wasn't going to refuse.'

'No strings? Except your job!'

He laughed and said, 'I can't remember much, but one thing I do remember is how utterly unimportant the job seemed. Everything except Lucy was shadowy, unreal. The rest of the world was illusion. I could have seen it fall into ruin without a pang.'

'And then?'

'And then she died and I was left alone in this illusory world.'

'Alone? You weren't alone!' she cried. 'I was there.'

'No. You were alone too in your own world. It was a world I wasn't strong enough to join you in. I had nothing to stay for, everything to flee from.'

'Including the internal investigation,' she said, feeling a sudden urge to hurt him. 'Might have been illusory, but I daresay the prospect of being jailed as a bent cop must have played a small part in your decision.'

He shook his head violently.

'I told you, there wasn't any decision. What I did had nothing to do with the threats, not the rat pack's at the Yard, not Goldie Gidman's either . . . '

'He threatened you too, did he?' she mocked. 'What was he going to do? Beat you up? Break a few bones? Pain or prison? No wonder you ran!'

It was proving hard to stick to her own proposal that apologies and recriminations should be saved for later. In her heart she believed he had vanished because he had no choice, but all that pain he had caused her surely deserved some punishment?

He didn't react to her mockery but said quietly, 'I felt threatened, certainly. Not long after the investigation started, I was opening the garage door one morning. A car pulled up at the gate and a woman got out and called to me. She said she'd heard the house was up for sale, I told her it wasn't, and she looked up at the house and said it didn't matter anyway, now she'd seen it, she thought the property looked as if it might be a fire hazard. She'd known a lot of houses like this go up in flames, everyone inside burnt to death, just because the owner was careless. She hoped I wasn't a careless owner.'

'You're saying she was from Gidman?'

'His name was never mentioned, but oh yes, I knew she was from Gidman. I felt angry, but there was a man sitting in the car, watching us. He didn't look the kind of guy I wanted to see getting out of the car, so I said I wasn't the careless type. I was just about past caring then,

347

but you were still at home.'

'So you were thinking of me?' she said. 'What do you want me to do now? Swoon with gratitude?'

'I was almost at a point where I wasn't thinking of anyone,' he said. 'What I did had nothing to do with you or anyone. I did it because I couldn't help it. It was like teleporting in the space movies. I was there, I wasn't there. I was now, I was years in the future.'

She felt drained. She didn't know how long she'd be able to go on with this, couldn't imagine where it was going to end. Her throat felt very dry. She coughed and glanced out of the window towards the pub.

She said, 'I could do with a drink.'

'Better we're not seen together in there. They know me. Here — '

He produced a bottle of water from the glove compartment. She opened it and took a swig. It was lukewarm but it eased her throat and renewed her strength.

'So that's what took you away,' she said. 'What brought you back?'

'Nothing. I mean, lots of things. I mean it wasn't just a blinding revelation: *Oh, I'm ex-DCI Alex Wolfe, I must have lost my memory.* It was gradual, confused. You see, I was really settled in my new life, I had a job, I had friends.'

'A job? Friends? Lucky you. What kind of job?'

'Casual work, to start with. In fact I started here at the Lost Traveller.'

'The what?'

'It's the name of the pub. I must have come here for a drink and seen the advert. Maybe it was the name that attracted me.'

'Oh yes? Might have made more sense if it had been called the Running Man.'

That came out more sharply than she'd intended, but she'd been provoked by the hint of pathos in what he'd said.

His reaction was a faint smile, the first lightness she'd seen in his features.

He said, 'Whatever, it helped me survive. I collected glasses and served behind the bar to start with. I was casual labour, money in hand, nothing in the books, so no questions to answer. Just as well, as I had no answers to give.'

'You must have had a name. They must have called you something.'

'Yes, they did ask me. I told them my name was Ed. Ed Muir. I'd no idea why, it just came into my head. For all I knew then it was my real name.'

She stared hard at him, looking for signs that he was mocking her, but found none as he went on: 'Later, when it started coming back to me, I realized where it came from. Back about a year before I got put on Macavity, I was on the team investigating that Hackney benefits scam. Way it worked, someone in the local social security office had to be involved, so I was delegated to go along and sign on to try and get a lead. I needed a name, so I called myself Edwin Muir. Remember? That Scottish poet you were so fond of? I'd just bought you a fancy edition of his collected works for your birthday.'

She said very quietly, 'I remember. You couldn't see what I saw in him, right?'

'That's right, but his name stuck and it came in really useful. Not only when I was working casual, but later, when things started coming back to me. I'd started doing a bit in the kitchen at the pub. I always enjoyed cooking, remember?'

Suddenly she didn't want to do any more shared memories, not at this level, not like a couple of old school friends who'd run into each other by chance.

She said, 'So you became a cook, is that what you're saying?'

'To start with. And as I stopped being casual, I needed a real back story. That's where Ed Muir came in handy. Way back then, I'd picked up a lot of tricks about how to manipulate social security. Turned out there were still some traces of Ed Muir on file from the Hackney op, so it wasn't too hard for me to build up the identity, particularly as I wasn't trying to get money out of them. In fact, they've probably got me in their books as a success story. Layabout turns the corner, gets a permanent job, starts contributing.'

Feeling his evident pleasure in his own smartness like a pain, she said abruptly, 'Do you still work here, at this pub?'

'No. Sometimes I come back to give a hand if they've anything big on. But I moved on. I'm in charge of a fair-sized catering operation now.'

He spoke with a quiet pride, but he didn't offer any details.

She said dully, 'So you got your memory back. And you decided you preferred your new life to your old one. Great.'

'It wasn't as simple as that,' he urged. 'At first, it didn't feel like recovering my memory, more like losing my mind. Then I met someone . . . '

'A woman, you mean.'

'Yes. We got together. I suppose, for me anyway, at first it was as much for comfort and warmth as . . . anything. But then she got pregnant. That was a waking point. Not the final one, perhaps, but a huge lurch back to reality; two realities, the one I wanted, which was here, and the other one that I'd escaped from but knew I'd have to deal with if I was to take my second chance.'

'Second chance?' she said. 'That how you saw it?'

'Oh yes,' he said seriously. 'I'd lost everything. Now I was getting it all back. How else should I see it?'

This was too much. *Second chance!* In all the joy of moving into a steady relationship with Mick, she had never ever thought of it as a second chance, an opportunity to replace what she had lost. Seven years of watching and helping her daughter grow, how could they ever be replaced?

'And me? What about my loss?' she cried.

'I told you,' he said patiently. 'I went back to check you out. I had to know what damage I'd caused. When I saw that you and Purdy . . . well, I knew that I couldn't change what had happened, couldn't offer any kind of reparation. All I would do if I showed myself was cause even more damage.'

'That was a very handy conclusion to reach,

351

wasn't it?' she sneered. 'Gave you the excuse to do exactly what you wanted to do.'

'That too,' he agreed. 'We'd both repaired ourselves, started new lives. It made sense not to risk shattering both of them again, didn't it?'

'Maybe. In which case, why are we sitting here?' she demanded.

He shifted in his seat and she could feel his relief at this step away from what had bound them together in the past to what had brought them together in the present.

'I know why I'm sitting here,' he said. 'I heard something breaking on the terrace at the Keldale and I looked up and found myself looking straight at you. The real question is, what are you doing here? This photo you mentioned, have you got it with you?'

'No. I gave it to the police, to the man I was having lunch with. His name's Dalziel. He's head of the local CID.'

'I've heard of him,' he said. 'And this was a picture of me in *MY Life?*'

'Yes. In the crowd, during the royal visit last week.'

'And that didn't strike you as odd? You know I wouldn't bother to cross the street to see a member of our clapped-out royal family.'

'That was the old you. What do I know about the new model, this happy relaxed guy with a good job in the catering industry? Listen. It was definitely you in the picture.'

'Looking like I look now?'

'No,' she said. 'It was like you as you used to be.'

'Anything else? Why did you choose to stay at the Keldale, for instance?'

'There was a message with the photo. On Keldale notepaper. I thought it might signify something. I had nothing else.'

'What did the message say?'

'*The General reviews his troops*. Remember?'

'Of course I remember,' he said with a reminiscent smile that made her want to hit him.

'But you're saying you didn't send the message or the photo?' she said.

'Why would I?'

'Why would anyone?' she snapped.

He stared at her gloomily for a moment, then said, 'I can only think of one reason. I've been a fucking idiot.'

'Why does that not surprise me? I'm sorry, I mean, how? What have you done?'

He took the water bottle from her and downed an inch.

'I told you, there's been a period — in fact, it's only come to an end today — like when you wake up in the morning but you're not really fully awake. I knew who I was again, but I wasn't yet totally back in the real world. I can't have been, otherwise I wouldn't have done it. But it seemed harmless. In fact it seemed stupid not to, like turning down a gift from the gods.'

'What the hell are you talking about, Alex?'

'I needed money. It seemed important to give her the best possible start, to show everyone how proud I was, to show God how grateful I was . . .'

'Who? Who are you talking about?'

'My daughter,' he said. 'I wanted to throw her a really splendid christening party.'

She looked at him with realization dawning, though perhaps the realization was that she had known this all along, but hadn't wanted to admit it.

She said with a calmness that frightened her, 'That's why you were in the garden. The christening party. It was yours.'

'Yes,' he said.

'For your daughter.'

'Yes.'

'What have you called her.'

'Lucinda.'

That was when at last she started crying.

18.10–18.15

Peter Pascoe entered the Keldale at a speed just short of a run and shouldered aside a middle-aged woman at the reception desk.

The receptionist didn't wait for him to speak but said, 'Room number 36.'

Pascoe was on his way up the stairs before the displaced guest had time to finish saying, 'What a rude man!'

Upstairs he saw the door marked 36 was open.

As he rushed towards it, the thought occurred that he was doing exactly what he'd tried to tell Dalziel not to do. But he did it all the same.

A figure stooping by the bed straightened up, alerted by the sound of Pascoe's entry. For a moment his imagination put a shotgun into the man's hands. Then he saw it was DC Seymour and he was holding a laptop.

'Oh hello, sir,' said Seymour. 'The Super's through there.'

He nodded towards a door connecting this room to the next.

Pascoe went through.

'What kept you?' grunted the Fat Man, shaking the contents of a drawer on to the floor, then stirring the scattered underwear with his toe.

'For Christ's sake, Andy, what are you doing here?'

355

'What's it look like? Trying to spot owt that'll tell me where these scrotes have gone. How about you, Pete? You following me, or what?'

'I'm trying to stop you getting yourself killed.'

'Nice of you. Apart from that, got anything new to share with me?'

'Nothing important,' snapped the DCI. 'Just that Novello's out of danger, if that's of any interest to you.'

He was immediately sorry for his shortness as the Fat Man sank on to the bed as if his legs had lost the strength to hold him.

'Thank Christ for that!' he said with a religious fervour that could hardly have been matched by an archbishop. 'I were starting to think . . . thank Christ for that.'

It was only now that Pascoe realized just how heavily the sense of his responsibility for Novello's plight had been weighing on his boss.

'So what have you found?' he said, trying to turn the subject.

'Bugger all, so far,' said Dalziel.

The phone rang.

He picked it up, listened, said, 'You're a star,' and dropped the receiver back on its rest.

'That were that bonny lass on reception. Think she fancies me. I got her to check if these Delays were in. Aye, don't look surprised, did you think I was going to smash the door down single-handed? When no one replied I asked her to check the car-park video, see if she could spot the Delays going out. I just missed the bastards!' He smashed his left fist into his right palm in frustration. 'They must have gone out of the car park minutes afore I turned in. They were likely around when we were here before, Pete. If only I hadn't waited till I were sure . . . '

He stood up, his strength restored.

'We'll need to put out a call,' he said. 'Nowt yet on Gina's car, is there?'

'No. Sorry,' said Pascoe. 'She could be halfway back to London by now.'

'I don't think so,' said Dalziel. 'Them two didn't take off out of here to go for a little sightseeing run.'

'Sir, I think you should look at this,' said Seymour from the doorway.

They went through into the next room.

'Found this laptop stuck under the bed,' said Seymour. 'Thought it was just plugged in to recharge the batteries. But there's this . . . '

He turned it so they could see a map-diagram with a pulsing green spot.

'That what I think it is?' said Dalziel.

'It looks like a tracking bug,' said Pascoe.

'And it's not moving. Jesus, Pete, I bet it's in her car, and she's parked somewhere,' cried the Fat Man.

'Andy, you're guessing,' said Pascoe. 'Let's work out where it is and I'll get a patrol car to take a look . . . '

But he might as well have been talking to the trees. Dalziel was peering close at the screen.

'Got it!' he cried triumphantly. 'That's the north road, and yon's that unclassified road that leads nowhere but a few farms and the Lost Traveller. Was a time when you really needed to be lost to call in there, but it were a good pint last time I was in. So she's about a quarter mile down the hill beyond. Come on, we can be there in twenty minutes if we move!'

'No, Andy!' commanded Pascoe with all the stern authority he could muster. 'Think about it. If your theory is correct — and very possibly it's not — then there could be an armed and dangerous man out there. I've got an ARU on standby, I'll whistle them up and we'll all take a look together.'

'You wha'?' cried the Fat Man. 'There's a bastard out there who put my girl in hospital and he's likely looking to do the same to yon lass Gina who came up here looking for my help, and you want me to sit on my thumbs while you follow procedure? You do what you want; you'll know where to find me.'

'Listen, Andy,' said Pascoe seriously, 'I can't let you do this. It's just a matter of minutes . . . '

'Minutes might be all we've got,' said Dalziel. 'And, Pete, what's all this *letting* business? There'll likely come a time and place when you can tell me what to do, but it's not here and it's not yet. I'm off. You coming or staying?'

Seymour, who had been watching this confrontation of giants with fascinated interest, mentally noting every phrase and inflexion for the historical record, now focused all his attention on Pascoe. Was this the moment when Spartacus threw off his chains? When Fletcher Christian put Captain Bligh in the longboat and set him adrift?

In the event the outcome was rather lacking in drama.

Pascoe shook his head, like a man waking from a dream, smiled wryly, even rather sadly, and said, 'Oh, all right then. But if you get me killed, I'm not going to be the one who tells Ellie! Dennis, ring Sergeant Wield, tell him what's going off and where, and get that ARU moving quick!'

'And then,' as Seymour was later to tell his enthralled audience, 'they went running off down the corridor like a couple of big kids on their way to a party!'

Once Gina Wolfe started crying, it felt as if she could never stop.

Alex Wolfe had made no effort to comfort her, just sat there, watching patiently.

That told her more than anything he'd said that for him the past was dead. She wasn't even a ghost, just a complication that threatened to damage his new life. While the barriers she had created between herself and the past had proved paper-thin, he had found a way to turn that pain into part of a process, the first chance which, though ending in disaster, left you better prepared to grasp the second if and when it came along.

It was this realization that finally dried the physical tears, though inside she felt as if she might be crying forever.

She began to repair her face in the rear-view mirror, taking her time as she tried to adjust to this new-found perspective. She had to try to match his apparent objectivity. If they could both walk away from this safe and sound, well and good. But if only one of them could survive, then she had to be pragmatic. This stranger and his family were nothing to her.

She said, 'Well, Ed, what was this stupid thing you did?'

Using his new name was a signal to herself of what she felt was their new relationship. He showed no reaction.

He said, 'When I went on Gidman's payroll, I set up an online account for the money to be paid into. Not in my own name, of course, and not using my own PC at home. Funny, as stuff started coming back to me, the details of that account and the passwords and everything, they came back bright and clear while other stuff about my actual life before I became Ed Muir was still hazy and fragmented.'

'Perhaps it says something about your priorities,' she couldn't resist saying.

He took her seriously and replied, 'Yes, I think so too. The money was for Lucy's treatment. That was always my priority. That was why I made no effort to use the account other than to establish it was still active. Spending Lucy's money on clothes, or booze, or living expenses, it didn't feel right.'

How could he talk about her so calmly? she asked herself.

Because, the answer came, he now had Lucinda.

She thought about what he'd been willing to do for the sake of his first daughter. What lengths might he now be willing to go to in the interests of his second?

'Then we had Lucinda. Naturally we got to talking about the christening. Ali didn't really want to go over the top . . . '

'Ali?'

'My partner. Doesn't earn a fortune. She's a

361

clarinettist with the Mid-Yorkshire Sinfonietta, and does a bit of tutoring too.'

'A music teacher. Like me.'

He looked surprised, as if the correspondence hadn't previously struck him.

'Yes, that's right. Don't make anything of it. She's very different. Small, talks a lot, quite bouncy.'

'That's supposed to make me feel better, that she's different?'

'No. I wasn't trying to make you feel anything. Just telling you. I mean, I know all about Mick, and I'm not going to get my head in a knot because, apart from being a cop, he's completely different from me.'

He was right, she thought. Mick was older and in physical build, in taste, in outlook, in *everything* very different from Alex. Was that significant?

She put it aside for later examination and said, 'You were saying about the christening . . . '

'Was I? Oh yes. Me, I get a decent screw, but nowhere near enough to push the boat out the way I wanted to. Like I said earlier, it just seemed important somehow to make the christening an occasion to remember. And then I thought of that account. The way I saw things, it seemed perfectly fitting to use it to celebrate Lucinda's day. I wouldn't take a penny more than I needed for the christening, I thought. I had my heart set on the Keldale, they do these things so well. I got a price from them and paid in advance by transferring the exact sum direct from this account. It did cross my mind that activity after seven years lying dormant might attract attention, but it seemed a very small risk. It wasn't as if I was clearing the account out, and the money wasn't coming direct to me, it was going straight to the Keldale. Anyway, I was old news, who'd be interested in me after all this time?'

He shook his head as if in disbelief at his own naïvety.

'And who is interested in you, Ed?'

He said, 'Goldie Gidman, of course. He's the one who knew about the account. The rat pack never got anywhere near it, I'm sure. I knew enough about the way these things are investigated to make sure I covered all my tracks. But Gidman must have put a watch on that account the day I disappeared. And he'd leave an alarm set. He always was a very careful man, Goldie. Hated loose ends. That's why it was so hard to lay a finger on him. He didn't really need to have me on his payroll. It was just an extra precaution.'

'A precaution that became a liability when the rat pack started investigating you.'

'That's right. Then after all these years suddenly the account becomes active. All he's got is a payment to the Keldale Hotel. So what does he do? My guess is he'd send someone up here to see if they could pick up my trail. There was an attempt to break into the Keldale office last weekend. I read about it in the paper. The manager going on about how pleased he was with their new state-of-the-art security system, installed on police advice. Wouldn't surprise me if that was down to Goldie, seeing if he could find what the payment was for. And when it failed, he thought, What do you need to lure a hunted animal out of hiding? Answer, a tethered goat.'

She said, 'Is that what I am? A tethered goat?'

'I'm afraid so. His people would have to be careful. The way Goldie would see it, if I got the slightest whiff he was on my trail, I'd be over the hill and far away. On the other hand, I'd probably react very differently to the appearance of my wife on the scene. Incidentally, are you still my wife?'

'Yes.'

'Why's that?'

'Mainly because for a long time I was hoping you'd come back,' she said. 'And then when I stopped believing that was a possibility, it seemed less complicated to hang on till I could become an official widow.'

'Of course. Seven years, presumption of death, then you'd be entitled to everything, not just a divorcee's share. Good thinking. Mick help you there, did he?'

'No. Mick's not mercenary, he would have preferred me divorced so we could marry straight away,' she retorted defensively.

For some reason this made him smile momentarily.

She went on, 'So you're saying Gidman arranged to have your face put into that photo and have it sent to me? Meaning he had a photo of you. Why didn't his people just flash it round the hotel?'

'Two reasons,' he said promptly. 'One was it would be an old photo. I doubt if anyone would recognize me.'

'I recognized you,' she said.

'Gidman's people have never been my lover,' he said.

There was no regret, no vestige of affection in his tone, confirming her sense that nothing remained of their old relationship.

'The other reason?' she said.

'Because they wouldn't want to draw attention to themselves by making overt enquiries in case they couldn't get rid of me quietly and they triggered a murder investigation. You, on the other hand, could flash the photo wherever you wanted. Stick it on lampposts, get it in the paper. They hoped someone might put you on to me. Or better still that I'd see it and make contact, and you'd lead them to me.'

'That's why you kept me sitting halfway up the hill so long,' she said. 'So you could make sure I wasn't being followed.'

'You've got it,' he said.

'And if they had followed me . . . you said *murder investigation*. You don't really think they'd try to kill you?' she said incredulously. 'For God's sake, this is Yorkshire, not New York!'

He laughed and said, 'You don't imagine Goldie has gone to all this trouble because he's been missing my lively conversation, do you? He sees me as a real danger.'

'But why? What could you do? Stand up in court and allege that seven years ago you were taking bribes to keep Gidman informed of the progress of a police investigation? Could you even prove that the money in this account came from him?'

He shrugged and said, 'Money always leaves a trail, as I'm finding out. But that's not the point. There's a big bag of shit with Goldie's name on it sitting around at the Yard. It's mainly rumours and allegations and the CPS won't touch it with a bargepole. But once get him in the dock, and anything goes. That was what Macavity was all about, putting together a case, any kind of case, that would get Gidman on the sharp end of a prosecution. And we might even have got there if I hadn't kept him ahead of the game.'

'That was seven years ago. He's had another seven years to make himself safe.'

'Of course he has. And I'm sure the kind of lawyers he can afford would tear my evidence to shreds. So not much chance of a conviction. But that bag of shit would have been emptied on the courtroom floor and the stink would stick to him for ever. Once he wouldn't have cared. But from what I read, another ten years or so, and Goldie could be visiting Downing Street to see *my son, the Prime Minister*. I could put an end to all that. The Tories would never forgive someone who'd tracked stinking estuary mud across their lovely royal blue carpet.'

Listening to him she was reminded of the bright, sharpminded young cop he'd been before their daughter's illness began to darken all aspects of their life. He could sum up situations in a flash, analyse possibilities, assess odds.

And he was passionate for justice.

Had that changed?

'So what are you going to do? Come forward and offer to testify?'

He exploded a laugh that was more like a bark, and not a friendly one.

'Don't be silly. I told you, I've got a second chance, a new life. Do you think I'm going to put it at risk by stepping back into the old one? You too, Gina. You've moved on, put all that dark stuff behind you. You wouldn't want to put your new life at risk either, would you?'

All that dark stuff . . . she wanted to scream at him that she knew now that *all that dark stuff* was part of her being forever. There was no space behind her she could ever put it.

She said, 'This isn't about me. Look, Ed . . . Alex . . . I know it would be much harder for you . . . '

That laugh again.

'You're right there. It wouldn't just be Goldie who ended up on trial. I'm sure they'd promise all kinds of leniency in return for my testimony, but the public don't like to see a bent cop going free. Trust me, Gina: it would be hard for you too — harder than you think. No, when you leave here, what you have to do is drive home, forget you ever saw me. You just decided what you were doing was pointless, someone's idea of a joke. You'll be safe at home.'

Again the implications of his words took a moment to sink in.

'Safe? Why wouldn't I be safe here?'

'Because when the tiger comes out of the jungle and the shooting starts, no one gives a fuck about the staked goat. They'd prefer not to involve you, of course. Much better for me to have a fatal accident, or simply vanish without trace. But if the choice was between risking losing me and blowing us both away right here, they wouldn't think twice.'

She stared at him for a long moment then said, 'I think you're trying to frighten me. Like Mick when I talked to him earlier.'

He laughed and said, 'Good old Mick, he'll see the big picture. Think about it. If you're not scared of Gidman, what about the press? I'm sure you had a taste of what those guys can get up to when I went awol. Imagine what a feast they'd make of this lot if they got a sniff of it. They'd tear you to pieces. Just think of the stories they'd make up. Wouldn't do much for Mick's career. As for you, I doubt if a parent anywhere would want to let her precious offspring take music lessons from a scarlet woman. So forget all of this, Gina. Go home. This hasn't happened. I don't exist any more.'

'You're right,' she said quietly. 'I thought I recognized you. I was wrong.'

'Great,' he said. 'Tell that to the fat cop. You made a mistake. That's your story. Stick to it and you'll be fine.'

'Even with Mick? You want me to lie to Mick too?'

'Oh no,' he said, with a smile closely related to his canine laugh. 'No secrets between lovers. In fact, I may give dear old Mick a ring myself to put him in the picture, so it wouldn't look good if you kept quiet, would it? You'll have his mobile number in your phone, I expect.'

'I've left it in the car,' she said. 'But I can remember the number.'

She recited it and he copied it into his phone.

'Always a good memory,' he said admiringly. 'Ali's the same. Must be all that music buzzing around in your heads. A real talent, memory. Except sometimes it's a real pain.'

He reached over and opened her door. His arm brushed against her breast. After seven years, that's the nearest we've come to intimate contact, she thought.

'Goodbye, Gina,' he said.

'But what are you going to do? They won't stop looking, will they?'

'They might. You never know. Things change.'

'For a man who thinks there's a hitman after him, you don't sound all that worried.'

'You're thinking of Alex Wolfe. He'd have been worried. I don't think I've got anything to worry about if you keep your mouth shut. Goodbye.'

He sounded slightly impatient now.

She said, 'Just one more thing. That general and the plucky little trooper game, did you ever tell anyone about it?'

'I don't think so. You?'

'No.'

'Never mind. One of those things, eh? A lucky guess.'

She got out of the car then stopped to take what she imagined might be one last look at him.

She said, 'Goodbye, Edwin Muir. *I pack your stars into my purse, and bid you, bid you so farewell.*'

369

He stared back at her uncomprehendingly. Why should he understand when she hardly understood herself?

He didn't say goodbye for a third time, just looked at her till finally she got out of the car. She closed the door behind her, firmly but trying not to slam it. She didn't want him to think she was leaving him in anger. Not that it would have mattered. Through the window she saw he had taken out his mobile and was dialling a number. For a second she thought he must be ringing Mick. Then someone answered and she saw a smile spread across his face as he started talking. It wasn't the guarded knowing smile he'd flashed as they spoke. This was a smile that turned him once more into the young man she remembered, the man she'd married.

He was, she guessed, talking to his new partner. Ali, the music teacher. The mother of Lucinda.

She felt all the pain of loss again as she hadn't felt it for years. Not that it had ever truly gone away, she realized now. There were things that had the power to obliviate the pain for a while. Music. Sex. But like a ground bass, it ran beneath all the variations of life, good and bad. Perhaps it was a necessary part of living. Perhaps humans needed a loss that felt worse than death to make the inevitability of their own death bearable.

But she would not wish this pain on anyone. She certainly did not want to have it dragged into the public domain once more. She recalled how intrusive the press had been in the aftermath of Alex's disappearance.

What Alex had told her about the threat from Goldie Gidman was hard to credit, it smacked too much of a TV thriller. But anything touching on the financier and his MP son would certainly be big news, and the thought of being besieged by journalists, midnight phone calls, cameras and mikes being thrust into her face whenever she emerged, her image appearing in newspapers and news items all over the country, was a horror worse than the threat of death.

No, though her own pain was not something she would wish on anyone, she was sure that if she had the chance to take the kind of pain journalists specialized in and turn it on them, she would not hesitate.

Alex was right. At least in this they were in accord. Silence was her refuge. She resolved that nothing would make her admit to the meeting and exchange that had just taken place. Nothing.

She set off down the hill towards her car.

18.05–18.15

Gwyn Jones's progress north had been slower than anticipated.

He'd stopped at the first service station on the motorway to ring Beanie. The conversation had gone pretty well, he told himself complacently. She had sounded really sympathetic as he span his tale of his grandmother's illness and the dutiful son heading back to the land of his fathers to take his place at the old lady's bedside. Then he'd bought himself a coffee and a sandwich to make up for his missed lunch, tried Gareth again without any luck, and rejoined the thickening traffic only to be held up by an accident a few miles ahead.

The next ten miles took over half an hour, but once clear he'd made reasonable time and now he was definitely *up north*, passing through what had formerly been known as the People's Republic of South Yorkshire where King Arthur lined up his coal-face knights to tilt against the great tyrant Thatcher.

A Welshman on a left-wing paper ought to have felt a frisson of fraternal nostalgia as he traversed this holy landscape, but Jones hardly spared it a thought or a glance.

He'd fed the Loudwater Villas details into his sat-nav. For most of the journey it had had nothing to do but tell him to keep going straight on. Finally it instructed him to turn off the motorway and soon the directions were coming thick and fast as he entered an urban environment.

The streets were pretty empty, not surprising at this time on a Sunday, but he indulged in a complacent sneer at this evidence that he was deep into the provinces.

In a few hundred yards he was warned he would need to turn right on to a road running alongside a river. Here was the turning and there was the river. Loudwater Villas should be in view in half a minute.

Ahead he saw flashing lights and some vehicles pulled on to the verge, among them a van bearing the logo of Mid-Yorkshire TV. Beyond them there seemed to be a barrier across the road. As he slowed, figures came alongside the car, some with cameras. A flashbulb directly into his face almost blinded him, forcing him to stop some yards short of the barrier. He wound down the window and swore at the cameraman. A woman thrust a microphone through the window and said, 'Excuse me, sir, MYTV. Can you tell us who you are and why you're here?'

He said, 'No, I bloody can't. Get that thing out of my fucking face.'

He pushed the mike away forcefully and a man's face replaced the woman's. It was a lean, weathered face with bright probing eyes that were scanning the contents of the car as if committing them to memory.

'Sammy Ruddlesdin,' said the man. '*Mid-Yorkshire News*. Sorry to bother you, sir . . . '

There was a pause as the man focused more closely on Jones's face.

Then he said in a lower voice, 'Don't I know you?'

'I doubt it. What the hell's going on here?'

'Just a little local murder. I'm sure I've seen your face somewhere. You're press, aren't you? Don't be shy. National, is it? Listen, you want local colour, I'm your man.'

He was being ambushed by reporters! The irony of the situation might have been amusing, but the man's words had roused emotions that left no room for amusement.

'What do you mean, murder? Who's been murdered?'

'That's what we're all trying to find out,' said Ruddlesdin. 'Look, if you're not here after the story, what the hell are you here for?'

He didn't answer but climbed out of the car and went up to the barrier with the media pack in close attendance.

A uniformed policeman confronted him.

'Can I help, sir?'

'Not in front of this lot you can't,' said Jones, who knew that every word he spoke was being recorded by those nearest him.

The policeman took his point and led him behind the barrier. Even here he took care to keep his back firmly directed towards the press pack and dropped his voice so that the policeman had to lean close to catch his words.

'Yes, I need to get into Loudwater Villas. I'm

374

visiting my brother.'

'Your brother, sir?' said the man, looking at a list in his hand. 'Can I have the name and flat number please?'

'It won't be on your list. He's staying with a friend. Alun Watkins, number 39.'

The man looked at him with new interest.

'And your name, sir?'

'Jones. Gwyn Jones.'

'Could you hold on here a tick, sir?'

The officer turned his back on the journalists and spoke into his personal radio. After listening for a moment he turned around and said, 'If you'd like to bring your car forward, sir, I'll raise the barrier.'

Ruddlesdin, who'd clearly got close enough to hear this last remark, fell into step beside him as he returned to his car.

'You must have clout,' he said admiringly. 'Else you're very clever. Any chance of a lift?'

Jones ignored him. There was a tight feeling in his stomach as if he'd eaten something so bad his digestive juices didn't even want to get to grips with it.

He got into his car and edged forward. The reporters were still taking photos. He found he hated them so much he could gladly have run them down.

As the barrier slowly rose, the passenger door opened and a young man slipped in beside him.

'Get the fuck out of here!' he yelled, thinking it was another journalist.

But the man was holding a police warrant card before his face.

'DC Bowler, sir,' he said. 'If you just drive towards the caravan there and park alongside.'

'What's all the fuss about?' Gwyn said as he drove slowly forward. 'I'm just visiting my brother, and he's only staying here, he's not a resident. Have you come across him? He's a lot like me, people say, only eight years younger. Have you seen him?'

It was as if by talking about Gareth he could create the cheeky young sod's physical presence.

'And his name's Jones, is it, sir?'

'That's right. Gareth Jones. Not surprising as Jones is my name too.'

'Yes, sir. Are you Gwyn Jones of the *Messenger*, sir?'

He said, 'Yes, I am,' hoping that the young cop would say, 'Thought I recognized you. Good try, mate,' then tell him to drive the car back to the barrier.

Instead he just nodded as if this confirmed something he already knew.

'What's going on?' he demanded.

'Just park here, sir. Now if you come with me, DS Wield will fill you in.'

He climbed slowly out of the car. He felt he was getting very close to a place he didn't wish to arrive at. He looked back towards the distant barrier and found himself longing to be on the far side of it, one of the assembled pack, chatting, joking, smoking, drinking, passing the boring hours that any decent reporter knows have to be put in if they are to get a decent story to put out.

Then in a sudden fit of revulsion he told

himself savagely that all that interested those bastards were bloody facts to grab their readers, saccharined with 'human interest' to make the readers feel less guilty about enjoying the gore.

'This way, sir,' urged DC Bowler, with an encouraging smile.

He was a nice-looking boy, with a fresh, open face, not at all the kind of messenger you'd expect to bring you bitter words to hear and bitter tears to shed.

Perhaps I've got it wrong, thought Jones as he walked towards the caravan. Perhaps this sense of ill-bodement clutching my heart is just some atavistic throw-back, as meaningless as those claims to foreknowledge always made by Great Aunt Blodwen twenty-four hours *after* any disaster.

Then at the top of the steps leading up into the caravan a very different kind of man appeared, this one with a face as illomened as Scrooge's door-knocker.

And as if in confirmation of this sudden downward lurch of his spirits, a voice cried, 'Gwyn, oh Gwyn boy! This is terrible, truly terrible!'

He turned his head in the direction of what he presumed was Loudwater Villas and saw a man running towards him, his face contorted unrecognizably. But Gwyn Jones recognized him.

So did Edgar Wield, standing on the caravan steps. Where the hell did he come from? This is getting to be a habit!

'Bowler, grab him!' he yelled.

But it was too late for any useful grabbing.

As Bowler intercepted and folded Alun Watkins in his arms, he was already close enough for his haggard, tear-stained face to be clearly visible. And now Gwyn Jones came at last to understand that though words could not create another's physical presence, they could certainly take it away forever.

'Gwyn, *bach*, he's dead!' cried Watkins in a voice powerful enough to carry all the way down to the straining ears at the barrier. 'He's dead. I'm so so sorry. Dear Gareth's dead!'

18.33–18.35

In the gathering dusk it seemed further back to her car than Gina remembered and it was with some relief that she finally reached it. As she opened the door, she saw a car speeding down the hill towards her. For a second she thought perhaps Alex had decided there were still things to say. Then she saw it was a blue VW Golf, not the dirty grey Astra.

It slowed to a halt as it reached her. A woman was driving. The man in the passenger seat spoke through the open window.

'Having trouble, darling?'

'No,' she said. 'I'm fine.'

'You sure?' said the woman, leaning across.

'No. I just fancied a bit of air so I had a little stroll,' said Gina.

It was kind of these people to be concerned, but she was not in the mood for kindness. She wanted to be left to herself in the private space of her car, to sit there till the darkness cloaked her completely, and to let flow all the still-unshed tears.

She turned to her open car door.

The man and woman exchanged glances, the woman nodded as if confirming a decision, and they both got out.

Even when the man grasped her arm Gina

379

couldn't believe that this was anything more than a really irritating excess of good Samaritanism. But when the woman opened the back door of the Golf and the man began to push her towards it, her mind did a somersault that brought all of Alex's warnings about the expendability of staked goats to the surface.

She tried to wrench herself free. All that happened was she felt her arm forced up between her shoulder blades and her head cracked against the frame of the door as she was forced into the VW. She screamed. The man slid in beside her, the door slammed shut, the car set off. She screamed again.

The man slapped her face.

She stopped screaming.

The man said, 'That's better, darling. Any more noise from you and I'll break your jaw.'

'Don't be stupid, Vince,' said the woman. 'How's she going to talk then? Let's find somewhere quiet, then she can scream all she likes.'

18.35–18.50

When Maggie Pinchbeck turned off the narrow country road to come to a halt before the high gates of Windrush House, the grey Jaguar that had been following her for the last half-mile turned too.

Maggie wound down her window so that the camera could get a better view of her face in the gathering dusk.

A voice she recognized as Milton Slingsby's said, 'Hi, Miss Pinchbeck.'

Then the camera adjusted, presumably to look at the car behind hers. Its driver decided to make life easier and got out and advanced till he was peering right up into the lens.

He was a tall imposing figure, in his forties, with a heavy jaw that looked as if it hadn't seen a razor for a couple of days and a shock of vigorous brown hair, beginning to be tipped with silver.

He glared aggressively at the camera, but didn't need to give his name as Slingsby said, 'Mick, hi! It's Sling. Long time no see!'

A short pause, then the gates swung open.

Maggie drove carefully up the gravelled drive, recalling Dave's warning about his father's pride in his lawns. She got the impression that if the man behind hadn't been constrained by her pace, he wouldn't have given a damn.

Outside the house she parked alongside Dave's Audi with the Jag on the other side.

I'm in the wrong business, she thought as she got out of her dusty Corsa.

The Jag driver nodded at her but made no attempt at introduction or conversation as they went up the steps together. Milton Slingsby opened the door. He gave Maggie a bright smile. But the other arrival he greeted with a cry of, 'Hi, Mick, how're you doing?' and a high-five.

'Sling,' said the man without any respondent enthusiasm.

Dave the Third came down the stairs as they entered the reception hall. He looked preoccupied.

'Hi, Maggie,' he said. Then he turned his attention to the Jag driver and said unenthusiastically, 'Who's this?'

Sling said, 'It's OK, Dave. This is Mick Purdy, come to see your pappy.'

Dave the Third frowned for a moment then managed a small official smile.

'Of course! It's *Commander* Purdy, isn't it?'

'Uh-huh,' grunted Purdy ungraciously.

'You gave evidence to a Select Committee I was on. Sorry I didn't recognize you straight off. You were in uniform then, I think.'

'Well, we know you lot like a bit of pantomime,' said Purdy.

Mick Purdy, thought Maggie. *Commander* Mick Purdy. Who had interviewed a woman called Delay about an assault allegation against Goldie Gidman. Who had been a friend and

382

colleague of the missing DI Wolfe. Who was now in a relationship with Gina Wolfe. Who was here to see Goldie Gidman. And who didn't feel the need or wasn't in the mood to be polite to Dave the Third MP.

She waited for her employer to express some curiosity about the purpose of Purdy's visit, but he just said, 'My father's busy with my mother just now, but he'll be free in a moment. Sling, show the commander into the lounge.'

The policeman nodded brusquely and followed Slingsby into a room off the hall.

Now Dave the Third turned to her and said, 'Maggie, I've got you here on a wild-goose chase, I'm afraid. My mother got a phone call about twenty minutes ago. Her sister, Belle, the one in Broadstairs, has had a stroke. It sounds serious and Mammy wants to get there straight away. She's just packing a few things, then I'm going to drive her down.'

'No problem,' said Maggie. 'Keep me posted, and I'll take care of things if you feel you ought to stay down there.'

'Yes,' said Gidman. 'I know I can rely on you for that. But can I ask you a really big favour, Maggie? Mammy's really upset at the thought of leaving Goldie on his own. It's Dean's night off, and when Dean has a night off, it really is a night, he won't show till breakfast. I know Sling will be here, but he's not all that reliable these days, so I wondered . . .'

He looks really uncomfortable to be asking me a favour, she thought. Have I made our relationship *that* impersonal?

383

She said, 'You'd like me to spend the night here, make sure Goldie gets properly fed and watered?'

'Yes, please. To tell the truth, he's not all that domesticated and, between the two of them, I think they're quite capable of setting the house on fire! Ma would be really chuffed if you'll stay. You know how high she rates you.'

'OK,' she said. 'No problem.'

'Maggie, you're a star,' he said with a warmth that faintly embarrassed her, mainly because it seemed so genuine.

Flo Gidman came bustling down the stairs, an old leather grip in her hand.

She registered Maggie, said, 'Hello, dearie,' then to her son, 'David, I'm ready, we ought to be on our way. I've said cheerio to your father, he says he'll manage, but I do wish Dean was here. Doesn't everything happen at the worst possible time, Maggie?'

She was saved from answering by Dave, who said, 'Mammy, I've got some good news, Maggie here says she'll stay the night and make sure Pappy's properly taken care of.'

'Oh, Maggie, will you?' cried Flo. 'That would be such a relief, you've no idea. It's not that Goldie's helpless, it's just that he doesn't bother. Unless there's someone here to keep him right, he'll sit up half the night in front of that telly, eating nothing but crisps and drinking rum. Like I say, he's not helpless, just hopeless.'

'Don't worry, Flo, I'll take care of him.'

'Lovely. He likes a glass of warm milk with a shot of rum by his bed, and when I'm not there

384

he usually takes one sleeping pill to help him get off. Just the one. They're in the tea caddy in the kitchen. He hates tea so he never looks in there. But don't let him talk you into giving him more than one. And don't let him take the rum bottle to bed with him. And make certain he don't smuggle a cigar in. I had a smoke alarm fixed right over the bed, but he's quite capable of switching it off when he's left to himself.'

'Mammy, you can't expect Maggie to be able to boss Pappy around like you do!' protested Dave.

'Why not? She gets the practice keeping you in line, don't she?'

'I'll do my best,' said Maggie. 'And I hope your sister's OK.'

'That's in God's hands. I'm more grateful than I can say, dearie.'

She folded Maggie in her arms and gave her a succulent kiss on the cheek.

Then she said, 'Come on, Dave, I'll just tell your pa that Maggie's going to take care of him, then we're off. I don't want to get there and find poor Belle's gone because of your dawdling.'

She went out. Dave the Third gave Maggie a wry grin then said, 'Oh, one thing more, you'd better know how to work the gate controls. Not that anyone's likely to come calling tonight, but sometimes Sling goes walkabout and it could be embarrassing if there's no one around.'

She followed him into a control room located to the left of the main entrance. She'd only glimpsed it through the open door on previous visits and now she was surprised to see how roomy it was. Perhaps the stark décor made it seem bigger. It certainly clashed with the rather self-consciously retro ambience of the rest of the house. The only furniture was a single office chair in front of a control panel. There was no window and the illumination came from a bank of TV screens filling most of one wall. Only two of them were active. One showed the area outside the front door, the other the main gate.

'You can talk to anyone at the gate by pressing this switch,' said Dave. 'And these two buttons open and shut the gates. OK?'

'Yes. All these other screens . . . ?'

'No need to bother with those unless an alarm sounds. Then you can bring up the perimeter walls and if necessary the house interior, though I shouldn't think they'll ever be needed. The alarm system links directly to the police and there's enough razor wire on the perimeter wall to shave a woolly mammoth.'

'David! Are you going to take all night? Get a move on or I'll drive this thing myself!'

The yell came from outside.

He grinned at her again. Sometimes she could see why he was such a successful womanizer.

He said, 'Open the gate, will you, then shut it behind me? I'll ring you later.'

He gave her a kiss on the cheek, not as warmly moist as his mother's, but more than a simple peck. That was a first too.

He left. She waited till she heard the Audi start up then pressed the button that opened the gate. A few moments later the car appeared on the TV screen. As it went through the gateway,

Dave's arm came out of the driver's window and waved a clenched fist farewell.

She pressed the *close* button. It was easy to categorize people, she thought. This was a side of her employer she hadn't seen enough of. With the right guidance, maybe he could make it all the way. The UK's first mixed-race prime minister. And he had the qualities to make a good if not a great one. With the right guidance.

Her shift of feeling about Dave made her feel suddenly guilty at the dark suspicions about Goldie that today's events had sent fuguing around her mind once more. If the combined efforts of Scotland Yard, the left-wing media, and Tory Central Office hadn't been able to lay anything on Gidman, then he really did have to be clean, didn't he?

Her phone rang. The display said *Number withheld* but she recognized instantly the voice that said, 'That you, Maggie?'

'Yes, Beanie,' she said.

She listened as the Bitch talked. After a few seconds she sat down on the chair in front of the control panel.

'Listen, hon, don't know why I'm doing this, except maybe you ought to know and also 'cos I gotta talk to someone about it. I've just had a call from Gwyn. I was ready to chew his balls off over lying to me, and banging that Huntley child and all, but I could tell something was wrong soon as I heard him. My ma used to tell me, never tell lies 'cos you never know when they'll come true. Gwyn said he had to deal with a family crisis. Well, he's really got one now. That kid brother of his, the one he was going to see up in Yorkshire, he's been murdered.'

'Murdered?' echoed Maggie incredulously. 'How? Why?'

'Shot in the face. And some cop woman who was there got put into hospital too. I don't know what's going on, but if it's anything to do with that stuff we were talking about, I thought you ought to know.'

'Do you have any more details?' demanded Maggie. 'Have they got anyone for it?'

'He'd have said if they had. He's really shook up. Never known him like this. He's even going on about the intrusive fucking press! Listen, hon, I've told you all I know, but you've heard nothing from me. And one thing more, that's you and me squared off, OK? Take care.'

The line went dead.

For another minute Maggie Pinchbeck didn't move.

Then she got up and went into the hallway just in time to see Sling leading Purdy upstairs, presumably for his meeting with Goldie.

The commander looked like a man with something important on his mind. She knew how he felt.

She watched them out of sight then went back into the control room.

18.20–18.48

As the old Rover sped north out of the city, Dalziel told Pascoe about his conversation with Purdy.

'Tried to hide it at first, but he's really worried,' said the Fat Man.

'Why wouldn't he be? With his girlfriend missing and these Delays on the loose, that would worry anyone.'

'I suppose so,' said Dalziel.

Pascoe frowned and said warningly, 'Andy, is there something else here, something to do with Purdy? I thought we agreed. No more secrets.'

You agreed, thought the Fat Man. It's me as makes the rules, remember?

But he didn't say it aloud. There would be a time for such reminders. Also it was good to have it confirmed just how fine-tuned his deputy's sensors were.

He said, 'I'm not keeping anything secret 'cos I really don't know anything. Remember, I've not seen Purdy for ten years and we weren't much more than drinking buddies back then. So the way this thing's panning out, I'm not taking owt for granted.'

'You think he might be more than romantically involved?'

'*Romantically involved?* You been at the

389

Barbara Cartland again? I've no idea, Pete. There's one thing, but. That stuff in the note Gina got about the plucky little trooper and the general. Two ways that might have got into circulation. One is the guy boasting in his cups to an old mate, the other is the girl reminiscing in her bed to a new mate. Mick Purdy fits both bills.'

They drove in silence for a while. Then Dalziel's phone rang. It was lying on the dashboard.

He said, 'Could you get that, else I might have to arrest myself.'

Pascoe picked up the phone and bellowed, 'What?' in a fair parody of the Fat Man's telephone style. His reward was a verbal assault that made him wince.

He held it away from his ear and said, 'I think it's your old chum Chief Constable Glendower, who seems to believe your mother had intercourse with a sow that was badly infected with both foot and mouth disease *and* swine fever.'

Dalziel laughed and said, 'Pass it here.'

Pascoe frowned and compromised by holding it up to his boss's ear.

The abusive rant was unabated. Dalziel listened with a widening grin on his face.

'Hooky, Hooky,' he interrupted finally. 'You should be careful, man of your age. Back seats are for teenagers. You'll give yourself a hernia if you're not careful. Nay, don't start up again. Just listen, will you? You know a journalist called Gareth Jones?'

There was a pause. Then Glendower's voice, more controlled now, said, 'Yes, I know a muckraker of that name.'

Pascoe, hearing the reference to Gareth Jones, leaned close so that he could catch the caller's words.

'And would it surprise you if it turned out he were doing a surveillance job on you while you were enjoying your romantic weekend?'

'What? The little shit!' Glendower's voice was now very alarmed. 'What's going on, Andy?'

Dalziel spelled things out with brutal economy.

When he'd finished, Glendower, his tone changed yet again, said, 'Oh Christ. And it's definitely Gareth Jones who's dead, is it?'

'Looks like it.'

'Poor bastard.'

'He wasn't looking to do you any favours, Hooky.'

'I know that. But he was just a kid. All right, he got on my wick, always hanging around my office, asking cheeky questions, making innuendos. Deserved to have his arse kicked, fair enough. But not this.'

'Aye well, does you credit, Hooky,' said Dalziel. 'But it's time to look out for yourself. Listen, I'm ahead of the game right now, but my DCI — him you met in the car park — he's a bright lad, he'll have to be told.'

He glanced across at Pascoe and winked.

'But he's not a blabbermouth,' he continued. 'And I'll do what I can to screw things down at the Keldale. Bit like you, eh? All right, sorry, no time to be frivolous. Listen, Hooky, there's bound to be some bugger who knows what young Jones were up to, so I doubt you're going to be able to keep the lid on this. But you can mebbe do a bit of damage limitation, right?'

There was a silence.

'Yes, Andy. You're right. Damage limitation it is,' said Glendower finally. 'Thanks, mate. Sorry I blew my top. I thought you were just having a laugh at my expense.'

'Nay, Hooky, if us old stagers can't look out for each other, who will? Listen, first thing I'd do is take a close look at your staff. You did the hotel booking and everything from your office, I suppose?'

'Yes. Well, I wasn't going to do it from home,' said Glendower defensively.

'Very considerate of you. But it means some bugger at work has probably been checking out your computer and phone and feeding this young reporter tit-bits. I'd look for someone who goes to chapel three times on a Sunday, sings in the choir, and reckons Sodom and Gomorrah are villages in Shropshire. But I expect you've got a lot of them.'

'Oh yes, but I reckon I know which one it is,' said Glendower vengefully. 'And with luck I'll have time to get the bugger sorted before I'm clearing my desk.'

'Nay, Hooky, it needn't come to that. A man's entitled to a private life. Unless you've been charging your naughties to expenses. You've not been doing that, have you? Tell me you've not been doing that.'

'There may have been some overlaps,' said

Glendower reluctantly.

'Oh, Hooky, Hooky. First rule of the game is pay for your own naughties else you really will end up paying for them. Listen, I've got to go. Got a murder case to investigate, remember?'

'Of course you have. Best of luck with that. I hope you catch the bugger. And, Andy, thanks again. Like I say, I thought that . . . well I thought some pretty uncharitable things . . . sorry. I'll not forget this.'

'Good luck, Hooky,' said Dalziel. 'By the by, signing in for your mucky weekend as Mr and Mrs Rowan Williams — loved it!'

He glanced at Pascoe again, looking to share a smile, but the DCI's face could have belonged to a Scottish Nationalist at the Glasgow Empire listening to an English comic telling kilt jokes on a Saturday night.

'So that's how you guessed the dead man might be a Welsh journalist,' he said.

'Aye,' said the Fat Man. 'Remember that bint in the white Mondeo? I clocked it had the same registration letters as Hooky's tank. So I checked if there were a wedding on at the Keldale over the weekend. There weren't. And when I saw there was no Glendower in the registration book, just a Mr and Mrs Rowan Williams, I rang our Control and put out a call on Hooky here and in Lancs. Guessed he'd be heading west.'

'You wanted to warn him,' said Pascoe accusingly.

'Aye. Why not?' said Dalziel. 'I'd do the same for you, and hope you would for me.'

'Maybe,' said Pascoe. 'But this is really going

to turn a spotlight on us. The press will love it. Top cop's dirty weekend gets teenage reporter killed. Jesus.'

'It's not Hooky's fault,' protested Dalziel. 'Any more than it's my fault for getting him bumped off that table. Any more than it's your fault for not checking up on me yesterday like you promised Cap you would.'

Pascoe looked at him in alarm and puzzlement.

'Did she tell you that she'd asked me?'

'No, but I'd lay money on it she did. You were too busy, though. Right?'

'Well, yes, as a matter of fact. But I don't see what on earth this has to do with anything.'

Dalziel thought of explaining that if he hadn't spent such a miserable Saturday he might not have woken on Sunday thinking it must be Monday . . . but it didn't seem worth the effort.

He said, 'All I mean is, if there's only one guy this is all down to, I reckon it has to be yon Tory milch-cow, Goldie Gidman.'

Before Pascoe could deconstruct this, his phone rang.

He said, 'Hi, Wieldy,' listened, said, 'OK. I'll let you know what we find,' and switched off. Dalziel wasn't surprised. A Wield call to give information was inevitably compact and comprehensive.

Pascoe said, 'Gwyn Jones has turned up. That idiot Watkins managed to give him the bad news before Wieldy could get to him. He's gone from being shattered to screaming that it's all down to Goldie Gidman and why aren't we sticking red-hot needles under his nails to get him to talk?'

'Don't often agree with a journalist, but maybe he's got something,' said Dalziel. 'Here we go!'

He swung across the carriageway to a fanfare of horns from the oncoming traffic and turned eastward down a narrow unclassified road.

'You're sure this is right?' said Pascoe a few minutes later, after he'd recovered his composure sufficiently to speak without a tremolo.

'When I were a young cop, you had to do the Mid-Yorkshire Knowledge,' said Dalziel. 'Find your way to every pub within twenty miles of the town centre. There. Told you.'

Ahead they saw a roadside pub with a sign swinging in the evening breeze. On the sign was painted a dejected-looking figure sitting at the foot of a bald hill.

'*The Lost Traveller*,' Pascoe read. 'After Blake, do you think?'

'As in, 'I've lost me way, send for Sexton Blake,' you mean?' said Dalziel.

Pursuit of this interesting literary divagation was prevented by the sight of a red car parked at the bottom of the steep hill that fell away from the pub.

Dalziel pulled in to the side and dug up a pair of binoculars from the clutter on the back seat.

'No sign of life,' he said.

He let the car roll down the hill and braked a few yards short of the Nissan.

The two detectives got out and approached cautiously.

The car was unlocked and empty, a mobile phone sat in its holder.

They looked at each other then went round to the rear.

Pascoe opened the boot and they both let out a sigh of relief when they saw nothing but luggage.

Dalziel headed back to his car while Pascoe got on the phone to Wield and told him what was happening. As they spoke, his eyes were on the Fat Man who was studying a map. Suddenly he nodded, hurled the map unfolded into the back of the car and called, 'Right, come on!'

'Where? Why? Andy, we should wait here. The ARU will be here in a couple of minutes . . . '

The Fat Man ignored him and bellowed in the general direction of the phone, 'Wieldy, tell 'em to follow us. Straight on down past the red car, T-junction, turn left, quarter mile on right, small quarry.'

When the flow turns into a tsunami, you've no choice but to go with it.

'Wieldy, you get that?' said Pascoe.

'Think they likely got it in Shetland,' said Wield.

The car was moving already as Pascoe scrambled in.

'Andy, where are we going?' he gasped.

'The sort of nice quiet spot a pair of psychos might take a woman to ask her some personal questions,' said Dalziel, leaning his considerable weight on the accelerator. In a less solid car, his foot might well have gone through the floor and hit the road.

'We can't know for sure the Delays have got her, and even if they have, they're certainly not going to hang around here,' protested Pascoe.

'Wrong,' said Dalziel. 'They'll be in a hurry, no time for subtlety. It'll be water-boarding from the start, or if they're short of water, they'll slap her around a bit to show they're serious, then stick a gun up her jaxy and start counting down from ten.'

Pascoe still looked dubious.

'You don't even know what direction they went in,' he said.

'They didn't drive back, else we'd have seen them. No, this is where they'll be, mark my words.'

He spoke with all the oracular authority of his prime, that long period during which his judgments, though often cloudily mysterious, almost inevitably turned out to be correct, a period that some posited had come to an end when he walked with godlike certainty straight into the blast of a terrorist explosion.

Pascoe felt the man's old power, but he also recalled the moment not long before when his legs had given way on hearing the news of Novello's recovery. That burden of responsibility had clearly weighed heavy. Was he now feeling the same sense of having let the Wolfe woman down? And was it himself he was trying to reassure by this assertion of confidence in what at best had to be a fairly wild guess?

The next few minutes would tell.

And which would be worse? Dalziel proved wrong and the quarry empty?

397

Or Dalziel proved right and the two unarmed policemen confronted by a killer with a shotgun?

Though perhaps, thought Pascoe with a kind of hysterical merriment as they approached the T-junction with no perceptible diminution of speed, perhaps the fat bastard's driving will kill us both first!

18.45–18.52

I'm not thinking straight, thought Fleur Delay. Too much pressure, too many pills.

The laptop had shown the Nissan standing still on an unclassified road.

A rendezvous, she'd decided. If they got there in time, they'd find the Wolfes sitting together in the car, talking. Or maybe in his car. When they separated, follow him and grab him. She didn't want any truck with the woman. Disappearing a guy who has already disappeared was no problem. Disappearing the blonde was going to raise complications.

Then they'd driven past the Lost Traveller over the brow of the hill, and a couple of hundred yards ahead of them there she was, just reaching her car.

Fleur had worked things out instantly.

She'd met Wolfe at the pub. They'd talked and separated. She'd walked back to her car, he'd driven off in his. They'd probably crossed with him as they drove towards the pub. She tried to remember the cars they'd passed after they left the arterial. There'd been two, maybe three. A year ago she'd have remembered details, but not today.

Anyway, it was too late and she had to decide what to do next.

Following the blonde was an option, but not an attractive one. If she'd just been talking to Wolfe, she was hardly likely to lead them back to him now.

As she braked alongside the Nissan she said to Vince, 'We take her.'

There had seemed no choice.

But now, looking at the terrified woman as she lay on the ground before them, Fleur knew she'd somehow reached a very wrong place.

Soon as Vince had shot the young journalist and laid out the policewoman, she should have followed her instinct and got out, to hell with The Man!

Her whole strategy, not just on this assignment but ever since the day she got the fatal diagnosis, had been based on a false premise.

Head for Spain, get Vince settled there before she died, and he'd be safe from The Man.

Maybe.

But there was nowhere in the world she could put Vince where he'd be safe from himself.

She looked at him now, standing astride the blonde, his sawn-off held in one hand, waiting for his sister's instructions.

She'd driven a couple of miles from where they'd snatched Gina Wolfe, looking for somewhere quiet and secluded to stop. At the T-junction she'd turned left. Right would take them south. Back towards suburban spillage from the city. North would be lonelier, emptier.

She was right. Half a mile on, she'd spotted a small quarry, not much more than a slice dug out of a hillside by some farmer looking for

400

hard-core, its upper edge visible from the road but with enough of a scattering of scrubby trees at the lower level to hide a car from passing eyes. In the dusky light, it was a desolate spot, fit for foul deeds.

Fleur stooped over the blonde and looked into the woman's fear-dilated pupils.

'All we want to know is where we'll find him,' she said. 'Tell us that and . . .'

She paused . . . *and we'll take you back to your car and let you go* . . . No, this was a bright woman, she wasn't going to believe that.

'. . . and no harm will come to you, I promise.'

Pretty feeble, but it might provide enough straw for a terrified woman to grasp at.

The dark blue eyes moved from hers to the shotgun barrel and back again.

'I don't know where he is,' gasped Gina. 'Yes, he rang me, or someone saying it was him, and he told me where to go, but when I got here, nothing happened. So after a while I walked up to the pub just on the off-chance he might be there, but he wasn't, so I went back to the car . . .'

'Vince,' said Fleur.

Her brother raised his right foot and stamped down hard on the blonde's left hand.

She screamed in pain.

'Look,' said Fleur, 'the more you make us hurt you, the harder it's going to be to let you go. I mean, once you can't move around by yourself and drive your car, what the hell are we going to do with you? All I want is to talk with Wolfe, find out what his plans are. If he's going to keep his head down and you're going to keep your mouth shut, then we're sorted.'

There were tears in the blue eyes now, and Gina Wolfe's voice trembled, but her words showed a mind still holding itself together.

'That's just what he wants . . . no fuss . . . me too . . . I just want things to carry on . . . no waves . . . I'll go back to London and that'll be an end to it . . . '

Fleur almost believed her, but she knew she'd never sell that to Goldie. He wanted closure, and closure did not mean leaving Wolfe alive to tell the tale.

Or this woman either.

There. She'd reached a decision that had been inevitable the moment they'd grabbed her.

She said, 'Vince.'

'What this time?' said her brother, grinning. 'Do her kneecap? Or mebbe . . . '

He reached down and flicked her skirt up around her waist with the gun barrel, revealing skimpy panties with a lace edging.

'None of that, Vince!' snarled Fleur, pulling the skirt back down.

For a moment this display of female sympathy brought a flicker of hope to Gina, but it was snuffed out immediately as Fleur Delay continued, 'We'll do her kneecaps if we have to, but let's give her a foretaste.'

She kicked her square-toed shoe violently against the woman's left knee.

Her scream echoed around the little quarry.

'Bad?' said Fleur. 'Imagine what it's going to

feel like when he blows it to pieces. Come on, dearie. What do you owe that lousy bastard anyway? He dumped you, he walked away, the only reason you got anywhere near him was us, and you want him dead so's you can marry your other copper. Don't be a stupid bitch all your life. Talk!'

She drew back her foot in preparation for another kick.

'Please, no!' cried Gina, pushing herself into a sitting position. Her gaze flickered desperately around the quarry as if in search of some impossible escape route, then her eyes focused on her captors.

'I'll tell you anything you want to know,' she gabbled. 'I'll do anything you want . . . anything!'

She was looking up at Vince now. Her hands went down to her skirt and she dragged it even higher than he'd pushed it with the gun barrel. Then she slipped her thumbs inside the waist of her panties and began to ease them down. As her bush started to come into view, as vigorous and blonde as the hair on her head, a broad grin stretched Vince's lips.

What the hell's she doing this for? Fleur asked herself. Not only was it out of character, but even if she let Vince fuck her, she must know that, once he was done, the questioning was going to resume. So why . . . ?

The answer was obvious. So obvious that on top form she'd have got there seconds earlier.

Distraction!

She turned in time to see a figure coming

towards them at a dead run. In his hand was a jagged stone.

She had time to scream, 'Vince!' before the man's shoulder hit her and flung her aside. Vince turned, the shotgun came up, Alex Wolfe swung his right arm and brought the stone crashing against the side of her brother's head.

His legs folded, his arms flung wide, the gun sailed through the air, he collapsed on to his knees then fell slowly forward till his head rested against the ground in a grotesque parody of a Muslim at prayer.

Wolfe dropped the stone and knelt beside Gina.

'You all right?' he said.

She fought to control the sobs that were suddenly fountaining up through her chest and gasped, 'Fine . . . oh Christ . . . I thought I was going to die . . .'

The sobs won and she leaned against him, crying uncontrollably.

He said, 'It's OK, I'm here, it's OK. I saw them as I drove away. I thought, I know those faces . . . I couldn't be sure, but I turned round anyway . . . things are going to be fine . . . you're safe now . . .'

As he threw words at her to calm her down, his thoughts were racing in furious counterpoint. Seven years ago his life had disintegrated and he had fled into a saving darkness. He had emerged to find that, somehow, with only the most shadowy awareness of how it had happened, he had created a new life, patterned on the old, but with promise of greater durability.

He had checked out that old life and, though he did not doubt that his actions had left scars, he had been able to convince himself that he would do more damage by re-entering it than by staying out of it.

And then by one act of stupidity, by a joy-fuelled desire to give thanks, to pour a libation, he had put everything at risk. In that first life, the gods had destroyed him. In this second life, he had come close to destroying himself.

But it was still possible to restore the balance. Gidman was a pragmatist. Once he understood there was more danger in pursuing his prey than leaving it alone, he would call off his hunters. All he had to do was get that message to him, and he knew just the man to act as messenger. But first of all he had to make sure the Delays got the message too, and with Vince still in his devout oriental position, he'd made a pretty good start with that.

Then Gina screamed, 'Alex!' and he shifted his gaze and his heartbeat stuttered in fear as he found himself looking at a creature like an escapee from *Dr who* with a high polished skull and black staring eyes in a face perfectly white except for the twin rivulets of red streaming from its nostrils.

It took a moment to recognize this as the woman he'd bowled over, dislodging her wig; and another to register that she was holding her brother's shotgun.

He stood up and stepped away from Gina, partly to keep her out of the firing line, and

405

partly to offer a moving target, though at this range and with this weapon, it wasn't going to be easy to miss.

He said, 'Fleur, Miss Delay, there's no need for this. Ring Goldie, it's all being taken care of . . . ' but even as he spoke he knew that yet again he'd let the chance of happiness slip through his fingers and not all the honeyed songs of Orpheus would be enough to soothe this wild beast.

18.57–19.22

Hendrix was singing 'Castles Made of Sand', but at the sight of this new visitor, Goldie Gidman did not hesitate to switch him off.

'Mick! Good to see you. It's been a long time. You're looking well. Sit down, have a cigar.'

'No thanks, Goldie. Gave up a long time ago.'

Purdy looked at the man seated in a deep leather swivel chair set in front of the huge TV screen. He hadn't seen him in the flesh for some time. Not a lot had changed. A few more pounds on his belly, a crisping of frost on his tight-curled hair, but he still created the same impression of controlled menace.

'Fell for the health propaganda, huh?' said Gidman with a laugh. 'Flo's got me dieting, but I won't give up my smokes. It's all bull, Mick. You ever notice it's always the good shit that's bad for you? Them bible-punchers got this government by the short and curlies. Iran thinks it's a religious state, they should come here!'

'That going to figure in the next Tory manifesto, Goldie?'

Gidman laughed again and said, 'Now how'd I know about that? Politics I leave to the boy. Sorry he couldn't be around to make your better acquaintance, Mick. Heard you got off on the wrong foot at that committee thing. He's had to take off with Flo down to Broadstairs. Her sister's taken bad. Flo's real worried. Me, I hope the cow snuffs it. Never did take to Flo marrying a nigger. Came round a bit when I got rich and respectable, but I got a long memory.'

'Everyone's got long memories since they invented computers, Goldie. I can remember when you had some very bad habits. I shouldn't like to think you're falling back into them.'

'Sure you won't have a cigar? You won't mind if I do? This is the only room in the house Flo let's me smoke in, can you believe that? She got smoke alarms fitted everywhere else so's the fire brigade will come running the minute I light up. Even got a specially sensitive one over our bed in case I should even dream of daring to smoke in there when she ain't around.'

He carefully snipped off the end of a cigar and went on, 'But I know how to turn it off, Mick. That's the secret to enjoying life, Not having no problems, nobody can manage that; but knowing how to turn them off, that's the trick. Wouldn't you agree, Mick?'

He put the cigar in his mouth. Slingsby, who'd followed Purdy into the room and taken up his stance by the door, came forward with a book of matches, struck one and moved it gently under the cigar's end.

'Never use a lighter, Mick,' said Gidman between puffs. 'You want a gentle flame for fine tobacco. Too sharp a flame and you start a bad reaction. Just enough and you get that slow, relaxing burn. There we go. Thank you, Sling.'

'I'm here to talk about Gina,' said Purdy.

'Gina? We're talking Lollobrigida here?'

'Don't fuck about, Goldie. What the hell are you playing at?'

Gidman drew on his cigar and let out a long sigh of smoky satisfaction.

'Not sure what you're getting at, Mick.'

'I'm getting at you faking a photo to get Gina shooting off to Yorkshire looking for her missing husband. And don't give me that old-fashioned bewildered look. I know your pet pair of psychos are up there looking too. And I know they've managed to kill one guy and put a female cop in hospital.'

'That's a lot of interesting stuff you know, Mick,' said Gidman. 'Let's suppose just for the sake of argument that I did send Fleur and that creepy brother of hers to have a little chat with DI Wolfe, if that's where he turns out to be. What's your problem? You got twice as many reasons as me for not wanting Wolfe to come back from the dead.'

'How do you work that out?'

Another long puff. The atmosphere in the room was getting a bluey-grey tinge.

'Well,' said Goldie, 'we both might have reasons to be a tad worried in case he started saying bad things about us. But at least I ain't fucking his wife.'

Purdy took a step towards the man in the chair. He didn't hear Slingsby move but suddenly he felt a hand on his shoulder.

'That's right, Sling, get Mick a chair. I think he's a bit over-wrought, he needs to sit down.'

A chair was pushed against the back of his legs

409

and he sank into it.

He breathed in deeply, grimaced at the taste of the smoke, and said in a low hard voice, 'Goldie, what you do about Alex is your own affair, but I don't want that pair anywhere near Gina. What the fuck do you think you're playing at, doing this without reference to me?'

'First off, didn't realize you were so serious about the woman. Thought you were just pleasuring yourself there till something better came along. I recall way back when Wolfe went missing, it was you told us all everything you knew about him that might help put us on his trail. Including that stuff he told you when you were pissed one night about the games him and whatsername, Gina, liked to play. That came in very useful getting her up there to winkle him out. She still like to play that plucky little trooper game, Mick?'

Purdy began to rise, but his buttocks hadn't got more than a couple of inches off the chair before he felt Sling's hand on his shoulder once more, this time accompanied by the touch of cold sharp steel at his jugular.

'Take it easy, Mick,' said Gidman. 'Don't mean to offend you. I consider you a friend. Always have done. That's why I made no fuss when you made it clear way back we were done, you'd chosen the path of righteousness and wanted to bury the past. I felt the same, Mick. That's why I respected your choice. You never had to look over your shoulder and see me there, right?'

'You were there when they set up Macavity,'

410

said Purdy accusingly.

'Come on, Mick. I knew that wasn't the kind of operation you were into. But no harm in ringing up an old friend and asking him if he could think of anyone might be interested in keeping me up to date with what was going on. And you gave me DI Wolfe. No pressure. You just gave him up.'

'And I've regretted it every day since,' said Purdy quietly.

'Don't take it to heart, Mick You weren't to know it would give me grief,' said Gidman, deliberately misunderstanding. 'And have I ever reproached you with it? No way. Anyhow, he did good work till he went sick in the head. Got well paid for it, too. That's what put us on to him in the end, the money. Funny thing about cop amnesia, you guys can forget everything except where you put the money.'

He laughed melodiously.

'All these years, I could have closed that account, got myself a full refund, but I didn't need the money. Hell, it was small change anyway. So I thought, leave it, Goldie, my man. That's where he'll go if ever he shows his head again. And that's what he did. Unfortunately, he just used the account to make a transfer to some hotel up there in the sticks. I thought maybe he's working at this hotel, or staying there, so I sent my gal Fleur to take a look. After a couple of days she says she can't get no lead on him. But I knew he was there, I could feel it. And that's when I got the notion of using your lady friend Gina to flush him out.'

'Not one of your better ideas, Goldie,' said Purdy. 'That's why I'm here. Tell them to stand down till I get Gina back home.'

'Does you credit to worry, Mick, but believe me, the nearest they'll get is to see if she leads them to Wolfe. Then they'll have a quiet chat with the guy, just check him out, know what I mean? No need for anyone to get hurt.'

'You know, Goldie, I think you probably got that right. No need for anyone to get hurt. No need for any of this. If Alex is up there, and there doesn't seem to be any evidence yet, what kind of risk is he likely to be? He's been away for seven years. Why should he want to show up and cause a fuss now? And if he did, what the hell can he say anyway?'

'Well, he could say that it was you recruited him on to my payroll. Now I wouldn't like that. But over the years I got used to people trying to put shit on me and no one's ever been able to make it stick. So I might be an incy bit embarrassed. You, though, Mick . . .'

He shook his head sadly, regretfully.

'What about me?'

'Hey, you know better than me what them whitewashed sepulchres you work for are like. Even if they couldn't prove anything, it would mean goodbye to your career, Mick. You done well. And you've done it clean, for the most part. Why risk throwing it away? And what about your lady friend? How do you think she's going to feel when she finds out the guy who's fucking her now had fucked her husband a long time ago?'

Purdy said quietly, 'I didn't come here to

listen to your crap, Goldie. I came here to tell you, anything happens to Gina, you're going to be a lot more than embarrassed. I'll raise such a shit storm, you'll end up in the Bailey and that boy of yours won't be a rising star at Westminster, he'll be a rising stink.'

For a moment Gidman sat stock-still, then he raised his cigar again, setting the heavy gold bracelets on his wrist jingling against the broad gold band of his Rolex.

'How you going to do that, Mick?' he asked. 'Macavity couldn't do it. And the *Daily* fucking *Messenger* can't do it. And all them professional ferrets at Millbank been over me with microscopes and even my shit came out smelling like roses. You think those guys are going to let themselves be proved wrong? No, I got tank-proof protection, Mick. So what can you say to hurt me?'

'You're forgetting I was around way back before you went corporate, Goldie. I was around when you were just a jumped-up loan shark, screwing your own neighbours into the ground. I watched your back then, God help me! Remember when that Polish tailor reported you for crushing his fingers with a hammer? It was me who warned you what was going off so you had time to fix the witness he cited, your lovely Miss Delay.'

'Got to interrupt you there, Mick. Fleur didn't need fixing. I said nothing to her, just wanted to see how she'd react when you interviewed her. 'Course, if she'd blabbed, I'd have had to send Sling round to arrange another accident. But she

413

did the right thing without needing to be told, and I knew I'd got myself a treasure. You've met her; you know how good she is, right?'

Purdy ignored this and said, 'Talking of Sling and accidents, you shouldn't forget it was me who did the tidying up after him back then. When he burnt the tailor's family to death, it was me spotted the butane spray he'd used to get things going and got rid of it before the fire inspection team got on the job.'

'Hey, man, didn't burn the whole family — the little girl got rescued, remember?' interrupted Slingsby indignantly.

'That's right, Sling,' said Gidman soothingly. 'Mick got it wrong, and I'm sure he's sorry. Right, Mick?'

Purdy felt the pressure of the knife at his throat intensify and he grated, 'Right.'

'Good,' said Gidman. 'Let's clear up this other thing while we're at it. You saying you kept that butane can all these years or something, Mick? Don't believe you. And even if you had, don't see how it can be tied in to Sling and me after all this time, not even with the wonders of modern science.'

'That will be for the courts to decide, Goldie. And it's not the only story I've got to tell.'

Goldie stubbed out his cigar and scratched his chin reflectively.

'Sounds like you're threatening me, Mick, That's not a friendly thing to do.'

'Just warning you, Goldie. The old days are over. For Christ's sake, you must see that. You can't go back to using your hammer again without it coming back to you. The Delays have killed one man already. The Yorkshire police know there's a link to you.'

'A very old link, Mick,' said Gidman. 'Let's see, how will my press statement go . . . ?'

His voice changed, became deeper, almost pontifical, as he intoned, ''Miss Delay once worked for me as an accounts clerk. As my affairs grew progressively more complicated, I found I needed a different kind and quality of financial help and she became redundant. So I let her go with a generous settlement well over a decade ago. Naturally I'm sorry to hear she's got herself into trouble, but really I don't think I can help the authorities any further in this matter.' How's that sound to you, Mick?'

'Sounds like a load of crap,' said Purdy. 'Goldie, I've said what I want to say. I came here to give you the chance to start tidying up while you still can. You'll be stupid not to take it.'

'Threatening me in my own house is what I call stupid, Mick,' said Gidman. 'As for tidying up, at the moment the only untidy thing I can see is you. Now give me a moment, I need to take a moment to think . . . '

It felt to Purdy as if the knife at his throat was nicking his skin. Certainly he could feel something warm trickling down his neck. Had to be sweat or blood.

'Take as long as you like, Goldie,' he said. 'As long as you like.'

And through his mind ran the thought that finally the fatigue of the weekend operation and the pills he'd popped to counter it had taken

415

their toll. What the fuck had he been thinking of, coming out here? This figure sitting before him might have adopted all the trappings of wealth and influence and respectability, but the very fact that he'd sent the Delays up to Yorkshire to clean up for him should have been a reminder that, beneath the surface, Gidman was the same ruthless, amoral gangster he'd always been.

It suddenly felt that it was going to take a divine intervention to get him out of this hole.

18.52–19.23

Sometimes what Orphic music would fail to soothe, a simple panic bellow can freeze in its tracks.

'HOY!'

The sound hit the back of the quarry, ricocheted off and rattled around, making direction hard to pinpoint.

For a second they all looked up, thinking such an ominous noise must have come from the skies.

Then Alex Wolfe saw that two men had appeared at the edge of the quarry. Straight away he recognized one of them: Peter Pascoe, who'd been at his daughter's christening.

The other looked vaguely familiar. That bulk . . . that ursine gait . . . that simian head . . . wasn't this the man Gina had been sitting with at the Keldale . . . ? Wasn't this the famous Andy Dalziel?

He was the one who'd shouted. No way such a sound could have emerged from the slender larynx of Peter Pascoe, who anyway seemed less bewildered by the presence of a bald-headed woman with a shotgun than the apparition of his christening party host.

'Ed, what the hell are you doing here?' he called.

417

Wolfe made no effort to reply. That was a question he'd need to think about. Unless things went really badly. In which case I won't need to bother, he thought, as he watched Dalziel advancing with the majestic instancy of a disgruntled rhinoceros.

'That the gun that shot yon poor lad at Loudwater? Best put it down, luv. It's evidence.'

This was almost an aside as the Fat Man walked past Fleur towards her brother, who had pushed himself up into a simple kneeling position.

Hard to say which of this trio was the most grotesque, thought Wolfe with that calmness which can sometimes follow terror: the pale bald woman, the bleeding man, or the megalithic cop.

'Vincent Delay, I presume?' said Dalziel. 'You the one who did the shooting and put my DC in hospital? How do you manage when you've not got a gun and you're not fighting a girl? Like to give it a try?'

'Andy!' said Pascoe. 'Leave it. He's hurt.'

'Call that hurt? That's a flea-bite. But I can wait. Or mebbe not. Murder, and him with his record, I shouldn't think he'll see the light of day in my lifetime.'

'Step away from him!'

It was Fleur, the gun trained on the Fat Man's belly.

Dalziel turned, a reassuring smile on his face.

'Nay, luv,' he said. 'Tek care. I warned you not to mess with that thing. Put it down afore you do yourself an injury.'

'Vince, on your feet. We're getting out of here.'

Now the Fat Man's smile broadened into a grin.

'Where to? Listen.'

He cupped an ear with his great hand. Distantly but rapidly getting nearer they could hear the sound of approaching sirens.

'Three of our lot, one ambulance,' Dalziel analysed. 'That'll be for Sunny Jim here, so's they can clean him up and get him looking pretty for the judge. You don't look so clever yourself, luv. Mebbe they'll take you along too, give you a bit of time to make your last farewells. Pity they don't have mixed jails, else you could do your time together.'

'Fleur!'

Vince was on his feet now. He wiped the blood away from his eyes.

'Shoot the bastard!' he croaked. 'We need to get away from here.'

Pascoe took a step forward and said, 'It's over, Fleur. Put the gun down. My men will be here any minute. They'll be armed. If they see you with that thing in your hand, they won't hesitate to take you out.'

The barrel moved uncertainly from the Fat Man to the slim DCI.

At least it's taken her mind off me, thought Alex Wolfe.

As if by thought transference the gun arced back in his direction.

'Make up your mind, luv,' said Dalziel. 'One shot's all you get.'

'Fleur, please! Let's go,' pleaded Vince, his voice almost child-like in its pitch and

419

intonation. 'I can't go back inside. They'll never let me out. We've got to get away, we'll go to Spain, I'll settle there, I'll like it there, I promise. Please, Fleur, please.'

He began to move unsteadily towards the blue VW. Dalziel stood aside to let him pass. The sirens were very close now.

The woman started to follow him.

Dalziel said musingly, 'How old is he? Not yet fifty? He could have a good thirty years inside if he keeps in shape. Never mind. He can catch up on all them GCSE's he missed out on.'

She kept on walking, though every step looked an agonizing effort.

The sirens had stopped. They heard the sound of car doors opening, voices shouting, feet running.

'Last chance, luv,' said Dalziel.

'Bastard!' she spat at him, and pulled the trigger.

The first of the new arrivals burst on the scene, heard the shotgun blast, saw the man slump heavily to the ground.

'Armed police!' he called.

The woman turned towards him, swinging the gun round with her.

'Drop it!' he called.

She brought it up to point at his chest.

He shot her through the heart.

'Oh shit,' he said, aghast at what he'd done. 'Oh shit.'

'Nay, lad, don't beat up on thaself,' said Andy Dalziel. 'She were on her way out anyway, you don't need to be a quack to see that.'

He looked towards Gina Wolfe. He wanted to speak to her, but she was folded in the shaven-headed man's arms and he was talking urgently into her ear. Somehow the Fat Man got the impression it was instruction rather than comfort that was being given.

'You know that guy?' he said to Pascoe, who had come to join him, looking rather shell-shocked.

'Yes . . . it's Ed Muir . . . it was his daughter's christening I was at . . . '

'What's he doing here then?'

'I don't know . . . in fact, I don't know anything . . . what's just gone off here, Andy?'

I've got to pull myself together, he thought. I'm sounding as pathetic as that poor bastard who just got shot by his sister!

'Nay, lad, don't get yourself in a tangle,' said the Fat Man, giving Pascoe an avuncular pat on the shoulder that made him stagger. 'Knowing stuff's the responsibility of the man in charge, and that's me, remember? What's your mate doing now?'

Pascoe looked to see that Muir had now moved away from the blonde and was talking urgently into his telephone.

'I don't know,' he said again. 'Probably ringing Ali, his partner . . . '

'Saying, 'Sorry, luv, I'll likely be late for supper, I've been held up by a pair of murderous sickos.' Hope she's an understanding lass.'

He walked forward to where Vince Delay's body sat slumped against the VW, a look of faint surprise still printed on his face.

'Talking of understanding lasses, yon Fleur did you a favour, son,' said the Fat Man, looking down at the corpse. 'Everyone should have a sister like her.'

'Loving, you mean?' said Pascoe, control of his voice restored.

'Dead, I mean,' said Andy Dalziel.

19.22–19.30

Goldie Gidman sat staring at the blank TV screen as if still watching his old favourite Hendrix strutting his stuff at Woodstock. The silence stretched into a minute. Things to say bubbled up in Purdy's head but they all sounded like pleas or provocation. He tried to think of ways of dealing with Slingsby. The guy was an old man with incipient dementia, but he was in the good physical shape that often goes with the condition, and in any case it didn't take much strength to slice through flesh and vein with what felt like a razor-sharp blade.

Cave in, he told himself. Make Goldie think you're backing off. But don't be obvious. He's no fool, he hasn't got where he is today by being a fool.

To which was added the uncomfortable thought, Nor has he got where he is today by being unwilling to remove obstacles in his path with extreme prejudice.

If that divine intervention were written into the score, it was time for it to play now.

His phone rang.

Its ring-tone, downloaded for him by Gina, was based on the aria from Bach's *Goldberg Variations*. He'd protested, 'Jesus, girl, they'll all think I've gone weird when they hear that.' And she'd replied, 'Yes, but you'll always think of me.'

He thought of her now.

The notes were repeated.

Goldie said, 'Better answer that, Mick. But be careful what you say.'

Moving carefully to keep the pressure of steel on his throat constant, he took the phone out of his pocket and put it to his ear.

'Purdy,' he said.

He listened. Gidman, watching him carefully, saw with interest that whoever he was listening to had caught his attention so absolutely that Slingsby and his knife had gone completely out of his mind.

After the best part of a minute, Purdy burst out, 'And she's OK? Is she there? Can I speak to her?'

He listened again, then said, 'OK, I understand. And that's both of them dead. You're sure of that?'

Another short period of listening then he said, 'Why don't you tell him yourself? Yes, he's here. Hang on.'

He took the phone from his ear and said, 'Goldie, I think you might want to hear this.'

Gidman stared at him for a moment then made a gesture. The blade went from his throat, he rose and moved forward and handed the financier the phone.

He said, 'Goldie Gidman.'

Now it was his turn to listen.

After a while he repeated Purdy's question.

'Both of them? You're sure?'

Another listen, then he said, 'If you can make

that play, then I'm OK with that. Believe me, I only ever wanted to talk.'

He switched off and handed the phone back. Then he smiled, gold fillings gleaming like Tutankhamen's tomb, and Purdy knew he was safe. He touched his neck then examined his finger. Blood *and* sweat.

Gidman said, 'You were right, Mick. Things got a bit out of control. We all have off days, right? But they've fixed themselves now. Thing I've found out as I've got older, nothing you can't fix by talking.'

Purdy put his handkerchief to his neck.

'Hard to talk with your throat cut, Goldie.'

Gidman laughed.

'Would never have come to that, Mick, Sure you won't have that cigar now? Drop of rum for the old days? OK, I understand. Don't mind me saying, but you look a bit peaky. I'd say the best place for you is back in your bed, get some sleep in before your woman comes home. Sling will see you out. And, Sling, when you've said goodbye to the commander, have a word with young Maggie who's volunteered to take care of me. Flo said she'd left one of her meat-and-potato pies for my supper. Show Maggie where she'll find it. And tell her I'll be honoured if she'll join me at the table. Bye, Mick. Don't be a stranger.'

Outside Mick Purdy watched as Slingsby, with the gentle smile that one uses to speed a parting friend, closed the door of Windrush House.

Then he took a deep breath of the evening air and looked up at the darkling sky.

425

Life felt good, even though there were difficult times ahead.

Alex had sounded confident he didn't need to break whatever cover he'd created for himself. Purdy could accept that, but harder to accept was Wolfe's assurance that Gina was going to go along with this. And if she did, what was going to be her attitude when she returned? Would she be willing to marry him, knowing that her husband was still alive? Would she let her lawyer go ahead with the petition for assumption of death?

And just how much would she by now have guessed about his role in recruiting Alex on behalf of Gidman?

These concerns he was confident of finding ways to deal with. They were mere midges in the ointment. But the one big blue-bottle potentially buzzing its way alongside them was Andy Dalziel.

How would he be reacting to all that had happened?

No doubt he'll let me know, thought Purdy. In fact, he'll probably be ringing shortly to tell me Gina's OK. Got to be careful I don't let him see I know already.

He was too tired for all this. Maybe he was too old for all this.

It was funny, but the one element he wasn't worried about was Goldie Gidman.

As on so many occasions in the past, including some he had personal knowledge of during the man's early career, some he guessed at in his latter corporate manifestations, Gidman had steered very close to the wind. But he carried with him an aura of invincibility.

Bit like Andy Dalziel, thought Purdy.

Two great survivors, two untouchables.

Pointless worrying about them any more than there's any point worrying about God.

Time to go home and sleep. The rest would keep till he awoke.

Shirley Novello opened her eyes for the second time since being brought to hospital.

The first time she had been surrounded by masked strangers who had bustled around her, poked and prodded, adjusted wires and tubes, until finally an unmasked man had introduced himself as her surgeon, asked a couple of simple questions, appeared delighted with her monosyllabic answers, then taken his leave, which she had read as permission to go back to sleep.

The second time she opened her eyes, there was no sound or bustle, just a single monumental figure sitting by the bed. She might have thought it was God if it hadn't been reading a Sunday tabloid.

'How do, luv,' the figure said. 'It says here that the Tory Party's put together a think-tank to take a close look at the recession and come up with ideas to fix it, and one of its five wise men is Goldie Gidman. Can you credit it?'

'Who . . . he . . . ?' she managed faintly.

'He's the bastard who's ultimately responsible for putting you in here,' said the apparition who might not be God but was a dead ringer for Andy Dalziel. 'And the bad news is, looks like it's going to be bloody hard making him pay for it. The good news is the bastard who actually

428

cracked your skull is downstairs in the morgue with his sister.'

This was all so surreal she decided it must be part of a post-anaesthetic delusion so she closed her eyes, but when she opened them again he was still there.

'The big question', said the Dalziel eidolon, 'is how much to believe of yon mate of Pete Pascoe's story. He says he were at the Lost Traveller talking to the landlord about a catering job, and when he were driving away, he looked down the hill and saw Gina being bundled into a car and he got worried so he followed. So, a real have-a-go hero, and modest with it, doesn't want any fuss. Gina says she'd gone for a drive, got lost, got out of the car to get some air and her bearings, then the Delays showed up and kidnapped her. Does owt of that sound plausible to you, lass?'

Novello tried closing her eyes again, but far from shutting up the speaker, this seemed to be taken as a comment.

'You're right, luv. Sounds bloody thin to me too. But the thing is, if I give 'em a dose of good old Andy Dalziel deep questioning, where's it going to lead but endless dole, eh? He's just had a babby by young Rosie's clarinet teacher, and Gina wants to get on home to claim a widow's pension and marry Mick Purdy. Now there's another problem, as you'll not be slow to point out.'

'Wa . . . er,' gasped Novello, opening her eyes.

'Eh? *What . . . her?* Is that like *who . . . he?*'

'Wa . . . er,' she repeated in exasperation.

429

'Oh, *water!* Right.'

He poured a glass of water from a bottle on her bedside locker, put his arm round her shoulder and set the glass to her lips. When she indicated she'd had enough, he gently set her head back down on the pillow.

She said, 'Is it really you?'

'Good question, luv. Kind of day I've had, I'm not sure how to answer it. We were talking about Mick. I've got me doubts there. Nobody hates a bent cop more than me, but we all cut a few corners when we're young, look the other way for a pint of beer here, a quick jump there. Could be straight as a die now. One thing I'm sure of is, it weren't himself he were worried about, it were Gina. He really loves that lass. Do I want to muck that up? She's not daft, but. I reckon she's going to be giving him a hard time when she gets back, and I don't mean that kind of hard either. So what should I do, lass? You're going to have to make these decisions afore too long. You're going far, I can always spot a good 'un, and you've got the makings. So what do you think I should do?'

She drew all her strength together and forced out the words very distinctly.

'Go . . . home!'

'Ay, you're right, Sleep on it. Except I can't go straight home. After we got most of it tied up back at the factory, Pete said he were going to buy the lads a drink down the Black Bull. I said I wanted to call round here, see how you were, but I'd likely look in on my way home. Not that there'll be anyone there now, it's well after

430

closing time, but Pete and Wieldy might hang on for me. I'll give them your best, shall I? Don't expect you'll be back for a couple of days. You don't want to hang about this place too long, but. Full of sick people, never know what you'll catch.'

She heard the chair being pushed back, large feet hitting the tiled floor as he proceeded slowly to the doorway. Was it all a delusion? Most of it had been incomprehensible, but there was one bit she wanted to cling on to and believe in. The bit where he said she was a good 'un and would go far. She could never ask him if he'd really said it, but some sort of authenticating sign that he'd actually been here in the flesh would be a comfort and an inspiration.

The footsteps paused. Distantly she heard the voice say, 'Oh, one thing more, Ivor. That forty quid I gave thee for tha lunch. In the circumstances, we'll not bother about the change, eh?'

Asked for and given.

Smiling, she fell asleep.

★ ★ ★

Dalziel left the hospital and drove through the quiet streets. It had been a hell of a day. Could have turned out a lot worse. That poor Welsh lad getting killed were bad, but he'd thought a lot about it and it weren't down to him any more than it had been down to randy old Hooky. But if Ivor's injuries had been fatal, if they hadn't got to Gina in time, then he had a feeling he'd have asked for his papers. Mebbe he wouldn't have had to. Mebbe they would have given them to him anyway.

He'd skidded close to the edge round a very dangerous corner, but he was still on the bloody road!

He pulled up on a double yellow in front of the Black Bull. Not another car in sight out here, it was well after closing. There was a dim light showing through a window and hardly any noise. Jolly Jack the landlord and his team of innumerate zombies would likely be clearing up. He almost pulled away but just on the chance Pete Pascoe had hung on, he got out and tried the pub door.

It opened and he stepped into the gloomy entrance hall, then turned right towards the doorway marked *Bar*.

First time I've come in here and not really wanted a drink, he told himself sadly. Nowt more depressing than a silent pub after throwing-out time.

He stepped pushed open the door and was hit by a cacophony of cheers and hoots and whistling.

They were all there, his motley gang, crowded into the raised area at the far end that CID had made its own. You could tell by their clothes what they'd been doing when news of the assault on Novello reached them. No one had paused to change. They'd all rushed in to offer their help, and though some of them had turned out to be superfluous to requirement, none of them had gone home. But why were they cheering so much? This was the kind of reception he might have expected to get at the successful end of a long and difficult case.

But somehow it felt different. Somehow it felt like they were welcoming him back after a long journey.

'You buggers got no homes to go to?' he demanded. 'Jack, draw us a pint and whatever this short-armed lot are having. Likely they've been waiting hours for some mug to come in and stand them a drink. Just the one, mind you. It's nigh on midnight and you've all got to be up for the crime-review meeting first thing tomorrow morning. Standards have been slipping. I'll have the bollocks off anyone who's late.'

He sat down in his wonted chair of state beneath an ancient Vienna clock whose eagle had long since flown at the end of some previous night of constabulary triumph, took a long pull at his pint, and delivered an optimistic bulletin on Novello that won another cheer.

'So all's well that ends well,' murmured Pascoe in his ear.

Was there just a touch of irony there?

'Not so well for Gareth Jones,' said Dalziel reprovingly. 'And I don't see a happy ending for Hooky Glendower. But it's ended a bloody sight too well for that bugger Gidman.'

'Nothing we can do about that, unfortunately,' said Pascoe. 'We'll have to leave it in the hands of God. Talking of Whom, sir, one question me and Wieldy were just wondering about. When taking Mrs Wolfe's statement, she said something about meeting you in the cathedral early this morning. That fitted in nicely with Mrs Sheridan's mistaking you for a kerb-crawler. Wieldy and I were just wondering, what in the name of all that's unholy were you doing in the cathedral? Sir?'

Pascoe had that look of deferential interest on his face which was his customary mask for a bit of not so gentle piss-taking. Wield's natural expression could have hidden anything. Both pairs of eyes were fixed on him.

He sipped his drink slowly, buying some time.

'That's right,' he said. 'We did meet in the cathedral. Often go there, specially on the Sabbath. Can't say I'm surprised you two irreligious sods didn't know that. Not much chance of running into you in church, is there?'

'But why, sir?' insisted Pascoe. 'You've not been born again or something.'

Wield hastily supped his beer. Something must have gone down the wrong way as he choked slightly.

Dalziel said, 'Born again? Nay. I'd guess it were a right painful experience for me mam the first time. Size I am now, I'd likely challenge an elephant. No, it's the music.'

His two colleagues exchanged glances then Pascoe said incredulously on a sliding scale that would have got him the part of Lady Bracknell, 'The music?'

'Aye. You ought to go there and have a listen some time. Smashing acoustic. And the organist were practising his Bach this morning: 'Art of the Fugue'. My favourite. Tha knows what a fugue is? Bit of a tune that chases itself round and round till it vanishes up its own arsehole.'

He whistled a series of random notes in alleged illustration. As if in sympathetic counterpoint, the old Vienna clock began to strike midnight.

Man and timepiece finished together. Dalziel stared at his interlocutors as if challenging response.

None came, and he said with some satisfaction, 'Aye, there's many a good fugue played on an old organ. You two might do well to remember that. Now, whose round is it anyway? I think some bugger must have drunk mine!'

5

con fuoco poi smorzando

Postlude

Midnight.

Splintered woodwork, bedroom door flung open, feet pounding into the room, duvet ripped off, grim faces looking down at him . . .

He sits upright and screams, 'NO!'

Even in his shock and terror a part of his mind is assuring him that this is a nightmare, not all that surprising in view of the evening's stresses.

A voice he recognizes says 'Hello, Goldie' and, despite the oddity of hearing it in his bedroom, the very familiarity helps soothe his fears, and he closes his eyes in relief and lies back, thinking that this must signal his awakening.

When he opens his eyes again, the duvet is tucked under his chin and the room is full of light. But the grim faces are still there on either side of the bed, men in their twenties or early thirties, dressed in dark sweaters and jeans; only two of them, it's true, but looking strong and active enough to dowse any thought of resistance, even if he had the strength.

He looks to the end of the bed and sees the source of the familiar voice and tries to rekindle the initial relief he felt at hearing it, but somehow it's reluctant to return.

'Maggie . . . that you?' he says.

It takes real effort to produce the words, like squeezing toothpaste from a nearly empty tube. What the hell's wrong with him? OK, he'd drunk

439

a bit more than he did when Flo was around, and he'd taken a sleeping pill like he usually did when she wasn't, but no way could that account for feeling like he was swimming in gumbo.

'What's . . . going . . . on? Something . . . happened . . . to . . . Dave? . . . crashed . . . that . . . fucking . . . car . . . ?'

Maggie Pinchbeck says, 'No, Dave's quite well, far as I know. Should be back from Broadstairs now. Hope he goes straight to bed and gets a bit of sleep before the police wake him up.'

'Why . . . police . . . wake . . . him?' asks Goldie Gidman, clinging to the fragile structure of conversation like a drowning man.

'To tell him about the fire, of course.'

' . . . fire . . . ?'

'The one at Windrush House that killed you, Goldie. That fire.'

It is both a comfort and a pain that in some remote part of his mind his thought processes seem to be working at normal levels of efficiency. So the nightmare continues, he comforts himself. All those years of sleeping sound while he was doing all that dodgy stuff, and suddenly a little crisis brings on the night sweats! Maybe he'd hit the rum even more than he recalled last night.

You been living too soft, man! he admonishes himself. Let this be a warning.

He tries closing his eyes again, hoping to slip back into sleep. A sharp prick in his left arm brings him back upright. One of the men is stooping over him with a hypodermic needle in

440

his hand. The other is filling the tumbler on the bedside table with rum. His hands are gloved.

'Don't worry,' says Maggie. 'Just a little Temezepam. Drugi here lives up to his name, I'm sorry to say. Knows how to get his hands on all kinds of shit. You've already taken a bit more Restoril than you thought. Think of it as a kindness. You should be out of it when the flames really take hold. But who knows, Goldie? Who knows?'

'Maggie, what . . . the . . . fuck . . . you . . . talking . . . about? Sling! Sling!'

He tries to kick off the duvet but doesn't have the strength and in any case the man with the hypodermic has no problem holding him down with one hand. Maggie Pinchbeck comes round the bed, picks up the TV remote from the bedside table. On the wall the flat-screen fills with colour.

'Say goodbye to Jimi,' she says, turning the sound down. 'Don't worry. We'll turn him up full blast before we leave.'

'Sling! Where . . . are . . . you . . . man? SLING!'

'He's outside, Goldie. But he'll be in here with you before you go. Faithful retainer makes brave attempt to rescue his old friend and master, breaks down locked door with axe, but the smoke gets to him and they perish together. The tabs will love it.'

'Why . . . you . . . doing . . . this . . . ?' he asks, terror fighting against the drowsiness spreading through his veins. Now the deep sleep he had so desired to slip into just a few moments

441

earlier looms like the mouth of a volcano. 'You men . . . what . . . she's . . . paying . . . I'll . . . double . . . '

'Come on, Goldie!' she admonishes. 'Double? You're a billionaire, for God's sake. You can do better than that. This is your life we're talking about here. What's it worth? How much did Mr Janowski owe you? Five hundred, was it? A thousand maybe? Surely your life's worth a lot more than a Polish tailor's?'

'What's . . . he . . . got . . . to . . . do . . . with . . . ?'

'Let's give you a clue. Say hello to the boys. That's Drugi who gave you your injection, and this is Kuba. Drugi's a plumber, Kuba's an electrician. He's fixed your smoke detector, by the way. They're brothers. Very strong sense of family. Have you guessed what family that is? That's right, the Janowski family. My family, Goldie. When you checked me out, that didn't come up, did it? Maggie Pinchbeck is the name I grew up with. But the name I was christened, the name I had before I was adopted, was Magdalena Janowski. I'm that baby girl you and Sling tried to burn to death with my mother and father, all because he complained that you'd crushed his fingers with a hammer over a little debt.'

'Not . . . true . . . not . . . true . . . '

'Yes, I found it hard to believe when I first heard it. That wasn't till fairly recently. I didn't find out I was adopted till I was eighteen, after Mum and Dad — that's my second Mum and Dad — got burnt to death in a car crash. I'm

442

sure they were going to tell me, but they left it too late. Maybe that's what started me working with ChildSave. It wasn't till seven or eight years later I felt able to start digging deeper and found I hadn't been abandoned. I was Magdalena Janowski and my real parents had died in a fire too. Oh yes, Goldie. Some things they say you can't experience twice. But thanks to you, I managed to be orphaned twice, both times by fire. That's one for the Guinness Book of Records, don't you think?'

She smiles, bitterly, humourlessly.

Goldie Gidman is fighting to keep his eyes open. The man called Kuba pours rum out of the bottle on to the duvet, then replaces the bottle on the table. There is a cigar case lying alongside it. Drugi takes a cigar out, carefully cuts off the end, looks at Maggie questioningly.

'Soon,' she says. 'So, Goldie, naturally I tried to find out more about my real parents. The street they lived in had long since been redeveloped — one of your projects, I think — and it was hard finding anyone who remembered them. I had better luck tracking down family connections in Poland. Hence my dear cousins, Drugi and Kuba.'

The men smile in acknowledgement of their names and she smiles back at them.

'I didn't revert to my original name because I didn't want to make my family history public business. But I did start taking a particular interest in the problems of immigrant children. Then quite by chance during the course of my work I met this old woman running a boarding house in Poplar. Not a very nice old lady; she was ripping off her mainly immigrant tenants something awful. But it turned out she'd lived in the same street as my parents. And when I mentioned their name, you know what she said, Goldie?'

Gidman forces his eyelids to stay open, as if by keeping them open he can keep her talking forever.

The two men look at each other, concerned that this is taking too long, wondering if Maggie is having doubts and is talking to put off the fatal moment.

Unperturbed she continues.

'She said, 'Oh yes, Janowski, the little Polak tailor that Goldie Gidman set on fire.' Just like that. Naturally I asked questions. She couldn't tell me anything else, just said it was common knowledge that Goldie Gidman had arranged the fire. She was a nasty, malicious old woman, so I wasn't going to take anything she said on trust. But I started asking around. Discreetly, of course; I can be very discreet. And you know what, Goldie? I couldn't find another soul to corroborate what she'd said.'

She shakes her head in disbelief.

'Not a soul. When you clear up after yourself, Goldie, you really do clear up, don't you? But I was able to establish that my father had made a complaint against you and Mr Slingsby. It came to nothing, of course. No evidence. And I did notice that from time to time some of the papers, the Messenger in particular, would make a few sly cracks about your early business methods.

444

Again, not a scrap of evidence. In fact, there was so little evidence that you'd ever done anything but spread sweetness and light, that I began to think, I must meet this guy and check him out for myself.'

Kuba looks at his watch and says, 'Maggie, we have been here too long.'

'I know. I'm sorry. I'm nearly finished. Goldie, you still listening?'

He nods his head. It is a real effort, but he wants to establish there is still communication between them. While he can hear, he is alive.

'To cut to the chase, Goldie, when I saw your son advertising for a new PA, I applied on the spur if the moment. I never thought I'd be seriously considered for the job, but maybe I could wangle it so I got a closer look at you. Well, you know how it worked out, Goldie. You were looking for someone who'd keep Dave on the straight and narrow. You checked me out and thought I might do the business, and at least he wasn't going to get horny every time he looked at me. In the process I got my closer look at you. And you know what? I was impressed! You really are good, Goldie. I thought, this is a guy who may play hard, but you can trust him. And all that stuff you do, community projects, kids' charities, refugee organizations — impressive! I found myself admiring you, Goldie. For God's sake, over the months I've worked for Dave, I even found myself liking you!'

She shakes her head in disbelief at her own gullibility.

'And then Gwyn Jones turned up today,

talking really strange. I had to check him out. That's my job, protecting Dave, isn't it? Some of my old worries started swirling round again. But it was all hints and guesses, no substance. I was ready to put it down to just another obsessive journalist ready to do anything for a story. Then I heard that Gwyn's brother had been murdered up in Yorkshire. And Mick Purdy, who's an item with Gina Wolfe, is paying you a visit.'

She nods at Kuba, who produces an aerosol and directs the spray at the duvet.

'Not too much. We don't want to leave traces,' she says. 'I knew I had to do something, Goldie. So I went into the control room downstairs and I switched on the in-house CCTV. That's right. While you and Commander Purdy were talking, I was watching and listening. When I thought that Sling was going to slit Purdy's throat, I got my phone ready to ring the police. Murder and accessory to murder would have done nicely. But something changed your mind, some message Purdy got. And from the way you acted last night, I could tell you felt that as usual everything in your garden was coming up roses. So I didn't ring the police. With the kind of friends you've got, no point, was there? I rang the boys instead. OK, Drugi. It's time.'

Drugi carefully wraps Gidman's fingers around the glass. For a moment he summons enough strength to hold it, then it slips out of his grasp and the contents spill over the duvet. Now the Pole moves away from the bed and takes out a lighter.

446

'Matches, Drugi. Don't you know a good cigar should always be lit with a match — isn't that right, Goldie?'

'I don't have matches, Magda,' says the Pole.

'Oh well. Can't have everything, can we? The lighter then.'

The young man flicks on the lighter and puts the flame to the cigar.

'One last thing, Goldie,' says Maggie. 'About Dave. Fortunately I think he's got more of Flo in him than you. Time will tell. Anyway, I'll take more care of him than you took of Mr and Mrs Janowski's child. I might even be able to help him fulfil all the aspirations you had for him. If he can keep his dick in his pants, that is. But I'll do my best, I promise.'

Gidman's eyes close. Maggie nods at Drugi.

He draws on the cigar till the end glows red, then he tosses it on to the duvet.

For a moment nothing happens. Then there is a gentle swoosh and a blue flame plays around the cigar, turning to yellow as the duvet catches fire.

The woman and two men open the door, drag in Slingsby's unconscious body, and drape it over the end of the bed. Already the duvet stuffing is producing a choking grey smoke.

The trio walk down the stairs and out of the house.

'Magda, we should not hang about,' says Kuba.

'Go, go. You don't want to meet the fire engines coming in.'

'We will see you tomorrow?'

'Oh yes. I expect I'll be round at Dave's flat,

447

seeing you do a decent job this time. Dave's going to be busy looking after his mom.'

In turn the two men kiss her on the cheek. Then they get into their old white van and drive away. Maggie returns to the house, goes into the control room and opens the gate for them. When the white van has passed through, she resets the DVR which she disabled before Drugi and Kuba arrived. The gate she leaves open for the fire engines.

The smoke is drifting down the stairs. Smoke alarms are going off all over the place.

She walks up the stairs, dialling 999. When she speaks, it's an effort to make her voice sound agitated. As she talks, she is running her fingers through her hair, dishevelling her clothes. She wants to stink of smoke when the firemen and the police get here.

Gidman's bedroom is an inferno. She stands and looks into the flames till the heat on her face becomes unbearable. Part of her mind is asking, does this make sense? Are you thinking straight? Is this the only way?

Too late now. She turns away and descends once more.

Outside, she breathes in deeply, letting the cool night air wash the taste of smoke out of her mouth. She looks up. In the black autumn sky, the crowding stars are shining so brightly that not even the undying electric glow of the great city stretching southwards for ever can put them out. Yet the astronomers assure us that many of them have been extinguished thousands of years ago.

Like our pasts, she thinks. *The light is always behind, meaning that even the few steps we can see ahead into our dark futures are obscured by our own shadows.*

She wonders how she'll feel in the morning. She tries to peer into the darkness but the harder she looks, the darker it gets.

It doesn't matter. At the moment she feels completely at peace with the universe.

She can hear sirens now. Soon in an oscillation of blue and silver light, with a glory like chrysanthemums, the great crimson engines will come sailing up the drive, casting bow-waves of gravel over Goldie's precious lawns.

She moves forward to greet them.

Other titles published by
The House of Ulverscroft:

THE ROAR OF THE BUTTERFLIES

Reginald Hill

A sweltering summer is always bad news for the private detective business. Thieves, fraudsters and philanderers take the month off and the only swingers in town are the ones on the nineteenth hole of the Royal Hoo Golf Course. The civilized reputation of the 'Hoo' is in trouble, however. Shocking allegations have been directed at one of its leading members, Chris Porphyry. When Chris turns to Joe Sixsmith, PI, he's more than willing to help (well, he hasn't got any other clients). Before long, though, Joe's on the trail of a conspiracy that starts with missing balls, and ends with murder . . .

A CURE FOR ALL DISEASES

Reginald Hill

Superintendent 'Fat' Andy Dalziel may have been in a coma, but he's not down for good. In the meantime a few weeks bedrest in Sandytown, a pleasant seaside resort devoted to healing, seems just the ticket. And when a fellow newcomer appears in the shapely form of psychologist Charlotte Heywood, Dalziel develops an unexpected passion for alternative therapy. But Sandytown's principal landowners are at war over grandiose plans for the resort. One of them has to go and when one of them does, in spectacularly gruesome fashion, DCI Peter Pascoe is called in to investigate — with Dalziel and Charlotte providing unwelcome support. Pascoe soon finds dark forces at work in a place where holistic remedies are no match for the oldest cure of all . . .

THE DEATH OF DALZIEL

Reginald Hill

Caught in the blast of a huge Semtex explosion, the only thing preventing Superintendent Andy Dalziel from stepping through Death's door might be his own size (and indomitable willpower). As he lies on a hospital bed, it falls on DCI Peter Pascoe to seek justice for Andy. The security services have written it off as an accident — the terrorist suspects have paid for their clumsiness with their lives. Who then, are the Knights Templar, a shadowy group exacting summary public justice on their enemies? Pascoe is certain of a conspiracy — but if the plot is complex, the climax will prove astounding . . .

THE STRANGER HOUSE

Reginald Hill

The slow life of the village of Illthwaite changes when two strangers arrive with the intention of digging up bits of the past that the locals would rather keep buried. Sam Flood is a young Australian whose grandmother was dispatched from Illthwaite as a child. Miguel Madero, a drop-out from a Spanish seminary, has come to the Stranger House in pursuit of an ancestor who had set sail with the Great Armada . . . The antipathy between them is instant, but their paths become increasingly entangled; with clashes metaphysical, and shocks natural and supernatural, as the tension mounts to an explosive climax.